I0527835

DEDICATION

To Kaky Black
*Who put me on the path to
becoming a better writer.*

To Sylvia Gann Mahoney
Who has kept me on that path.

UYLESS BLACK

THE CEPEE DIALOGUES

A Modern Fairy Tale

THE CEPEE DIALOGUES
A Modern Fairy Tale
BY
UYLESS BLACK

Available at online booksellers and local bookstores

To communicate with the author:
Ublack7510@aol.com
or
UylessBlack@gmail.com

For additional information on works by Uyless Black
Blog: Blog.Uylessblack.com
Web: www.UylessBlack.com
Facebook: Uyless Black Books
Pinterest: Uyless Black Books, https://www.pinterest.com/uylessblackbook

Information and Entertainment Institute
9323 N. Government Way, #301
Hayden, Idaho 83835

ISBN: 978-1-62737-011-0

Publicist: S. G. Mahoney
Cover & Book Design by Arrow Graphics, Inc.
info@arrow1.com
Printed in the United States of America

Epigraph

The Humans: Beings who evolved over thousands of years to dominate earth. Their design was chiseled onto their genome and gray matter with the imprints of ancient human tribal hierarchies.

The **Cepees:** Changed entities, programmed for extended eons. Their design was to overcome the humans' shortcomings, as well as exploit and celebrate the humans' accomplishments.

Was the transformation of the human to the Cepee an inevitable course, one with never-ending changes to first, the human, and later, the Cepee? Were they exploiting human's preordained fates? Were they following God's will or a will of their own making?

Read for yourself. Make your own judgment.

CONTENTS

PROLOGUE

The Cepee Dialogues: A Modern Fairy Tale is organized into 65 chapters, admittedly a rather large number of chapters for a single book. You may be relieved to know they are short chapters containing what I hope you discover to be compelling stories of the humans and their successors on earth, the Cepees. For convenience in reading, I have shortened the title in the chapters to *The Cepee Dialogues*, or simply *The Dialogues*.

The chapters contain three kinds of events. They are interwoven to present examples of the behavior of humans, who later became Cepees.

The book is organized as follows: (a) *Data fills* (Information gleaned from the humans' massive archives, which contain a history of their race). (b) The Cepee *Dialogues* (Conversations between two greatly modified humans during the year of 2084). (c) *Coming to you Live, from the Dead* (The playback of television programs, made by the humans in the early 2000s).

You will likely discern which kind of chapter you are reading. Nonetheless, in each chapter title, I have indicated if the chapter is a data fill, a dialogue, or a show.

Another thought about the short and plentiful number of chapters. Perhaps as an over-reaction to the Twitter world of abbreviated correspondence, it may appear I succumbed to the world of short attention spans, and the desire to parallel process more than one stream of information at a time

The construction of the chapters has nothing to do with the Twittering Society, but a different way to tell what I hope you will find an interesting story.

xi

The Dialogues are based on conversations between two Cepees. As mentioned in the epigraph, *Cepee* is an acronym for <u>c</u>hanged <u>e</u>ntity, <u>p</u>rogrammed for <u>e</u>xtended <u>e</u>ons.

A young student, in his early teens, is called the *Student Cepee* (the Student) and has been tasked with learning about his ancestors. The other Cepee is an astute and incisive guru, called the *Mentor Sage* (the Sage), whose job is to offer advice and counsel to the Student. The Student and the Sage are helped in their chores by a third party, the *Hologram Sage*, (the Hologram).

The narrative is based on the Student Cepee accessing and studying the Human Archives, as directed by the Sage Cepee. His learnings are called *data fills*, as his greatly improved computer-enhanced brain is able to store considerable archival information similar to that of computer memory.

The Student has been assigned a curriculum by the Sage, including the study of specific subjects from the archives. The Student is to retrieve and study this information, after which he will enter into dialogues with the Sage about his findings.

During this education program, the Sage will also direct the Student to watch a variety of the humans' now antiquated television programs. They are an important part of the Student's curriculum, as they will reveal much about the behavior of his ancestors.

If the Student completes the curriculum successfully, he will be allowed to assume responsibilities for helping his fellow citizens make planet earth an even better place in the cosmos.

To enhance the plot, the Student has been captivated by a fair and becoming member of the opposite sex. It is his goal to capture her biosynthetic heart.

As described in this book, earth's beings conduct their lives based on the *Rules of Life*. They are described throughout the narrative and summarized in a section at the back of the book.

You may be wondering why I have included the phrase, *A Modern Fairy Tale* in the title. It might conjure-up images of Snow White and Pinocchio, hardly close to the themes of this book. I chose the subtitle because the plots of fairy tales often involve quests for the common good.

The Dialogues do indeed describe many human quests, although some of them were happenstance and inadvertent ends unto themselves without consideration for one another. Only later in this book do the main characters take on a focused quest to save themselves from social oblivion. Thus, the term *fairy tale* is appropriate.

Some writers use fairy tales to address modern issues. That approach is what I have done with this book. Fairy tales often have happy endings. For *The Cepee Dialogues: A Modern Fairy Tale*, based on your philosophical and religious beliefs, that is for you to decide.

Notes on some Punctuation, Gender use, and the Time Line

This book contains many passages of quoted conversations.

For dialogue, one convention used to signal the omission of a word or phrase is to insert an ellipsis [...] to identify the omission within the sentence.

An ellipsis used at the end of an incomplete quote indicates that the sentence has been deliberately left grammatically incomplete.

Dialogue with faltering speech, incomplete thoughts or even confusion, insecurity, or contemplation is indicated with an internal or an end of sentence ellipsis.

The relative position of the ellipsis and other punctuation is meant to provide insight into the dialogues between the conversing participants.

In this writer's view, while quoting a conversation, the identification of pauses in the talk makes the quote representing the speaking seem more natural.

With guidance from the reference guide, Chicago, and to address this problem, I have adapted the use of three dots (...) to identify a pause in an utterance or a pause before the person begins to speak. Here are three examples:

She said, "He is pushing up daisies...so to speak."

He responded, "...Eh, okay, if you insist."

She replied, "But I was going to say..."

The characters in the dialogues in this book are often at a loss as to what to say because of the nature of what they have learned. The three dots reflect their natural oral reactions, as well as their being interrupted by another person during a conversation.

In identifying a human, the pronoun *he* or *his* is used. This convention does not mean that *she* or *her* is not important in this story. She is, but her male counterpart plays a bigger role in the dialogues dealing with aggression, one of the main themes of this book.

The names Student Cepee, Sage Cepee, Mentor Cepee, and Hologram Cepee are proper names and begin in upper case, including the use of part of the name. Examples: "Hello, Sage; greetings, Student; I see you once again, Hologram."

These same words begin in lower case when generic references are used.

As examples, "The Sage says hello to a student. ... The Student and a sage say hello. They view another hologram."

This book describes events taking place over the last decades during the 20th century, and 84 years into the 21st century. This time might seem too short for all the changes to take place as described in this book. However, the idea of exponential changes is an important part of this story. Humans are making extraordinary progress in changing our brains, DNA, and bodies.

Here is an example of exponentiation: Frogs are proliferating exponentially in a pond. One day the pond is half-full. The next day, it is full.

Synthetic biology was unknown a few short years ago. Now, it is a prevalent technology.

Nonetheless, who can know what might exist eight decades from now? As always with the future, we can only guess. This book is no exception. It is a guess, but I trust you will find it to be at least an educated guess.

PART ONE

HUMAN NATURE

CHAPTER 1

INTRODUCTION

The time is 2084. The dominant beings who dwell on planet earth are no longer humans. They are Cepees. The name of Cepee is derived from the term: _changed entity, programmed for extended eons._ The lengthy name is pronounced as "CP."

The Cepees did not eradicate the humans. Quite the opposite. For many decades, the humans made extensive changes to themselves, with the goal of improving their physical and mental capabilities.

In making these improvements, the humans gradually transformed themselves into a different race: the Cepees. While remaining a member of the _Homo sapiens_, they willingly modified themselves to become an extended lineage of their human ancestors.

They began this process gradually, as far back as the year, 1980, when they began to make modifications to their genetic makeup and alterations to their bodies and central nervous systems. The changes they made to themselves accelerated with each passing year. Alterations led to more alterations.

Thus, as time passed, the devolving human evolved into the Cepee. The borrowing from the old human line with a lending to the new Cepee line led to a greatly improved species.

Even though the Cepees are different from their predecessors, they share many of the humans' traits. They listen to their music, read their books, and watch their movies and television programs.

Many reminders of human existence are stored in the Human Archives. The Cepees study this vast library to learn more about

3

their curious ancestors. The Cepees are particularly fond of one song they found in these files. It is titled "Heaven on Earth." They like the tune because its title describes a world the humans desired and a world the Cepees have attained: a never-ending life on earth.

To achieve this goal, the Cepees took to heart the thoughts of one of their human predecessors, Julian Huxley, "The human species can, if it wishes, transcend itself—not just sporadically, an individual here in one way, an individual there in another way, but in its entirety, as humanity."[1]

The Cepees have fulfilled this destiny, one that was initiated in a somewhat happenstance manner by their ancestors, but later refined by the Cepees themselves. It was a world that was predicted by another forebear, E. O. Wilson, "Earth, by the twenty-second century, can be turned, if we so wish, into a permanent paradise for human beings, or at least the strong beginnings of one."[2] As told here, the Cepees' coming to dominate planet Earth was more than a strong beginning. It was an equally strong ending, as they took over the reins from the now defunct humans.

This permanent paradise for human beings began to come to fruition in the latter part of the twenty-first century. The startling progress the humans made each year of that century toward the improvement and prolongation of human life surprised almost everyone, even those who had a hand in making it happen.

In this latter part of the 21st century, the humans had begun to congratulate themselves. They had made remarkable progress in their battles against perpetual self-imposed war, self-induced totalitarianism, and their near ceaseless propensity for engaging in gratuitous violence.

In a touch of irony, the humans themselves had created these so-called Orwellian ills—named after a noted human writer who wrote of the folly and foolishness of his fellow world citizens.

---

[1] Julian Huxley, Transhumanism, "*New Bottles for New Wine*," 1957, in Leonard Roy Frank, *Quotationary* (New York: Random House, 2001), 253.

[2] E. O. Wilson, *The Social Conquest of Earth* (New York: Liveright, 2012), 297, Kindle edition, loc. 4777.

The humans were now trying to correct their mistakes. Thus, 2084, a century after George Orwell's book, *1984*, was published, provided a fitting benchmark for these beings to proclaim to themselves, "Well done." By this time, the human race was dramatically different from what it had been a century before. While still vulnerable to some shortcomings, by 2084, Homo sapiens were well on their way to fixing themselves and becoming a more laudable and less murderous species.

What did 2084 and beyond hold for these beings? Would the race finally lay to rest its self-imposed nightmares? Or would the humans' ancient legacies, subscribed to them through nature yet assisted by their own hand through nurture, win this battle?

To help answer these questions, we will be accompanied in our journey by three Cepees. One is a young male student, who is engaged in studying the Human Archives during the year 2084, yet another milestone in the Cepees' existence. The other is his teacher, a sage who guides this student through the humans' complex lives. Later in this narrative, we are joined by a young female student, leading the Student to conclude there is more to life than dialogues and data fills.

To round out the cast, the Sage sometimes enlists a hologram image who acts as the sage's proxy when the wise one is busy with other sage-like affairs. The Student affectionately calls this set of light shows the Hologram Sage, or simply Hologram.

Thus, our story begins in the year of 2084.

CHAPTER 2

THE HUMANS' CHANGE PROGRAMS
(Data Fill 1)

The Cepee student has not yet met his Cepee mentor and teacher, a noted sage. After all, sages in the Cepee race are esteemed beings. Their time is precious and must be spent on performing sagacious deeds, such as guiding, counseling, and providing leadership for non-sage Cepee citizens on earth, such as students and others. Thus, the Student only receives a message from the Sage about what his first data fill is to be.

A data fill will entail accessing the huge information repository of the Human Archives and gleaning information about the obsolete humans. It is a vast library containing the history of the Cepee's ancestors, the humans. These data fills will be an integral part of the Student's educational program.

The Cepees believe it is important to be knowledgeable of their past. They know they can continue to improve themselves by knowing more about their legacy, the human race. Thus, each young Cepee is taken through a rigorous educational program devoted to the study of their ancestors.

The Student smiles, as he thinks: *I must have an old-fashioned sage as my teacher. He is still using wireless email! My Wi-Fi brain chip could have easily taken in his instructions. I hear he is an elderly sage. Maybe he never opted for wireless Internet to be part of his brain. Oh well, he is in charge, and I'm to do as he says.*

Little does this presumptuous student know that his assigned sage has enormous capabilities. Cerebral Internet is part of his

6

makeup. However, this particular sage is, like his human ancestors, a (partial) creature of habit. Besides, the Sage keeps his capabilities under wraps, to be dispensed at appropriate times.

Before he begins the archival retrievals, the Student, a thoughtful but somewhat flippant being, again thinks: *Hm, I'm called a Cepee, for changed entity, programmed for extended eons. One of those "e's" means "extended." But my life is not just extended, it's endless. My name is wrong!*

He decides to do an ad hoc query to the archives. He asks, "Why are Cepees called Cepees if our lives are not extended, but infinite?" He receives this response.

> As a result of the evolution of the Cepee from an existence encompassing extended eons to that of infinite eons, our name could have been changed to Cepie: changed entity programmed for infinite eons.
>
> However, we Cepees retain the original moniker because, over many years, we have embedded this name into millions of computers, including those in our bodies and brains. Even in our advanced times, software changes are difficult and sometimes perilous to make.
>
> By the way, Student Cepee, you are not accessing the Human Archives in the manner directed by the Mentor Sage. Ad hoc access to the archives is permissible, only if it is approved by your sage-in-charge.

Thus both placated and chastised, and wondering what his Mentor Sage is all about, the Student absorbs and studies this data fill from the Human Archives.

The Student Cepee learns that the Cepees evolved to replace the human based on four major programs initiated by the humans and refined considerably by the Cepees. Their rather long names were usually identified by these acronyms: EGO, ILLS, SANE, and ASSES.

The result of these initiatives was profound. Before long, it became less costly and time consuming to make repairs and improvements to worn-out body components (nicknamed by the scientists as the humans' *peripherals*). With the development of regeneration and restoration mechanisms, the repair or replacement of a bodily member became a routine matter. The operations were simplified as many pieces of the emerging Cepee became biosynthetic, replaceable parts, subject to a long existence.

In addition to the astounding improvements made to the humans' peripherals, neurosurgeons and genetic engineers developed ways to greatly enhance the humans' central nervous system—the brain, spinal cord, and nerves throughout the body—which was dubbed by the scientists as the humans' *mainframe*.

EGO (Enhancements to Glorify Ourselves)

The humans' goal for the EGO programs was to eliminate humans' physical shortcomings, such as ugly, damaged, or worn-out body parts. Alcoholism, drug addiction, and other maladies were removed from the humans' inventory of miseries. Cosmetic surgery became as common as paying a visit to the dentist. Unattractive noses, sagging buttocks, slumping chins, ugly wrinkles, sagging breasts, and unsightly warts were altered or removed to improve a person's appearance.

Starting modestly in the twentieth century, the alteration to the human assumed a life of its own. Before long, internal parts in the body, such as organs, that were starting to show some wear-and-tear, were being repaired or replaced. The frequency of changes accelerated as success led to more success. When mid-twenty-first century came about, the human was taking on a distinctive character from what he or she had been in the past. By late-twenty-first century, the Cepee's mental and physical compositions had become quite different from that of the conventional human.

Notwithstanding this transition, some of the earthlings, residing in a transmutation purgatory around the time of 2070, were both amused and bemused with their situation. They were not yet the Cepees of the future, because they were still partially mired in the human past. A noted commentator of that time named this period the EGO epoch: Enhancements to Glorify Ourselves.

Nonetheless, in their later times on earth, the humans had eliminated the word *ugly* from their vocabulary. All citizens were well above average in their looks.

ILLS (Incurable Latent Labile Sicknesses)

By the early part of the twenty-first century, the human race had come to understand it might very well be losing the battle against a large number and variety of diseases. Germs were adapting themselves to more accommodating residences in the human body. These organisms were mutating and adapting to drugs and medicines faster than supposed cures could be developed.

The battle was hindered by the delay of first, inventing medicinal cures; second, having the medicines approved by government agencies; and third, creating drugs whose side effects were not harmful. Unlike the EGO programs, which were important but not essential to the preservation of the species, the operations associated with ILLS were fundamental to the species' long-term survival. Consequently, many ILLS programs were initiated to counter the attacks of microorganisms such as bacteria, protozoa, and viruses.

Genetic engineering slowed and eventually eliminated the aging process. Uncooperative organic residue was removed from the human's flesh container, soon to be replaced with biosynthetic material. In many instances, replacements came from natural human parts; some harvested from other humans; others grown and often modified in Petri dishes. Eventually, faltering or failed functions were taken over by human, and soon, Cepee designed components using artificial intelligence (AI) technology and 3-D printers.

A medical expert coined the term Incurable Latent Labile Sicknesses (ILLS) to describe these problems and the programs to solve them: Incurable, because some of the human's diseases had proven to be intractable. Latent, because several of the diseases lay dormant for years, suddenly appearing to do damage to the victim. Labile, because many of the viruses changed often and rapidly, resulting in high rates of mutation that offset previous treatments. Sicknesses, because being sick and miserable were the end results of the process.

In a nutshell, the frequent rate of change enabled a germ to adapt to new medical milieus in order to escape the human's natural immune system and medicines' antidotes. Therefore, the ILLS initiatives took a new approach: Modify the human's genome to make it more resistant to germs *and* modify specific germs to make them, as one scientist quipped, more "user friendly" to the humans' gene pool.

SANE (Supplying A New Ego)

The humans took the ILLS programs to another level as they learned more about the regions of the brain and parts of DNA that had an effect on insanity and psychopathy. But these initiatives went further than combating mental illness. The scientists and researchers came to understand the cerebral and genetic underpinnings of mental well being, even optimism.

These programs entailed the manipulation of genes as well as making changes to both ancient and recently evolved parts of the brain. They resulted in the creation of powerful counter measures to combat mental miseries. The humans dubbed these initiatives as SANE, for Supplying A New Ego.

The acronym and its derivation implied the humans had artificially manipulated their genome and central nervous system to give themselves new and enhanced mental functions. In spite of the acronym, SANE not only fixed the brains of the insane, it also repaired the mental functions of many who were sane. Maybe a bit off kilter, but sane.

ASSES (Alterations to Save Society from our Egregious Selves)

If the humans had not changed themselves because of EGO, ILLS, and SANE, by mid-21st century, many of the changes would have occurred anyway because of reason number four, dubbed by the pundits as ASSES.

By this time, many humans recognized they had no choice but to drastically alter their make up. No choice, because the race was annihilating its societies. Humans had begun using nuclear weapons, as well as deadly gasses and poisons, on large populations in both urban and rural parts of the world.

Reactions of the Student Cepee

The Student has had considerable information—that is, data fills—downloaded previously into his brain and ancilliary brain chips. But synthetic cerebral circuitry, as advanced as it is, is not up to the task of integrating completely with the Cepee's natural neurons. Consequently, the Student Cepee looks forward to his first meeting with the Sage Cepee. He has many questions to ask, and the Sage has many answers.

CHAPTER 3

INTRODUCING
THE STUDENT AND THE SAGE

(Dialogue 1)

The Student Cepee, 13 years of age, is a relatively recent addition to the Cepee race. Nonetheless, his vast assemblage of protein-based computer parts and tailored genes give him an impressive array of mental powers and an imposing head start in life. But he needs guidance from more experienced Cepees. After all, he is a student.

He has been selected for a special education program because of his impressive intellectual skills. His advisor for these activities is the Sage Cepee, also known as the Mentor Sage, or simply, teacher, a wise and knowledgeable being by virtue of his long existence, his extensive data fills, and his expansive studies of the human and Cepee races. The job of the Sage is to counsel the Student and answer questions the Student has about the humans.

The Sage is also to be the Student's mentor. For this specific project, the mentor's task is to mold a somewhat naïve and overly self-assured student into becoming a wise and contributing member of the Cepee society. The two beings are, even in the Cepee world, a special combination.

As mentioned, the Student has been selected for this program because he has been evaluated as having exceptional potential. The Sage has been selected because his fellow sages know he is indeed an extraordinary Cepee.

12

Thus, one exceptional Cepee, who possesses a partially filled mental tabula rasa, will engage in dialogues with another exceptional Cepee, one whose mental tabula rasa is replete with knowledge and wisdom.

The first exchange takes place after the Student has accessed the Human Archives a few times.

Sage Cepee, "Greetings, Student."

Student Cepee, "Greetings, Sage. I understand I am to begin a learning program, and you are to be my teacher."

Sage, "Yes. You will come to me with questions about the humans. I will answer your queries and review the progress of your learning about these beings. By the way, to clear matters at the start, we do not consider ourselves as a separate species from the humans, the *Homo sapiens*. One of our comedians distinguished ourselves from them by categorizing ourselves as *Cepee sapiens*, a play on words."

The Student thinks, *Clever, but inaccurate, even to a student. But these dialogues might actually be interesting. I hope they are also fun.*

The Sage continues, "For our dialogue today, we will concentrate on *Cepee sapiens*, so to speak, not humans."

Student, "Fine, Sage, you're in charge. You're in the driver's seat. And yes, I have several questions."

The Sage thinks: *No shyness about this student. I will see how he handles his glibness as we proceed through his program,* "I know you do. Proceed."

Student, "How did you know?"

Sage, *This one might be a bit of a challenge,* "Because I am a sage, and you are a student. Stop your unnecessary postulating and get to your questions."

Student, "Well, that question was a question!" But the Student knows he might be overstepping a bit, a common practice with students. "OK, Mentor Sage, I'll get with the program. As a relative newcomer to the Cepee race—I'm only a teenager, how can I have such mental powers to be so young?"

Sage, "First, you started your existence like the humans did theirs: Procreation was a joy to the humans. It is a joy to the Cepees. But your mental and physical make-up reflect many decades of alterations to humans' and later Cepees' brains and genomes.

"Like humans, you came out of your mother's womb, but unlike humans, we Cepees operate with bioengineered, organic-based chip sets in our brains. These chips are not of silicon. They are of human matter."

The Student looks surprised. Sage, "Yes, Student, even in the early 21st century, humans had begun to make Boolean logic gates out of human matter, research they started in the previous century. You will learn more about this later. You are also born with many other genetic enhancements over that of your human ancestors.

"Your initial abilities are reflective of this technology, and some of your capabilities are bootstrapped into biosynthetic components. Thus, your first few years of existence have been devoted to self-study with the data fills. Your upcoming data fills and our dialogues will enhance the foundational attributes you have obtained. As discussed shortly, part of the Human Archives you will access contain old movies and television programs made by the humans. They will be an important part of your education, especially during the humans' late 20th and early 21st centuries."

Student, "Great! I love videos. …Hm. Why don't you sages just load everything into us students at the onset? It seems my idea would be more efficient than your approach."

Sage, "Because of the uniqueness of your query, you answered your own question. We do not want to standardize everything about our behavior. Even if we wanted to, we could not, because we do not yet understand certain fundamental aspects of the operations of the brain and genome. Anyway, we recognize the value of diversity. Members of our race exhibit contrasting characteristics—such as the questions and thoughts you just offered to me.

"Our race retains many of the mental features of the humans. Indeed, many of our cranial components and DNA strands are identical to the humans. Our philosophy has been to retain the beneficial components of the humans' mental and genetic compositions, and at the same time, eliminate the negative and destructive characteristics that proved to be so ruinous to the humans—at least those characteristics that we understand."

The Sage emphasizes, "Student, throughout your program you will learn there are many components of our ancestors' behavior we have not altered because we do not know the mechanisms that contributed to their behavior in the first place. For example, we do not know how the brain enables the so-called soul. We do not understand the physiological aspects of the cerebral concepts of self and free will. I doubt we ever will. We know much about the machinations of the brain, but we do not yet fully understand the hows and whys of many of those machinations. We have been wise enough to leave well enough alone.

"Nonetheless, as you recently learned, we Cepees are sufficiently unique that we consider ourselves a different race from our ancestors. Mind you, not a different species, but a different race. You will learn more about this subject in your education program."

Student, "So, I am unique, but I am also not unique?"

Sage, "Correct. But then, this situation is no different from the outdated human."

Student, "Outdated. What happened to the human?"

Sage, "It became the Cepee."

Student, "Why did the human become the Cepee?"

Sage, "That is the purpose of your studies and dialogues with me: to discover why."

Student, "How did the human become the Cepee?"

Sage, "That too shall be revealed in your education program."

Student, "What did the human look like?"

Sage, "The human resembled you and me, although our ancestors were, on the whole, not as attractive as Cepees. But the composition of the human—its constituent parts—were quite different from the Cepee. You will also learn about this topic during your education program."

Student, "Fine, but it would be easier to just load up all this information automatically into my brain chips. Seems like a lot of work on my part. I won't have much free time to myself."

Sage, "First, we do not know how to perform such a 'load up.' We have yet to fully grasp all the cerebral mechanisms for learning. Certainly, our brains are greatly enhanced in comparison to the humans, but we do not function as if we were an ordinary computer. The operations of our natural organic matter still offer mystery in relation to the structure of integrated circuits.

"Second, your complaint is the common lament of all students. Looking for an easy way out! As your teacher, I will require you to show initiative in your studies. I will enjoin you to record—or as the humans would say—*write-down* your thoughts on your research about the human race and share those thoughts with me. So yes, you have work to do."

Student, "Writing? That will be an exertion on my part. As you know, I am not versed in writing a full sentence. If I even write, I prefer to use what the humans called *twittering*. Mostly, I just use the Wi-Fi chip in my brain to 'talk,' but not 'text.' Writing? With respect, Mentor Sage, writing seems worthless to me.

"If I want to 'write,' voice recognition does the writing for me. Besides, is any of this work going to be any fun? Any laughs along the way?"

The Sage, coming from an old school of Cepees, ponders how the Student remains able to read in the first place. The Sage also concludes the Student may have more than his share of lazy genes stranded on his tailored DNA.[3] He says to himself, *But this one appears bright. I will see how he progresses though my program.*

---

[3] In the early part of humans' 21st century, they found clues about the behavior of procrastination. By temporarily suppressing a gene affecting the brain's processing of dopamine, researchers were able to suppress a monkey's often natural motivation *not* to work—even if the work brought forth enticing rewards. Before long, scientists had succeeded in transferring this procedure to humans, who had been excelsior models for sloth. The end result was startling. All humans began to perform useful, society-enhancing functions. Unions no longer struck. Its members came to loathe picket lines. The number of people in government bureaucracies declined dramatically, and the bureaucrats began to answer their phones to help inquiring citizens. Voice message companies went broke. The couch potato industry withered away as well. Later, the Cepee race brought the concept of productivity to a fine art and science. Their thumbs became even more prominent appendages to their hands as texting became more frequent than talking on the phone. However, still later, entering Twitter input became strictly by voice, and the humans' thumbs atrophied to their original sizes. See Eric Nagourney, "Hurry Up and Procrastinate," *The New York Times*, August 17, 2004, D6.

Sage, "That's up to you. Let's see how you react to the following quote as it relates to your concern. A human writer once said, 'I am deeply involved in researching the subjects of sloth, idleness, and procrastination. However, the subjects prevent me from writing about them.'"

Student, "Ha! I like the quote."

Sage, "Then you will do fine with your data fills and studies. I suspect you will find some humor from them, as well as considerable information. The television programs of the humans will amplify your upcoming data fills and our dialogues."

Student, "Thank you, Sage."

Sage, "That's my job, Student. To teach you. Yours is to learn. Now, let's get to work. Here is an illustration that you should retain during your training."

The Mentor Sage retrieves and displays a hologram image of the figure below, "This image will be helpful to you during your studies. Presently, I recognize only some of it makes sense. But as you proceed through your curriculum, this information will be key to your understanding the sequence of major events that led to the creation of us Cepees."

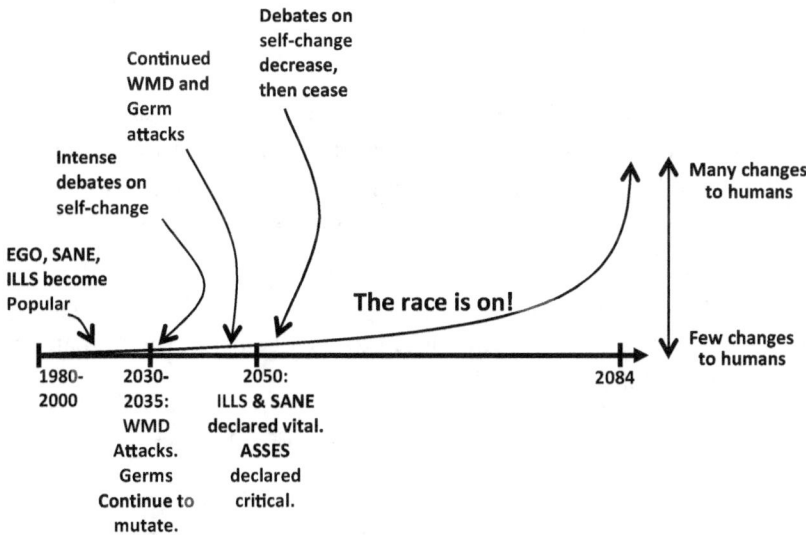

The Human Exponential Consequences Curve.

The Student Cepee examines the figure, "I recognize EGO, ILLS, SANE, and ASSES. They were part of my initial data fills. I understand their general ideas as well. But some other parts of the picture are new to me."

Sage, "Yes, I understand. Eventually, this figure and its other entries will become clear."

Student, "Fine, but I'm curious about the notation, 'WMD.'"

Sage, "WMD are the initials for weapons of mass destruction. As you will learn, these instruments played a key role in the humans' self-change projects."

Student, "And the phrase, 'The race is on!'?"

Sage, "This phrase will become evident as you perform your data fills—and if I can succeed in getting you away from my office for you to begin your work! Are you procrastinating?"

Student, "No, Sage, just curious. By the way, I understand some other parts of the picture. To the right, I see the notations 'Few changes to humans' and 'Many changes to humans.' In relation to the curved arrow, it appears their changes to themselves became more frequent. Am I correct, Sage?"

Sage, "Indeed you are, Student. In fact, the changes accelerated exponentially. Well done. And during your training, you will encounter this curved arrow frequently. Get along now, and continue your data fills.

"As I stated, for part of your training, I have scheduled you to view several humans' television programs. They will provide more background for your training. They will give you a different learning tool, perhaps provide some laughs, and especially show the folly of the humans."

Student, "Folly, Sage?"

Sage, "Yes, folly that contributed to the decline of the human and the ascension of the Cepee."

CHAPTER 4

ORIGINS OF STUFF AND HUMAN-ENGINEERED FOOD

(Show 1)

The Mentor Sage directs the Student Cepee to watch the first in a series of antiquated human television (TV) shows. During sessions with his teacher, the Student will watch a number of these programs of images on humans' primitive TVs, but rendered in three dimensional hologram representations. They were recorded many years ago and are now maintained by the Cepees for their studies of the humans. The Cepees have named these programs *Coming to you Live, from the Dead*, because the humans' former live productions are now about dead people.

This program is titled, "Origins of Stuff and Human-Engineered Food." The program explains how the humans evolved from hunter-gatherers to food producers and warriors. Here is what the Student sees.

A moderator introduces the program, "How many of us do as we wish during our waking hours? How many of our ancestors did what they wanted to do during their time on earth? For example, consider our early hunter-gatherer forebears. Positioning ourselves in a cave thousands of years ago, we overhear the following conversation between a man and a woman."

[The hologram rendered TV program shows the inside of a cave, which is occupied by two early humans.]

The woman, "I'm running low on saber-toothed tiger. Get off that stone mat for a change. Fulfill your role as the hunter in this family and kill us something to eat."

TV moderator: "This man is not necessarily a couch potato, as couches do not yet exist. He could be known in his time as a mat potato, but potatoes don't exist either. But marriage, in some fashion or another, does exist."

The male primate says to himself, "Someday, someone will say, 'Marriage is the triumph of hope over experience.' Whoever says it, I wish he would have said it before I had the experience of marriage."

Moderator, "Actually, it was said by an 18th century Samuel Johnson, a distant relative of our cave dwellers."

The man, "We've hunted the region almost clean of game. Not much left but small mammals and some wild cattle. You're the gatherer in the family. Go pick some fruit."

The woman is not all that happy about her lot in life either. She thinks, "Someday, someone will say, 'The difference between war and marriage is that in marriage, you sleep with the enemy.' Whoever will say it, I wish it would have been said before I did any sleeping."

Moderator, "Actually, no one knows who said it."

The woman counters, "We've exhausted the current crop of wild berries, at least locally. There's some ill-tasting green fruit available, but they're a couple mountains away. It's too far to go for a few pieces of a bitter berry. Besides, I'm just now learning to walk upright. It's a hassle to half-walk, half-stoop over every hill and dale for a tasteless fruit that may be picked clean by the dying-out *Homo erectus* living over there."

Moderator, "We see played out in those old times why our predecessors moved from the hazardous occupation of hunters and the insecure occupation of gatherers to food producers, leading to the invention of *stuff*."

Woman, "I have an idea. Let's look for one of the few remaining *B. primigenius* in our area. (Moderator's voice-over, "That would be a cow, albeit a wild cow.") We then milk it and have a source of food available when we need it. We can settle down and accumulate stuff.

After all, we won't have to pack our meager gear and move to another place to search for hunting grounds we have not yet depopulated. We won't have to look for berry bushes we have not yet denuded. Our staying in one place will allow us to produce additional children, eventually overpopulating our habitat. What is more, being sedentary, we can become increasingly acquisitive; a little stuff here, a little stuff there. Who knows? Someday, we might have enough stuff to fill two caves."

Man, "Not a bad idea. We can increase our population to the extent we begin to specialize. I milk cattle, and you become a cave wife. Eventually, we will be able to stratify our occupations and develop hierarchies of dominance. We can develop tools, some of which we give to selected tribe members working in a new occupation, the warrior class. They can dedicate themselves to maiming and slaying fellow humans in order to acquire their stuff! Thus far, our intraspecies violence, while widespread, is not very well organized. At this stage of our evolution, we don't have much stuff to covet."

Woman, "I agree, and the wild berry will be more pleasant to eat if I grow, graft, cross-strain, and otherwise modify it into an edible sweet pea. What is more, we can eventually domesticate wildcats and jackals! We can live day-to-day with these animals, as well as reside in close quarters with other humans of our expanding population. With this new life style, we can more easily contact the animals' diseases, add some of our own, and eventually evolve into a hierarchical, stratified, disease-ridden race."

Moderator, "Thus, the early humans began the changes from the dangerous job of wild game hunters and the tedious job of gatherers to the relatively safe occupation of food producers...depending on the weather, of course. After some experimentation, spanning over several centuries, humans succeed in housebreaking animals and plants—thus rendering our first domesticated food."

[Cameras pan out of the cave, and focus on a bucolic sunrise, thus implying a bright future for the human race.]

As the TV program demonstrates, the increased population of humans, with dense concentrations in smaller places, coupled with their occupation of food producers, fostered further movement to a sedentary life and a less dangerous day-to-day existence. It also led to the accumulation of more stuff and the eventual booming storage locker industry.

CHAPTER 5

PECKING FOR POKING

(Show 2)

As part of his studies, the Student Cepee is directed by his teacher to another *Coming to You Live, from the Dead* TV show, titled "Pecking for Poking." As mentioned, its low resolution format—a human contrivance—has been changed by the Cepees to playback as a three-dimensional hologram presentation.

Indeed, holograms driven by artificial intelligence (AI) software have become a prominent part of Cepee culture. One could call them AI robots, but they are too ephemeral to do much hard labor, which is left to AI-driven, powerful machines. Shortly, we come across a unique hologram, one controlled by the Mentor Sage.

The program explains the relationships of a hierarchical pecking order to the opportunity for having sex and perpetuating the species. Here is what the Cepee sees.

[The TV camera shot closes in on a group of early human males, squatting around a fire. The time of day is in the early evening, just before sunset. In the background, a group of early female humans is seen sitting behind the males. The camera cuts to the leader of this tribe. He arises from his squat to address his assemblage.]

"Fellow tribe members. As you know, because I am the strongest and most virile man of our lot, I have been given the responsibility of protecting the females and wimps in our tribe. This position gives me precedence over the other males to spread my sperm and genes into as many women as possible. However, my vice consul informs me there have been complaints among the males of our tribe about the paucity of sexual encounters in their day-to-day lives. Let me remind everyone of our Human Tribal Hierarchy pecking order."

[The TV camera closes in on a drawing of the figure below, rendered on a stone slate with charcoal markings.]

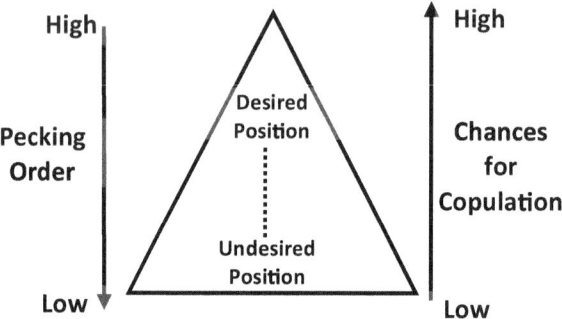

The pecking order for poking.

The tribe leader continues, "As you know, a direct relationship exists between the position one occupies in our hierarchical pecking order and the chances of mating with our females. I am in the 'Desired Position' in this hierarchy. The rest of you are positioned on the lower rungs. If you are unhappy with this arrangement, you are welcome to lead the next hunt for a wooly mammoth, take command of the next raid into our neighbor's caves, or fight me for my position in our tribe. Any takers? ...I thought not, so I remain the 'main man' for our women," as he points to the group of females.

The tribe leader briefly and silently reflects, *One man to twenty women, a fitting example of The Disproportionate Ratio.*[4] *No question; I'm a contented human male...but a bit tired in the morning.*

[The TV screen reveals the males in this circle are not happy with their leader's lecture, and disgruntled mutterings are heard from the females. Both groups are dissatisfied with the 1:20 ratio and consider it quite disproportionate.]

The tribe leader continues, "I recognize the need for a diverse gene pool. Can't have our children growing three ears. I also know I must keep all you campers as happy campers. I have decided to grant

---

[4] Defined as n : m, where n is very small and m is very large.

the males in our tribe a specific number of copulation privileges. Let's look at the stone tablet again. Guuuug, you are just below me in the desired position in our Pecking Order/Chances for Copulation hierarchy. So, you are number two in our tribe's copulation queue."

[The TV screen reveals smiles appearing on the faces of Guuuug and the female members of the tribe.]

"On the other hand, Harold, you are our resident wimp, resting at the 'Undesired Position' of our pecking order. I have thought of banning you from the tribe, but we need you as live bait for our tiger traps. Therefore, you will be given the last place in the queue. Your ejaculation privileges with our females are once a year."

[The TV screen shows looks of indifference appearing on the faces of the females and a pronounced frown on Harold's face.]

"I am writing on this slate the number of times per year, with the associated dates, that each of you men will be given an opportunity to lower your testosterone levels with the females in our tribe. I must place a limit on these numbers because we can't afford to have your testosterone drop beyond the assertiveness threshold. If so, your aggressive tendencies will diminish, and we'll end up as the tigers' suppers or slaves to other tribes. Well, that's it. Early to the stone mat everyone. We're running out of meat and must sally forth tomorrow morning to hunt for fat and protein."

[The screen shows Harold and his friend, Oooorg, walking toward the slate to study the copulation schedule.]

Oooorg commiserates with his friend, "Wow, Harold, too bad. I'm sorry you're at the bottom of our pecking order and therefore, positioned at the concomitant last place in our copulation queue. But better you than me. ...Say, why are you smiling? You can have sex only once a year."

Harold responds, "Sure, but look at my sex schedule. Tonight's the night!"

[The camera pans out of the campfire scene and focuses on a romantic sunset, thus implying a pleasant evening for Harold, and due to his prolonged abstinence, a busy night for one of the females in the tribe.]

CHAPTER 6
THE HUMAN TRIBAL HIERARCHY
(Data Fill 2)

Notwithstanding the Student's increasing inventory of downloaded data from the Human Archives, and notwithstanding his assimilation of this information, including the television shows, he begins to understand the complexity of his ancestors' lives. But he also thinks—quite prematurely—that he has a firm grasp on the subject.

He reflects: *My Mentor Sage has started me on a program to learn about the humans. I think I already know enough to move on to other things in life. I know that thousands of years ago, the humans evolved from hunters and gatherers to sheepherders and gardeners. They eventually became the dominant large-bodied species on the planet. We Cepees then took over. That's it. What else is there to know? The next time we visit, I'll demonstrate my knowledge to my teacher. For certain, he will promote me to a position of more importance and prestige.*

In the meantime, the Student begins a data fill dictated to him by an established curricula set by the Mentor Sage. Here is what the Cepee learns.

Tribes and the Human Tribal Hierarchy (HTH)

The increased population of humans, with dense concentrations in smaller places, coupled with their occupation of food producers, fostered a change to a sedentary life. It also led to the proliferation of diseases, the development of specialized occupations, stratified societies, and the emergence of *tribes*.

26

Each human belonged, or aspired to belong to many tribes, some based on common ancestors; others based on common customs and traditions; still others based on a diverse array of human traits and dispositions.

Humans also evolved to create the *Human Tribal Hierarchy* (HTH)—in practice, a pecking order. The result was the desire for each human to be on top of his or her tribal pack; to be superior to the other humans in the tribe; to ascend the pecking order in a given tribe.

Maslow's Hierarchy of Needs

The Human Tribal Hierarchy was the foundation for the Maslow Hierarchy of Needs, developed by the psychologist Maslow in the humans' 1940s, and summarized as a general scheme in the figure on the next page. The bottom of the hierarchy represented the fundamental, basic needs of a human, such as water, food, shelter, and clothing.[5]

After these requirements were satisfied, the human needed sex to insure his/her genes were passed to subsequent generations. Sex was secondary to some of the other basic needs. After all, copulation was not very high on a person's list of needs if that person were starving or freezing to death.

The Student is relieved to learn that his ancestors considered sex to be one of their most important activities. He says to himself. *OK, so I don't know everything yet. I don't know enough about sex to fully appreciate all that it meant to the human race and what it means to my own Cepees. But I do know enough to know I want to know more. Oh well, back to my data fills.*

---

[5] Maslow's hierarchy is more detailed than the hierarchy shown in the figure. I have substituted the word "need" for Maslow's word of "motive," and separated sex into a separate entry. I have also added the word "power" to the hierarchy. Here is Maslow's complete hierarchy: (1) physiological; (2) security and safety; (3) love and feelings of belonging; (4) competence, prestige, and esteem; (5) self fulfillment; (6) curiosity and the need to understand. Sourced from Microsoft's Encarta Reference Library.

Maslow's Hierarchy of Needs (a general view).

After these essential physiological needs were met, humans sought ways to satisfy their egos, such as attaining prestige and esteem, and garnering power. These aspects of behavior did not contribute directly to the survival of a human, but they did have an indirect role to play. For example, a male who was held in high esteem by his tribal members would more likely find success in spreading his genes than a male who was shunned by the tribe. And a powerful tribe member, one who held sway over others, was more likely to survive and procreate than a powerless underling. Nonetheless, this male had to succeed in the lower, basic needs before he could aspire to the higher rungs of prestige, esteem, and power.

The "loftier needs" shown at the top of Maslow's Hierarchy became important after the aforementioned basic needs and ego-satisfaction requirements were satisfied. As examples, many humans strived for self-fulfillment by creating works of art or by gaining an understanding of a religion or science. Others wished to engage in politics, perhaps write a book, or play music.

Most members of the human race took to the idea that love and affection toward others were important to their lives; that it made them and the recipients of these emotions happier and more fulfilled.

The Student Cepee reflects: *That pretty female that came to my teacher's office after my first session. She's...well, I understand this part of my data fill...attractive. I think she might have found me attractive until I said, "Hello, Cepeeette!" That seemed to turn her off a bit. I don't understand why. Maybe I'll ask my mentor about it. Hm. No. I don't want to show my ignorance. I'll let it be.* As he continues with the data fill.

These behavioral attributes were laudable, because their existence led to a more harmonious species, one capable of improving not only the human who practiced them, but other humans who interacted with the practitioner.

In addition, as the race became farmers and animal tenders, they began to have idle time on their hands. Idle time had a significant impact on the race. With more free time, and with a food surplus, the humans could ascend onto higher positions in the Maslow Hierarchy (as mentioned, also called the Human Tribal Hierarchy): creating music, sculptures, and paintings; inventing religions; discovering gravity and electricity—overall making the world a better place in which to live.

But along with these noble and laudatory accomplishments, the abundance of free time also gave the human the freedom to engage in less meritorious pursuits: committing rape and murder; inventing torture devices; discovering weapons of mass destruction—overall, making the world a more dangerous place.

The Luck of the Geographical Roll of the Dice?

Some humans held the view that human tribes who had the good fortune to live in accommodating climates for growing food, or lived in regions abundant with large domestic mammals, gained a head start on other societies— a favorable position with significant consequences for the human race. The proponents of this theory postulated that eventually, this roll of the geographical dice led to a competitive advantage and affected various tribes' positions on the power and wealth hierarchies throughout much of the humans' modern times.

The notion of geographical determinism as the sole factor for the creation of tribal hierarchies was viewed with skepticism by the Cepees. After all, they were a separate race within the Homo sapiens. Indeed, the great distances that separated the early human tribes resulted in their evolving in different ways—both genetically and physically—leading to different races with different capabilities.

Regardless of which school was correct—and there were elements of truth to both views—with less time needed to keep their larders full, humans were free to invent new tools. Two such tools were steel and gunpowder. Eventually, they became one of the most important factors in a tribe assuming dominance over other tribes. After all, a wooden spear was no match for an iron blunderbuss. Many conquests a tribe (perhaps even a large tribe, such as a nation) obtained over another was because of superior firepower.

The Autocatalytic Process

The humans also began to conduct much of their behavior under the influence of The Autocatalytic Process. It was a feedback cycle wherein a process reinforced another process and vice versa. Also, the cycle went exponentially faster, resulting in the human race increasingly leading a faster-paced life, eventually encouraging the fantastic—and fantastically fast—changes the humans began to make to themselves in the 20th and 21st centuries.

The Autocatalytic Process also resulted in the humans increasing exponentially the power of their weapons. The time between the invention of a deadly weapon and its replacement by a deadlier weapon became exponentially shorter in time.

The Threshold Lowering Syndrome

This syndrome described an act by a human, who by committing an act, made it easier for this person or another person to repeat the act. The act could have been beneficial or detrimental to the parties involved. But regardless of its merit, the party who committed the act received positive reinforcement from carrying it out, such as applause, infusions of adrenaline or dopamine, perhaps self-satisfaction, maybe self-preservation.

Unfortunately for the human race, this syndrome, in consonance with The Autocatalytic Process, led to the acceptance of using increasingly deadly weapons on increasingly large populations.

The Immediacy Syndrome

The humans had a relatively brief stay on the 4.54 billion year-old earth. The Human Archives documented their race was about 200,000 years of age, and their more modern societies were only 6,000 years old before they began their initially gradual, and later rapid transformation to the Cepee.

Since those earliest times, the Immediacy Syndrome had a great influence on their behavior. This characteristic affected most of the population and manifested itself in the desire for an immediate fulfillment of a wish. In some instances, the wish was a genuine need, such as a craving for water or warmth. In other situations, the wish was associated with less important matters: a craving for status, an appetite for pride, a hankering for religious succor.

Whatever was desired—such as pride, sex, food, money, or spiritual fulfillment—its consumption or realization, and (often) satiation required immediate satisfaction. The human had been programmed over many centuries to focus on the present. The future was of no importance.

Until late in the human era, long-range considerations of almost any need or desire were irrelevant to the well-being of the human. Delaying the acts of eating, drinking, or copulating made no sense. Why wait to eat if one were hungry? Why delay an orgasm if copulating couples were trying to expand their gene pool or for that matter, taking-in pleasure? To the early humans, today was important. Tomorrow would be today soon enough.

To a great extent, this short-range view persisted throughout human history, even into humans' modern times in the 21st century.

CHAPTER 7

I'M PRE-PROGRAMMED FOR SPONTANEITY!

(Dialogue 2)

Thus bolstered by the first meeting with the Mentor Sage, the data fills, and the *Coming to you Live, from the Dead* shows, the Student Cepee continues the curriculum to learn about his ancestors, the humans.

Upon approaching the podium in the sanctuary of the Mentor Sage, the Student Cepee encounters a sage-like image. Therefore, the Student Cepee pays careful attention. After all, a sage is sagacious.

However, this dialogue is executed with a sage rendered as a hologram. The Mentor Sage is not present. This sage is not genuine, of course, but its artificial intelligence (AI) components give it a real-life appearance. The hologram image is rendered as a standing sage, positioned just a few feet from the sitting Student. Here is what the Student Cepee learns.

"Greetings, Student. I wish you well during your exploration of the Human Archives." The Hologram Sage smiles, "I also hope you reach an understanding of the subject matter of your studies, the human beings."

Student, "What's so funny?"

The Student knows the sage is not a real Cepee. Nonetheless, because of the artificial intelligence software directing the presence and behavior of the hologram image, the Student also knows this simulated sage can interact with the Student in a sophisticated fashion. The Student queries, "Why the smile?"

Hologram Sage, "Because I presented you with a sentence containing a contradiction in ideas. Even we Cepees have never achieved a complete understanding of our ancestors."

Student, "Then what's the point? Why don't I proceed to the next phase of my education program? Why should I spend my time studying a subject I will never fully understand? And where is the Mentor Sage?"

Hologram Sage, "I am standing in for him, under his direction. He is busy doing sage-like things. By the way, don't be so insolent! You cannot skip this part of your education. As you progress through it, you will come to understand why. Furthermore, learning about the humans, dealing with their behavior, understanding their motives, comprehending their actions is like standing in a raft in the middle of an ocean: You never sink, but your feet are always wet."

Student, "So you're telling me this part of my education is important. You are also warning me I will understand the humans, and at the same time, I will not understand them?"

Hologram Sage, "Right on! You will often find the behavior of our predecessors incomprehensible. Usually, their conduct could be explained. But again, not always. In addition, you will examine them from the perspective of a Cepee and, therefore, with a different set of values than those of the humans."

The Student thinks: *Right on?* "I think I understand the idea. I will be entering a more contradictory world than the Cepee's. I must accept more ambiguities."

Hologram Sage, "You got it! Let's get on with it. As you are becoming aware, the searches into the Human Archives will be filled with data...data crucial to your understanding the human race. Of course, your curriculum is not a self-study program. Your Mentor Sage will help you assimilate these data into meaningful information."

The Student wonders about: *You got it!* "My Mentor Sage tells me our ancestors are extinct. Why?"

Hologram Sage, "Take that question to your Mentor Sage. He has set up a dialogue with you about this subject."

Student, "I did, and my teacher said to wait awhile. I thought you might throw some light on the subject."

The Hologram Sage does not respond to the joke, but answers, "Then don't be so impatient. Your data fills and your Mentor Sage will reveal the answer to your question. By the way, I can field some of your questions, but we holograms are not designed to be completely interactive."

The Student silently agrees.

Hologram Sage, "Actually, my specialty deals with the humans' popular music during their latter times on earth. I'm filling in for another hologram for a while. The primary hologram for your tutorials encountered a glitch this morning during a software download. It is proving to be a bug to fix, so you may have my presence in your studies for a while."

Student, "Sorry to inconvenience you. How is your backup performance coming along?"

Hologram Sage, "OK, I guess. I'd rather be rock and rolling. It fits in with my light and mirrors personality. But I've been downloaded with a couple of special routines that should get us through our talks. Anyway, as our rock and roll ancestors would say, your Mentor Sage is, 'Boss'…Well, maybe 'King'…eh, perhaps 'Prince.' Anyway, the Mentor Sage will provide you with everything you need. I am here to assist when he is occupied with other matters."

Student, "Ah, so that's what's behind 'Right on.' and 'You got it.' You're so-programmed?

Hologram Sage, "Yo, bro!"

Student, "Maybe we should try another subject?"

Hologram Sage, "That might be a bit taxing to my subroutines, but I'll give it a go. Your Mentor Sage has purposely restricted the number and variety of apps I can use. He does not want my AI operations to get out of control."

Student, "Hologram Sage, my teacher informs me that Cepees are good looking. So, it stands to reason that we have opportunities for a lot of sex. Right? …Say something, Hologram Sage."

The silence from the Hologram Sage is the result of its executing several million lines of software code trying to come up with an appropriate response. Finally, it responds, "No can do. Pose your question to your Mentor Sage." (In spite of the year being 2084, artificial intelligence is still called artificial intelligence for good reason.)

Student, "Very well. But I wouldn't mind a little data on the subject, or a little bit of the subject itself."

Hologram Sage, "Something like your desire to experience an immediate data fill?"

Student, "Ha! Hologram Sage, I thought you did not have humor pre-programmed into your presentation?"

Hologram Sage, "I'm not pre-programmed for humor, but I am pre-programmed for spontaneity."

Student, "That's a contradiction in logic. How can something be pre-programmed for spontaneity?"

Hologram Sage, "It cannot. Your Mentor Sage directed me to pose the statement to you to test you. I suppose you passed. Anyway, I am also pre-programmed to remind you to stay focused on your studies. Your subject of the human race will have you encounter some unusual behavioral patterns."

Student, "Such as?"

Hologram Sage, "Humans killing other humans."

Student, "What! Killing one another? Why? It must have been to keep themselves fed, clothed, and sheltered; to meet the physical needs of their lives; to satisfy the lower rungs on the humans' Maslow Hierarchy of Needs."

The Hologram Sage executes a number of possible response routines from its software library and finally replies, "No. Some killed for the pleasure of killing. Your Mentor Sage has more information for you."

The Student thinks, *Another paltry response from this virtual sage. Computer-based education is not very effective. I'd like to be taught by a non-computer, a real sage.* (Which of course, is not possible because all 'real' sages operate with organic-based computers in their skulls.)

The Student then protests to the hologram image, "Hologram Sage, this stuff is ponderous."

Hologram Sage, "I'm only a light show. What do you expect me to do? Make something up that assuages your attention-deficient, juvenile neocortexes? What's the matter, Student, too taxing? Am I asking you to actually think? Would sound bites make you happier? Perhaps a human MTV millisecond sequence? How about canned laughter? Maybe a five-second musical jingle? Did I use a verb in a sentence? Not enough audio Twitter? You're just like our ancestors, unable to focus on much of anything for more than a second or so.

"Student, this tutorial is explaining several important traits of the humans. If you are to understand why we are here, and why the humans are not, I suggest you pay more attention and exhibit a morsel of patience."

Student, "You sound like my Mentor Sage."

Hologram Sage, "True! The Mentor Sage downloaded that missive for playback to you."

Finally realizing he is in a learning environment, the Student—as with most students—feels trapped, "Well, I might as well get into the spirit of things. Looks like my Mentor Sage is a real teacher."

With a new perspective on the situation, the Student Cepee and the Hologram Sage wrap up their meeting with this final instruction from the Hologram, "Student, your teacher wishes me to inform you of another human term. You will encounter it during your surfing of the Human Archives. It is called The Disproportionate Ratio Effect."

Student, "A ratio, such as n-to-m?"[6]

Hologram Sage, "Yes, and disproportionate in that the value of n is very small and the value of m is very large. For example, the ratio of (n) persons doing harm to (m) people. As in the ratio of Iraqi terrorists in Iraq to Iraqi citizens in the humans' 1990s: 3,000:25,000,000, or the ratio of IRA gunmen in the humans'1970s to Northern Ireland citizens: 400:1,800,000.[7]

"As another example, the ratio of a lone killer in Las Vegas murdering 58 people in the early 21st century. For an extreme example,

---

[6] Introduced in footnote 4.

[7] Bruce Hoffman, "Plan of Attack," *Atlantic*, July/August, 2004, 43.

the killing of hundreds of thousands of people with a weapon of mass destruction, by only one person pressing a button."

The Student is stunned. He has not yet been exposed in any detail to this aspect of his ancestors' behavior. The Hologram informs the Student he will have ample opportunity to learn about this ratio and related matters.

Student, "OK, Hologram Sage, I'll remember this ratio idea. Whew. Sobering. ...Eh, can you present me a disproportionate example that is not so tragic...maybe even funny?"

The challenge is taxing to a software-impaired light system. Still, the Hologram Sage grinds away, "OK. How about this: The ratio of Wilt Chamberlain (n) to Wilt's sexual partners (m)."

Student, "I don't know about Wilt or his partners. But I know about the subject. My ratio requirements are quite modest. I'd settle for 1:1."

Hologram Sage, "Take your problem up with your teacher. Stay put. He will arrive shortly."

CHAPTER 8

THE IGNORANT, THEREFORE, DOCTRINAIRE SYNDROME

(Dialogue 3)

The next exchange between the Student Cepee and the Mentor Sage takes place after the Student had completed his data fills on key phrases, definitions, and concepts, as well as his first enlightening dialogue with the Hologram Sage.

Student Cepee, "So many terms!"

Sage Cepee, "True. But you will find them useful as you become more involved in learning about your ancestors. They will become mental short cuts for your analysis."

Student, "I find the description of tribe to be interesting, especially the idea that almost any human affiliation had a tribal slant, as well as a hierarchy, a pecking order."

Sage, "Correct. Practically every human relationship, and almost every human encounter, was based on a tribal hierarchical pecking order. Some of the tribes were small, such as a family unit. Others were larger, such as a religious sect. Some were huge, such as a nation. Many were disguised with language and gesticulatory manipulations. But underneath the surface, humans looked to assume a dominant position in practically every tribe to which they belonged."

Student, "Why? We Cepees do not react this way."

Sage, "We Cepees have no need to. As you will learn in your education, over thousands of years, the humans evolved to focus their efforts on survival and spreading their gene pool to subsequent generations. A dominant human was more likely to survive and pass his or her genes to children. An acquiescent, subservient human did not fare well in the humans' competitive world. However, Cepees are not concerned about survival, because we never die. Nor are we obsessed with spreading our gene pool because genetic tailoring obviates the process."

The Mentor Sage continues, "Student, do not discount the efficiency of the humans' tribes and their Human Tribal Hierarchies. The practice made them the most dominant species on earth."

Student, "Oh? Then why aren't the humans still around? It doesn't appear to me they were all that dominant...to just die out with hardly a whimper."

Sage, "It was not a whimper! It actually started with some very big bangs.

"At this point, you know very little about the subject of how the humans, as you say, 'died out.' Therefore, you should not make a comment, or express an opinion on something about which you have no knowledge. This mode of behavior is an unfortunate holdover from our ancestors.

"Let me teach you about one of the more vexing habits of the humans, one I find a trace in you. We Cepees have dubbed it The Ignorant, Therefore, Doctrinaire Syndrome. It was a common human behavioral trait in which a human who was devoid of any knowledge whatsoever on a subject held an unyielding—and often belligerent—opinion on the very same subject."

Student, "May I offer an opinion on this syndrome?"

Sage, "You may."

Student, "Pathetic."

Sage, "And worse. Many humans formed an opinion about a subject and held this opinion throughout their lives, regardless of circumstances demonstrating the opinion was invalid, incorrect, or harmful."

Student, "Why did humans take this approach?"

Sage, "As you will learn, it was often because of pride and the loss of face. Be patient. We will have other dialogues on one of the biggest deficiencies of our ancestors, their pride."

Student, "Am I permitted another opinion?"

Sage, "Of course. You are permitted opinions if they are based on something besides thin air or Twitter nonsense." (The Mentor Sage is not fond of this ancient human anti-intellectual contrivance, even the audio version that works with a wireless chip embedded in the Cepee brain.)

Student, "What a pointless approach. How could our ancestors solve a problem if they could not change their views on a matter?"

Sage, "Unfortunately for them, often they could not. Just consider how long they held on to the belief that the earth was flat. They imprisoned one of their geniuses, Galileo, for postulating the earth was not the center of what they thought to be the universe.

"One of their more modern examples of this syndrome was a United States President, named Donald Trump. He denied that a phenomenon called global warming was causing the sea levels to rise—until his golf courses near the sea coasts became 18-hole water hazards. His resort, Mar a Lago, became an apt name for the place."

Student, "What does Mar a Lago mean?"

Sage, "In Spanish: Sea to Lake. Mr. Trump's property ended up being appropriately named. "

The Mentor Sage continues, "The unveiling of new facts proving an opinion to be incorrect was frequently ineffective in altering the opinion. The person holding the opinion fell back to The Ignorant, Therefore, Doctrinaire Syndrome, thus saving the person's pride and keeping the person in good stead with equally stupid members of the same group."

Student, "As I thought when I watched the Hologram Sage's presentations, I'm beginning to detect some cracks, maybe holes, in the human dam."

Sage, "Yes, and you will see many more cracks and holes. As you receive your data fills, try this experiment. Tabulate how many times you come across a situation in which a human says something to the effect of, 'I have studied this issue in more depth, and I have decided there is another way to look at it. I could be wrong. No, I am wrong.'"

Student, "Will do, Mentor Sage. I have another question. My last data fill revealed that humans continued to lower their thresholds for acceptable levels of behavior. I cannot understand this fact. Can you help me?"

Sage, "As you learn more about the importance of the humans' positions on the tribal hierarchies, you will begin to understand why our ancestors began killing one another for reasons other than physical survival. Without getting too far ahead in your program, this uncontrollable propensity eventually led to the Cepees' ascension to replace the human. Again, be patient. The information is forthcoming."

Student, "I understand. I'll stick with the program. ...Mentor Sage, the Hologram Sage mentioned sex. Is sex part of my education program?"

Sage, "My records indicate it was you who brought up the subject. You are an impatient student. Remember your study of a human trait called The Immediacy Syndrome?"

Student, "Yes. They defined it as the need for an immediate fulfillment of a desire or wish."

Sage, "Don't succumb to this syndrome! Sex will come into your life. All in due time, Student. All in due time."

Student, "Easy for you to say. You're a sage. Not so easy for me. I'm a student. Very well. What's next?"

Sage, "A thank you will do."

Student, "Thank you, Mentor Sage."

Sage, "It is my job, Student Cepee. For now, we take a short break. Come back in a few minutes. We will have another dialogue."

Student, "Eh, any chance of the other student showing up anytime soon?"

Sage, "You mean the female student you saw earlier?"

Student, "Yes, the one I saw after our first session. I didn't know her name, so I just called her 'Cepeeette.'"

Sagacious sages are patient beings, but this student is pushing his luck. The Mentor Sage responds, "She had come by to register for a program with me. During your encounter with her, you did not exhibit The Ignorant, Therefore, Doctrinaire Syndrome, you displayed The Ignorant Syndrome! You've so much to learn, Student Cepee. You are dismissed for a few minutes to think about your insult to that damsel."

CHAPTER 9

THE TABULA RASA RULE

(Dialogue 4)

The next exchange between the Student Cepee and the Mentor Sage takes place after the Student has completed his data fills on the early humans, their evolution from hunters and gatherers to food producers and other specialists, as well as the many terms associated with his ancestors.

The non-hologram sage admonishes his student, "Don't you understand you insulted the Cepee female by referring to her as 'Cepeeette?' There is no such name for a Cepee being."

Student, "Just having some fun, Sage, pointing out that she was a female."

Sage, "A Ms. would do. It would be the same situation if she called you maleette to distinguish you from her."

Student, "But, Sage! I *am* a male. There would be no need to use the word *maleette* to identify me. ...Say, how about if I call her *little woman*? That was a term our ancestors liked to use."

Sage, "How about if she calls you *little man*?"

Student, "No way, Sage! I'm not little. That is a degrading term."

Sage, "Perhaps *little woman* is also degrading; if not degrading, then condescending. Nor was there any need for you to have used Cepeeette. The next time you see her, I suggest you apologize."

The Student is eager to have such an opportunity. "That I will do, Mentor Sage."

Sage, "What are your questions and thoughts for today?"

Student, "I came across the idea that idle time was a contributing factor to our ancestors' intraspecies murders. The notion seems a bit far-fetched."

Sage, "Keep in mind the humans evolved into a stratified, hierarchical race. As they learned to store away their excess larder for later use, they did not have to work all the time. They had idle time on their hands. Some of this time was taken up in extraordinary pursuits: art, music, writing, and inventions. Other times were taken up by our predecessors imbibing in a lot of mischief."

Student, "But my data fills do not explain why some of this idle time was spent in mischief."

Sage, "That is because you have not finished your data fills. Be patient, Student! The information is forthcoming."

Student, "Very well, Sage. I noticed from my data fills that many humans seemed to shirk their responsibilities to one another. I gather the statement, 'My mind went blank,' was just an excuse for their inactions."

Sage, "Correct, Student. We Cepees call this malady, The Tabula Rasa Rule. It was the humans' age-old practice of denying responsibility for an action—a sin of commission—or an inaction—a sin of omission—because the humans' mind apparently went blank: They supposedly forgot. Indeed, the rule was so prevalent in the human race that we Cepees play an amusing game, at the expense of the humans, to parody their behavior."

Student, "May I play? I could use a break from my data fills and studies."

Sage, "Certainly. Here is how it is played. The challenge is to fill-in parts (a) and (b) of this sentence: (a), I had no intention of (b), my mind went blank. The challenger furnishes (a); in turn, the challenged furnishes (b). Because you do not yet know very much about the human, you will present me with an (a) entry. In turn, I will respond with an (b) excuse. As you proceed into your studies, you will come to understand humans and can compose some (a) and (b) clauses yourself."

Student, "Cool! OK, here goes. Eh, 'Your honor,'"

Sage, "'I had no intention of insulting the Jews. I drank too much tequila, and my mind went blank.'"

Student, "Hm. 'Your Grace,'"

Sage, "I had no intention of violating the altar boy. We were doing catechisms, then my mind went blank."

Student, "Sage, how can you come up with such responses so quickly?"

Sage, "Experience with the humans' history, Student. Try another."

Student, who is getting into the spirit of the game, "'Fellow citizens,'"

Sage, "'I had no intention of altering the Bill of Rights and compromising the Geneva Conventions, but I was fighting terrorists, and my mind went blank.'"

Student, "I've archived this subject, Sage. This man Bush had to gather intelligence, and another president even suspended the Americans' *habeas corpus* during their Civil War."

Sage, "If you have studied the subject, then you may recall America had two other branches of government?"

Student, "Yes."

Sage, "His actions being declared unlawful would have been helpful, Student."

Student, "Well, OK, you're a sage, and I'm not."

Sage, "Indeed, now it is your turn: 'Dear listeners of my talk show,'"

The Student must react if he is to pass this test, "Eh… 'I had no intention of getting my maid in trouble, but someone other than myself needed to buy my drugs, and my mind was blank from too many drugs anyway.'"

Sage, "Very creative. Try this one: 'Dear listeners of my talk show,'"

Student, "That's not fair!"

Sage, "Neither was the humans' treatment of one another. Get on with it."

Student, "I had no intention of hiding my erection problems, but someone other than myself needed to buy my drugs. After all, I was famous. People *rushed* to my shows, so I could not be seen purchasing erection medicine. How deflating it would have been to my fans... not to mention, me."

Sage, "I'm impressed. One more: 'My fellow stockholders,' "

Student, " 'I had no intention of defrauding you, but greed made my mind go blank, and I got careless.' Sage, The game is a pretty harsh indictment of our ancestors."

Sage, "Indictment? Yes, but the game makes nothing up. It simply reflects aspects of our ancestors' behavior."

Student, "Did the humans also play this game?"

Sage, "Yes. But they sometimes had to stay out of harm's reach when supplying the (b) entries. As you have observed, the game could expose raw subjects."

Student, "Yes! This is fun. How about: 'I had no idea my dismissal of global warming would result in massive hurricanes, floods, fires, and the loss of life of thousands of humans...not to mention, my Mar a Lago becoming a mar and a lago.' "

The Mentor Sage chuckles to himself, *This student is justifying my choosing him for my program. In spite of his cheekiness, I am growing fond of the lad.*

The Student continues, "Can we Cepees play this game with ourselves as the subjects?"

Sage, "Of course not. Our minds are never blank. To the Cepee, there is no such thing as a tabula rasa. Certainly, we may not have sufficient information to account for every eventuality that comes into our lives. But we are programmed not to make excuses for our behavior."

Student, "Sage, I had no intention of skipping that last data fill. My mind went blank."

Sage, "Ha! Nice try. Now get back to work. The next phase of your study of the humans is about a subject that was instrumental in bringing about their altering themselves, which eventually led to us Cepees."

Student, "What will that be?"

Sage, "Aggression that was not linked to their well-being, progress, or survival. More accurately: violent, gratuitous aggression."

CHAPTER 10

HUMAN AGGRESSION

(Data Fill 3)

The Student Cepee returns to his study of the Human Archives. His study guide directs him to focus on the terms and concepts described in this data fill, and then discuss them with his teacher. Here is what he learns.

As 2030-2035 appeared on the humans' calendars, it became evident several characteristics had to be modified or eliminated from subsequent members of their species. If possible, one trait had to be culled completely. It was the humans' propensity to engage in violent, gratuitous aggression against one another.

In the past, aggression had been beneficial to the species. It kept humans alive and in competition with other animals and with one another. However, as the human changed over thousands of years, many manifestations of what was once species-enhancing aggression degenerated into pathological behavior contrary to the betterment of their species. The behavior was a form of *retrograde evolution* because it became an evolutionary dead-end alley.

Humans began to behave in a self-destructive manner. Competition, aggression, sexual selection, and breeding began to take place without any relationship to species survival and enhancement. They became ends unto themselves.

Tools for Aggression

During the early development of the human, the tools of aggression were muscle power, body speed, and mental agility.

46

Later, external mechanisms such as clubs, knives, spears, and arrows became a key part of the aggression toolbox. As the human learned more about the development of these tools, he learned to use more sophisticated methods for playing out his aggressive tendencies. Thus, tools evolved from instruments of limited capacity to tools that could destroy entire cities.

Moreover, before the advent of tools, the humans had little need to breed inhibitory behavior into their mental makeup. The gestures of submission with various kowtowing motions, or retreating from a threatening situation were usually (but not always) sufficient to ward off aggression from other members of the species.

The Law of the Instrument

The human invented many tools as instruments to abet his aggressive motives. To be fair, most of the humans' tools were used for tasks such as tilling the earth, scraping hides, digging holes, and hunting mammals, reptiles, birds, and fish. But other tools were invented for hunting humans.

Tools eventually became extensions of the human's mind and body—the human assumed a tool was part of his makeup. Unto itself, this concept was not deleterious to the human. But it became unhealthy when combined with The Law of the Instrument: *Exemplified by the child who picks up a hammer and looks for something to pound.*

The Aggression Cycle

With less risk, accompanied with *the absence of an evolved inhibitor in the brain*, the invention of a weapon as a tool for destruction upset the aggression apple cart, leading to The Aggression Cycle: A process where humans became increasingly aggressive with increasingly destructive tools. The cycle operated as follows: 1. Acquire a tool. 2. Use it successfully for aggression. 3. Thus reinforced, acquire a more destructive tool. 4. Use it for aggression. 5. Repeat the cycle over and over again.

As the tools for aggression evolved to distance the human from the object of his mayhem, the human became less inhibited to mitigate his behavior. After all, disemboweling a human with a remote controlled missile was much easier on the conscience than performing the operation with a knife.

The Noble Savage

The term *Noble Savage* was often used by the humans to describe a noble and gentle human who lived in natural surroundings, far removed from the cruelties of civilization. The so-called Noble Savages were the same as other humans. But they evolved from hunter-gatherers to food producers—much later than, say, the Europeans evolved—and started off lower on the Human Tribal Hierarchy pecking orders. Unfortunately for them, they came up with "snake-eyes" with the place-of-birth roll of the dice.

Humans routinely abused these unfortunate people, thinking them as beings less equal to other humans and less worthy of respect.

The Revenge Cycle Token Passing Protocol

The humans also routinely practiced The Revenge Cycle Token Passing Protocol, shown in the following figure. The idea behind this cycle was simple: After a tribe had been attacked by another tribe (which could be large tribes, such as nations), the attacked tribe was obligated (even expected!) to strike back and avenge the assault. After the revenge had been taken, the tables were turned: the avenger became the avenged, and the avenged became the avenger, and another battle took place.

Then, the tables were turned once again. It never stopped. Humans kept the cycle going until one of the tribes admitted defeat, was subjugated, or was killed off. This cycle was abetted by the aggression cycle, as well as the continued improvement of weapons of mass destruction…coupled with The Law of the Instrument, discussed earlier.

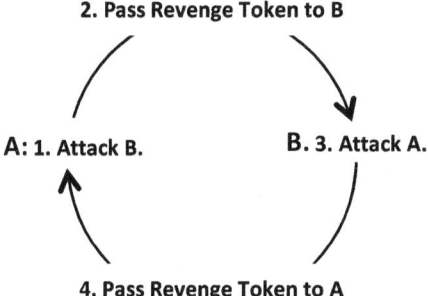

The Revenge Cycle Token Passing Protocol.

The Deadly Trinity + Tools for Mass Destruction = Chaos

The availability of weapons of mass destruction to non-nations as well as nation states altered the fate of the human race. Because of the diffusion of the threat into many disconnected sects, clans, and ethnic groups, previous methods of obtaining security became ineffective.

Confrontation of a nation often did little good. Invasion of the state often provoked hostility among the citizens of the invaded country. Even worse, many nations eventually found themselves populated by individual killers, who were bent on destroying the internal fabric of those nations' societies.

Consequently, the 21st century human race found itself in jeopardy, in danger of falling prey to The Deadly Trinity, summarized here and illustrated in the figure on the next page:

• The Revenge Cycle: The desire of a person or tribe to attack anyone who had previously attacked that person or the person's tribe.

• The Aggression Cycle: The successful execution of an aggressive, violent act that led to more aggressive and violent acts.

• The Law of the Instrument: Tools (instruments) of mass destruction became easier to create, obtain, and use, so the humans naturally enough, used them. Succumbing to The Threshold Lowering Syndrome, humans committed increasingly violent acts with these weapons.

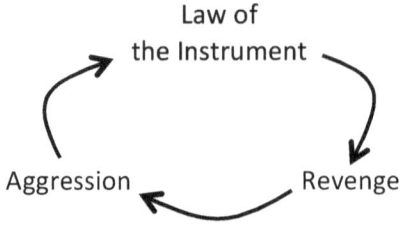

The Deadly Trinity.

Eventually, the rising death tolls and the disintegrating societies of the human race forced humans to come to grips with the perils of their situation. They began to realize the only way out of this dead-end alley was the mental/genetic alteration of their species, a process already underway with EGO, ILLS, and SANE.

Using these projects, the faltering generations of humans and the emerging Cepees also took advantage of life-altering and life-sustaining technologies to make many other changes to the human, eventually-to-be Cepee. By mid-21st century, they began to understand they had to eradicate The Deadly Trinity before The Deadly Trinity eradicated them.

The Student Cepee takes a deep breath: *My ancestors became little more than killers of their own kind. I've learned in other data fills that many animals killed their own species, but the deaths were for long-term survival of the killer. The archives tell me humans killed simply for the sake of killing.*

I read in the archives about a saying the humans had, "You can choose your friends, but you cannot choose your relatives." Based on what I am learning about the humans, I am far from certain I am glad they were my relatives.

I wonder what the Mentor Sage can tell me about this sickness?

CHAPTER 11

THEY'RE RIOTING EVERYWHERE TRUISM

(Dialogue 5)

The Student Cepee has completed the data fills on his ancestors' pathological aggressive behavior. He remains mystified how the humans could have been so murderous when the Cepees are just the opposite. While he is preparing for the dialogues on this subject with his Mentor Sage, the Hologram Sage lights up next to the Student Cepee's desk.

Hologram Sage, "Whoa, here I am again! Greetings, Student. Your Mentor Sage is aware the last data fill was not a bed of roses. So, I have been retrieved from an optical disk and plugged into a laser to give your synapses a break from firings."

Student, "Big deal. If you actually gave me a break, my synapses would not be firing at all!"

Hologram Sage, "Ha, I meant firings from the humans' guns, not firings across your synapses."

Student, "I know what you meant, Hologram Sage. I was making a joke."

Hologram Sage, "As you know."

Student, "Yes, you are not fully loaded for humor."

Hologram Sage, "You got it. Just keep in mind…eh, just keep in mainframe— the limitations of software. Anyway, as you know, I am an expert on the humans' popular music. In keeping with the theme of your current studies, here is a song about the humans' inclinations for maiming one another. It's titled, 'They're Rioting Everywhere.'"[8]

Playing a hologram guitar, the Hologram Sage launches into this song:

Strum, strum, strum....♫♪♪♫
They're rioting in Pakistan.
There's strife in Iran.
There's killing in Baghdad,
and Israel wants land.

The whole world is festering
in one gloomy stew.
The Jew hates the Arab,
the Arab hates the Jew.

Palestinians hate Israelites,
Jordanians hate them, too,
...And the Jews don't like anybody very much!

But we are now certain and can just assume,
that someone will send us a very toxic fume.
And friends they all tell me, that some happy day,
someone will turn the tap on,
and we will all be gassed away.

They're rioting in Palestine.
There's strife in Iraq.
What nature doesn't do to us,
man will do behind our back.

---

[8] If you want to sing along, the melody for the song is an old Kingston Trio tune, *They're Rioting in Africa*. I take blame for the new lyrics, whose cadence is based on the original song. Thank you "Trio." I remain your fan.

Student, "An appropriate song, perfect for my studies and a welcome break from my synapse firings about human firings. Yes, I see our ancestors tended to riot and kill almost anywhere."

Hologram Sage, "Eh, your ancestors, not mine. My ancestors were more along the line of a light bulb."

Student, "Funny, and you probably didn't even know it. Anyway, I am still confused about the violent and aggressive nature of the humans. I'll take it up with the Mentor Sage. ...Any more songs in your data base?"

Hologram Sage, "Sure. I'll appear as needed, as your Mentor Sage so directs."

Student, "Fine. Say, do you know about the humans' The Revenge Cycle?"

Hologram Sage, "I don't know much of anything but what is downloaded into my system. Why?"

Student, "While accessing the Human Archives, I often come across quotes from my ancestors. Here is one from a human's description of The Revenge Cycle:

" 'The Revenge Cycle (also known as The Reciprocal Kick Ass Effect): The instinctual desire to kick the ass of anyone who has previously kicked your ass, or who has fondled the ass of your sister. In turn, the person whose ass was kicked returns the favor by kicking your ass. You reciprocate; so does the kickee/kicker, eventually resulting in a never ending spiral of ass kickings.' "

The Student continues, "This part of the archives even provides references for further study: 'Northern Ireland; Bosnia/Serbia/ Croatia; Haiti; Iran/Iraq, Iran/Saudi Arabia; Greece/Turkey/Cyprus; Tutsis/Hutus. Multitudinous factions in the Middle East as well as Africa, South America, Asia, Europe, and Australia. That is, any area of the world inhabited by humans.' It appears my ancestors were an accomplished ass kicking species."

The Hologram Sage does not have a lot of light to shine on the Student's recent observations. However, it is perceptive enough to offer, "Student, if I were you, I would not characterize these kinds of observations as 'kick ass'. Sages are not fond of human profanity."

Student, "What is profane about the passage? Besides, I am doing research. Who knows what I might unearth about the humans' earth, so to speak? I am merely reflecting the thoughts and speech of my ancestors. What is the point of my research if I cannot speak about my findings?"[9]

But the Hologram fades away, and the puzzled Student makes his way to the desk of the Mentor Sage.

[9] The student has encountered one of the more recent maladies of his ancestors: political correctness.

CHAPTER 12

THE MISPLACED PRIDE AND PREJUDICE PARADOX

(Dialogue 6)

The Student Cepee pays an unscheduled visit to the Mentor Sage. The Sage is surprised to see the Student, "Student, I thought you would be immersed in your data fills on the humans' malpractice of their living practices. But I find you at my sanctuary once again."

Student Cepee, "Yes, Mentor Sage, I've been thinking about our dialogues. Before continuing my next studies, I have another question about our ancestors' behavior. Thus far, I have noticed their conduct toward one another was often vicious. The humans were especially hostile toward their Noble Savages. I have learned the so-called Noble Savage was not considered noble and became a subject of ridicule, exploitation and abuse by other humans, whom I call the non-Noble Savages."

Sage, "Non-Noble Savage? A nice turn-of-phrase, Student. Yes, the Noble Savage was rarely treated nobly by the non-Noble Savages. The problem stemmed from the Human Tribal Hierarchy, which you have studied. Do you recall the Noble Savage concept?"

The Student takes umbrage with this question, "Of course, it played a big role in the progress of the early humans and their positions in their pecking orders. The term was not coined by a Frenchman named Rousseau, but he claimed the primitive humans living in the 1700s existed in an innocent state of nature and were

55

corrupted by the 'unnaturalness of civilization.' Yet these humans were no more or less noble than others."

The Student continues, "And the point of the Human Tribal Hierarchy was to teach me the dominance exhibited by some humans over others. Yet, some of the humans began to behave as if their superior place in life made them better than others, especially other races, cultures, and religions."

Sage, "Well stated, Student Cepee. And correct. It came about because of genetic mutations over many centuries in different parts of the world. That is a topic for later data fills and other dialogues.

"Part of this increasing mental hubris refers to a term we Cepees use to describe this moral shortage: The Pride and Prejudice Paradox. This paradox described a human affliction in which people attributed their self-worth and pride to their origins and where they ended up living. It dealt with circumstances over which they had no influence or control.

"Irrespective of their merit, and because of their good fortune, some humans lived lives of affluence and privilege. Of course, their situation should not be…as the Hologram Sage would say…dissed. Using a human phrase, their 'life style' was not the problem. After all, we Cepees live in very comfortable accommodations.

"The problem was the prejudice they held toward other people who were born in less fortunate circumstances, who emerged from the womb with different skin color, who took on a different religion, or spoke a different language. To use another human term, often the human had no control on which 'side of town' he or she came from, yet their worth was judged by other humans based on this factor."

Student, "Hm. Life's roll of the dice. Didn't our ancestors have an influence on which 'side of town' they lived? I have learned about the humans' competitive spirit and their reliance on merit for advancement up their pecking orders. It seems The Pride and Prejudice Paradox implies our ancestors' self-worth and pride had nothing to do with their merit."

Sage, "Not at all. Our ancestors displayed considerable spirit and thrived on competition. Their pride was instrumental in their successful ventures. Your point is well taken, but The Pride and

Prejudice Paradox must be interpreted very carefully. This paradox states that humans all too often displayed *misplaced* pride about something they did *not* create—over which they had no control. Conversely, they exhibited prejudice toward other humans who had no control over who they were, or little control over their position in life. Remember, Student, pride is one thing; misplaced pride is quite another. I reproached you earlier about this problem."

Student, "Yes, I remember your advice. Perhaps the paradox under discussion should be named The *Misplaced* Pride and Prejudice Paradox. The existing title might lead one to believe pride is always associated with prejudice. Such is not the case."

Sage, "Your point is noted. I will take it up with my fellow sages, and for now, we will use your addendum."

Student, "Thank you. Sage, I take it you are not very high on The Misplaced Pride and Prejudice Paradox and its consequences?"

Sage, "Your assumption is correct and another understatement. As you continue your studies, you will learn our forebears advanced their often misguided causes based on misplaced pride and associated prejudices, which manifested themselves in mindless acts of bigotry, chauvinism, intolerance, injustice, unfairness, and discrimination.

"These travesties against one another were nothing more than camouflages for their deficient DNA and aberrant gene mutations. ...Which we Cepees fixed."

Student, "I must learn more about this aspect of our ancestors."

Sage, "Fine, and we will have another session soon about a closely related subject, which we Cepees have dubbed The Pride Paradox."

Student, "A shorter version of The Misplaced Pride and Prejudice Paradox?"

Sage, "Yes, but with a different twist."

Student, "Thank you, Sage."

The Sage is a bit surprised. The Student uttered another unsolicited thank you. But this teacher, being a sage, must remain sagaciously stoic. He responds, "That is what I do. My job description, if you will."

CHAPTER 13

THE AGGRESSION / SUBMISSION QUANDARY

(Dialogue 7)

The seventh Cepee dialogue takes place after the Student Cepee has listened to the Hologram Sage's song about human riots and mayhem and the teacher's wisdoms about misplaced pride.

Student Cepee, "Sage, I find the information in my data fills confusing. They deal with our ancestors' inability to control their deadly aggression and violence. I understand the facts, but I cannot grasp why they did not come to grips with the problem. They killed one another almost indiscriminately. Can you clarify this point?"

Sage Cepee, "Yes, and at times, you can delete the word *almost*, because they *often* killed each other indiscriminately. Student, as the humans liked to say, 'Hindsight is 20-20.' We Cepees can look back on the past with considerable wisdom. After all, we have the advantage of reflection to view the consequences of their behavior. Humans did not have this luxury. Our ancestors had another saying that is apropos to the situation you describe, 'When you're up to your ass in alligators, it's hard to remember your job was to clear the swamp.'"

Student, "Whoa! So, it is permissible to use human slang during these dialogues?"

Sage, "Of course. After all, you are doing research on humans, so you must occasionally use their clichés and idioms. And we Cepees

58

honor honest talk, even though we might not like some of that talk. Why do you ask?"

Student, "It deals with statements this hologram makes. But the thing is just a bunch of light. ...Eh, fine, Mentor Sage. I know its reflections are your reflections. I sometimes forget about this fact, as a hologram's ideas and guidance seem, well, so transparent. And Could it be true that the Hologram is programmed with some AI software that is even beyond the control of Cepee sages? Do sages sense that AI has gotten out of hand? Personally, I have come to like the Hologram Sage. Given it's not much more than light beams, it's... as it would say, pretty cool!

"Anyway, when I was doing some surfing of the archives, I came across an incident where a noted and respected authority was to give a lecture on the subject of rape to an academic institution. She was admonished for using the word *rape* in her presentation. How could that be?"

Sage, "As mentioned a short time ago in your program, the humans went through a condition called *political correctness.* It was a sad state of affairs and resulted in pointless assaults on the idea of free speech, which we Cepees revere. We will take this subject up later in our studies. For now, let's return to the humans' uncontrolled aggression, one of their major failings."

Student, "Yes, Mentor Sage. So, another aspect of their behavior is perplexing. It appears a human who did not strike back and take revenge from an insult or an assault was considered a...I think the word I learned is *wimp.* And it seems to have applied, not only to a human, but to tribes as well. It appears if one did not return a blow, one was dishonored. One lost one's pride if revenge was not extracted.

"Yet, where was the line drawn? How did the human distinguish between aggression and submission? With few exceptions, I gather submission was dishonorable and not an effective approach to making one's way in the humans' competitive world."

Sage, "Let us be clear about the matter. If a human allowed another human to dominate, the dominated human was destined for the genetic backwaters. That is simply the manner in which the humans evolved.

"An example should be helpful. Some human historians believed a once mighty empire, Rome, lost its place in the world after its emperor, a man named Constantine, forswore the martial arts for 'love thy neighbor.' "[10] Other reasons contributed to Rome's downfall, but the Christian concept of submission was not an effective tool for repelling the attacking Goths and other pagan warriors."

The Sage continues, "By the way, Student, the word *wimp* is slang, and a word the humans often misused. A more-fitting word is *coward*. And you have come across one of the dilemmas inculcated into the human over their many years of evolution. We Cepees call it The Aggression/Submission Quandary.

"The humans were often in a state of uncertainty about how to behave. Should they be assertive? Or submissive? Or aggressive? To what extent? In what situations? Sometimes, our predecessors acted wisely. Sometimes, they did not. But they never resolved how to dispose of The Aggression/Submission Quandary. That is why it is called a quandary in the first place."

Student, "OK, I suppose I must learn to accept the gray world in which my ancestors lived. Still, Constantine adopted a religion that embraced peace and submission. His act must have had a pacifying effect on that part of the world."

Sage, "It did not happen, Student. 'That part of the world' did not change very much.

"And as the humans evolved, our ancestors continuously twisted their religious dogmas to accommodate their pre-ordained dispositions toward acquisition and violent aggression. Your data fills on humans' religions will provide more information on this matter."

Student, "I see your point about the complexity of our ancestors. But we Cepees do not have to deal with these dysfunctional maladies, do we?"

---

[10] Pat J. Buchanan, *Where the Right Went Wrong* (New York: St. Martin's Press, 2004), 2.

Sage, "No. Earlier versions of our race removed them from our DNA and certain parts of our mainframe."

Student, "I have another question. Who started The Aggression and Revenge Cycles?"

Sage, "No one knows. No one will ever know for certain. We Cepees think they began in a piecemeal fashion, little by little, in separate episodes over many centuries. Aided and abetted by The Threshold Lowering Syndrome."

Student, "Sounds logical. OK, Mentor Sage, one last question: Why aren't we aggressive and violent?"

Sage, "If one has everything one needs; if one is everlastingly happy; if one is not fighting for food, turf, sex, and the other desiderata incipient in our ancestors—aggression and violence are irrelevant."

Student, "Yes! I'm proud to be a Cepee!"

Sage, "No, Student. You misuse the word *proud*. You are *lucky* to be a Cepee. Proud implies you had something to do with being a Cepee. You did not. Do not make the mistake of your forebears and succumb to inappropriate pride."

Student, "Maybe I need more data fills. For now, I will remember your advice. By the way, I think I could use some of your sage knowledge. It might ease my task of learning about the humans. Any chance for some shortcuts?"

Sage, "No. I am a sage, a title I have earned. As a student, you've not earned that distinction. Such cheek. How do you think we Cepees stay busy and occupied? We have our roles to play. For now, you are a student. Later, the Cepee Design Committee will decide your future role in our race."

Student, "Well, it never hurts to try, and the sage job looks pretty attractive to me."

Sage, "Get back to work."

Student, "I will, and thank you, Sage."

Sage, "Don't mention it. As you know, it is part of my job description."

CHAPTER 14

THE DOGGED PRINCIPLE AND THE BELL-SHAPED CURVE LAW

(Dialogue 8)

The Student returns to his teacher before he finishes his specific assignment on studying required parts of the Human Archives.

Sage, "Back again? Fine. I notice your interest in our ancestors is increasing. And you appear to be focused on your studies. Your attention span has increased. I am pleased."

Student Cepee, "Thanks, Sage. Yes, the humans' behavior fascinates me. Before I continue my data fills, I would like to discuss in more depth the 'being average' idea, the concept that most humans were average in their behavior. The resulting Bell-Shaped Curve from the archives looks like this." The student uses a hologram generator to display this image:

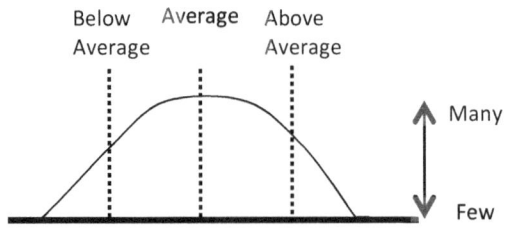

The Bell-Shaped Curve.

Student, "Mentor Sage, it appears most humans were considered average in any given pursuit, such as doing math or running a race.

62

Others were better than average and others were below average. Most of the data fills indicate the humans possessed many of our characteristics.

"For example, I have learned most humans were altruistic and nonaggressive. Yet some of them were very altruistic, and some were just the opposite. So, the use of the Bell-Shaped Curve can be applied to just about anything. The idea is quite helpful for this part of my training."

Sage, "The humans' Bell-Shaped Curve is a valuable principle. And yes, the curve for 'acceptable behavior' was skewed significantly to the right. That is, more humans were 'decent' than not."

Student, "Was there a Bell-Shaped Curve for malevolence? After learning about our ancestors' violent aggression, I have concluded the human population contained a significant number of deranged individuals. Am I correct?"

Sage, "In relation to the Cepees' ethics and morals, yes. However, for the humans, what constituted malevolence—that is to say evil—often depended on the situation. For example, your upcoming studies of the humans' malpractice of their religions will reveal the acts of so-called holy war killings of non-combatants were considered to be evil to some tribes but noble to others.

"We Cepees have drawn the line about this matter. Using a human cliché, you will also learn later, 'A rose by any other name is still a rose.' We Cepees believe, 'Murder by any other name is still murder.' As you will see in your studies, the issue of evil made no difference to many humans, which is an example of The Threshold Lowering Syndrome that you learned earlier."

Student, "Fine, Sage. But their behavior is still confusing. It appears the humans were always trying to change one another. If the efforts were not successful, they often tried to eliminate an opposing person. But who was right, Mentor Sage? Who was wrong? Was one cause more just or more equitable than its alternative?"

Sage, "I know you have already made judgments about some of these matters. To amplify your ideas, I emphasize once again that what was right to one group of people was often wrong to another—a conflict we discussed earlier. Let's have the Hologram Sage interject some verse that will enlighten you about this matter.

"We Cepees make fun of our ancestors with this doggerel. It is spoken or sung by a human who lived in the Middle East and was acclimated to theocratic, undemocratic cultures. His way of life was threatened by the life styles of other societies. Like most humans, he refused to give up what he and his forebears had embraced for centuries.

"We Cepees call this aspect of the humans The Dogged Principle: Their propensity to be persistent, resolute, single-minded, steadfast, tenacious, stubborn, and indefatigable in holding on to their views of life and their ways of living. It goes like this…"

Student, "Wait one moment, Sage! What was wrong with having this characteristic? It seems to me it was an admirable trait to possess."

Sage, "Student, I am making no value judgment about this aspect of our ancestors. The Dogged Principle simply represents facts about the humans. But to your question, sometimes this principle was beneficial to the humans and sometimes it was not. Anyway, you interrupted me. As I was saying, the doggerel goes like this."

The Hologram Sage materializes beside the Mentor Sage and launches into this ditty:

Doggerel of the Dogged

There is little that can be done.
You only make things worse
trying to sway our tribe,
with your Jeffersonian verse.

Our way of life is set
by the Human Tribal Hierarchy.
All that you do to us
is create yet more anarchy.

You pacified Iraq, Christianized Sudan.
What remains for you to do,
is 'liberate' Iran.

Just leave us alone.
And stay out of our houses.
We'll keep our daily kneels,
in spite of your causes.

Yes, just leave us alone
We're tired of your charity.
Try as you will,
it will never lead to parity.

Student, "With respect, Sage, I could add to your doggerel some of my own verse which makes just the opposite point, and spoken from the viewpoint of those humans who were committed to improving the lives of others.

Doggerel of the Dispossessed

Japan and Germany;
Luxembourg and Poland.
They all were rid of evil.
Not to mention Holland.

The Falkland Islands come to mind.
So does Franco's Spain.
Our noble deeds made them free,
and took away their pain.

The backward Balkan people,
imprisoned, as you see.
They were once bound up in chains,
Then we gave them liberty!

And yet you say we must be wrong.
You deny our noble stance.
Then try to see it this way, my friend:
We liberated France!

Sage, "Hm, not bad verse. Doggerel is a better description, but good points nonetheless."

Student, "What say you, Hologram Sage?"

The Hologram Sage, programmed to disregard a non-programmed question, remains mute. Its image fades away. Of course, the wise Mentor Sage had this exit programmed beforehand.

The Mentor Sage offers, "As you should know, no response. Anyway, the claims in both doggerels are valid. And that is the point I am making to you. What was just to one human was unjust to another. What was an appropriate mode of behavior, be it for religion, for governance, for sex...whatever...was a bone of contention among most humans.

"To illustrate this point, during their latter stay on earth, some of the Noble Savages in America—who were called Native American Indians—proclaimed they had been fighting terrorists since 1492... when they were visited and taken over by Europeans. Of course, their 1492 adversaries held the opposite view. They proclaimed they were liberating the Indians from ignorance, and coincidentally, their land."

The Sage continues, "However, as I stated, clearly many of the humans' laws, ethics, and morals were laudable. Nonetheless, and judging from your studies thus far, you are beginning to understand that some of the practices of our ancestors were quite counterproductive to the betterment of their race.

"Intraspecies violence, to cite the prime example. Let's summarize their plight by using two Bell-Shaped Curves. First, as we discussed, most of our ancestors were far removed from engaging in violence against their own kind, as shown here:"

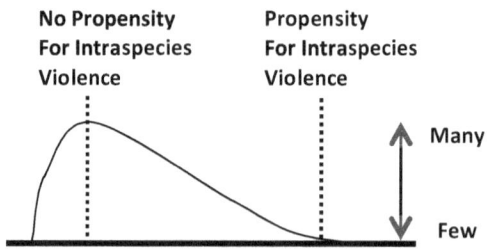

The Bell-Shaped Curve for intraspecies violence.

The Sage then introduces the second curve, as seen below, "As you will learn in your data fills, a very small number of humans succeeded in creating mayhem with weapons of mass destruction by annihilating huge populations.

"Of course, before weapons of mass destruction (Pre-WMD) became available to the terrorists, zealots, insurgents, and sociopaths, the humans' destructive capacity was rather limited, as shown on the left hand side of this curve. However, with the post WMD era and the time leading to it,—as nuclear, biological, and chemical weapons found their way into the hands of terrorists and rogue states—the situation changed, as shown on the right hand side of this curve:"

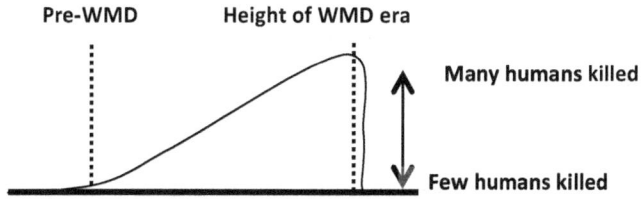

The Bell-Shaped Curve for destructive capabilities of humans' weapons.

Student, "A good example of The Disproportionate Ratio in action. I think I know the answer to these questions, but I will ask them anyway. Couldn't these humans' grievances be addressed peacefully? Couldn't they be controlled?"

Sage, "Before I answer your questions, these points are cogent to your education: Some of the humans who used WMDs were insane. Some were malevolent. Others were genuinely oppressed. Others were social malcontents. Others were attempting to scale their assorted pecking orders. Still others were various combinations of these traits.

"Now to answer your questions. Your first question, 'Couldn't these humans' grievances be addressed?' Student, you are an example of The Dogged Principle! The human race never really attempted to solve this problem. And we Cepees will never know. Given the genetic and cerebral dispositions of the humans, the problem may have been unsolvable. Still, the humans never really tried.

"To your second question, 'Couldn't these humans be controlled?'…Think, Student! For you already know the answer to your question."

The Student replies, "Ah, the answer is yes. During their latter times on earth, they were already moving toward methods of fixing and improving themselves with the EGO, ILLS, and SANE programs. The nuclear and biochemical attacks, which I have only touched on in the archives, and the subsequent ASSES initiatives completed the process."

Sage, "Precisely. The humans sometimes used this cliché, 'If you can't beat'um, join'um.' With ASSES, the devolving humans and the ascending Cepees modified this cliché to, 'If you can't beat'um, change'um.'"

Student, "These facts are becoming increasingly clear. Thanks again, Sage."

Sage, "Return to your studies, Student."

CHAPTER 15

WATER, AIR, LAND, AND POPULATION

(Data Fill 4)

The Student's attitude toward his ancestors has darkened since the Cepee's last data fill and dialogues with the Sage. After all, he *is* a Cepee, even if an inexperienced one. Thus, the Student's ancestors' seeming pathological propensity for pointless violence has taken him aback.

He moves on to another subject: the earth's environment during the humans' time. The news for the Cepee does not make him any happier as he retrieves this information from the Human Archives:

While the humans were busy killing off one another, they were also killing off their earth's biosphere. Signs pointing to the deterioration of the planet were in evidence for many years. The earth had begun to react to the humans' aggressive onslaught on its vital organs. It gave warnings about this assault, contaminated water, air, and land as examples. But generally, the warnings were ignored.

Controversy about Global Warming

The humans could not reach consensus about one key variable in the biosphere deterioration equation: global warming. Some people believed warming of the earth's surface was occurring because of humans' toxic emissions into the atmosphere. Other people believed these emissions had little or no effect on the land, the water, or the atmosphere.

Controversy about Population Growth

The number of people living on the planet was similar to the global warming debate: widespread disagreement on the subject. Was the number of people on earth too great, too little, or just right? The problem was not overpopulation in general, but overpopulation in specific parts of the planet. Many of the densely populated areas or places of cultural/religious importance became arenas of deadly contests between various sects, cultures, and nation states.

The Lag Effect

The problems associated with the earth's environment were greatly complicated by The Lag Effect, as seen in the figure below. This effect represented the time lapse between the occurrence of an action (event A) and when the consequences of the action revealed themselves (event B). The time between events A and B was called the lag window.

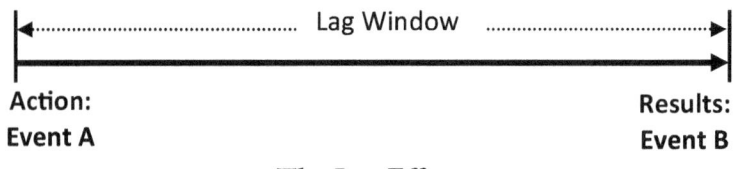

The Lag Effect.

The Exponential Consequences Curve

Another aspect of the lag window was called The Exponential Consequences Curve. Depicted in the next figure, it shows an arrow beginning at the start of the lag window and proceeding to the end. Toward the end of the window, the arrow takes a sharp curve upward, a nonlinear, exponential increase. The slope of the arrow illustrates the magnitude of the consequences of the action taken at event A.

The curve often manifested itself as The *Unintended* Exponential Consequences Curve. The accumulating results of an action were not accurately foreseen. Thus, the humans often remained blissfully unaware of the future consequences of their behavior and their despoilments. Issues were also clouded because the effects of human induced global warming and population growth encompassed a lag window of many years. This lag effect resulted in greater delays in recognizing, then dealing with the problems.

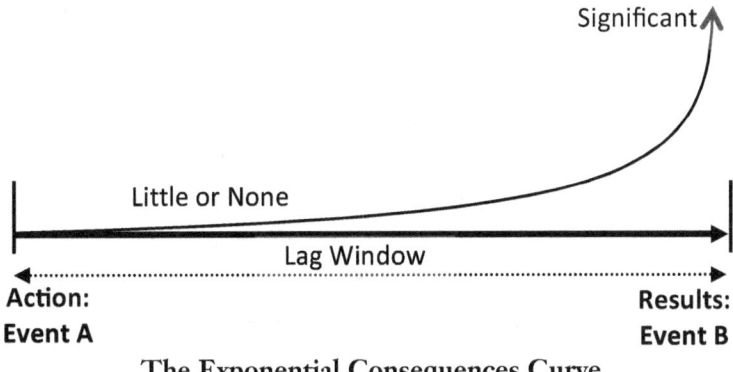

The Exponential Consequences Curve.

If so, who could fault humans if their primary concern was the lag window of their short time on earth? Why should Joe and Josephine Citizen, residing in the safe environs of their gated community in Connecticut, care about the greening of remote Greenland?

Even more, Joe and Josephine lived inland, away from oceans. Why should they care about the tail-end of The Exponential Consequences Curve showing the oceans were becoming polluted; that the sand traps at Mar-a-Lago were becoming water hazards? Likewise, why should Joe and Josephine care if remote China had too many Chinese?

The answers to these questions were, with few exceptions, they did not care. But they should have. In the early part of the 21st century, irrefutable evidence proved humans were creating serious biospheric problems, and these problems would have severe consequences for...if not Joe and Josephine, then certainly their offspring, not to mention Mar-a-Lago.

The Pigsty Paradox

The reality of the situation became clear. Regardless of the debates on global warming, regardless of conflicting computer simulations, emulations, models, and lab experiments, these facts were uncontested: Real-life, practical observations revealed many humans were breathing dangerously dirty air, drinking contaminated water, eating filthy food, and walking on urban and country landscapes that appeared to have been dumped on by a junkyard skyhook.

It was painfully plain to see: The humans were destroying their habitats, another example of The Threshold Lowering Syndrome. Yet people seemed oblivious to their surroundings. Consider pigs living in their sties, heedless of their surrounding muck and swill. Consider the back hills of states such as West Virginia, Pennsylvania, and Virginia where acres of land resembled garbage dumps.

Consider abandoned oil fields in New Mexico that left poisonous chemical scars in the soil and on the landscape; dwellers living near dried-out lake beds and forced to wear masks to filter deadly particles in the air; fetid canals in Bangkok, too dangerous to swim in; submerged islands and coasts, courtesy of melting ice bergs.

Deserted strip mines in Montana gave off poisonous wastes into local water supplies, resulting in an enormous toxic lake next to the city of Butte—larger in area than some towns (one mile long, one-half mile wide). Factories on the Shenandoah River dumped carcinogens into the water to be enjoyed by the downstream citizens of Georgetown and Washington, D.C. Tons of used needles and discarded hospital waste washed up on New Jersey beaches. The Russians contaminated Lake Baikal, which contained one-fifth of the world's fresh water.

On and on. It became a never ending litany of humans abusing the very places in which they lived. The apathy of the human race, aided by The Lag Effect, and reinforced by The Immediacy and The Threshold Lowering Syndromes, eventually created a pigsty habitat on many parts of the planet. Yet a substantial number of humans did not care or were oblivious to it all, a human condition called The Pigsty Paradox.

As time went on, some humans began to understand they were contributing to biospheric catastrophe. Eventually, these people no longer questioned that the earth's air was becoming unpleasant to breathe; that many bodies of water were too dirty to drink; that chemically contaminated land was dangerous to walk on. They finally accepted that humans had created a serious problem. The challenge was how to get the problem fixed.

CHAPTER 16

THE ACQUISITIVE SYNDROME

(Dialogue 9)

The next dialogue takes place after the Student Cepee has finished the data fills covering studies about the water, air, land, and population controversies.

Student Cepee, "Sage, I have finished my data fills about the issues surrounding our ancestors' habitats. During the humans' later times, I gather some parts of earth were being cleaned up and other parts became more polluted, or were destroyed by severe storms.

"Also, it appears the population problem receded as the humans' birth rate fell. Yet, my studies reveal overpopulation on parts of the earth remained a problem throughout the humans' stay on earth. So, it seems I have contradictory information."

Sage Cepee, "No, your data fills and your inferences are correct, although I will explain that the population problem did not completely recede. I will also address your confusion by explaining how the humans related to one another and their material possessions.

"With few exceptions, humans wanted to be around other humans. Like Cepees, they were a gregarious lot. Consequently, they clustered together in cities, leaving many parts of the world sparsely populated. You missed the picture about one aspect of the human."

Student, "What's that, oh wise one of many data fills?"

Sage, "Your fawning does not become you, and we discourage its use. Cepees do not go for flattering—but then you are still in a bootstrap stage of your existence, so you are not quite tuned yet.

"To continue, the problem of overpopulation stemmed from the humans' need for convenience. They wanted to be near stores. Humans were addicted to what they called *stuff*, a subject you studied earlier. Their behavior is what we Cepees call The Acquisitive Syndrome: the instinctual propensity of a human to acquire stuff. When combined with The Autocatalytic Process and The Threshold Lowering Syndrome, this tendency became pathological to many humans, which as you now know, led to cities being populated with thousands of storage lockers containing unused wares.

"But we must not be judgmental, Student. Acquisitiveness had been a necessary part of our ancestors' ability to survive their harsh lives. In order to eke out a living, much less to prosper, many of our ancestors—a great many of them—kept some reserves on-hand. Yet, they did not want to store their goods in, as the Hologram would say, stuff lockers, which were often robbed. In irony, some humans needed to safeguard their meager possessions into semblances of their ancestor's caves. Some poor tribes actually hid food.

"Moreover, if a human lived in a remote part of the earth, he or she had to travel many miles to acquire his or her food. Not a pleasant way to spend one's time—traveling back and forth to find something to eat."

Student, "Those vast unused areas you are describing were located in more remote parts of the world. So, say, Montana and Siberia remained mostly uninhabited?"

Sage, "Only partially. Migrations took place to these remote places because the cities became dangerous places in which to live. Just be patient and do your data fills as instructed."

Student, "Okay, Sage, but I have another question about the pictures I viewed of the humans' cities in the mid-21st century. The cities look quite similar to one another. I don't see much diversity. And their stores—they're the same in all the cities. Didn't our ancestors become bored with the sameness of their environment?"

Sage, "Some did. Some did not. Two factors played a role in the humans' evolution to sameness. First, the humans believed in economies of scale, especially the people who sold stuff to consumers. So, by building and manufacturing stuff that did not vary, the sellers could capitalize on making everything look alike—a far less expensive approach than building diversity into their stores and products.

"Second, the consumers were obsessed with buying stuff at the lowest price. Therefore, the merchants who mass-produced inexpensive stuff edged out the merchants who had different but more expensive stuff."

Student, "Okay, I understand. By the way, here is a photo from the Human Archives of the humans' Los Angeles."

The Student hands the picture to the Sage, who views an image of the entire downtown of L.A. populated with Walmarts and Taco Bells.

Sage, "Yes. A fine example of the humans' fondness for the economies of scale and lowest price factors."

Student, "One more question. Why weren't more of the humans' hunters and fishermen in the camp of the environmentalists? I think they had more to gain from a clean environment than many other humans."

Sage, "Some of these people were environmentalists. But many were not because they thought a pro-environmentalist stand was… what word comes to your mind, Student?"

Student, "Wimpy?"

Sage, "A Hologram Sage term, but certainly accurate."

Student, "I see, and the term *tree hugger* was not very masculine—much too wimpy."

Sage, "Exactly."

Student, "Their attitude was shortsighted."

Sage, "Indeed. And you will learn that our ancestors evolved to hold the view, 'In a world of tribes and thugs, manliness goes a long way.'"[11]

Student, "Oh? Who were the thugs?"

Sage, "Almost anyone who belonged to another tribe: The other group across the river, across the mountain, and just as likely, across the street. …Or just anyone who disagreed, who had a different opinion."

---

[11] Robert D. Kaplan, "Supremacy by Stealth," *The Atlantic*, July-August, 2003, 69.

The Sage returns to the population issue, "I stated earlier that the population problem never completely receded. Let's amplify your data fills on population. In certain parts of the human's world, areas remained sparsely populated, while others became dangerously over populated. The dense populations created excessive demand for the sparse amount of resources that limited acreage offered. Consequently, different tribes began to fight one another over the land, sometimes resulting in mass killings. On occasion, thousands of people died because of too many people occupying too little space."

Student, "Thousands?"

Sage, "Correct. For now, I've arranged for you to view some human television programs on the subjects of our dialogue today."

Student, "Thank you, Sage! The programs are welcome breaks from…"

Sage, "Yes, I know from actually doing work. Nonetheless, you will find them informative."

Student, "By the way, Mentor Sage, I have not seen that girl around here since our first meeting. Is she in the vicinity?"

Sage, "She is busy with other activities, Student. All in due time."

Student, "You keep saying that, Sage."

Sage, "And I will continue saying it until an appropriate time comes for you to meet her. You are not ready. For now, you are too full of yourself. Get along."

CHAPTER 17

TO BREATHE OR NOT TO BREATHE

(Show 3)

The Student Cepee's retrievals (data fills) from the Human Archives regarding the biosphere problems lead him to conclude the humans could not agree about one key variable in the biosphere deterioration equation: global warming. To gain a better understanding of the issues involved, the Cepee retrieves a table titled The Global Warming (GW) Conundrum Matrix, shown below.

The Student Cepee consults the human's dictionary to learn about the word *conundrum*. He reads this definition, "A word used by certain humans, called pedants, to describe an unresolved opinion or a riddle whose counter opinion or answer involves the humorous use of a word or words."

Global Warming (GW) Conundrum Matrix[12]

Opinion	Counter opinion
a. GW causes earth surface temperature to rise. (1)	a. Not! (2)
b. GW causes melting of glaciers and rising of sea levels. (3)	b. Not! (4)
c. GW causes rise in carbon dioxide levels in atmosphere. (5)	c. Not! (6)
d. GW causes increase in soil moisture and greening of earth. (7)	d. Not! (8)
e. GW also causes water shortages. (9)	e. Not! (10)

See footnote 12 for explanation of notes (1) through (10)

---

[12] The notations of (1) through (10) pertain to the following references, from

Upon examining the matrix, the Cepee reads five opinions about the effects of global warming, followed by five counter opinions. The latter are all the same, answered with a grammatically incorrect adverb, and followed by an inappropriate exclamation point...and therefore, humorous!

The Cepee notices this matrix has been used in another *Coming to you Live, from the Dead* TV show, titled, "To Breathe or not to Breathe." It downloads the show, and here is what he sees.

[The TV camera shot pans to a group of humans sitting around (logically enough) a round table. Their scowls and overall demeanor imply they are carrying the weight of the world on their shoulders. They resemble scientists, perhaps social workers, or evangelists; maybe timeshare salesmen, or offshore oil well operators during the hurricane season.

[Notwithstanding the unpleasant mood of the group, the director of this show has music playing in the background. Because music has been found to be a powerful mechanism for altering the moods of television and movie audiences, this show is playing the pleasant, but appropriately serious "Morning Mood" movement of Grieg's *Peer Gynt Suite*, thus implying hope for the meeting. Presently, one of the humans, the moderator for the meeting, speaks up.]

"Good afternoon, fellow serious, pondering people. We are here to exchange views on the controversial issue of alleged human-induced global warming and its alleged consequences. I say 'alleged' because some of you believe global warming is nothing more than

---

which the issues are sourced: (1) National Academy of Sciences (http://yosemite. epa.gov/oar/globalwarming.nsf/content/climate.html); (2) Testimony of S. Fred Singer before Senate Committee on Commerce, Science, and Transportation (http://www.nationalcenter.org/KyotoSingerTestimony2000.html; (3) See Note (1); (4) See Note (2); (5) "Global Warming, the 'Greenhouse Effect'," http://www. solcomhouse.com/globalwarming.html; (6) "Global Warming: The Origin and Nature of the Alleged Scientific Consensus," a paper by Richard S. Lindzen for *The Cato Review of Business and Government*; (7) See Note (5); (8) See Note (2); (9) Questions and Answers on Global Warming, Global Warming Information Center (http://www.nationalcenter.org/KyotoQuestionsAnswers.html; (10) See Note (2).

an overheated discussion about ongoing, natural, cyclic biospheric events.

"For efficiency and brevity, we will use the Global Warming (GW) Conundrum Matrix, prepared by the Windows Opinion Cross-Checking/PowerPoint software. Even though the material, facts, and ideas for this matrix originated from the scientists who sit at this table, the Planet Software Dictator has placed a reading royalty licensing fee on anything that passes through his company's software. It is not Mr. Gates' intellectual property, of course, but because he owns most of the software in the world. Well, you know about *that* problem.[13]

"Therefore, please read the Matrix only once and commit it to memory, because we have already overspent the 'Paying Someone Else for Our Ideas' line item in our budget. OK, let's get started. We first hear from our colleagues, the Believers, who state global warming is the fault of humans and is causing the earth surface temperature to rise."

Global-Warming-Believer Spokesperson, "Thank you, Dr. Moderator. Global warming is the fault of humans and is causing the earth surface temperature to rise."

Moderator, "Eh, that is what I just said."

Believer, "Yes, we know. We are glad to learn we have persuaded you to accept our view."

Moderator, "Fellow scientist, you know I must remain neutral in this debate. My comment was a way of introducing you. Please expand your view. Then we will hear a counter-opinion from the Non-Believer group."

[Music volume increases and continues to rise, ever so slightly, with each sentence uttered by the Believer spokesperson.]

---

[13] For the forerunners to Bill's ideas, see Apple icons, trashcans, etc. Nonetheless, for the forerunners to Steve Job's ideas, see Palo Alto Research Center (PARC) icons, trashcans, etc. Xerox PARC started it all, and in the end all of us have benefited. Satire aside, well done Bill Gates and Steve Jobs. Your borrowings have been of great benefit to the users of your products.

Believer, "Fine. Our findings indicate the earth's surface temperature has risen by approximately one degree Fahrenheit during the past century. In addition, over the past twenty years, the warming has accelerated. This warming trend is attributable to human-based emissions. These activities have contributed to the buildup of greenhouse gases, such as carbon dioxide, methane, and nitrous oxide."

The Global Warming Non-Believer Spokesperson responds, "Not! Our findings indicate no appreciable warming has occurred for over sixty years. The tree ring records for Siberia and Alaska show no warming has occurred since 1940. Indeed, our findings often show a cooling trend. Furthermore, certain parts of the world are actually getting colder!"

[Gradually, the volume of the "Morning Mood" movement fades out and *Peer Gynt*'s "Aase's Death" is now heard in the background, implying increased tensions and a more ominous turn in the mood of the round table discussions.]

The Student Cepee wonders how two scientific studies using similar data could reach opposite conclusions. He continues to watch the show.

Believer, "Furthermore, our findings indicate human induced global warming is causing the melting of glaciers and other ice formations, leading to the rising of sea levels. For example, Alaska's major glaciers and icebergs began to melt very rapidly in the late 1900s and early 2000s.[14] At the turn of the 20th century, the earth's icebergs were experiencing an annual loss of 24 cubic miles of mass, and studies indicate the melting is occurring at twice the rate than in the mid-1950s. This melting is in turn leading to a steady rise in the sea water around the globe. As another example, a collapse of Antarctica's ice sheet will raise sea level by five meters—among the

---

[14] *USA Today*, July 22, 2002. Life Section, 6D.

flooded areas of the world will be Florida. If present trends continue, about a third of the state will disappear underwater."[15]

[The background music changes from "Aase's Death" to the ominous sounds of *Peer Gynt's* "In the Hall of the Mountain King."]

Non-Believer, "Not! Nonsense! And balderdash! May a human-induced plague contaminate your findings. *Our* findings show the global average sea level has risen about 400 feet in the past 15,000 years. Why? Certainly not because of human based emissions. It is the result of the ending of the Ice Age, which is still happening. The world is stuck with the rise in sea levels, and there is nothing that can be done about it. Antarctica? Why parts of this continent are actually experiencing an increase in the thickness of the ice sheet."

Moderator, "Fellow wise persons, regardless of who or what is causing the oceans to rise, all of you agree that seas will indeed rise, probably flooding our coasts and submerging the shorelines of our southern states, most of San Diego, and New York's subways. There-fore, is it not incumbent upon us scientists to offer a solution to this impending disaster?"

Believer, "Nope. Our job is to predict disaster, not avoid it."

Non-believer, "For once we agree. Besides, it's time the Miami Dolphins and Mar-a-Lago earned their names."

[An audio feed plays happy background music and canned laughter, thus implying a note of frivolity to the proceedings. This cheery melody is immediately followed by music from "In the Hall of the Mountain King," thus signifying a return to a tense, dramatic meeting.]

Non-Believer, "Furthermore, I resent being the defender for all these questions. The fact is that many years ago, we humans started adding gasses to the atmosphere.[16] Without our ancestors' actions,

---

[15] Robert L. Bindschadler and Charles R. Bentley, "On Thin Ice?" *Scientific American*, December 2002, 98-105.

[16] William F. Ruddiman, "How did Humans First Alter Global Climate?" *Scientific American*, March 2005, 46-53.

current temperatures in northern Europe and North America would have been cooler by three to four degrees Celsius! Such a change has made it much easier to foster our productive agricultures in those parts of the world. Therefore, global warming has been a blessing to us.

"Even more, if every signatory to the Kyoto Protocols adhered to these agreements, it would prevent no more than $0.126°F$ of temperature rise every 50 years!"[17]

Believer, "So, we do nothing?"

Non-Believer, "Precisely."

Moderator, "Very well, let's address the third issue in the Matrix. It's…oh my, I have forgotten it. No! Don't anyone say it out loud or write it down. If you do, we must pay another usage fee to the Software Dictator. You there, sign it to me. Hmm, no that's too visible, better whisper it to me. …Thanks. OK, the global warming Believers hold global warming is causing a rise in the carbon dioxide levels in the atmosphere. Your podium, Believer."

Believer, "Thank you. Yes, our findings indicate emissions from vehicles, factories, humans, cattle flatulence, and Boy Scout campfires will double, perhaps even triple, the amount of carbon dioxide in the atmosphere in the next 30 years."

Non-Believer, "Not! These levels will not increase to those hypothetical, preposterous levels, because we humans will stop burning coal, increase our dependence on nuclear reactors, and cease breathing. Furthermore, even if CO_2 does increase, its effects will be to stave off yet another ice age."[18]

[Once again, the music increases in volume, implying increased stress and drama in the round table discussions.]

Moderator, "The last two issues in our matrix for discussion will be debated as one topic."

---

[17] Patrick J. Michaels, "Live with Climate Change," *USA Today*, February 2, 2007, 8A.

[18] Ruddiman, 53. Mr. Ruddiman does not make this statement categorically, but suggests it as a possibility.

[Music changes to the first movement of Beethoven's *Fifth Symphony*, with its opening four notes of: DA DA DA DA.]

Believer, "Thank you. Our findings show human induced global warming is causing more rain in some parts of the earth, leading to the greening of the areas. Ironically, some parts of the world are experiencing water shortages."

Non-Believer, "Not! Not!...and Not! Your findings are based on contradictory simulation models. I suspect your algorithms, if applied to the 1880s, would find America's cites buried in horse manure by the 1920s. For example, some models show North and South Dakota losing 85 percent of their average rainfall. In another, these states gain 75 percent! Other models are equally conflicting and confusing. Besides, even if greening is occurring, it's time Greenland earned its name."

[The Believer and Non-Believer scientists are brought to a state of high agitation by their arguments and the music. This music, now playing in full volume the concluding scores of the first movement of *The Fifth Symphony*, demonstrate typical human behavior toward a frustrating situation: violence.]

[Spurred by the inspiring music and the demonic comments of the opposition, both sides of the table (insofar as there two sides to a round table—the subject of a future TV show) start hurling their notes at one another. Luckily, little damage is done with the paper missiles, until one scientist throws the notes stored on his computer onto the head of his adversarial counterpart across the table, who sinks to the floor with a concussion. In the past, these frequent scientific melees resulted in the launching of shouts, obscenities, and harmless slide rules. But sometimes a price must be paid for progress.]

[The TV screen fades from the round table scene to a commercial about beautiful, black, huge 12-cylinder SUVs, outfitted with TVs, refrigerators, maxi-bars, and images of a charred Smokey the Bear on the dashboard. This commercial is followed by a PBS debate (and therefore, a miniscule audience) on the alleged relationships of low gasoline prices in the United States to the booming sales of oversized SUVs.][19]

The Student Cepee turns off the show and thinks: *No wonder my ancestors could not solve the biosphere warming problem. They could not agree on anything.*

---

[19] Low in relation to much of the world.

CHAPTER 18

NO MORE BREAD AVAILABLE? LET THEM EAT GRASS

(Show 4)

The human race would not stop creational and recreational copulation—which was a good thing not to stop because both interpretations of the act led to the perpetuation of the species and to more humans. But the number of people living on the planet was similar to the global warming debate: widespread disagreement on the subject. Was the number of people on earth too great, too little, or just right?

The Student Cepee has reached the conclusion the humans were genetically disposed to argue about any subject whatsoever. For every Yin, there was a Yang. For every opinion, there was a counter opinion. The Student's study of his ancestors finds another TV show titled, "No More Bread Available? Let Them Eat Grass." The program is accompanied by the Population Controversy Matrix, shown below.[20] The Student wonders if this show will also

---

[20] The sources and references on the issue of population are as numerous as the earth's human population and humans' opinions. This matrix and the show are based on http://www.ourcivilisation.com/aginatur/prog2.htm, and Chapter 16 of Jared Diamond's, *Collapse*, specifically see pages 511-513 that pertain to point f of this Matrix; and a few comments of my own. Jared Diamond, *Collapse: How Societies Choose to Fail or Succeed* (New York: Viking Press, 2005), 511-513. I respect Diamond, but I have grown increasingly skeptical of his geographic determinism.

demonstrate the human's propensity toward habitual arguing. Here is what the Cepee learns from the downloaded program.

Population Controversy Matrix

Claim	Counter claim
a. Many parts of the world are overly populated.	a. There is no such thing as over-population, the more the better.
b. Humans are encroaching on the habitats of trees and animals.	b. Humans have dibs on everything on earth.
c. Overpopulation is leading to over-farming.	c. New techniques obviate over-farming.
d. Overpopulation will lead to widespread famine.	d. New techniques avert wide-spread famine.
e. There are not enough animals in the world.	e. "My neighbor was killed by an elephant!"
f. Population trend is leading to a non-sustainable level of people on earth.	f. Population "problem" is solving itself.
g. Congested habitats tend to produce pissed-off people.	g. Why were tranquilizers invented?

[The TV camera focuses on the TV program moderator, who bears a striking resemblance to a moderator, and two other people, who bear a striking resemblance to two other people.]

Moderator, "Tonight, we present a symposium on the alleged subject of alleged overpopulation. I mention the *alleged* word twice, because some citizens believe it is not really a subject, and if it is, the subject is spurious, and therefore, alleged.

"Our debate this evening is between the Tree Huggers, known as Greens or the Green Party, and the Tree Cutters, known as Browns or the Brown Party. We shall see they have an axe to grind, although the Greens believe the axe should be grinded and applied metaphor-ically. Whereas the Browns believe axe grinding is a forerunner to slash and burn. OK, Greens and Browns: the podium is yours."

Greens Spokesperson, "Thank you. We believe the world is dangerously overpopulated with people and woefully under-populated with Spot Owls and Protozoa. As examples, the population of the earth has almost doubled since 1970 and is expanding at a rate of 86 million people per year. This growth translates into somber facts: Three babies are born every second; another Birmingham is created every four days; another United Kingdom is generated every seven months."

Browns Spokesperson, "So what? Your statistics are numbers meant to scare people. They mean nothing. 'Three babies a second?' Is that good or bad? Is doubling the population a problem? Or for that matter, is another Birmingham every four days positive news or negative news? You throw out statistics indiscriminately, and you make certain they are large enough to impress a population that thinks any number beyond four digits is an awesome magnitude."

Browns Spokesperson continues, "Your innumerate numbers aside, we disagree with your premise. More people means there will be more ideas, better technology and better standards of living. In the West, every indicator of quality of life has improved as the population has grown. You Greens claim Africa is underdeveloped because it is under populated. How can an infrastructure be built to support a population that does not exist?"

Greens Spokesperson, "It is contrary to our biases and prejudices for us to agree on this question. We've made our point, substantiated by our numbers. Let's move on to point b of the Population Controversy Matrix. Humans, with their inexorable propensity for procreation, are encroaching on the habitats of trees and animals. The profusion of the human presence is leading to the displacement of other forms of life on the planet."

Browns Spokesperson, "Again, so what? In the pecking order of existence, humans are rightfully on the upper rungs. Trees, flowers, insects, fish, reptiles, wild animals...they are at the bottom of the pecking order. Eh, as well as the Noble Savage. This also includes plant life and plankton, as well as house pets. (See Chapter 10 for a description of the Noble Savage).

"And trees? The world is awash with trees. We're even planting them in strip mall parking lots. Next thing we know, you will be asking us to paint asphalt green!"

Greens Spokesperson, "How callused! And speaking of the Noble Savage, there are too many of them. Take a look at points c and d of the matrix. Their proliferation is leading to disastrous over-farming, profligate use of deadly pesticides, and deforestation problems, which result in the denuding of hundreds of thousands of acres of rich soil. It also results in chemical runoffs into streams and rivers, surely a forerunner to famine and death."

Browns Spokesperson, "Nonsense. America is proof that the intelligent use of concentrated farming and animal husbandry, accompanied by wise use of chemicals and aggressive genetic engineering, can produce safe and tasty food. America is the 'bread basket' of the world. This distinction did not come from the Greens' Pollyanna views of reality. It came from realistic assessments of the earth's ability to feed its inhabitants. Our transgenic crops can easily feed a world full of people."

Greens Spokesperson, "Malarkey! Your genetically modified Frankenfood plants will end up producing nothing more useful than superweeds. Let's move on to point e in the matrix. We believe the overpopulation problem is contributing to the demise of the creature, critter population. We believe the loss of wild life, while not a factor in the preservation of the physical aspects of our race, will eventually lead to the loss of something almost as important: Our spiritual, ethereal yet fragile ties with the fragile creatures who share earth with us."

Browns Spokesperson, "Fragile creatures. Drivel! Let me relate a story told to me by a person who lives in an area that contains the open zoo you propose. He resides in the foothills of Mount Kenya. Wild animals are allowed to roam freely around his home. He is currently recovering from an elephant attack! And four of his friends were killed by these animals."

Greens Spokesperson, "Ridiculous! Anecdotal rubbish. My neighbor was run over by a child on a bicycle, so let's cage up all those dangerous adolescents. You're hopeless."

Browns Spokesperson, "My turn. Addressing point f in the matrix. The population 'problem' is not really a problem anyway, because the rate of increase in population growth is declining. It is accepted that the population of the world will level off to a rate less than double its present level."

Greens Spokesperson, "I tend to agree with your projection, but this prediction, even if it becomes true, has led you to miss the point.

The current population size is proving to be unsustainable. Just look at the current situations in Africa: mass starvations. Consider the rapidly diminishing rain forests, the depletion of top soils, the death of coral reefs and lakes. Factors brought forth largely because of population pressures on the environment—and of course, the better standards of living for many people. Projecting your predictions into the future means adding more people to an already over-burdened planet."

The Greens Spokesperson continues, "Let's address the last point in the matrix, point g. It has been demonstrated many times that humans do not behave well when they are forced to live in highly populated, constrained environments, such as large cities. They tend to become more aggressive. They complain about their confined, congested spaces and the loss of freedom of movement. They suffer from maladies such as depression and 'road rage.'"

Browns Spokesperson, "Your last point first: If overpopulation is creating 'road rage,' why do people continue to drive cars on congested freeways? After all, they could take the bus, ride a bicycle, walk, quit their job—any number of alternatives. Next, addressing your first point of overly populated cities. Why do people flock to New York? Why is Hong Kong and El Paso inundated with immigrants? Why don't the people in London's Mayfair district avoid people-crushing sidewalk traffic and shop for their purchases on the Web? Have you visited crowded Tokyo lately? How about swarming Bangkok? No problems in those cities either. The Browns' motto is 'High rises for high living!'"

Greens Spokesperson, "Idiot!"

Browns Spokesperson, "Imbecile!"

Moderator, "Hm. We've run out of time for our program on the thorny population issue. I hope you viewers learned as much as I did during this half hour about the perplexing subject. Also, I wish to thank the two spokespeople for their calm, insightful...Hey, you there! Put away that ax!"

[The television screen changes to a commercial asking for donations to fend-off the starvation of Biafra's and Sudan's children population. The ad is followed by a news clip of rioting in Haiti and a terrified child fleeing from a pillaged store with a piece of raw beef in her arms. The report is followed by a travelogue about luxurious hotels built on the branches of the trees in the rain forests of South America.]

CHAPTER 19

DO THE SORES AND LESIONS ON FISH HAVE PROTEIN VALUE?

(Show 5)

The Student Cepee has been directed to another TV show titled, "Do the Sores and Lesions on Fish Have Protein Value?" The Student is puzzled by the title of the program because he has not yet executed data fills about the subject. But the Student's education has been directed by the Sage. Thus, he stays with his studies, and here is what the Cepee learns.

[The TV screen shows several humans sitting at a rectangular table. All but one person is arranged along the two long sides. This lone man sits at one of the short sides. The scene implies this male is an authority figure and in charge of the other humans in the scene. Indeed he is. He is in charge of Couch Potato TV Dinners, Inc. The Cepee surmises a TV show he had recently watched should have used this kind of table, instead of the egalitarian round table.

The director of this show is into unembellished reality: no background music. Consequently, because the 21st century human mind has been conditioned to receive continuous, constant, incessant, ceaseless, uninterrupted, endless, perpetual, enduring auditory stimulation, each person, including the authority figure, is listening to music through a headset—attached to an iPod or similar piece of gear.

The TV camera shows the authority figure raising his hand, at which time he removes his earplugs.]

Authority Figure, "Headsets and earplugs off everyone. ... Thanks. We can now receive auditory pollution from the spoken words of *actual* human beings. As always, our discussion today must be short. This brevity will allow us to avoid communicating excessively on a personal, face-to-face basis—too much angst.

"Frankly, it would have been preferable if we could have resolved the issues pertaining to this meeting on Facebook, thus allowing us to multitask an Internet chat session with our smart phone-based video games. However, because I write your pay checks, I insist we meet face-to-face occasionally, just to make sure my email and money are being sent to a live person. OK, let's proceed.

"We are here today to discuss pollution. ...Oops, I should say alleged pollution. Let's lay it out on the table. Our company is under government investigation for the alleged pollution of several bodies of water.

"We fish from these waters to provide the meat for our frozen TV seafood dinners. Coincidentally, the waters are located near our chicken farms, cattle ranches, oil refineries, and a couple of strip mining sites.

"The problem? Our company is accused of contaminating our products with our very own products! The government charges our farms and factories have created toxic runoffs into nearby rivers, lakes, and streams, thus contaminating the fish and frog legs we sell to our customers."

[The TV camera cuts to another human, located on a long side of the rectangular table. His name is Subordinate A.]

Subordinate A replies, "My department has been monitoring the reports of these government investigations. A few weeks ago, Uncle Sam issued warnings about eating a popular fish taken from these waters. Unfortunately, this fish is the flathead catfish we place in our TV dinners. Uncle Sam has warned fish eaters to be careful eating fish if they are caught from specific lakes and associated downstream rivers in one of the areas where we have our farms, ranches, plants, and factories."[21]

Subordinate A continues, "The government contends our fish are contaminated with polychlorinated bihenyls (PCBs). They say this chemical has been used for many years as coolants in our factories and oily sprays to keep the dust down on our dirt roads. How were we to know PCBs were harmful when we first started using them?[22] It's all very unfair.

"Their pernicious press releases claim PCBs have been linked to cancer. The government even recommends pregnant or nursing women forego eating our fish! To add insult and injury to our profit/loss statement, the government also warns anyone from eating more than eight ounces of our flathead fish per month."

The Cepee pauses to think: *Their government was saying it was OK to consume a certain amount of carcinogen—just don't overdo it. Why eight ounces? Did nine ounces produce instant illness or death? Were seven ounces of PCB-filled fillet harmless?*

Authority Figure, "I will call President Donald Trump. He's dismantling the Environmental Protection Agency anyway. Before long, we can sell this poison to anyone. For now, we can turn this problem into a marketing bonanza. We repackage our twelve-ounce TV dinner to only seven ounces and advertise the 'new' product as meeting the government's maximum requirement for consuming carcinogenic fish.

"So, we offer less fish in each TV dinner package, but we increase the price and cite government regulations as the reason for the increase. Problem solved. Donald will be proud! Less government intervention. Next item on the agenda."

---

[21] *The Roanoke Times*, October 30, 2003, A1.

[22] Lag effect example number one, in which the consequence of an action does not show itself until the perpetrators of the action are retired, dead, or otherwise held harmless for their action.

[Applause and complimentary comments spring fourth from the subordinates. Small wonder the Authority Figure has amassed so much authority: He is the quintessential make-a-deal salesman.]

Subordinate B, "I have good news to report this morning. The cattle shit and sheep urine that has been permeating the wetlands of some of our property in Florida for the past sixty years has resulted in a fortuitous mutation of the frogs down there.[23] They are now growing five legs!"[24] As a minor aside, some of these mutants are croaking along the tees of local golf courses and scaring the golfers. They've even taken residence in the water hazards of the nearby local Mar-a-Lago golf course.

Authority Figure, "That is indeed good news. With no effort or expenditure of additional capital, we have increased our frog leg inventory by 25 percent. Our restaurant chains will welcome this turn of events. So will our French café markets. So will our stockholders."

The Authority Figure continues, "We can turn this problem into another marketing bonanza. We expand our seafood TV dinners with a new offering. We sell five frog legs for the price of four. The mutation gives us leverage on our competitors' four-legged frog products. Problem solved. Next item on the agenda."

[Once again, applause and laudatory remarks spew forth from the subordinates. The camera spans to President Trump, who is a chief stockholder in this company and is monitoring the meeting from the White House. He twitters a laudatory message, while he dines on non-shit laden frog legs produced by another company. In spite of his chauvinism, he admires the former queen of France, Marie Antoinette, who proclaimed to her subjects, "Let them eat shit."]

Subordinate B, "I regret to inform you my good news is accompanied with bad news. Some of the mutated frogs are growing only three legs."

---

[23] Lag effect example number two.

[24] Scott Allen, "Widespread Abnormalities Stump Scientists. Pesticides, Parasites Among Explanations," *The Boston Globe*, July 28, 1997, B01.

[Gasps, followed by silence, followed by a frown from The Donald.]

Subordinate B continues, "However, the head of our Defecation and Urine Waste Department has informed me the three-legged frogs appear to be doing their mutating in only one river, and this body of water is adjacent to our chicken farms. So, I am happy to report we are divesting ourselves from our chicken shit, three-legged frogs problem. We're selling our adjacent three-legged-frog operation in this river to our prime competitor in the frog leg market!

"Besides, the EPA is on the verge of being closed by President Trump, so we might be able to wait out the storm and continue feeding our customers shit. After all, that is what our president has been doing with Americans."

Subordinate B continues, "A minor problem about this transaction has been solved. The prospective buyers made comments to me that this river wasn't exactly pristine. Its dark green ooze seemed to raise their suspicions. I put their concerns to rest by informing them the profuse presence of green frogs gives the water a green appearance!"

[Gasps, followed by applause.]

Subordinate C, "I regret to report more bad news on the seafood market front. Because the chicken waste from many farms, including our own, has been flowing into the Chesapeake Bay for fifty years, the Bay's water is now contaminated.[25] What is more, a significant number of fish have been caught with deformed heads, as well as sores, lesions, and strange looking bumps on their bodies.[26] We are getting bad press on this matter. To complicate the problem, some fishermen have taken ill after they have handled the fish. They complain of skin lesions, fatigue, and light-headedness."

---

[25] Lag effect example number three. I assume you catch on and can now spot The Lag Effect in action. If you have not caught on to the idea of this effect, you are likely suffering from it. As a side note, the lag effects in this chapter reflect facts that have been reported in respected media.

[26] www.usgs.gov/themes/FS-189-97/.

Authority Figure, "You say 'handled.' The fishermen did not eat the fish?"

Subordinate C, "No."

Authority Figure, "That is not our concern. We are *not* in the business of selling fish for our customers to *handle*. We are in the business to sell fish for our customers to *eat*. And I have another brilliant marketing idea. All these extra growths on the fish surely increase their nutritional value. Let's fire up a sales campaign to advertise a new fish in our product line, one with more protein content than our previous product."

Subordinate C, "Right away, sir, but what about the deformed head?"

Authority Figure, "Is the head bigger or smaller than the head on our premutated product line?"

Subordinate C, "Bigger."

Authority Figure, "There you go. More bang for the buck. We can't miss!"

[The TV camera pulls away from the scene and a commercial begins. The moderator explains the dedication of the Couch Potato TV Dinner Company to the quality of its products. This segment is followed by video shots of happy looking fish, happy looking frogs, happy looking company stockholders, and sick looking customers. The commercial ends with President Trump lauding the idea of alternative facts and deregulation.]

The Student returns to his studies of the Human Archives for another data fill.

CHAPTER 20

THE UNIVERSE AND RELIGION

(Data Fill 5)

The next assignment for the Student Cepee is to study the humans' views of the universe and their religions. It is not an easy task as their thoughts on these subjects are almost as diverse as the cosmos itself, including their theories about the origins of the universe.

Clouding the discussion was the religious leaders' opposition to many of the scientists' views about the universe and the possible reasons for its existence. For this data fill, the Student learns about the humans' theories on how the universe came into being. He learns that his ancestors, being contentious and curious creatures, engaged in unending debates about the universe and their religions. Many of these debates ended with the debaters killing one another. Religious wars became the order of the day.

Theories about the Universe

The inability of a human to accept another's beliefs or a society to accept another society's way of life was partially attributable to the customs associated with their Human Tribal Hierarchy. A key component in the hierarchy was their religious incompatibility with one another. Time and again, religion had the lead role on the stage of deadly aggression.

These conflicts often stemmed from the basic questions of how and when the universe was created and for what reason. From these questions, the inevitable thorny issue of the intervention or absence

97

of a divine power—a god or gods—in this process led to confrontations and conflicts.

Regardless of these quarrels, humans were never able to answer fundamental questions about the universe. They were baffled by the possibility of a universe of seemingly infinite size with a seemingly infinite existence. The word *seemingly* is fitting because some humans believed a limit existed on the size and life span of the universe, even though this limit was in the framework of billions of light years in size and billions of years of existence.

Others believed the size and life span of the universe were infinite. Some theorists stated the universe was never ending, that it wrapped back onto itself. Still others held the view that the universe was only six-thousand-years old and nothing existed beyond earth except a cloud-filled heaven guarded by angels at a pearly gate.

The Big Bang

Numerous theories about the universe had been formulated in the past, and they continued to persist into the Cepee era. One prominent hypothesis, the Big Bang theory, championed the idea of a universe that was at one time extremely compact. Then, according to one (and dominant) school of thought, about 13.75 billion years ago, a cosmic explosion occurred, and the universe began expanding very rapidly.

Thus, this school considered the universe to be a bit less than 14 billion years old. The original supposition of this theory held that the universe would eventually stop expanding and begin contracting. This contracting theory was later (largely) discounted.

Regardless of the theories, most everyone agreed that the universe was big. A distant galaxy observed by astronomers (from its emanated light) revealed that the light had traveled over 13 billion years to reach the earth—at a speed of 186,000 miles per second.

Very big indeed. It was determined that one galaxy was 100,000,000,000,000,000,000,000 miles away from earth. The expansion from the Big Bang caused the universe to cool, allowing energy to be converted into various subatomic particles, such as protons, neutrons, and electrons. It would take millions of years for these particles to create atoms and compositions called elements.

This division among learned scientists, the inability to agree on such fundamental concepts, further alienated many religious communities from the scientific society. They looked upon these academic disputes as silly and atheistic. They believed the Big Bang and results from the bang required a divine creator. The detractors of a god-created universe claimed the cosmology of the Big Bang and its aftermath made the idea of a creator superfluous.

The religious mountebanks countered by asking, "In your view, who or what powered the bang itself?" They had a point. The Big Bang theory and Einstein's equations broke down when applied to the universe's earliest moment.

To attempt to answer these skeptics, the scientists came up with the theory of *inflationary cosmology*. This theory put forward the idea that a cosmic fuel could have created the Big Bang. The religious leaders came back with a similar question, "Then who or what created this cosmic fuel?" The scientists had no answer. They retreated to their equations to devise more postulations.

A variation on the Big Bang theory stated the universe was a four-dimensional system. Its conventional three dimensions were extended by a fourth dimension of time. Others came forth with theories about even more dimensions. Regardless of how many the humans thought might have existed, the dimensions were said by some humans to be infinite, supporting a universe with no boundary and an ad infinitum existence.

These explanations took many years of research and discovery. They represented feats of startling intellectual achievements. Still, what was out there beyond the observed cosmos? Other than theoretical explanations, no one could say, as it could not be observed. This puzzle pleased some of the religious people. One religious pundit offered, "I told you so. Beyond those light beams is a cloud-filled heaven."

Most members of the scientific community rolled their eyes about heavenly clouds in silent defense of their beliefs. Meanwhile, some members of the religious community loaded their guns in non-silent defense of their dogmas.

Religious beliefs about the universe spilled over into widespread killings as humans confronted one another about the subject: "I am killing you—you infidel!—to keep my religion pure from your poisoned blasphemies."

It became less a matter of one's secular beliefs about the universe than a person's religious beliefs about what existed in the cosmos. In a great and tragic irony for the human race, the humans were never able to reconcile their limited time on earth to their ephemeral heaven, yet they maimed and killed one another to advance their cause and theory.

In pursuit of their goal to have a heaven on earth, knowing they were laboring under the constraints of a limited life span, they set themselves up to further extend their life time.

CHAPTER 21

THE ZEALOT'S LOT IN LIFE CONUNDRUM

(Dialogue 10)

After the data fill on the universe and the religious confrontations among his ancestors, the Student Cepee finds the Hologram Sage hovering about in translucency and waiting for him at the student's study. At the direction of the Mentor Sage, the Hologram Sage informs the Student, "Dude, the Sage has directed me to provide you with another tutorial," as the Hologram Sage fires up a concert and starts the music with:

Strum, strum, strum...♫♪♫♪
I'm a bomb tottin' warrior for jihad,
And I'm doing it for my only God.
    Oh, Allah, you are great,
    and you dictate my fate,
which makes killing for hate a fine job!

The Student Cepee observes, "You're pretty hung up on the Muslim terrorists, aren't you?"

"Nope, just playing out my duties as required by your teacher. He's the conductor, I'm the orchestra...eh, make that the band. Anyway, I take it all lightly."

"Lightly? Yes, that I can see. But why just the Muslims?"

101

"Oh, don't be concerned. It goes both ways:"

Strum, strum, strum...♫♪♫♪
I'm a Bible-tottin' warrior for the Lord,
And I'll give you Christ's way of a reward.
　　Oh, Jesus, you are great,
　　and you dictate my fate,
for all other creeds lead to discord.

Student, "There's nothing new in these ditties. Mentor Sage and I have discussed their suppositions."

Hologram Sage, "Nothing new! I made them up from scratch... well, sort of. I searched the human libraries and downloaded into my optical memory some important facts, not to mention verse... and then forgot about it. Then later, all those thoughts and ideas unconsciously came back to me, and I was able to sing these brilliant platitudes."

Student, "First, how can a platitude be brilliant? It is pointless and empty to begin with. Second, how can you forget and then remember? You remind me of a human singer. He 'stored up' prose written by a Civil War poet and later used the verse and phrases in his songs. He said, 'I crammed my head full as much of this stuff as I could stand and locked it away in my mind out of sight, left it alone.'"[27]

"So what? We musicians borrow others' stuff all the time."

"Yes, but this musician offered no attribution to the poet."

"That's show biz, Student. Anyway, the Mentor Sage directed me to sing and talk about religious zealotry. The subject is out of my league, so I'll plagiarize here and there."

Student Cepee, "That sounds familiar."

Hologram Sage, "Right on, bro. Anyway, your teacher wishes me to recite this quote from the Human Archives: 'To be a zealot in defense of one's beliefs is to be a patriot.'"

---

[27] See my "Odes to Bob Dylan" (with references and footnotes) at Blog. UylessBlack.com.

Student, "Yes, Hologram Sage, and my Mentor Sage has led me to understand those human zealots did little but destroy one another and themselves. It was pointless."

The Hologram responds, "Not if the human was a crusader. The humans took the view that being a zealot in the defense of Christianity was to be a crusader."

Student, "Christianity? Many humans did not practice Christianity."

Hologram, "Ah, right. No problem. Here's another: To be a zealot in defense of one's beliefs is to be a jihadist."

Student, "I must say you are putting on an impressive light show. It is intelligent, even ironic. And as I learned from my studies, one set of zealots thought all other sets of zealots were evil and had to be converted or destroyed."

Hologram, "Yep, no solutions! It was one big puzzle that the humans were incapable of solving. How 'bout this one:"

Strum, strum, strum...♫♪♫♪
Nothing succeeds like success.
Nothing exceeds like excess.
    And the zealots themselves proclaim
      that their small and modest aim,
is removing all of those who might transgress.

Student, "Yes, and I have learned that this 'modest' aim was impossible to attain. How could they convert the millions of people who practiced Hinduism, Confucianism, Buddhism, and others? How could they convert nonbelievers? They could not, yet they never gave up trying. How ridiculous and self-defeating. They never backed off from their excesses in trying to be successes."

Hologram, "Hey, dude, you're rhyming! There's hope for you. Want some lessons?"

The Mentor Sage makes his appearance, "Hologram Sage, you're not following my instructions. I have been monitoring your session with the Student. I directed you to read a quote from one of the defunct humans. It addresses how these opposing camps evolved. Here it is:"[28]

> I think fortunately the majority of Muslims today will not commit acts of terrorism. But to argue that there is nothing in Islam that leads to violence—that would be a weak argument to a false argument, because if you define *Islam* as "submission to the will of Allah," then you find out what that submission means...you find out that... the sixth obligation is to convert others to Islam, first by peaceable means, then by violent means.
>
> So when Islam is violent—you can't argue...that it's not a violent religion. Then you will say, "What about Judaism? What about Christianity?" Now, adherents of these religions over the centuries have been pacified to understand and accept the separation of the divine and the worldly...Nowhere in the Muslim world has that profound pacification of Islam...taken place. And I think that is the difference.

Student, "Hm. Some zealots softened. Some did not. Very enlightening. Am I reading this quote correctly, Sage?"

Sage, "Yes, you are, Student. There were still violent zealots in all the religious tribes. But the radical Muslims were the most violent in humans' modern times."

Student, "The quote provides a fine summary of the problem. Thank you, Mentor Sage."

Sage, "Very well, the Hologram will wrap up this session. I must get back to my dais to meet with another student, and you must continue your data fills.

"But before I depart to impart wisdom to others, consider these three pairs of questions. They relate to the humans' inability to

---

28 "Ideas and Consequences," Aspen Institute's Aspen Ideas Festival of 2007, *The Atlantic*, October 2007, 54. This quote is also included in the Uyless Black, *2084 and Beyond* book.

resolve their religions to the universe in which they lived. Hologram Sage, light up your display."

The Hologram turns on the following exhibit:

A scientific idea: An unknown number of universes created instantaneously from near nothingness?
A religious idea: A son of God created from a human virgin?

A scientific idea: A never-ending universe?
A religious idea: A never-ending afterlife?

A scientific idea: A black hole from which nothing leaves?
A religious idea: An earth, from which Jesus leaves, but later returns?

The Student ponders: *Which are more surreal? None? All? Some?* The Sage departs. The Hologram prepares to turn off its light show. First, it fires up a final non-award winning song to reinforce this dialogue:

Strum, strum, strum...♫♪♫♪
I'm a zealot, that's how I live my life.
I vow to sow mistrust by sowing strife.
If you disagree, you will surely pay my fee,
for the blade of my knife will make you see.

The Student Cepee has come to the conclusion that the humans' debates about the universe fed on debates about the religious interpretations of the universe, and vice versa. It was a never-ending cycle of conflict. The Student wonders how much violence was created among the humans because of these disagreements. The Student is about to find out.

CHAPTER 22

MISSIONARY FERVOR

(Data Fill 6)

The Student Cepee returns to the Human Archives, where he continues to study his ancestors' practice of their religions.

With few exceptions, the humans' religious tenets should have mitigated the humans' disposition to harm one another. Without question, some passages in the religious holy books countenanced slavery, stoning a person to death, and other inhospitable practices. Nonetheless, the majority of the prevalent religions forbade killing, covetousness, acquisitiveness, and other antisocial traits that had been built into the humans' genomes over many centuries. Even so, humans never stopped killing other humans because of their religious beliefs.

Conversion Contagion

Many of the origins of warfare could be traced to the belief that members of a religious tribe, say tribe A, were obligated to become missionaries and convert persons of other religions to tribe A's religion. As one example, the Christian's Bible contained a section known as the Great Commission. The "Gospel According to Matthew" stated, "Therefore go and make disciples of all nations, baptizing them in the name of the Father and of the Son and of the Holy Spirit, and teaching them to obey everything I have commanded you."[29]

---

[29] David Van Biema, "Undercover: Christianity in Muslim Lands," *Time*, June, 30, 2003, 39.

Other religions had their own views about some matters that also led to serious conflicts. For example, "...the annihilation of Israel 'is not only a religious and national duty, but also a universal human duty, from which no Muslim or free human being can be exempt.'"[30]

Mass Assassins Misinterpretation of their Holy Books

The religious fanatics did not discriminate between civilians or military, between white, black, or yellow races. What was good for the goose was good for the gander. What was good for the Christian was good for the Jew, the Hindu, and the Buddhist. Their rule: all people remotely associated with their enemies fell under their sword. Men, women, children, all were beneficiaries of the terrorists' programs.

The humans often justified their murderous actions by quoting passages in their holy books. They avowed to practice their religions in accordance with the dictates of those religions cited in these books. But they often did not. For example, the word *jihad*, often cited as meaning "holy war," actually meant "striving" in the Quran. (Writer: used in this book to mean a war.) In addition, the word *shariah*, often interpreted as "law," actually meant "path," as to be on the right path, as in "Allah's reassurance to Muhammad that he is on the right path." In addition, the Quran never mentioned "veils."[31]

On and on. It was not just the misuse of the Quran, it was the misuse of the Bible and the Torah, as well.

In fact, the humans' practice was not the practice of religion. It was the malpractice of religion. They used convenient sections of these books to justify their barbarous actions. One of the better-known religious warriors, Osama bin Laden, had no religious justification for the killing of noncombatants, including women and children. He made it up as he went along.

The radical Islamists' wantonness seemed to have no end. In the early 21st century, these depraved people attacked a school in

---

[30] David Remnick, "Danger Levels," *The New Yorker*, July 31, 2006, 22.

[31] Lesley Hazleton, "Close Reading," *The New York Times Book Review*, December 24, 2017, 10.

Pakistan and murdered "141 people, nearly all students…867 educational institutions were attacked by Islamists between 2007 and 2015, often because these places had the temerity to teach science—or worse, educate girls."[32] Small wonder so many parts of the Muslim world were behind the times and mired in obsolescence.

Armageddon

The stage for war between differing religious factions had been set. For certain, history had revealed similar acts. Religious wars over irresolvable differences did not just happen in the humans' modern times. They existed centuries before. But this situation was different. In the past, the conflicts were resolved with primitive instruments of war: swords, knives, and spears, resulting in the deaths of a few hundred to a few thousand people here and there. In more modern times, the instruments were TNT bombs, and shortly thereafter, nuclear bombs and biochemicals—instruments that could and did kill hundreds of thousands of humans.

The Disproportionate Ratio came into play again: A very small number of people (n) did great harm to a very large number of people (m). In addition, one bomb of mass destruction (n) killed thousands of people (m). These two ratios, acting in concert, altered the fate and future of the human race. They became key components to The Deadly Trinity.

The Student sits at his desk, stunned by what he has just learned.

---

[32] "Pupil Power," *The Economist*, January 16, 2018, 9.

CHAPTER 23

THE TURF TUSSLE TRUISM

(Dialogue 11)

—————

The Student Cepee seeks out his Mentor Sage. He is still taken aback by how the interplay of two executions of The Disproportionate Ratio could have had such devastating consequences.

The Student is also perplexed about the many passages in the Human Archives describing how land—turf—gave rise to countless battles among his ancestors, especially the battles for religious turf.

The confusion is understandable. The Cepees are turf-agnostic. Having learned from their ancestors about hundreds of debilitating wars fought for land and sea supremacy, they have long since defined turf and surf boundaries within a defined set of unambiguous laws.

If a Cepee happens to live in an area for a while, the Cepee does not automatically become entitled to that area. Tenure means nothing. Squatter rights do not exist.

Why? Because for centuries, humans killed one another—resulting in millions of dead bodies—because of their tussles about whose turf belonged to whom. The Cepees have long since learned if there was turf for taking, there should never be a deadly tussle for taking it.

The Student arrives at the podium and office of the Sage.

Student Cepee, "Sage, I have been studying the humans who lived in the Middle East during the twentieth and twenty-first centuries. Once again, I learn of our ancestors' fixation on land. Why? They never really needed miles upon miles of land for their existence. They…"

109

Sage, "Student, they did need a lot of land. They needed soil to grow their crops and raise their stocks. Also important was the fact that the more land a nation possessed, the more people the nation could sustain. Larger populations meant a larger tax base as well as more soldiers. Land and its possession became not only a source of survival, it became a source of pride."

Student, "Eh, you interrupted me, Sage."

Sage, "I'm a sage. You're a student. I can interrupt. You cannot."

Student, "Does not seem fair."

Sage, "It is not fair. If you wish to acquire my privileges, you must earn them. Let's bring in the Hologram to assist with this learning session," as the Sage plugs into his Sage console and light images appear before the Student and the Sage.

Hologram Sage, "Dudes! I've been dimmed for a long time. Why the blackout? I'm not dim-witted. I can throw a lot of light onto those meaty subjects you two discuss. So, where's the action?"

Sage, "I wish to instruct the Student about the deadly consequences of our ancestors' fixation on turf, on an obsession that had over time, become less relevant to their wealth and well being."

Hologram Sage, "I'm not programmed for…"

The Mentor Sage enters keys on his console, which sets the stage for the Hologram to play and sing what is titled, "Turf Tussles."

Strum, strum, strum…♫♪♫♪
This land is my land, and never your land,
From the Dead Sea shores, to the Galilee.
From the Negev sands, to the Haifa sights.
From the Gaza Strip, to the Golan Heights.
From a Jerusalem view: anything in sight.
This land was made for only me.

Student, "The tune and cadence sound familiar. …Woody Guthrie?"

Sage, "Yes, and aside from the Hologram's borrowings, Student, this mentality greatly influenced the leaders of the Israeli and Arab factions for several decades. They gave no quarter. The Israelis deceived most everyone into thinking they would give in to help those they displaced, that they would relinquish what they captured during the six-day war. They did not."

Student, "They baited everyone?"

Sage, "Yes, and in the end, they baited themselves."

Student, "What do you mean?"

Sage, "You'll see. For now, go back to the Human Archives and study a passage...Never mind. Hologram, display Human Archives item 434c34234."

Hologram Sage, "Yo, bro!" As the following image appears to recite a quote from the Human Archives:

We are the only people who have lived in the Land of America without interruption for 12,000 years. We are the only people, except for a short U.S. Cavalry Kingdom, who have had independent sovereignty of southwest America. We are the only people for whom all our land has been a capital. We are the only people whose sacred places are only in the lands of America.

Student Cepee, "And?"

Sage, "And therefore, the Native American Indians laid claim to all of America."

Student, "I am somewhat knowledgeable with this part of the archives history, but not your statement. With all respect, I am skeptical of your quote."

Sage, "Very observant, Student. I made it up only to provide a teaching point for your studies. Throughout human history, the claim to turf of the turf's supposedly original inhabitants was routinely ignored.

"It had to be! Migrations and immigrations made this claim moot because it was impossible to implement. Once a tribe left its homeland, other tribes took it over. The original tribe lost its claim."

The Hologram Sage reinforces the Mentor Sage's lesson with a flashing image: "Possession is 9/10th of ownership!"

Mentor Sage, "Well done, Hologram. We sages should consider giving you holograms more programmed spontaneity. …Anyway, one cannot go wandering around the world, perhaps occupying others' home turf and expect to come back and displace those who had moved to this turf."

Student, "But, Sage, the Native American Indian never moved voluntarily. Yes, they were nomadic, but they were forced away from their hunting grounds to make way for the migrating white people."

Sage, "Yes, the newcomers committed acts of genocide."

Student, "Genocide? That is a severe statement. These people were not murdered. They were moved to reservations."

Sage, "Many were indeed murdered, Student. Besides, 'genocide' is not just the killing of physical beings, it is also the killing of the culture of those beings. The Europeans who took over the land of the Native Americans committed acts of genocide. But then, so did the Huns in Asia, the Mongols in Asia, the Muslims in Spain, the Crusaders in Jerusalem, the…"

Student, "I get your point, Mentor Sage."

Sage, "And you interrupted me again. Teachers are never interrupted by students. Mind your tongue!"

Student, "Sorry. …Hm. I've been studying the Zionist movement and the migration of the Jews into the so-called Holy Land. The Zionists claimed that land rightfully belonged to them because they were the original occupants."

Sage, "Since what time, Student?"

Student, "Since around 4,000 years before the early 2000s, the period I am now studying."

Sage, "In the context of our ancestors' life on earth, 4,000 years in the past was not so long ago. Who was there before them?"

Student, "The Assyrians were there at about the same time, maybe slightly later. No one knows for sure. They settled in the area, which included the Jewish Holy Lands, sometime in the 9th century BC. Before the Assyrians, I learned that King David conquered Jerusalem when it was home to the Jebusites. They were there before the Jews came along to pronounce the turf as 'holy.' …This is getting a bit heavy, Mentor Sage. Our readers might be thinking of turning the page."

Sage, "Fine. Let's close this lesson with the Hologram replaying its hologram image with a another quote.

"It's your go, Hologram Sage, display Human Archives item 434a34234. It is the Jewish view of the issue." The Hologram Sage lights up and plays:

> "We are the only people who have lived in the Land of Israel without interruption for 4,000 years. We are the only people, except for a short Crusader Kingdom, who have had independent sovereignty in this land. We are the only people for whom Jerusalem has been a capital. We are the only people whose sacred places are only in the land of Israel."[33]

Student, "True and not true. The Jebusites lived in that area for several centuries before the Israelite tribes arrived. But I have not seen in the Human Archives that Jerusalem was a capital for the Jebusites, or that they considered this land a sacred place."

Sage, "Therefore?"

Student, "The Jews had right of possession?"

Sage, "How about the displaced people from the invasions of Huns, Mongols, Muslims, not to mention the Navajos in New Mexico? Did they have the right to repossess the land where their ancestors once lived?"

Hologram, "Possession is 9/10th of ownership!"

Sage, "Yes, you've made your point...twice. But the Hologram echoes the hard reality of this issue. After decades of living in the Holy Land, the Muslims were gradually displaced by the Jews. In the 20th and early 21st centuries, the Jews colonized Jerusalem and the Golan Heights, formerly held by non-Jews."

---

[33] Patrick Tyler, *Fortress Israel* (New York: Farrar, Straus, and Giroux, 2013), 344-345.

Student, "Colonized? That is a bold claim to make about anyone! I've not seen evidence of this type of behavior."

Sage, "Student, go back to the archives and retrieve more information on two of Israel's Prime Ministers: Benjamin Netanyahu and Ehud Barak. I will be waiting for the results of your research."

Student, "I'll just open my tablet and…"

Sage, "And? …and have your teacher waiting around while you dig for answers? Such cheek! I've other students to see. Off you go. Take the Hologram with you."

Student, "He's not around. You pulled the plug on him after his 9/10th statement."

Sage, "Very well, then take along the plug. I've had my fill of impertinent students and holograms for today. I'll see you first thing tomorrow morning."

Off the chastened Student goes, regretting he did not prepare for this last meeting with his Mentor Sage. He vows to be ready tomorrow.

—Morning appears. So does the Student at the Mentor Sage's podium and office.

Student, "Sage, I unearthed some disturbing facts from the Human Archives.[34] May I proceed?" …The Sage nods yes. "Prime Minister Netanyahu acknowledged his goal was to create a Palestinian Bantustan. I discovered Bantustan was territory set aside as part of South Africa's policy of—it's hard to believe—apartheid.

"Netanyahu also ignored the petition of over fifteen hundred military officers who called for Israel to abandon the illegal settlements in Palestinian land. He sought to force the Palestinians to live on less than forty percent of the land they were granted by the United Nations."

---

[34] The dialogue regarding a Palestinian Bantustan and Ehud Barak are sourced from the following: (a) https://www.haaretz.com/opinion/.premium-1.794087, (b) Ari Shavit, *My Promised Land*, (New York, Random House, 2013), and (c) Patrick Tyler, *Fortress Israel* (New York: Farrar, Straus, and Giroux, 2013), 344-345, 406, 412.

Sage, "Good work, Student. What did you find on Ehud Barak?"

Student, "Upon his being elected as Prime Minister in 1999, he addressed a large crowd and announced Israel would move to separate itself from the Palestinians by drawing four lines in the sand.

"Line one: A united Jerusalem, but under the sovereignty of Israel. Line two: Under no circumstances would Israel withdraw from its illegal settlements. Line three: No army would be permitted in the Palestinian parts of their U.N. mandated turf. Line four: Israel would extend its sovereignty farther to accommodate more settlers into the Palestinians' turf."

Sage, "And your conclusions?"

Student, "Facts are facts, Mentor Sage. It is evident that the practice of at least some facets of apartheid became part of Israel's nature. I also discovered that other prime ministers took similar stands."

Sage, "Why did the United States not intervene into this situation?"

Student, "America's politicians could not afford to lose the Jewish vote."

Sage, "Your research was well done. As you study in more detail the archives' material dealing with the humans' twenty-first century, you will see the consequences of our intransigent ancestors. Continue your studies. In the meantime, let's have the Hologram play out Mr. Guthrie's verse as we Cepees have embraced it."

The Hologram Sage fires up once again:

Strum, strum, strum...♫♪♫♪
This land is my land, and only my land
From the Golan heights, to the West Bank sites
From Jerusalem's walls... including Arab halls
This land was made for me and only me

Student, "No periods?"
Sage, "Artistic license."

CHAPTER 24

THE MISSIONARY POSITION: PROS AND CONS

(Show 6)

For a break in his immersion in the Human Archives, the Student has been directed by the Sage to watch additional human television programs. The wise Mentor Sage knows these programs reveal much about the behavior and nature of the humans. The Student is directed to watch a show about the effectiveness or ineffectiveness of the human missionaries' ideas on disciple-making, baptizing, and obedience training. It is titled, "The Missionary Position, Pros and Cons."

The program begins with the image of a matrix coming into view, as seen on the next page.

[The camera closes in on a talk show host who is standing before a large, adoring audience. The crowd is clapping and cheering the host as she introduces the program.]

Host, "Folks, this program is what you have been waiting for. In addition to my attempts with my book club to raise the pathetic literary IQs of my fans, I am now providing time on my TV show for even more serious, contentious subjects. For today, we tackle a controversial topic: religious missionaries. As you noticed, our program title is, 'The Missionary Position, Pros and Cons.'"

[Guffaws and prurient laughter stream forth from the audience.]

116

The Missionary Matrix
(Pros and Cons of Giving and Receiving Religious Missionary Deeds)

	Pros	Cons
Missionaries	-Conversion of infidels to correct religion. -Fewer contestants in the religious turf battles (therefore, more turf). -Up the odds of getting to heaven. -Experience feel-good feelings. -Accrue more power. -Attain more wealth (tithes, offerings).	-Pissing-off large populations of other religions; therefore, -invoking resistance; therefore, -provoking conflicts, wars, and death. -Thus, experiencing feel-bad feelings.
Missioned	-Conversion to the correct religion, thus a lock on heaven. -Resisting missionaries, resulting in a shorter time on earth; thus a faster path to heaven (The Pizarro Effect). -Upon (possibly) surviving The Pizarro Effect, a better standard of living.	-Conversion to the wrong religion; thus relegation to hell. -Resisting missionaries, resulting in a shorter time on earth; thus, a faster path to hell (The Reverse Pizarro Effect). -Worse standard of living (The Slave [aka Noble Savage] Effect).

"Ha! Me, too. The title is a *double entendre*. The sexual aspect of the title is covered tomorrow when the late Hugh Hefner was on an earlier show. For our program today, we are privileged to have on our panel two imminent experts on the subject of the religious missionary position. However, due to the sensitive, controversial nature of the subject, and the associated risk of assassination to anyone who makes a stand on any religious topic, we must keep their names and faces secret. So, here we go. Let's examine The Missionary Position!"

[The scene cuts to a hologram-rendered version of the Missionary Matrix, followed by a close-up view of two panel members, who are silhouetted in shadowed profiles.]

The Missionary, "Thanks, Oprah. It's great to be on your show. Naturally, I favor the 'Pros' column and the 'Missionaries' row of the Missionary Matrix because my fellow missionaries and I save the infidels from eternal damnation by converting them to our correct religion. As a side benefit, we expand our power and wealth, augment our turf, and increase our odds of getting to heaven. After all, our Good Book tells us to get out there and convert those infidels! Besides, it just feels good to do good."

The Missioned, "Wait one minute. We understand your view of an 'infidel' is someone who has no religious beliefs. We practice a religion, just as you do, but it is different from yours."

The Missionary, "No, you are not correct. Our view of an 'infidel' is someone who does not practice *our* religion. If you want to spin wheels on lexical nuances, we will be here all day. In fact, I might just call you a pagan."

The Missioned, "Fine, I think your answer makes my point. With your definition, we consider *you* to be the infidel, even a pagan. OK, let's move to the 'Cons' column and 'Missionaries' row of the Matrix. To put it bluntly, your missionary missions tend to piss-off the missioned folks. We have our own religions, thank you, and had been doing fine with them until you came along."

The Missionary, "Nonsense. You lived in spiritual squalor until we conquered your people, castrated your cultures, and killed off your pagan priests. Our religions uplifted your societies and put you on the path to heaven."

The Missioned, "Pagan priests? Is that a reverse joke? Anyway, killing aside for the moment, 'spiritual squalor' brings us back to the circuitous argument of who is the infidel in the infidel-noninfidel relationship. Besides, you interrupted me. I've not finished with the 'Missionaries' items in the 'Cons' column.

"It is simple. By imposing your religion on us, you insult us and injure our pride. We resist, provoking wars—leading to death, destruction, famine, and poverty to us. *But not to you.* All-in-all, your actions result in frequent occurrences of feel-bad feelings to *others*."

The Missionary, "What a narrow-minded view you have. To expose your faulty logic, Oprah, permit me to refer to the 'Pros' column and the 'Missioned' row of the Matrix. First, sure we piss you off, with the resulting wars of which you speak. But your newly-found religion gives you a pathway to heaven—a virtual lock on the pearly gates. Shoot, our shooting into your population translates into a shorter time on earth for your tribe, thus, a faster path to heaven. What is more, if some of your people survive our rapacious marauding, we will guarantee them a better standard of living, even if they don't gain the initial fast path to heaven."

Oprah, "The faster path to heaven. You must be referring to part of the Matrix with the notation of The Pizarro Effect, a reference to a 16th century missionary effort in South America resulting in the killing of thousands of missioneds."

The Missionary, "Right you are, Oprah. Soldiers killed off those infidels in just a few hours. Sent them on their way to salvation—almost instantly."

The Missioned, "*Au contraire*. I call your attention to the 'Cons' column and the 'Missioned' row of the Matrix. First, our view is you end up converting us to the wrong religion, thus consigning us to hell. Second, assuming your religion is 'correct,' you kill us *before* you have so-called 'saved' us. So, we don't get to heaven at all. In your eyes, we are still infidels, and thus relegated to hell."

Oprah, "That would be The Reverse Pizarro Effect entry in the Matrix?"

The Missioned, "Yes, and another point: About this better standard of living entry in the Matrix. In many instances your goals are to make us slaves, decidedly a step down in our life styles."

Oprah, "Ah yes, that would be 'The Slave Effect' entry in the Matrix, also known as The Noble Savage Effect."

[The camera pans to a somnolent audience.]

Oprah, "We have run out of time, folks. I hope we got those little brain cells jingling just a bit with this panel discussion. Hm, most of the audience is asleep. Not to worry. Tomorrow, we will replay an interview I once had with Mr. Hugh Hefner of *Playboy* magazine. Hugh is pushing up daisies now but not much else. However, his legend lives on. Thus, I will tell you about the other Missionary Position, with visuals far more stimulating than the boring Missionary Matrix."

[A camera close-up reveals the audience perks up, especially the people who have tickets for tomorrow's show.]

Oprah's show is followed by a special program featuring a singing performance by a Frank Sinatra-like person. He is dressed in a subdued black tuxedo, and accompanied by a thirty-piece band. The performance is taking place on a beautiful Las Vegas-type stage. With eyes closed, almost caressing the microphone in his hand, he is singing a love song with the verses of, "What a God you are. You are the master of everything."[35]

The Student realizes the singer is not Mr. Sinatra, as Frank had passed on before this program was being made. The singer is a TV evangelist. Still, he looks very Sinatra-like, crooning and all. But the absence of Frank's Rat Pack is a giveaway—not to mention the song's lyrics.

Immediately following the song, the singer appears on a different stage, dressed in a black suit with a red tie, red shirt, and red handkerchief. He begins his talk by stating, "I'm afraid is a way to say, 'I believe.'"...Followed shortly with, "All the sins you piled up couldn't keep you from being born again." ...Followed later with, "I am not going to be insubordinate to Jesus, my commander-in-chief."...Followed still later with, "There is no thing as a spiritual birth defect."...Followed later with, "Are you following me so far?"...Followed by the Student, who turns off the program, his mind overloaded with clichés.

---

[35] I watched this program on Channel 14, Hawaii, a few years ago. I was so amazed by the performance, I lost track of time and the date of the show, but I did take notes. The quotes are taken from the program.

CHAPTER 25

GOD IS GREAT, AND MINE'S GREATER THAN YOURS

(Show 7)

The Student realizes the data fills thus far on the humans' religious wars and subjugations might be painting an unfair picture of the humans. He knows the missionaries in the latter part of the humans' reign on earth were more benevolent than Pizarro, the Crusaders, and the zealots of the Inquisitions. As a whole, these later humans were more compassionate. Still, the question lingered: Why were large numbers of the earth's inhabitants destroyed because of religious beliefs?

To the Student, the answer seemed to be that a few humans, some who acquired weapons of mass destruction, contorted their religions to distort their existence, as well as the existence of their fellow humans. They killed for pride, power, turf, and to pass The Revenge Cycle Token back to their enemy, a concept explained in Chapter 10.

But another idea came into play: a revenge cycle—*without* the passing of the token; perhaps more accurately described as The Aggression Cycle, also introduced in Chapter 10. The Student is aware of this similar effect from the earlier data fill, but that previous study had focused on warring tribes passing a killing token back-and-forth, taking turns murdering one another: "They killed some of us. It's our turn to kill some of them!" The Aggression Cycle did not involve any token passing.

That must be the reason the Mentor Sage directed the Student

Cepee to watch another *Coming to you Live, from the Dead* TV show titled, "God is Great, and Mine's Greater than Yours." (Subtitle: "And While You're at it, Give me my Land Back!"). Here is what the Student sees:

[The TV camera closes-in on a news journalist. He is dressed in a reporter-like trench coat and is standing in front of two heavily armed men. As an aside, the Student wonders why so many of those earlier reporters wore trench coats, even in the summer.]

Journalist, "Tonight we examine two Middle East factions. We learn how The Aggression Cycle is being used to keep this region in a state of despair, death, poverty, misery, terror, and turmoil—with the exception of those citizens at the top of the power, wealth, and pride pecking orders—who become even wealthier from the mayhem. Our guests for the program are representatives of the Israelite and Palestinian tribes.

"In order to fit this show into our miniscule time allowance, along with the associated profligate advertising slots, we must restrict our discussions to the Israelites and Palestinians. Later in this series, we will introduce other key players in the Middle East Aggression Cycle, such as the Saudis, Sunnis, Sufis, Salafis, Shiites, Turkomans, Wahhabis, Jordanians, Assyrian Christians, Kurds, Syrians, Iranians, and various Lebanese tribes. For now, we start the discussion by looking at the Aggression Cycle."

[The camera is positioned to show the cycle, illustrated in this figure.]

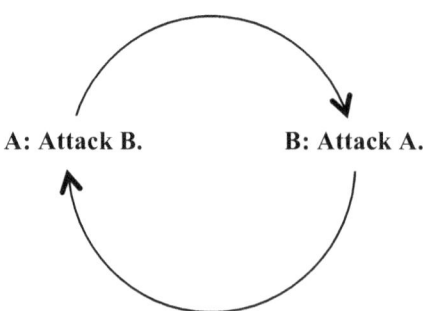

The Aggression Cycle: dispensing with passing a revenge token.

Journalist, "For this discussion, the Israelites are party A, and the Palestinians are party B. Party A, even though we are discussing the idea of a tokenless aggression cycle, I pass the discussion token to you."

Israel Spokesperson, "Well, where does one begin when discussing a cycle? It's impossible. Just look at the visual. It has no beginning. I can only surmise that's why it is called a cycle. Perhaps I should start by discussing the cycle at its termination, but the cycle has no end either. Why do you present me with a circular riddle, as if I did not have enough of them already in my daily life? What is this, a conundrum or something?

"Anyway, my complaint is: Several years ago, party B set off bombs on my turf, killing members of my tribe. Therefore, I retaliated, extracted revenge, and killed party B's people. With my mission accomplished, I felt much better."

Palestinian Spokesperson, "Your turf! I won't question why you are in the Middle East—on *my* turf— in the first place. I will focus on your tribe members killing my tribe members. Aside from your illegitimate residency on my land, you have repeatedly violated UN rulings on this issue, thus giving my tribe ample justification for attacking you at any time. It is fruitless to wait for passing a revenge cycle token back-and-forth. Those times have passed."

Israel Spokesperson, "I will address your distortions shortly. For now, an important aspect to this situation has been overlooked in the newspapers and other media. Aggression is the occupation of our warrior class—a powerful and influential element in our society, one that often overrides our legislature.

"In fact, I am a member of this class, and our specialty is attacking you at anytime that suits us. It is our job description. It is the *only* entry in our job description: to preempt your attacking us. If we stop our attacks, we are out of a job. It is in our own self interests to keep the Tokenless Revenge Cycle cycling."

Palestinian Spokesperson, "Amen! ...uh. Right on! We have the same job description problem. Besides, the only tools I know how to use are guns and bombs. Plow shares and hoes? I never learned to use them."

Journalist, "It appears you two have an intractable problem. Anyway, I am curious. Party A, why don't you keep possession of the Revenge Cycle Token Passing idea, discussed earlier. You know, so you can continue to attack Party B?"

Israel Spokesperson, "It does not work that way. We must make up a reason for our attacks—the same for Party B. No exchange of any ridiculous token. Of greater consequence, we would lose the financial support of our backers if we became too passive and waited to avenge an attack. Our backers insist on more aggression; sells more weapons.

Palestinian Spokesperson, "I agree. Besides, our most ardent supporters will support only so much mayhem and murder. The idea is to extract enough carnage to outrage the other party, who will then support its warriors launching an attack on us. Consequently, we end up inciting revenge—without the use of a fatuous token.

"We just attack!...thereby keeping our job description up-to-date, as well as our employment status."

Journalist, "What is to be gained by this cycle? How can your people benefit from this never-ending violence? Will the cycle never end?"

Party A, "Sure, just tell party B to embrace our religion, stop invading our turf, cease killing our people, give us back our land, and admit our god is greater than their god!"

Party B, "Sure, just tell party A to embrace our religion, stop invading our turf, cease killing our people, give us back our land, and admit our god is greater than their god!"

[As the TV screen fades away from the warriors to the moderator, the Student begins to understand the full meaning of The Aggression Cycle.]

Journalist, "There you have it, folks. And as we promised, the other contending factions and tribes in this factious arena are now highlighted. Oh, we are running out of time. But due to the fantastic responses we are getting from this program, our website has shut-down from too much traffic. What?...Eh, I have just been informed the shut-down occurred because it was bombed.

"We will return later to this subject with a detailed look at the Sunni/Shiite Aggression Cycle. And to really titillate your appetite for religious killings, we will also present a program on holy wars, the martyr Osama bin Laden and his al Qaeda warriors. Until then, peace."

[The TV camera cuts to a scene showing help groups performing missionary work in a religious war region and attempting to bring the world together, while attempting to convert the world to their "correct" religion. The scene is accentuated with doves flying into and out of the foreground, punctuated with gunfire, bombs, and flying body parts in the background. Occasionally, one of the doves is downed by an errant bullet.]

CHAPTER 26

THE EXPONENTIAL BUTTERFLY EFFECT

(Data Fill 7)

During the study of his ancestors, the Student has learned about The Unintended Exponential Consequences Curve. He has also watched an archived TV show in which a stand-up comedian defined The Interrelated Principle.

This principle is closely associated with The Butterfly Effect in which a butterfly flaps its wings in South America and causes a hurricane in the Gulf of Mexico. The idea of this metaphor is that anything that might happen in the world can affect anything else in the world.

The Cepee thinks, *The point of the principle is the interdependencies of actions and events. I can see the relevance of this principle and The Exponential Consequences Curve in the data fill I am currently studying.*

Let's see what the Cepee is up to. The Student retrieves the chart depicted in the figure on the next page. It accompanies an explanation of how several seemingly unrelated events came together, resulting in an attack on the United States, called 9/11. Already familiar with the event itself, the Cepee examines this figure as he reads the following explanation.

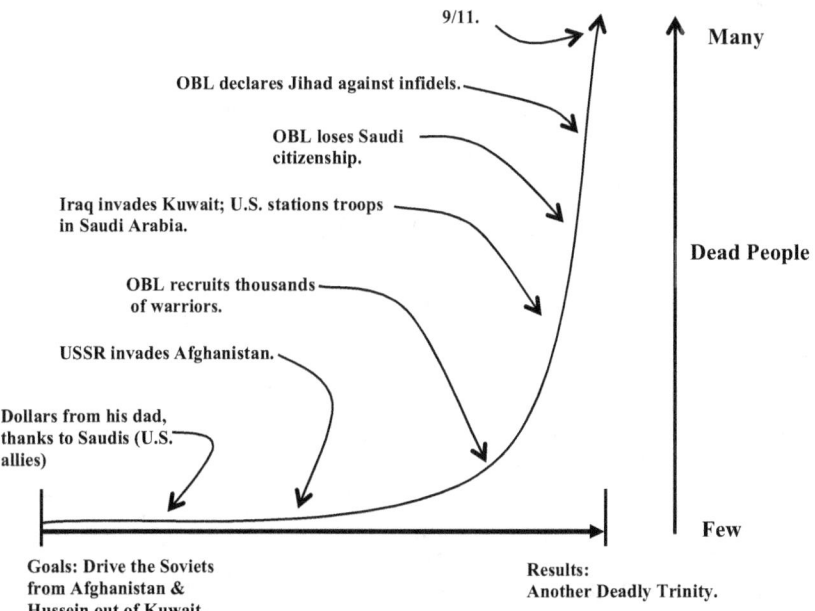

Exponential consequences of dollars from bin Laden's father.

• Thanks to his father, Osama bin Laden (OBL) became a multimillionaire. Thanks to the close connections his father had with the Saudi Arabian government, the family construction company prospered. In a touch of irony, bin Laden acquired his wealth and power because of the largesse of an American ally.[36]

• In 1979, the USSR invaded Afghanistan, an act bin Laden considered to be an attack on Muslim land—and an act justifying a jihad. (As noted earlier, the word *jihad* did not mean holy war in the Quran.) As a consequence of his interpretation of Islam, bin Laden relocated to Afghanistan to fight the Soviets. He was joined in this effort by the United States in a worldwide effort to recruit from the Arabic-Islamic world an infrastructure to combat the godless Soviets—who were also the USA's principal competitors. This competition was one reason for America's participation. The CIA alone

---

[36] Bin Laden did not use his wealth to any great extent to fund his wars. He was a gifted fund raiser of others' money.

came up with approximately $3 billion in aid to the Afghanistan fighters.[37]

• Little did anyone know Osama's money-raising and people-management skills, along with substantial contributions of dollars, expertise, and arms from America (to combat its Cold War nemesis, the Soviet Union) would lead to the defeat of the USSR in Afghanistan—as well as the creation of another terrorist and insurgent infrastructure—one that did not exist before the Afghanistan war.[38] In another touch of irony, bin Laden and the United States were on the same side during the USSR occupation of that country. The American support during this war would also result in the arming of thousands of Muslims. These former farmers, students, merchants, and couch potatoes changed their job descriptions to warriors. This mobilization, abetted by the United States, made use of the Muslim communities to create thousands of ideologically trained warriors and thousands of sympathizers to the militant Islamic cause.[39]

• The Iraqi invasion of Kuwait and the decision to place U.S. troops in Saudi Arabia, displeased bin Laden. His complaint pertained to the presence of non-Islamic people (nonbelievers) on Islam territory, another invasion of Muslim land. Ironically, the American presence insured the secular apostate, Sadam Hussein, would not harm Mecca and Medina, the Islamic sacred cities. No matter, bin Laden's religious sand box had been invaded. He was displeased—so were the Saudis. They had earlier revoked Osama's citizenship. These acts of the backsliding Saudis led Osama to declare war on his home country.

• Having been kicked out of formerly friendly countries, what was Osama to do with his ideology, money, arms, and vengeance?

---

[37] Emran Qureshi, *The Washington Post*, August 25, 2004, C1 and C9.

[38] Ibid., C9.

[39] Ibid., C9: An estimated 35,000 warriors from 43 Muslim countries were in Afghanistan. And more than 100,000 additional Muslim radicals visited Afghanistan and Pakistan during this war.

Answer: Invoke the catchphrase of jihad and declare war on all infidels. Noncombatants were in his crosshairs. Even children were not exempt from his killings.

• Osama bin Laden began attacking noncombatants and civil buildings to advance his views on religious fiefdoms. He targeted U.S. warships as well. In a major intelligence failure, the United States did not connect the dots (the terrorists' pilot training, their taking multiple trips between America and Afghanistan and Saudi Arabia).

The result? 9/11, an event the Student had studied previously in the Human Archives. The Student Cepee reflects: *America would never be the same. It took on a permanent war footing, and the Muslim jihadists declared a permanent religious war against, not only America, but any non-Muslim on earth. Why am I not surprised?*

By now, the Student is thinking more often of how fortunate he is not to have been born in the humans' early 21st century

Meanwhile, other occurrences of The Exponential Butterfly Effect were taking place. Other countries were arming themselves with weapons of mass destruction.

CHAPTER 27

THE EQUAL EXTERMINATION OPPORTUNITY (EEO) PROGRAMS

(Show 8)

The Student is beginning to understand and appreciate the magnitude of the problems the humans' religions brought on their race. Nonetheless, with some exceptions, it appeared the humans were misinterpreting their holy books. The Student turns-on the television show titled, "The Equal Extermination Opportunity (EEO) Programs," and this is what he learns.

[The TV screen shows a reporter walking along on a city street. She introduces her show.]

Reporter, "Hello, folks. Your reporter is standing on a corner of a busy thoroughfare in Baghdad, Iraq. Believe me, I am earning my pay today (as large and small arms fire is heard in the background). Anyway, standing beside me are three Iraqi citizens who have agreed to appear on television and offer their opinions about the treatment of prisoners who have been captured during the war in their country and surrounding areas, such as Syria. They have also agreed to offer their views on the subject of jihad."

The reporter continues, "A news item in the early weeks of the U.S. invasion of Iraq reported on the capture of an Islamic American Marine by Islamic terrorists in Iraq. Previous hostages of Western extraction have been decapitated by their captors in this region of the world. Until now, these hostages have been civilians. This hostage, as I said, belonged to the Marine Corps and practiced Islam. Just after

130

the capture, the world was buzzing about the fate of this man. The situation, now passed, is still relevant to current issues. We begin our report with Mr. Assad.

"Mr. Assad, can you tell our viewers your opinion about this capture and what the fate of the captured person should have been?"

Mr. Assad, "I find it rather surprising the insurgents...not terrorists, mind you...would be going after Islamic soldiers when there are so many infidels to behead. It seems a waste of effort."

Reporter, "So, you draw a distinction: Beheading a human should be based solely on religion?"

Mr. Assad, "Yes. And this Marine is a Muslim, so he should not be beheaded."

Reporter, "And, Mr. Agras, how do you react to this situation?"

Mr. Agras, "He is also Lebanese and Arab. These additional variables should be considered in the EEO beheading equation."

Reporter, "And Mr. Aman?"

Mr. Aman, "I would definitely say to the captors, 'He's a Muslim brother. Let him go for the sake of Allah. Make an exception to the EEO rule.'"

Reporter, "And if he were a non-Muslim?"

Messrs. Assad, Agras, and Aman, "Off with the infidel's head!"

Mr. Assad adds, "Nonetheless, the beheading of another person is unfortunate, but sometimes necessary."

Reporter, "In several Muslim countries, I understand Muslims behead Muslims frequently as part of their penal code."

Mr. Assad, "The situation with the war prisoner is quite different. This man was a participant in a battle against Muslims."

Reporter, "Oh? He was in a military unit participating in a war against the secular ex-ruler of your country, Saddam Hussein, whom many Muslims consider a Muslim backslider—an apostate."

Reporter continues, "But regardless of who fights whom, I understand the Prophet Mohammed said to treat prisoners of war kindly."

Mr. Agras, "True, but maybe this man was a deserter and not a prisoner of war."

Reporter, "But Mohammed directed Muslims not to kill any soldier who had turned his back to battle. It appears his remonstrance describes a soldier who is in retreat as well as a deserter."

Mr. Aman, "You do not understand. Muslims can take up arms and kill if they are threatened. Killing in self defense is permitted by the Quran and Mohammed."

Reporter, "I understand, but this is not about self defense, nor am I speaking of threat. I am speaking of murdering a single, solitary unarmed prisoner who was not attacking a Muslim, and who may have been defecting. In addition, other executions were performed on civilians, such as the 9/11 attacks. Thus far, you have not been able to justify these acts in relation to your religion."

Mr. Aman, "As you would say, let's cut to the chase. Beheading one another is a tradition for Muslims. For example, the Shiite tribes in South Iraq are promising to behead the Sunni citizens of Falujah." (Note from author: They fulfilled their promises.)

Reporter, "Let's be clear. I am not questioning the execution method. Beheading is likely more humane than, say, hanging. I am asking you to explain your views on the rationale for the terrorists' executions of people whom Mohammed quite clearly says should not be executed."

Mr. Agras, "I once again correct your use of the word *terrorists*; the correct term is *insurgents*. Moreover, let us also be clear. I quote from the Quran Chapter 47:4, 'When ye meet the Unbelievers in battle, smite at their necks. At length, when ye have thoroughly subdued them, bind a bond firmly on them: thereafter is the time for either generosity or ransom: Until the war lays down its burdens.'"

Reporter, "Yes, 'generosity' or 'ransom.' But this text from the Quran makes no reference whatsoever to killing. The Quran teachings also advise that the pain of the sentence be less than the pain inflicted by the murderer upon his victim."

Mr. Assad, "But don't forget, Osama bin Laden declared a fatwa. In so-doing, he declared a World Islamic Front, and stated '...America had declared war against God...and he (bin Laden) called for the murder of any American, anywhere on earth.'"[40]

---

[40] *The 9/11 Commission Report* (New York: W.W. Norton, 2004), 47.

The reporter, "Many citizens in America might take issue with bin Laden's claim of American's battling God. Anyway, a fatwa is issued by a respected Islamic authority, a trained scholar, about an interpretation of Islamic law. Bin Laden is hardly an Islamic scholar. He is an engineer by training. Yet, he issued his own fatwa, which your faith does not allow."

Mr. Agras, "You need more education. A collective jihad is proclaimed by a Caliph. There has been no Caliph since 1924. For an attack on Muslims or Muslim territory, there is no need for anyone, including a Caliph, to authorize a Muslim to fight. The individual jihad is the duty of each Muslim, Caliph or no Caliph."[41]

The reporter continues, "Once again, I am not speaking of a war. The focus of this interview has been and continues to be on the issue of *aggression against noncombatants*. I ask you to quote a Quran passage in which Mohammed directs the killing of unarmed civilians or defeated foes."

Mr. Aman, "Then permit me to quote from the Quran, Chapter 2: 190, 'And slay them wherever you catch them, and turn out from where they turn you out. For oppression is worse than killing. But fight them not at the Sacred Mosque, unless they fight you there. But if they fight you, slay them. Such is the reward of those who oppose faith.'"

Reporter, "But you left out the important identifier of 'them.' You did not include the sentence *preceding* your quote. It reads, 'Fight in the cause of God those who fight you, but do *not* transgress limits, for God loves not transgressors.' Gentlemen, defeated foes, civilians, noncombatants, women, and children can hardly be classified as 'those who fight you.'"[42]

Silence from Messrs. Assad, Agras, and Aman.

Reporter, "There you have it. I'll see you later on my next report."

---

[41] Michael Scheuer, *Imperial Hubris* (Washington, DC: Brassey's 2004), 7.

[42] This revealing, misleading reading of the Quran by Jihad apologists was pointed out to me by Sohaib Nazeer Sultan, who also wrote The *Koran for Dummies* (Hoboken, NJ: *Wiley Publishing*, 2004), 273-282.

CHAPTER 28

EGO, ILLS, AND SANE

(Data Fill 8)

In earlier surfings of the Human Archives, the Student Cepee has become familiar with the EGO procedures, as well as the ILLS and SANE therapies performed on the humans in the early 21st century. They were instrumental in lowering the threshold for making yet more changes to the species.

For example, cosmetic surgery was once performed in secret and a person undergoing this procedure stayed in hiding until the scars healed. Shortly thereafter, the younger looking person rejoined his circle of friends and colleagues, ostensibly having returned from a wrinkle removing vacation in Hawaii. Before long, this hush-hush maneuver became passé and a prospective makeover patient would proclaim, "It's time for another facelift." No one cared, as long as they had equal access to the cosmetic surgeon's knife.

The ILLS programs eased or eliminated the day-to-day miseries of a person, and in many cases, prolonged his or her life. Humans were quite vulnerable to germ-induced sickness. Eighty percent of their infectious diseases, such as the common cold to the deadly Ebola virus and AIDS, were transmitted by touch. ILLS eventually kept the germs at bay, while allowing the humans to continue their disposition to touch, hold, and love one another.

Fat Deposits. A large part of the population in the non-Noble Savage countries, overburdened with discretionary income, consumed enormous amounts of food. Some of these fat humans recognized the errors of their indulgence and attempted to diet and

134

exercise themselves back into a reasonable facsimile of a human. Others had surgeons remove their fat. Still others had their stomachs stapled in order to reduce the size of their gluttony reservoir.

In contrast, the Noble Savage country citizens were blessed because they did not have to worry about obesity. They experienced no anxiety about tummy tucks or stapled stomachs. They had no concern with clogged arteries. Their lot in life was much simpler. They did not worry about eating too much food. Their concern was eating too little.

EGO and ILLS Produce

The EGO programs were a valuable fix to the humans' unwieldy and unreliable bodies and minds. The ongoing changes that became part of the Cepee would solve most of the problems the EGO initiatives had begun to address.

The ILLS initiatives complimented EGO's agenda, and they went to the heart of the issues associated with human's health. These tasks were complicated and sometimes did more harm than good. But in the long run, the many experiments and research projects yielded positive results.

Eventually, the genetic underpinnings to aging were discovered, leading to the ability of a being to never die. Coupled with the fantastic progress made in body parts replacements, heaven on earth was just around the corner.

SANE and Genetics: A Bigger Challenge

The SANE programs presented a more challenging problem. They dealt with the humans' brain and genetic makeup. They also dealt with the humans coming to terms that their species was actually made up of different races. The notion was politically incorrect in some circles, but its genetic underpinnings were unassailable.

The fact that the human race did indeed consist of different races had nothing to do with the worthiness of one race over that of another. It had to do with the relative isolation of humans from one another in their ancient times, and the consequent changes Mother Nature made to their respective genetic makeups.

Nature and nurture were cooperating roommates in the human's body.

CHAPTER 29

I GREW BREASTS FOR THE SUPER BOWL HALF TIME SHOW

(Show 9)[43]

At the direction of his teacher, the Student surfs the humans' archives for a TV program about steroids. He finds scores of serious documentaries, but he wants a less ponderous treatment of the subject. A *Coming to you Live, from the Dead* show is available titled, "I grew Breasts for the Super Bowl Half Time Show." The Student is intrigued by the show's title. He downloads the show, and here is what he sees.

[The TV screen shows a news journalist sitting at his desk, facing the camera. The standard news music is playing. This weird melody, mimicking a Jean-Michael Jarre composition on a bad day, is supposed to remind the viewer of clicking telegraph machines or electrons flying through a wire. The journalist looks up from the blank piece of paper he is holding and turns his attention to the teleprompter.]

Journalist, "Hello, folks. This is D.A. Newes. Welcome to our show. Tonight, we examine the controversy surrounding the use of steroids. We will be checking with several of our station affiliates

---

43 The side effects of anabolic-androgenic steroids discussed in this *Coming to you Live, from the Dead* show are sourced from the FDA website. Search for "the dangers of taking steroids."

around the world as we expose the seamy side of bodies...eh, body-building. Joining us on the broadcast is Mary Contrary, a steroid specialist and a militant advocate of the Yin side of the Yin/Yang conflict between females and males.

"Also on hand, in our studio in Washington, is a member of the Federal Communications Commission (FCC). This gentleman will monitor our telecast to censor any statement, innuendo, or four-letter word that might offend the viewing public. In keeping with the stereotype of a 'nameless bureaucrat,' he will remain nameless."

D. A. Newes continues, "Let's visit our sister station in Los Angeles, where journalist I.M. Roving is interviewing Horace Harold, a former major league all star baseball player, recently retired and contemplating his next career move. Over to you, I.M."

I.M. Roving, "Right, D. A. ...Horace, you have admitted you used steroids during your stellar baseball career. Can you tell us why you took these pills?"

Horace, "Sure. For performance enhancement. I could never have slugged all those home runs by just eating spinach. And for money. Look at me! I'm rich, and I owe it to anabolic-androgenic steroids."

I.M. Roving, "With respect, Horace, I am looking at you, and you don't look so good. By the way, can you tell us what anabolic and androgenic mean?"

Horace, "Well, I don't feel so good either. Sure, anabolic refers to muscle building and androgenic means a tendency toward increased masculine characteristics. So, my steroid pills pumped me up in more ways than one!"

FCC person, "Censored! No sexual innuendoes are allowed on the public airways."

I.M. Roving, "Eh, O.K. Horace, as you know, the pills you took for over ten years are known to produce several unwanted side effects. Care to comment?"

Horace, "Yeah. But first, you there on the split screen, with FCC underneath your face. What's your name?"

FCC person, "It's immaterial."

Horace, "Well, Mr. Immaterial, I was not referring to that kind of 'pumping up.' In fact, after a few months of taking steroids, I noticed my testicles began to shrink, and…"

FCC person, "Censored! No references to sexual organs are permitted during the family hour."

I.M. Roving, "Look, Mr. Immaterial, this program is not 'Family Feud.' It is a serious journalistic investigation. We are trying to discuss a major problem facing our society. Besides, testicles is not a four-letter word."

FCC person, "Hm. Good point. OK, but watch your language. For example, you can use the word *testicle*, but you can't use the word *ball*, because it's four letters."

I.M. Roving, "How about 'balls?'"

FCC person, "Sure, that's five letters."

Horace, "Anyway, I also noticed I was starting to grow. …Uh, am I allowed to use the B word?"

FCC person, "Is it four letters?"

Horace, "No."

FCC person, "OK, proceed."

Horace, "Well, it's downright embarrassing. I couldn't even take a shower with my teammates after a game. I had started growing …b…br…breasts!"

[The split screen shows gasps coming from all parties except the journalists, who must maintain their journalistic composure of nonchalance and aloofness. Many in the audience know about gynecomastia, the development of enlarged breasts on a man. They also know gynecomastia is a permanent condition. It cannot be suckled away.]

Horace, "You know, I put up with my breasts while they were small, and training bras did the trick for a while. But they kept getting bigger. Before I knew it, they were starting to interfere with my game and…"

Mary Contrary, "Chauvinist! Pig!"

Censor, "Censored! You cannot make sultry, inaccurate, outrageous remarks about breasts and sports performance. A sports commentator was banned from the air for a similar snide remark."

Horace, "Wait a minute! First, these are *my* breasts we're talking about. Second, how do you think you would react if you woke up one morning and discovered your hard-earned, steroid-laden pectorals had morphed into breasts!? Besides, my breasts didn't affect my *swing*, they affected my *psyche*.

"Sure, maybe if I had started out with breasts, I would not have been so conscious of them. Maybe I wouldn't have worried if my bra was showing when I was at bat. You know, concerns like that pile up. After a while, as my bra slipped, so did my batting average."

[The TV screen shows Mary Contrary and the FCC censor relaxing a bit. They are satisfied Horace's comments about the sports performance of his breasts are not the same kinds of statements that led to the dismissal of a famous male sport commentator, who from all appearances, seemed a bit buxom himself.]

FCC person, "OK. You can continue your story, but you are on notice to be more careful about the remarks you make about your body."

Horace, "Fine. Well as time went on, my performance started going down the tubes. In addition, I began to suffer from dizzy spells, and my skin began turning a shade of yellow. I started balding, and my doctor told me the steroids had damaged my liver. So, I decided to quit the game and try another sport."

I.M. Roving, "What was the new sport? How did you do with the career change?"

Horace, "It was golf. I was a good golfer in my youth, and I even earned my card on the professional tour. I did OK for a couple years, but my past steroid use continued to plague me. In addition to the other problems, my doctor told me the pills were a big factor in my mood swings, including anger, aggression, and depression. I started seeing or hearing things that weren't there, and I had problems sleeping. Funny, but I had attributed these problems to playing golf. Still, I played well and made some money for a while."

I.M. Roving, "Interesting. What was your biggest adjustment moving from baseball to golf?"

Horace, "The biggest adjustment was getting out of shape."

I.M. Roving, "Golfers might take you to task on that statement."

Horace, "Yeah, but they are too out of shape to do much of anything about it. Anyway, my main problem was taking in a few opioids here and there. Got picked up for driving 'under the influence.' It put my career under water."

I.M. Roving, "Tiger Woods would like to talk to you after the show. Back to you, D. A. Newes."

D. A. Newes, "Now we hear from our correspondent in Berlin. She tells us about the steroid problems of the former East German women's track and field team who a few decades ago, dominated their competitors. Over to you, Barbara."

Barbara, "Right, D. A. Newes. Let's go to our correspondent onsite. Over to you Deborah."

Deborah, "Right. And back to you, Barbara."

Barbara, "Right. And back to you, D. A. Newes."

D. A. Newes, "Eh, nothing happened. I think Deborah is actually supposed to say something."

Deborah, "Ah! These 'over to and back to' handoffs can be confusing. OK, I am holding a picture of the East German women's track team during the time these girls were winning all the women's track and field medals in the world, except those won by the USSR team. By the way, the USSR team looks like a clone of the East German team."

Barbara, "Deborah, I think you made a mistake. You're holding a picture of East Germany's *men's* track and field team."

Deborah, "Nope. I double checked the picture with other records. You see, the use of steroids also has negative effects on females. Their usage can lead to growth of facial hair, male-pattern baldness, deepened voice, and loss of feminine body characteristics, such as shrinking of the breasts."

Censor, "Censored!"

Mary Contrary, "Oh, shut up!"

Deborah, "And some of these women have experienced health problems attributed to steroid usage. Fortunately, many of the complications went away over time. OK, that's all from Germany. Back to...whomever."

D. A. Newes, "I'll take it from here. As we have learned folks, anabolic-androgenic steroids are known to have serious side effects on both males and females. Without a prescription, their use is illegal, but the black market is thriving. Adults, keep away from steroids, and keep steroids away from your kids, both girls and boys.

"To wrap-up this expose, we want to update you on Horace Harold's career path. He has left professional golf. His breasts had nothing to do with his decision. But they did influence his decision to get into show business. He informed us last week he has interviewed for next year's Super Bowl half time show.

"We sign-off now with an endorsement from the Lance Armstrong Cycling Enterprise Devotees fan club...known as LACED... to keep Deadly Steroid Stuff (DSS) flowing through your increasingly contaminated veins, arteries, and brain."

[The TV screen fades away from the program, followed by an advertisement for the Super Bowl—not the game itself, but for the smoke and noise (mistaken for talent) of the half time show. Several entertainers, displaying a flair for rendering music into a banal cacophony, are shouting into microphones and displaying various parts of their bodies—all to divert attention away from their voices.]

Once again, the Student Cepee marvels at his odd ancestors, the humans. He thinks, *They seemed to specialize in agitating anything they touched. Yet as the Coming to you Live, from the Dead shows demonstrate, they were interesting creatures. They were certainly not boring.*

CHAPTER 30

AN OUNCE OF AVOIDANCE IS WORTH A POUND OF CURE

(Show 10)

Once again, the Mentor Sage directs the Student to view another television program about the humans and their off-beat behavior.

During his surfing of the Human Archives on the ILLS program, the Student has learned that millions of years before the humans made their presence known, there were germs, some of the oldest forms of life on earth.[44] The student has also learned these facts about germs.

Like humans, germs were living organisms and endured the ageless process of birth, growth, reproduction, death, and decomposition—the inevitable food chain cycle. Unlike humans, who displayed a modicum of discernment about where they lived, germs were not as demanding about their habitat.

Germs lived almost everywhere. In food, drink, colons, throats, mouths, lips, teeth, hair, skin, sweat, tears, coughs, sneezes, urine, feces, and semen. On door handles, telephone handsets, steering wheels, café napkins, movie theater seats, pencils, pens, paper—and much to his chagrin, Howard Hughes' coffee cups.

The humans were a dependent lot, relying on an extensive inventory of the earth's flora and fauna to assist them in consummating

---

[44] A rock unearthed in Australia, contained a fossilized germ. Specialists declared this Rip Van Winkle germ to be about 3.5 billion years old.

142

the ritual of their food chain cycle. Germs helped the human make its way through this cycle. "Make its way" is interpreted in two ways.

Interpretation one: Germs sometimes hastened the human's entry to a latter phase of the cycle: death from the germs' diseases. And after the human was dead, germs, with their enormous appetites, assisted in getting rid of the body.

Interpretation two: Many benevolent germs helped the human postpone inevitable death in that they helped the human combat other germs that were deadly parasitic.

Therefore, germs were both a blessing and a curse to the human. They were indispensable companions during life. Yet they often caused death...and they definitely kept dead human carcasses from piling up.

The student has been directed to a television show about the subject, titled, "An Ounce of Avoidance is Worth a Pound of Cure." Here is what the Student Cepee sees.

[The television screen displays a radio studio with a talk show host speaking into a microphone. The speaker is promoting a miracle drug his company has developed recently in Tijuana, Mexico. The product is also sold from off-shore ships anchored beyond the 200-mile limit of the U.S., as well as drug stores in Canada and Mexico.]

Talk show host, "Good evening, my devoted hypochondriacs. This is your insightful, fraudulent host, Doctor Doctor, once again on the air to sell you just about everything you do not want or need to ingest in your intestinal tract to combat those irksome germs. As always, I must state that in spite of my name, I am not a licensed doctor. My first name is Doctor. My last name is Doctor. My middle name is also Doctor. Thus, I am fully named Doctor Doctor Doctor. But you can just call me Doctor, or shucks, just Doc.

"Tonight, we have a special show for you. The Food and Drug Administration (FDA) has challenged our company! The FDA says our claims about our miracle medicine are based on false facts. We are calling their bluff this evening. We state our claims are based on true facts as well as factual facts, and true to our President's view of reality: alternative facts.

"Our current President is a bit disappointed to learn we do not deal with alternative facts…which we indeed do! But we call them falsified truisms. The words are a contradiction of reality, but so is the behavior of our President.

"Facts aside, and true to alternative options, the show this evening is devoted to our highly touted and egregiously profitable MiracleKillMedicine™ and its life saving and otherwise life altering components, MiracleKillIngredients™.

"To rebuff the FDA, we will dedicate the program to an examination of the effectiveness of our fantastic medicine; its wonderful ingredients; its germ killing power; its assuaging side effects, and its falsified truism remedies."

[The TV screen is now split, with Doctor Doctor on the right side and a telephone caller on the left, thanks to Skype.]

First Call In. Call in person A, "Doctor Doctor, I'm in awful shape. I feel bad all over more than any place else. I'm dizzy, nauseous, suffer diarrhea, have high blood pressure, can't sleep at night, urinate almost continuously, and…uh…have lost interest in my wife's affections."

Doctor Doctor, "Don't forget, my dear sickee, this evening is devoted to a discussion of the ingredients and effectiveness of our product, not to cure you through the air waves. Besides, we leave the telecures to our competitors, the teleevangelists—who don't use medicine, other than snake oil.

"Anyway, our mail order wonder, MiracleKillMedicine, will be helpful to your condition. You should take one MiracleKill pill each morning. Just be aware of possible minor side effects. As examples, you may experience dizziness, nausea, diarrhea, elevated blood pressure, occasional sleeplessness, perhaps incontinence, and some erectile dysfunction. And for certain, your hair will not fall out."

Call in person A, "Eh, Doctor, with the exception of the hair falling out, you just described the very problems that prompted my call to you."

Doctor Doctor, "Ah, I see. You're not having problems with your hair falling out?"

"No."

"Well, there you go! You will continue not to experience hair fall out problems."

Recognizing a potential discontented customer, the talk show host launches his most effective sales tool: obfuscation, "Not only that, our lab tests show you will not experience all these side effects at the same time. Even better news for you, the first three of the seven side effects will occur independently of the last four. Thus, the possible combinations of these side effects number only twelve!

"For example, you may experience dizziness accompanied by incontinence, but you will not experience dizziness accompanied by erectile dysfunction.

"Isn't life grand with your dependence on our drugs! Thanks for calling in. I'll now turn your call over to our order fulfillment and fleecing department."

Doctor Doctor concludes this part of the show, "Before we take the next call, let me say that due to pressure from the FDA, I am obligated to make the following statement on the air: 'Some people should not take MiracleKillMedicine because of the possible side effects of its ingredients.'

"There, done. But I assure you MiracleKillMedicine is indeed a miracle medicine. Nonetheless, it might have side effects on the sides, fronts, tops, bottoms, backs, and insides of certain people. OK, next caller. You're on the air with Doctor Doctor's MiracleKillMedicine!"

Second Call In. Call in person B, "I think I need your medication, but I am not sure all the ingredients in your drug are compatible with my body."

Doctor Doctor, "I understand your concern, and in spite of my pain killers, I feel your pain. Also, I am required by the FDA, the FCC, the AMA, and my nearly atrophied conscience to state

MiracleKillMedicine should not be taken by people who are allergic to its ingredients."

Call in person B, "What are its ingredients?"

[Doctor Doctor silently finds the tab in his "Medicine Manual" labeled "Side Effects, To Be Discussed Only When Threatened By Anyone Who Can Take Away Your FCC-Sanctioned License to Extort the Public."]

He then responds, "Our MiracleKillIngredients for Miracle-KillMedicine are cellulose, lactose, magnesium stearate, iron oxides, talc, titanium dioxide, starch, with butylated hydroxyanisole added as a preservative."[45]

Call in person B, "I'm not familiar with some of those ingredients, but I know about the others. Look, I'm already overweight. I don't need any more cellulose…just had several pounds removed from my stomach last month. I prefer to use talc on my armpits and private parts, and confine the use of starch to my laundry. In addition…about that preservative…preservative for what, your medicine or my body?"

Doctor Doctor, "Ha! You certainly have a pithy sense of humor Caller in B. Sure, as individual agents, acting alone, those ingredients you mention are associated with fat, body odor, and stiff shirts. But collectively, they congeal in your body to equal more than the sum of their parts. They interrelate with one another to produce a powerful antidote to your ills. Besides, one of our subsidiaries owns several magnesium, iron, and titanium mines and factories. Can't let this stuff go to waste. Next caller! You're on the air with Doctor Doctor."

Third Call In. Call in person C, "Doctor Doctor Doctor, I've…"
Doctor Doctor, "You can't call me a doctor!"
Call in person C, "I didn't. I addressed you by your three names. If I had called you a doctor, I would have said, Doctor Doctor Doctor Doctor."

---

[45] These ingredients are advertised for an FDA-approved medicine.

Doctor Doctor, "Hm. OK, sorry. I have to be careful not to openly camouflage myself. What is your question?"

Call in person C, "Right. Well, as I was saying, I've been taking your pill as you prescribed and..."

Doctor Doctor, "You can't say prescribed! I prescribe nothing. I am not allowed by the government to 'prescribe.' I only advise. Dear devoted sickee, remember that I am a talk show host. Even though my ill-informed falsehoods and drivel affect millions of people; even though I abuse the very medicines I disavow; even though I castigate those who are as afflicted and hypocritical as I. ...Well, I am not responsible for my behavior because I advertise myself as 'entertainment!' And I can't help it. MiracleKillMedicine—and some uppers furnished by my maid—give me a real *Rush*."

Doctor Doctor continues, "And after all, who doesn't want to let off a little steam now and then!"

Call in person C, "Look, you're the host, I'm the caller. I'm supposed to be the one with problems. Anyway, I've been taking the pill you're pushing on your show. I'm pregnant, have liver problems, and I'm also breast feeding. I just read the label on your bottle. It states your pill might be dangerous to people in my condition."

Doctor Doctor, "Well, as a sidebar, I suggest you ease up on your sex life and cut down on the Johnny Walker. But..."

Call in person C, "One moment, Doc Doc Doc. Here is some more information. After taking one of your pills each day, I began to experience muscle pain, tenderness, and weakness. I have also experienced a breakdown of my kidneys."

Doctor Doctor, "Well, yes, MiracleKillMedicine might create muscle and kidney problems, at least according to the FDA. But do not be concerned. If any of these conditions occur in your muscles, kidneys, or breasts, just let us know, and we will double your dosage to two pills a day.

"By the way, my lovely sicksters, if any of you are a bit overweight and that likely includes most of you, one aspect of my products is that they are guaranteed to cause a severely upset stomach. It is likely you will vomit repeatedly after swallowing one of my pills. Just think, you can shed your pounds because you can't hold anything in your now distended belly! Plus, you will not have to buy those expensive diet pills or have an expensive stomach stapling operation.

"Folks, it's time for a commercial break. Let's hear more about MiracleKillMedicine, then I will accept your call-in orders for our wonderful pills. Oh yes, no calls are accepted from third-world countries, Detroit, or Newark. Poor folks can't afford the medicine, so don't bother using the phone at your strip shopping mall to call us."

TV announcer, "Thank you, Doctor Doctor. Friends, you just heard about some of the wonderful condiments in the MiracleKillMedicine recipe. We only have one minute of advertising time to tell you about its virtues, because, due to FDA regulations, we must give you a *full* disclosure of its side effects.

"First, its virtue is that its side effects allow us to sell you more drugs to counter the side effects. Second, the side effects are many and varied, thus providing diversity to our product line.

"So friendly, sick consumers, here are the possible side effects of taking MiracleKillMedicine. For your convenience, they are grouped according to the parts of your body they affect:[46]

"**Digestive system**: upset stomach, gas, heartburn, stomach pain/cramps, constipation, anorexia, loss of appetite. **Liver and pancreas**: inflammation of the pancreas, hepatitis, jaundice, fatty changes in the liver, possibly liver failure, cirrhosis, and liver cancer. **Skin**: hair loss (sorry Doctor Doctor, this is a recent discovery); rashes, itching, discoloration, growth of nodules on skin, dryness. **Bones and muscles**: muscle cramps, aches, pains, and weakness. Joint pain and muscle breakdown. **Nervous system**: headaches, dizziness, insomnia, tingling, memory loss, damage to nerves, anxiety, depression, tremor, loss of balance, psychic disturbances. **Eyes and taste**: altered taste sensations, blurred vision, eye muscle weakness, progression of cataracts. **Allergic reactions**: shortness of breath, wheezing, low blood pressure (even shock), swelling of face/lips/tongue/throat, bruises, sensitivity to sunlight, fever, chills, difficulty

---

[46] With the exception of the upset stomach, all side effects in the disclaimer, as well as those cited earlier, are associated with one medicine. This information was taken from an advertisement for a cholesterol remediation pill.

breathing, burn-like shedding of skin all over the body—including the mucous membranes and the lining of the mouth. **Other side effects having to do with joy, contentment, and happiness**: loss of sexual desire, impotence, and breast enlargement. Fortunately, the breast enlargement possibility is not as serious as it may sound: It pertains to only half of the population: the male half."

The TV announcer concludes his pitch with, "Thanks to the FDA, we had to spend most of our allotted time informing you about the possible side effects of MiracleKillMedicine. So, before returning to Doctor Doctor, may I conclude with our motto, 'An ounce of our medicine is worth a pound of side effects!' Back to you, Doctor Doctor."

[TV screen cuts back to Doctor Doctor, who is sitting idly beside a bank of telephones. The phones remain silent.]

Doctor Doctor, "Keep those calls coming in folks and don't forget, we stand behind our product. If you are not satisfied with MiracleKillMedicine, just call our toll-free number, and we'll send you another bottle at half the price."

[The camera moves back from Doctor Doctor and the screen fades to black.]

The Student Cepee remains almost mesmerized by the surreal nature of humans and their dependence on drugs and medicines. He continues to look at a blank space where there was once a hologram rendition of the television program. He thinks, *My poor ancestors. Taking their drugs was almost as dangerous as not taking them.*

He then turns his attention to another dialogue, where he discovers his Mentor Sage has the Hologram acting as his proxy.

CHAPTER 31

FAT PEOPLE GOT NO REASON TO LIVE RULE

(Dialogue 12)

The Student Cepee has completed his initial studies of the humans' EGO and ILLS programs. Later, the student will learn more about the changes the humans undertook during their journey to become Cepees. For now, as the student prepares for a dialogue with his Mentor Sage, the Hologram Sage makes another appearance.

"Hey, Student, how 'bout them humans!"

Student, "They were certainly unusual. Their fixation on taking drugs was amazing. So were their problems with being fat. I'm glad we Cepees don't have to worry about the humans' organic offal. By the way, you use language differently from my Mentor Sage."

Hologram Sage, "Really? Far out. My specialty, the humans' popular music, requires I playback different clichés and idioms than those used by your Mentor Sage. He is far too sagacious to stoop to my light and mirrors shows."

Student, "I understand your position. Anyway, what's up? I am actually on my way to visit with my Mentor Sage."

Hologram Sage, "He is busy just now, doing some interviews with potential students. I am again to be his proxy for this dialogue."

Student, "Oh! These potential students. Is one of them...?"

Hologram, "Yes, one of them is the girl who resides in your chip-laced brain fantasies. The Sage directed me to inform you that

150

you are too self-serving and arrogant to warrant any interactions with her."

Student, "Yeah...'All in due time.'"

Hologram, "Yep. In the meantime, here's a song about the subject you studied recently: Fat."

Student, "Fine, I haven't had a break for a while."

The Hologram Sage fires up a hologram piano and launches into a song titled, Fat *People got no Reason to Live*.[47] Here is what the Student Cepee hears:

Plunk, plunk, plunk...♫♪♪♫
Fat people got,
fat people got,
fat people got,
no reason to live.

They got tiny little arteries,
and great big hearts.
Their adipose tissue,
it gives me the starts!

Their cholesterol level,
is much too high.
Their angina rhythms,
make their loved ones sigh.

Don't want no fat people,
don't want no fat people,
don't want no fat people,
to die.

Student, "Catchy. And contradictory. In the first verse, the song claims fat people have no reason to live. The last verse has the song stating that fat people should live."

---

[47] My thanks to Randy Newman for his *Short People* song from which I borrowed heavily.

Hologram Sage, "Right on! You see, modern human popular music made no sense at all. As long as the verses rhymed and the melody contained no more than three chords, it was considered a masterpiece."

Student, "What happened to Beethoven? I listened to his *Ninth Symphony* a few days ago. His music contained rich scores."

Hologram Sage, "No way. *Roll over Beethoven* was a very simple score."

The Student remains silent. The Hologram Sage, oblivious to the lack of response from the Student, continues, "Your Mentor Sage knows you have been reading about the humans' fast food industry. So, the Mentor Sage thought you might enjoy another ditty about fat and health."

Student, "Sure. I like your fat people song, but I think you need some downloads on Beethoven. OK, go ahead."

The Hologram Sage sings:[48]

You deserve a stroke today.
So get out and get away,
to McDonald's.[49]

Student, "Ha, but I recall McDonald's began selling salads."

Hologram Sage, "Yes, which resulted in new customers who were lean and wanted to stay that way."

Student, "A keen observation. Well, I must leave now to visit with my Mentor Sage."

The Student Cepee walks away as the Hologram Sage fades away.

---

[48] Please McDonald's, no lawyers. Lighten up!...in more ways than one.

[49] Uyless Black, "Traveling America (I)," 2006, 10.

CHAPTER 32

THE FEEL GOOD LAW

(Dialogue 13)

The thirteenth Cepee dialogue also takes place after the Student Cepee had spent some time thinking about the humans' use of feel-good and look-good pills.

Student Cepee, "Sage, I'm back. As you know, I have been studying our ancestors' use of drugs and medicines, and I would like to clear up some matters before moving to another subject."

Sage, "Very well."

Student, "I came across a human saying of, 'No pain, no gain.' Is this idea an oxymoron?"

Sage, "An oxymoron is defined as having two contradictory words. You are close. Let's call the saying a contradiction of ideas, perhaps a four-word oxymoron. Anyway, 'No pain, no gain' did not mean the human believed he or she had to suffer conventional pain to gain an advantage in life. The word *pain* meant to exert much effort, perhaps resulting in some discomfort, such as exhaustion or muscle fatigue—but not the pain sensations of, say, a dangerous injury."

Student, "So, the human did not mind suffering a bit, as long as the suffering could have a positive result? Perhaps another saying describes this feature of the human, 'Nothing ventured, nothing gained?'"

Sage, "Correct to your first question. And yes, 'Nothing ventured, nothing gained' could apply here, although the humans usually used this cliché in the context of a business or social venture. But your idea is valid."

The Sage continues, "However, many humans did not adhere to either saying. They were lethargic in their approach to their lives, always looking for an easy way out. Using your saying, we could express the behavior as, 'Nothing ventured, nothing lost.' A low risk approach to life. Any more questions?"

Student, "Just one. Many humans took pills and drink to make themselves feel better. We Cepees do not need this kind of stimulation, do we?"

Sage, "No, the same effect is part of our genetic tailoring. The humans to whom you refer succumbed to The Feel Good Law. This Law served as a palliative and mollifying influence for the human race, who were frequently forced to live in unpleasant, often painful conditions. "

Student, "Is this law another secret, known only to anointed sages?"

Sage, "Patience, Student. The law stated that many humans would disregard almost any taboo or prohibition in order to feel good. ...And in accordance with The Immediacy Syndrome, to feel good as quickly as possible. ...By the way, the correct grammar is 'feel well,' not 'feel good.' But slang is a productive and pleasant part of language. Our conversations are more enjoyable with the use of idioms, clichés, and slang. Just do not overdo their usage."

Student, "No problem! Anyway, it appears as if this type of human was above average on the Bell-Shaped Curve for hedonism."

Sage, "With a few exceptions, our ancestors were not ascetics. And given their lot in life, if I were in a human's shoes, I would be the first in line at the Feel-Good Pill Counter."

Student, "I understand. Compared to our forebears, we Cepees have an easy go of it."

Sage, "Indeed we do. The Feel-Good Law is built into our genome."

Student, "Thank you, Sage."

Sage, "I look forward to our next dialogue."

CHAPTER 33

THE TOWERING EGO CONDITION

(Dialogue 14)

———

The Student Cepee has completed another study of the Human Archives. He is eager to talk with the Mentor Sage about the humans' SANE programs. He saw the irony of the acronym. After all, a significant number of his ancestors were far from sane.

The Sage and the Student have spent time discussing a human's ego and why it was both a blessing and a curse. During his data fills on this subject, the Student came across information about Donald Trump, a former real estate developer, TV personality, and later in his life, a president of the United States.

Student, "Hello again, Mentor Sage."

Sage, "Greetings, Student. It has been noted you did several data fills on the humans' EGO, ILLS, and SANE initiatives. Do you have any more thoughts or questions about these programs?"

Student, "Yes. I learned about this man named Donald Trump and a building he named after himself! Trump Tower."

Sage, "You seem surprised."

Student, "Mentor Sage, I have done many hours of research on the humans. I cannot recall any of them building something—a bridge, a highway, or such—and naming it after themselves. The humans liked to honor other humans by placing a person's name on an airport, a stadium, and yes, a building. But such a designation was carried out for others, not the person who was so-honored."

Sage, "Hm. You seem particularly chagrined by this action. I will..."

155

Student, "I am, Mentor Sage! As just one example, did another American president, Ronald Reagan, rename an airport for himself?"

The Sage, who is a fountain of knowledge, patience, and persistence replies, "Interrupting your teacher…again…is not a productive way to conduct our dialogues. We will have to do a bit more work with your DNA, although we have not had much success finding the genetic combinations contributing to incessant interruptions. On the other hand, your comparison is apt, Student. Well done. I will bring in the Hologram Sage to amplify your point. "

The Hologram Sage lights-up. The Hologram has taken on the image of President Ronald Reagan, standing at a podium, making an announcement: "Fellow Americans, because of my greatness, I am re-naming the National Airport the Reagan National Airport."

Student, "That is my point, Sage. Reagan did not name the airport after himself. The hologram show is a parody and a reflection of Trump's ego, which was often out of control."

Sage, "You make an astute observation, Student. It points to a great deficiency of some of the humans. As you have learned, we have spoken of the dangers of excessive pride. But the trait we are addressing masked a more dangerous aspect of our ancestors: grandiose narcissism.

"Narcissism so extreme, it clouded a human's view of reality. This man, Donald Trump, was obsessed with exhibitionism, attention-seeking, and huge demands of entitlement for himself. He denied having any weaknesses.

"Leaders of our past were usually more narcissistic than the average human. As well, some of America's presidents were noted for their narcissism. Student, a high level of narcissism did not disqualify a person from being the United States President. But we Cepees have learned that a human could exhibit narcissism that was so excessive it disqualified the individual from carrying out the duties of a leader."

Student, "My studies reveal a person who I am certain was an extreme narcissist but a brilliant leader: Napoleon."

Sage, "Go on."

Student, "First, his intellect was astounding, something akin to Cepees' mental powers. Second, he was an extreme self-promoter.

He wrote letters in which he exaggerated the magnitude of his victories, just as Mr. Trump did. However, unlike Trump, Napolean, although a killer, was also sensitive to the needs of others. He developed loyalty because he was also genuinely concerned for his soldiers and those citizens he ruled. And unlike this Trump person, Napoleon rarely insulted or demeaned anyone, even his enemies."

Sage, "What have you learned by comparing these two men?"

Student, "Other than what I have told you, Mentor Sage, is this: Trump and Napoleon were certainly extreme narcissists. Whereas Napoleon only occasionally 'bent the truth,' Trump bent it with regularity, so much so that he began to lose some of his supporters."

Sage, "But only some, Student. How so?"

Student, "Mentor Sage, it comes back to one of the rules you taught me about the behavior of the humans: The Ignorant, Therefore, Doctrinaire Syndrome: A human who was devoid of any knowledge on a subject held an unyielding—and often belligerent—opinion on the very same subject."

Sage, "Yes, Student, once this kind of human formed an opinion about something, it was set in mental stone. No amount of persuasion about the error of the opinion would have any effect."

The Sage continues, "Napoleon sometimes declared great exaggerations. But he performed."

Student, "Is that so, Sage? I could mimic your comment: "Trump often declared great exaggerations. But he performed."

Sage, "You are challenging me. Just remember, Student Cepee, there are different interpretations of the word *performed*. Napoleon changed the humans' western world. He put his life in jeopardy several times to achieve his goals. He transformed politics, legal systems, and ways of governance in many countries. In that sense, he performed.

"Trump performed on television and the humans' Twitter. He never went to battle; never led an army across Russia; never re-wrote civil code for the western world. He had a penchant for tearing down others. He expressed this thought about a man who was captured by an enemy, when his airplane was shot down over the enemy's territory: 'He's a war hero because he was captured. I like people that weren't captured, OK?' "

Student, "It is amazing that someone could make this statement and not be ostracized from politics. Yet he kept his fan base. He even publicly bragged about assaulting females and got away with it! Time after time, his followers unwittingly adhered to The Ignorant, Therefore, Doctrinaire Syndrome."

Sage, "Yes, and he did have some solid ideas on trade. He also recognized the dangers of uncontrolled immigration. Often, the problem was how he presented himself as a head of state to the public.

"He lied repeatedly, Student, which were generously characterized as 'false or misleading claims.' When caught with his mis-statements, he discounted them as 'jokes.' He debased the presidential office. He was an extreme unilateralist, and made many efforts to dismantle over sixty years of America's successful efforts to construct foreign relations and domestic infrastructures. Before you execute your next data fill from the Human Archives, here is another *Coming to you Live, from the Dead* television program, which will amplify our dialogue today."

CHAPTER 34

THE ALTERNATIVE FACTS FARCE

(Show 11)

The Student has been instructed by the Sage to download another human television program. This is what he learns.

[The humans' antiquated TV screen, once again rendered as a three-dimensional hologram image, displays a moderator introducing the program.]

Moderator, "Good evening to all. Tonight, we have a special treat for you. President Donald Trump is the featured guest. He will interact with a panel of distinguished reporters about the subject of alternative facts.

"To set the stage, President Trump's staff has claimed the attendance for his presidential inauguration was the 'largest audience to witness an inauguration, period. Both in person and around the globe.' This statement was found to be false.

"A White House advisor was criticized for creating the phrase alternative facts during a TV interview.

"She later explained that alternative facts are not lies, but different ways to view the same information. She said: 'Two plus two is four. Three plus one is four. Partly cloudy, partly sunny. Glass half full, glass half empty. Those are alternative facts.'"

The Student Cepee puts the television show on pause. He thinks, *Those are not alternative facts! They are just another way to state the same fact. In fact, there can be no such thing as alternative facts. Facts are facts.*

When the Student releases the pause button, he witnesses the guest interrupting the moderator:

President Trump, "You sniveling journalist. There are two sets of facts: Those put out by a media who wish to destroy me and those put out by me. Let's face the facts. Mine are factual facts. Yours are false facts, designed to undermine my presidency. Let's call a heart a spade! Alternative facts are alternative ways of getting ahead in life."

Moderator, "Let's hear from journalist number one."

Journalist number one, "Mr. President, it has been documented that since your taking office, you have told a lie, or in less harsh terms, misinformed the public almost every day."

President Trump, "Wrong! Give me examples."

Journalist number two, "I'll join in here. This is a chart showing only five days of your presidency. The underlines state the facts about your quotes:"[50]

- JAN. 21 "I wasn't a fan of Iraq. I didn't want to go into Iraq." *(He was for an invasion before he was against it.)*

- JAN. 21 "A reporter for *Time* magazine — and I have been on their cover 14 or 15 times. I think we have the all-time record in the history of *Time* magazine." *(Trump was on the cover 11 times, and Nixon appeared 55 times.)*

- JAN. 23 "Between 3 million and 5 million illegal votes caused me to lose the popular vote." *(There is no evidence of illegal voting.)*

- JAN. 25 "Now, the audience was the biggest ever. But this crowd was massive. Look how far back it goes. This crowd was massive." *(Official aerial photos show Obama's 2009 inauguration was much more heavily attended.)*

- JAN. 25 "Take a look at the Pew reports (which show voter fraud.)" *(The report never mentioned voter fraud.)*

---

[50] These findings and the quotes in this discourse are courtesy of *The New York Times*.

President Trump, "Once again, the media is out to get me. My facts are as valid as yours."

Journalist number three, "Mr. President, one set of facts cannot be valid if they conflict with another set of facts! Is that *not* evident?"

President Trump, "No. Your facts are false facts. Mine are true facts. You media hounds are vermin!"

Moderator, "Let's move on to the related topics of 'untrue facts' and 'false facts.'"

The Student turns off the program and says to himself, *Fantastic, yet the American public was taken in by this charlatan.*

The Mentor Sage, whose multiprocessing skills are in evidence, takes over, "Student, contrast some comments made by America's first president, George Washington, to those you just witnessed by America's forty-fifth president, Donald Trump.

"Washington said, 'Every action done in company ought to be with some sign of respect to those that [who] are present.'

"Trump said the media were 'sick,' and disparaged anyone who displeased him. He spoke harshly about professional football players and movie actors who held different views about politics. Those comments turned off many Americans."

The Mentor Sage continues, "The first U. S. President, George Washington, ennobled those around him. The forty-fifth President, Donald Trump, demeaned those around him. Washington was an inspiring leader. Trump was a shallow narcissist."

Student, "Sage, had our ancestors devolved so much in only a couple centuries or so?"

Sage, "No. In fact, most of our ancestors became more civil and benign toward one another. But the combination of The Threshold Lowering Syndrome and The Disproportionate Ratio Effect resulted in unfortunate consequences for our ancestors. Again, Student, this fact—a true fact, if I may make light of the subject—is key to understanding what contributed to the demise of the humans."

Student, "Debilitating to them. Exhilarating for us."

Sage, "Don't be flippant. Get back to your studies."

PART TWO

KILLING, INC.

CHAPTER 35

BOMBS AWRY AND BOMBS AWAY

(Data Fill 9)

The Student Cepee has been endowed with genetic manipulations designed to give him a positive outlook on life. After all, who could not feel positive about life if one's living was one of security and one of infinity? A time without end, forever lounging in a metaphorical hammock with lemonade at one's side. It was a pleasant way to think about aging, as old age death did not exist.

Nonetheless, the immediate and all-consuming job of this young being is to learn about his ancestry. He could indeed lounge on lawn furniture and take in drinks, courtesy of his comfortable life style. But he is not focused on lounging and drinking.

He is a special Cepee. He is consumed with learning more about his ancestors who lived long ago. In his consideration, it is his job to improve the Cepees. After all, part of this process of his special curriculum is to learn about humans in order to improve himself, but in his mind, to also improve his race.

And he is always subject to the scrutiny of the Mentor Sage.

The Student thinks, *The Sage is a pain in my cerebral ass. But he has taught me much. I will stay with the program.* (As if he had a choice, after all, he is a youngster and a student.) Thus, the Student begins his surfing the Human Archives once again to learn about his ancestors.

Dangerous Neighborhoods

By the early years of the 21st century, many humans, especially those living in urban areas, began to suffer a common fear. Increasingly, a human, acting alone or in concert with a few other people, would stake claim to infamy by wiping out groups of people who lived in a large city. Starting modestly, the Tylenol bottle poisonings led to other murders: the Tokyo subway sarin nerve gas attacks, the Oklahoma City bombing, the D.C./Virginia snipers, the Ohio freeway killings, the 9/11 attacks, the Anthrax mailings, the Madrid railway bombings, the London subway and bus attacks, the slaughter of Amish school children, the Mandalay Hotel, Las Vegas assaults. These killings were precursors to even more deadly attacks.

However, courtesy of The Threshold Lowering Syndrome, these "modest" assaults were followed by thousands of deaths occurring when religious/political zealots or simply lunatics unleashed bombs and biochemicals in several urban centers. Targets of the attacks were amusement parks, gambling casinos, financial institutions, shopping malls, even schools.

Dangerous Societies

Initially, the humans who were bent on destroying other humans were relatively small in number, such as the attacks cited above. Without question, these people were disruptive and caused considerable trauma to their victims and financial strife to those nations who were attacked. But overall, their aggression tool box contained a relatively modest inventory of gasses, rifles, and bombs.

However, this equation changed when weapons of mass destruction became available to individuals and non-nation tribes. Where once a madman or a tribe who possessed a modest killing tool box could murder only a few people, this single person or a small tribe could now kill hundreds of thousands of people—all in one attack; all in conformance with The Disproportionate Ratio Effect.

The single-shot arrow of many years ago was followed by the single-shot musket, later by gattling guns, still later, AK-47s. The curve was bending upward toward the creation of increasingly deadly weapons. And the curve was bending upward...exponentially.

The Gradual Momentum of Lowering Thresholds for Violence

The Student learns that much of the tragedy of the human race came about because they gradually lowered their thresholds for committing gratuitous violence on one another, often in battles for turf and power. The Student comes across two studies on this idea: the Holocaust and the Rwandan genocide. A researcher of these events offered these thoughts about genocides:

> The first time a human kills another human, the experience is horrific: perpetuators describe reactions that include vomiting, shaking, recurrent nightmares, and profound trauma [sociopaths excepted]. ...But, over time, the physical and emotional horror at participating in violence subsides. This, then, is when the moralizing rationale that draws on dehumanizing propaganda comes into play. How does one adapt to participation in violence? By calling on culturally available repertoires that frame violence as the morally right thing to do.[51]

The Student recalls from his studies the genocides committed by Adolf Hitler and Joseph Stalin.

The Attacks with Weapons of Mass Destruction Begin

The culmination to the human species' self-destructive madness came with the first attack since WWII with nuclear weapons. The detonation was in Washington, DC.

The DC attack was not an isolated incident. In keeping with their multitasking approach to their jobs—as evidenced by the 9/11 and Madrid attacks—the terrorists also bombed the cities of Tel Aviv, London, and Moscow, the repositories of secular, sinful backsliders. The toll of dead numbered in the hundreds of thousands. Many more

---

[51] Aliza Luft, *The New Yorker*, December 11, 2017, 5.

were seriously injured and thousands of humans eventually died of radiation exposure.

The Revenge Cycle began another cycle. Those who were thought to have attacked America's bastion of democracy were subjected to the United States' nuclear arsenal, as well as the reprise of other nations who took umbrage with these assaults. Before long, other cities were nearly annihilated.

In addition, some nations or non-nation state tribes in the mid-21st century used chemical and biological weapons on military and civilian populations. In Syria, Muslims gassed fellow Muslims who had a different view of their take on Islam. The same carnage held for the Sunni in Iraq by their chemically decimating their Sunni Kurds kinfolk in north Iraq. "Kissing cousins" took on a new meaning: "killing cousins."

Given these inevitable Human Tribal Hierarchy conflicts, it was the use of nuclear weapons that caused the human race the most traumas.

Aftermath and a Sobering Assessment

The nuclear attacks, the resulting counter attacks, the ongoing wars between the religious factions, as well as other tribal killings around the globe eventually became the proverbial straw that broke the camel's back. The camel's back was the refusal of a sizable and influential part of the human race to accept or support radical genetic engineering or brain alterations. The straw was the colossal human death toll, with the expectation that the mass slaughters would never stop. Even countries that were not bombed were decimated as the trade winds carried nuclear particles into the air above them.

After this wholesale destruction, it was only a matter of time before the human genome was altered to "disinfect" the human's makeup of any vestige of deadly aggressive behavior. The magnitude of the attacks, the number of dead humans or those with radiation sickness, the burying of friends and loved ones (those who could be found), the knowledge that more attacks would follow—the horrific magnitude of it all spurred the humans to "fix themselves." They had to eradicate The Deadly Trinity before The Deadly Trinity eradicated them.

A Pause for Reflection

The Student Cepee remains amazed at the inability of his predecessors to curtail their disposition toward self-destructive acts. These actions entailed not only outright warfare, but the despoilment of their bodies and minds, as well as their seas and land.

As intelligent as the Cepees are, they have difficulty comprehending how the humans' centuries of evolution could have led them to a dead-end alley of self-destruction. The Cepees have concluded human genetic anomalies got out of hand until the Cepees began to emerge from their ancestors' EGO, ILLS, and SANE programs. Nonethelesss, the Student remains in a state of reluctant dismay about his ancestry

As well, for a while, the Student opts to spend more time with the Sage. The Mentor Sage has no objection. After all, his job description is to mentor young Cepees. He looks forward to the student's questions and the opportunity to guide the development of the youngster...and to display his sage-endowed sagacity.

In the meantime, the Sage has directed the Student to view another *Coming to you Live, from the Dead* television show.

CHAPTER 36

IT ONLY HURTS FOR A LITTLE WHILE

(Show 12)

The Student welcomes the Sage's direction to take a break from studying the Human Archives. The recent studies on weapons of mass destruction have been disturbing, even though they took place many decades ago. Luckily, the Student has been directed to view a *Coming to you Live, from the Dead* TV show on the subject of chemical and biological warfare. On the other hand, maybe he is not so lucky, as the topic is somber. But he decides to see if another human TV satire can make the subject entertaining.

The student learns the title of the show is taken from the humans' country song, "It Only Hurts for a Little While." The program director has added a subtitle, "But While it Hurts, it Really Hurts." The Student also downloads a table titled Chemical Weapons Taxonomy for use during the program but is not available to the participants in the show, only to the studio audience and the TV viewers. Here is what the Cepee sees.

[The TV camera first displays this screen:

Chemical Weapons Taxonomy (Not all inclusive)

Chemical Agent	Effect
Incapacitating agent	Incapacitates eyes and nose functions
Choking agent	Attacks respiratory system, putting a damper on breathing
Blistering agent	Creates large skin blisters, with the goal of discomfort and infection
Blood agent	Creates convulsions and respiratory failure
Nerve agent	Attacks central nervous system

170

Next, the camera closes in on a quiz show host, who cannot be identified because he or she is wearing a biochemical warfare mask and suit. The host stands in front of three contestants of unknown sex and identity because they are also outfitted with masks and suits. Muted music can be heard as the host begins his/her introduction to the camera and the live audience. The soft melody is the famous country song, "It Only Hurts for a Little While."]

Host, "Hello, folks! Tonight we have a very special show for you. We decided to reflect the name of the famous show, *Jeopardy*, with subjects that are just that, jeopardous! Our topics are chemical and biological weapons, also called CBW, surely fitting subjects because they place the recipients of their effusions in jeopardy. Our emphasis will be on weapons that are falling into the hands of terrorists. (Writer: Thanks to the Jeopardy show and Alex Trebek for their fine work.)

"Because our category is limited to one subject, I will pose the answer to our panel of three contestants and their response will be 'What is so-and-so?'... the 'so-and-so' is the correct question to the answer. The Chemical Weapons Taxonomy table you can see on your screen cannot be seen by our contestants. So, we can evaluate the accuracy of the contestants' answers.

"Oh yes, about our masks and suits. During rehearsal, one of the chemical/biological samples you will see during the program fell from a table. Its container cracked from its impact with the floor."

[The live audience becomes restless because it would like to continue to be a live audience.]

Host, "Don't worry! It was just a small crack, and we participants have this protective gear on because as they say, 'The Show Must Go On.' For you nonparticipants, if any of you suffer ill effects and must be taken to the hospital, after—or if—you have recovered, we will give you a free pass to another educational show. So, either way, you can't lose!

"I have several samples of CBW agents in the vials here." [He points to a table on which rest several small bottles.] "The ingredients in just one of these bottles, if opened and let into the air in this studio, are sufficient to kill us all, or make us so sick we might wish for death.

"Do I have your attention? OK, here we go. First answer: Creates large skin blisters, with the goal of discomfort and infection."

Buzzer from contestant one, "What is acne?"

Host, "No, sorry."

Buzzer from contestant two, "What is a blistering agent?"

Host, "Right you are! Next answer: Attacks central nervous system."

Buzzer from contestant one, "What is rap music?"

Host, "No."

Buzzer from contestant three, "What is your office mate's cell phone?"

Host, "Time's up. It is: What is a nerve agent? That was a tough answer I gave you. Here is the next answer: Attacks respiratory system, putting a damper on breathing."

Buzzer from contestant one, "What is oxygen?"

Host, "Eh, no."

Buzzer from contestant two, "What is a choking agent?"

Host, "Correct! And the next answer is: Invokes convulsions and respiratory failure."

Buzzer from contestant one, "What is oxygen?"

Host, "Eh, no…maybe contestant one should not be so fast with the buzzer."

Buzzer from contestant two, "What is a blood agent?"

Host, "That is correct! One more answer before a commercial break: Incapacitates eyes and nose functions."

Buzzer from contestant one, "What is incapacitating agent!"

Host, "Ha! Nice recovery contestant one. Your question is *a* correct one, but not *the* correct one. You did not frame your response in the form of a question." (The host has impressive perception skills.)

Contestant one, "Sure I did. I said, 'What is the lack of oxygen!'"

Host, "Yes, but you did not use a question mark at the end of your sentence. You used an exclamation point. Your response was not a question."

Contestant three, "What is an incapacitating agent!?"

Host, "You are correct! It's time for a commercial break. When we return, our answers will be a different category. The focus will be on biological weapons."

[The TV screen fades from the quiz show scene as a commercial appears. This advertisement entices the audience to purchase music CDs, such as rock and roll, classical, rap, and country.]

The announcer makes his pitch, "If you buy ten of our discs, we will ship you a free CD of that country-terrorist classic, 'It Only Hurts for a Little While.' Of course, you will want this little masterpiece as a nostalgic reminder of tonight's show. Here is a sample of this wonderful melody."

A Willie Nelson-type voice can now be heard, blending in with the complex cadence of three cords, played over and over in sharps and flats...but mostly flats.

Strum, strum, strum...♫♪♪♫
(The first three lines are the refrain)
It only hurts for a little while.
That's what they tell me.
That's what they say.

It only hurts for a little while.
But you will hurt 'till I can have my way.

You see my problem is my pride,
that's why I blister up your hide.
Your problem is that you're so vain,
until I liquefy your brain.

(Refrain)

These lands you claim were always mine,
You even claim my lakes and rivers.
Claim my turf and sea as yours,
and I will poison up your livers.

It only hurts for a little while.
That's what they told me.
That's what they said.
It only hurts for a little while.
And you will hurt till you and yours are dead.

Announcer, "Just what you need to cheer you up on those rainy, lonely afternoons. And folks, a new offering: If you purchase twenty CDs, we will send you another famous country-terrorist song, 'The Hurtins' All Over, All Over You.' Now, back to our show."

The Student sees another table appear on the screen, which is invisible to the panel members, as the Biological Weapons Inventory. The screen then displays the host and the three panel members.

Biological Weapons Inventory (Not all inclusive)

Biological Agent	Effect
anthrax	Aches and pains, fever, fatigue, cough, chest pain. Inhalation is fatal.
botulism	Affects central nervous system and interrupts nerve impulses. Difficulty in walking and swallowing, impaired vision and speech, occasional convulsions, ultimately paralysis of respiratory muscles, suffocation, and death.
salmonella	Typhoid fever, food poisoning, abdominal pain, fever, nausea and vomiting, and diarrhea.
smallpox	Skin rash develops on face, chest, back, and limbs. Rash develops into pus-filled pimples resembling boils; death is common.
tularemia	Chills, followed by enlarged glands. Death is rare but can occur.
yellow fever	High fever and jaundice, possibly death.

Host, "OK, panel contestants, your correct questions to my answers will now double in value. Here is the first answer to our second round: Affects central nervous system and interrupts nerve impulses."

Buzzer from contestant one, "What is MTV?"

Host, "Right you are, but not what I am looking for. Good to see you off the oxygen fixation."

Buzzer from contestant two, "What is botulism?"

Host, "Right. Next answer: Chills, followed by enlarged organs and glands."

Buzzer from contestant one, "What is too much Viagra?"

Host, "Not that kind of organ!"

Buzzer from contestant two, "What is tularemia?"

Host, "You are again correct. Well done. Next answer: Aches and pains, fever, fatigue, cough, chest pain. Long term inhalation is fatal."

Buzzer from contestant one, "What is a cigarette?"

Host, "Brilliant but incorrect question."

Buzzer from contestant three, "What is cocaine?"

Host, "Incorrect."

Buzzer from contestant two, "What is anthrax?"

Host, "Absolutely! Contestant two is pulling away. Next answer: Skin rash develops on face, chest, back, and limbs. Rash develops into pus-filled pimples resembling boils; death is common."

Buzzer from contestant one, "What is a bad tattoo?"

Host, "No. And you were doing so well with your brilliant, incorrect questions."

Buzzer from contestant two, "What is smallpox?"

Host, "Right you are. I see we have run out of time, and we have not exhausted our inventory of biological weapons. Contestant two, you are the winner and will return to the show tomorrow when we feature another topic that is putting our society in jeopardy: off-the-shelf nukes. Just be aware these weapons are available only in areas of the country that allow Walmart, Costco, and Best Buy to sell armaments—which, due to the tax revenues, takes in all our glorious states—including Israel, Taiwan, and South Korea—our recent additions. Ahem, Puerto Rico has been dropped from our list of itinerant states, as it is mired in chaos and debt. So, 'till then, goodnight everyone."

The Student Cepee turns off the hologram television. He ruminates on what he just watched, *It was a sad state of affairs: our ancestors started killing off one another, which forced themselves to create us Cepees. I'd hate to think the damage they could have done if they were still around.*

CHAPTER 37

VIETNAM BOOGIE

(Dialogue 15)

The Student Cepee is still trying to fathom his discoveries about the human race and their modern wars. In so far as a Cepee could be dumbfounded, the Student is just that: dumbfounded. He is preparing to go to the Mentor Sage when the Hologram Sage appears.

Hologram Sage, "What's happening, S.C? Oh, you don't have to explain. Your Mentor Sage knows you are befuddled and will clear up your confusion the next time you two meet."

The Student realizes his conversation with a hologram must necessarily be limited in their intellectual content, but he knows the Hologram has appeared for a reason, "I have many questions for my Mentor Sage. As for you, what's up?"

Hologram Sage, "I have a song for you about the humans' wars. It contains a message about wars in general. Your mentor wishes to know if you can infer the message from the verse, if you are gaining in your cognitive powers."

Student, "Fine. But thus far, your songs have not been very subtle, although I do admit, I enjoy listening to them. OK, as you would say, lay it on me."

Hologram, "Cool. By the way, this song is done to the beat of rap music. Have you had a data fill about rap?"

Student, "Yes. I learned it was an off-shoot of rhythm-and-blues and that it emphasized verse over the music itself. I listened to some rap tunes. It seems as if the rap bands succeeded in rendering the three chords of rock and roll music to no chords at all. Do you agree?"

176

Uh oh, the Student had committed a software *faux pas* by asking the Hologram to make an improvisational response. The Hologram Sage replies, "Eh, the Mentor Sage has me programmed to remain discordant on this matter."

Student, "Never mind, I should have known. Go ahead. Sing your rap to me."

Hologram, "Will do. First, some background. The song is about the Resistance War, so named by the Vietnamese, or the Vietnam Conflict, so named by the Americans. It is titled the *Vietnam Boogie*, although it is really the *Vietnam Rap*. Here we go!" as the Hologram raps out this song:

...♫♪♪♫, sort of...
Danang, Chu Lai, Phu Bai, Hue!
Take a city with each day.

Capture Quang Nga, that's our duty,
while we dance the *Vietnam Boogie*.

Haiphong, Hanoi, Khe Sanh, too!
They'll be ours when we get through.

Student, "That's it? I know the names of the cities in the song are places in Vietnam, sites the Americans and Vietnamese fought over. So what?"

Hologram Sage, "I'm not finished, Student. The Mentor Sage directed my routines to pause and inform you the first verses were written to depict the time in the mid-1960s when the Americans were deploying troops *into* Vietnam. During this time, the Americans thought they were winning the war.

"The next verses were written to describe the times in the mid-1970s when the Americans were deploying troops *out of* Vietnam. The American leaders kept telling their citizens that America was winning the war, but the Viet Cong and Vietminh were taking on offensive deployments and starting to control aspects of the conflict:

...♫♪♪♫, again, sort of...after all, it's rap:
During these times of guns and smoke,

how about a fun time toke?
Dancing! Prancing! Tuti Fruiti!
While our troops do the *Vietnam Boogie.*

Hey! Where did all those Vietcong go,
while we watched the Bob Hope show?[52]
They can't do our boogie dance,
but look out soldier, they kicked-ass France!

Soooo…

Hello, Saigon,
Du-wa-ditty.
Well, wha'da you know?
You're now Ho Chi Minh City!

So long Saigon, your name's sunset.
Lowered by the tune of the Vietnam Tet.

Danang, Chu Lai, Phu Bai, Hue!
Lose a city with each day.
Goodbye, Vietnam, you're now broke!
We'll see you later with our Macs and Cokes.

Student, "I had better consult with my Mentor Sage…unless you want to help me out."

Too late, the Hologram's light has been turned off. So the Student Cepee prepares for his next dialogue with the Mentor Sage.

_____

[52] During the Vietnam War, this writer watched a USO show from the deck of an aircraft carrier. The ship was anchored in the South China Sea, a short distance from the coast of South Vietnam and the ship to which I was temporarily assigned. Bob Hope was not in attendance for this performance, but several Playboy Bunnies were. The huge speakers and accompanying amplifiers were almost deafening. As I listened and watched the show, I wondered if the Viet Cong ashore were also listening. They were likely planning their next attack on our shore-based troops, while we USO customers on the carrier deck were fantasizing about the bunnies. It was at that moment that I realized America would not defeat the Viet Cong and Vietminh. We could escape reality with a USO show. The Viet Cong had no escape route. They had no choice but to stick it out. For us, we could go home if things got too rough. They stuck it out. We went home.

CHAPTER 38

NOTHING EXCEEDS LIKE EXCESS

(Dialogue 16)

The next Cepee dialogue takes place after the Student Cepee has finished his data fills and studies about the 21st century intraspecies wars among the humans, and after he had watched the Hologram Sage perform the *Vietnam Boogie*.

Student Cepee, "Sage, I have questions. But before I pose them to you, the Hologram informed me there was a message in the *Vietnam Boogie* song. I suspect the last line about 'Macs and Cokes' was the message. Maybe the Americans could have achieved their aims in Vietnam without going to war?"

Sage Cepee, "No one will ever know. But some humans believed America's pre-WWII creed of, 'The business of America is business,' became one of its Cold War creed of, 'The business of America is the business of spreading Christianity and democracy...if needed, through war.'"

Student, "I know I am a student, and you are a sage, but I must disagree. America was no more disposed toward war than any other country."

Sage, "I agree. It was not I who made up this saying. It was spoken by humans who were against war in general. As you are learning, if it were not the Americans who, as the Hologram would say, 'kicked ass,' it was someone else. Throughout the humans' history, The Law of the Instrument held sway: Those who had the dominant instruments of war were the ones who applied those instruments and thus dominated the landscapes."

179

Student, "Yes, so I have learned."

Sage, "About the *Vietnam Boogie*, here is a fact for your consideration: After this war, America became Vietnam's number one trading partner."

The Student has been reflecting on his learning from the data fills and his dialogues. He responds with a near sagacious utterance: "Hm."

Sage, "Yes, and as you learned, many parts of this earth were rendered uninhabitable for many years because of the humans' wars."

Student, "What made our ancestors change their path toward self destruction?"

Sage, "I assume that is another one of your flippant remarks. You already know the answer to your question."

Student, "Yes, Mentor Sage. I was practicing being a sage by posing a sagacious question. The answer is their realization they were on the way to their Deadly Trinity, one of self destruction."

Sage, "Correct. Besides, as time went on, with or without their wars, they were changing themselves to eventually become us. Their aggression and wars with weapons of mass destruction merely hastened the process of their altering their genetic and cerebral makeup to save themselves from themselves.

"Their excess led to us, Student. They redesigned themselves to shield themselves from one another."

Student, "Quite sobering, Mentor Sage,"

Sage, "Yes. Their ultimate behavior was akin to their approach of fighting one another: destroying a village in order to save another village; destroying a nation in order to save another nation. Ultimately, it led to the possibility of destroying the earth to…what, Student?"

Student, "To save the earth in order to save another earth? Which could not be done."

Sage, "Yes, our ancestors embarked on an unintended journey, to destroy the very road on which they traveled for centuries. It was a road that had made them a great race but one that led to their demise and our ascension.

"Their road forward in time was accompanied with The Threshold Lowering Syndrome, The Creeping Momentum Law, and The

Disproportionate Ratio Effect. Which meant: They gradually built more lethal weapons, while lowering their ethics on how they were used. These weapons found their way into a small part of human populace...a small number of people who wreaked havoc on our ancestors.

"It was a road paved with irony, Student. The irony was the humans' brilliance to build a road with stones of extraordinary and effective accomplishments, yet that same road was lined with self-destructive pavers."

Student, "A contradiction in ideas, Mentor Sage?"

Sage, "Somewhat, Student. More to the point, a contradiction in behavior. More specifically, a mix up in gene mutation and evolution, which we Cepees fixed."

CHAPTER 39

THE S-SHAPED CURVE CANON
(Dialogue 17)

The next Cepee dialogue takes place after the Student has done more research in the Human Archives. He wishes to discuss with the Sage an idea he has come across that is titled: The S-Shaped Curve Canon. It is a complex set of laws, grouped together to identify a body of facts and described by a horizontal S-shaped curve. The Student sketches this drawing, taken from the archives. It is far from an artistic rendering, but the Student is not an artist.

Laying the S down.

He learns from the Human Archives: "If the relationship of the S-shaped curve to the letter "S" has escaped the reader, here is the S-shaped curve, resting at its conventional, readable, upright position:"

The upright S curve.

Laying the S-shaped curve down again, its canon-level significance is explained with these notations [see next figure]: (a) An idea

182

is embraced with wild enthusiasm, as it presents an overly simple approach to an overly naive population. (b) Regardless of its merits, positive or negative, it is followed by ridicule and/or ignored, as humans are inclined to do. (c) It once again gains favor, as public relations propaganda deceives a gullible populace. (d) Eventually, it fades into the sunset, suffering from obsolescence, overuse, disinterest, or satiation—usually accompanied with ridicule.

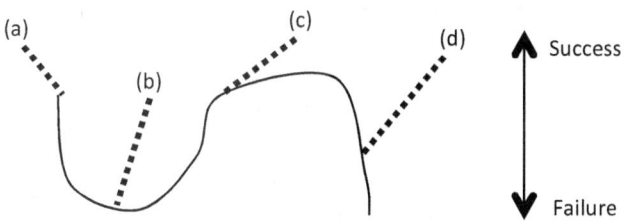

S-Shaped Curve in general.

The archives provide some examples: Example one: HDTV. (a) Fantastic idea; beautiful picture! (b) Initially, no one can afford one. (c) Mass market reduces price and people buy HDTV. (d) Replaced by YouTube and Facebook.

Example two: Free love. (a) Always popular in theory and usually very popular in practice. (b) Religion and pregnancy discourage wide practice. (c) Birth control devices, acting in concert with The Feel-Good Law, overwhelm religious reservations. (d) Herpes, HIV, evangelicals, the Pope, and China put a damper on the practice.

Example three: Presidential administrations: (a) President is elected, undergoes obligatory honeymoon. (b) President is discovered for what he is: a politician. (c) Electorate forgets President is a politician (or who is the President) because they are too busy Twittering. (d) The consequences of poor decisions and The Lag Effect of the *previous* administration catch up with the *current* administration and the incumbent President is defeated in the next election, hounded from office, or impeached.

To complete the cycle, his administration's malpractices lie in wait for his successor, to be sprung when The Lag Effect raises its head years later.

The Student then consults with the Sage, "If you don't mind, Mentor Sage, while discussing the humans' 21st century wars, I would like to revisit the S-Shaped Curve Canon. I have been thinking about it in relation to the Middle East."

Sage, "Of course. I encourage your initiative."

Student, "OK. Let me draw the curve and place some notes on it," as the Student renders the following:

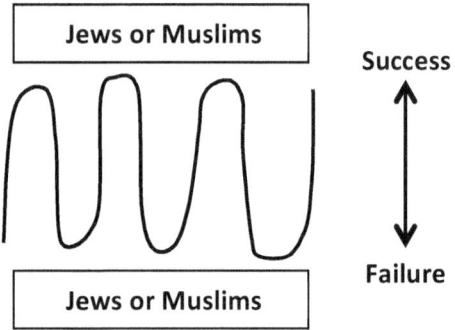

S-Shaped Curve for occupation of Middle East "Holy Lands."

Sage, "Your work are not works of art, but drawing is not your job. Hm. I see you have been studying. But I must advise you that your drawing is an over simplification of the history of that part of the world. It doesn't show the rise and fall of other tribes and sects: the Canaanites, the Greeks, the Romans; the British to name a few."

Student, "My intent is to depict the Middle East problem during the latter times of the humans' stay on earth. The turf battles became a bone of contention between Jews and Muslims, not Canaanites, Greeks, Romans, or British. My studies are leading me to believe the humans' 21st century wars with weapons of mass destruction had many of its roots in these so called Holy Lands because of the Jews and Muslims never ending battles for their religious turf."

Sage, "Correct, but are your conclusions restricted to the contentions between the Jews and Muslims?"

Student, "I'm not following you."

Sage, "I will re-render your graphic:"

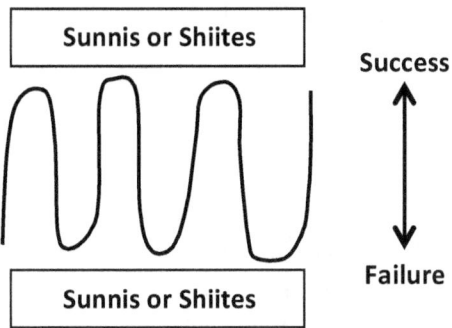

**S-Shaped Curve for the best position in the
Islamic religious hierarchy.**

Student, "I see your point, Mentor Sage. I have learned there were other factions contributing to the nuclear and biochemical mayhem that came about. In fact, looking around the globe of the 21st century, there were many factions."

Sage, "Yes, and the various warring factions often battled *within* their tribes as often as they battled other tribes. A Sunni took as much pleasure in beheading a Shiite as taking off the head of a Jew. Same with the Shiite. Even more, within the Sunni and Shiite sects themselves, there were further subsects and conflicts among them. And your take on The S-Shaped Curve Canon is another way of showing…?"

Student, "The Revenge Cycle in action?"

Sage, "Correct again."

Student, "How about us Cepees? On whose side did we land?"

Sage, "We Cepees have embraced many of America's tenets: freedom of expression; freedom from the fear of the State; freedom of movement; freedom of choice, as long as the choice does not damage someone else. So, in many respects, the American humans' model was a success. Yet, in much of the Americans' practice, they often exhibited self-delusionary hypocrisy, a dialogue for another time."

Student, "But we're here and the Americans—and other humans—are not. They're in the Human Archives."

Sage, "We will address your point in our next dialogue. For now, I have other students to attend to. I am impressed with your progress. Keep up the good work, Student."

Student, "Thank you, Mentor Sage. Say, I have not seen, as you said, that 'fair damsel' around your sanctuary. Is she, eh, still in the vicinity?"

Sage, "Student, you are on a special program designed by your especially selected teacher and mentor. Your 'biosynthetic heart-throb' is a member of another program. Keep your biosynthetics under control. …All in due time."

The Student leaves his mentor, grumbling about the 'all in due time' nonsense. He says to himself, *My heart may be biosynthetic, but my heartbeat is real*…as the writer of this saga silently groans for having written that last statement.

CHAPTER 40

ONE MAN'S TERRORIST IS ANOTHER MAN'S FREEDOM FIGHTER

(Show 13)

While studying his ancestors' habits of regularly bombing and otherwise mistreating their neighbors, the Student Cepee wonders about the accuracy of the term *terrorist* as used in the Human Archives. Its meaning had a negative context to the humans, although many names and terms were used to describe people who engaged in activities leading to the deaths of other people. These humans were called assassins, terrorists, zealots, extremists, freedom fighters, insurgents, and so on.

A *Coming to you Live, from the Dead* TV show is available on this subject, and the Mentor Sage explained the program would shed a lot of light on the subject (in spite of the absence of the Hologram Sage). The Student downloads this program, titled "One Man's Terrorist is Another Man's Freedom Fighter." Here is what the Student sees.

[The TV screen shows a talk show host in the foreground with six contestants standing at their respective podiums in the background. Five podiums are aligned on one side of the stage, facing the one remaining podium, positioned on the other side.]

Host, "Good evening to you all. Our show tonight will be based on the famous 'Name that Name' format. I will pose a question to our panel, and they will provide a person's name who fits the

187

question's clue. To help our panel and our viewers, this table provides the definitions of the terms I will use in the questions."

[The camera cuts to the table shown below.]

Confusing Terms and Definitions

Term	Definition
Freedom fighter	Participates in an armed revolution against a political system regarded as unjust.
Terrorist	Uses violence or the threat of violence for political purposes.
Anarchist	Tries to overthrow a society's formal system of government.
Revolutionary	Committed to a political or social revolution.
Guerrilla	Committed to the overthrow of a government.
Insurgent	Involved in uprising against a government or ruler of a country.
Militant	Active in the support of a cause; engaged in fighting or warfare.

Host, "Our six panel contestants are an international assemblage. We have citizens from the United States, the Republic of Vietnam, the United Kingdom, Russia, Cuba, and Afghanistan. However, in keeping with the current unilateralist, go-it-alone posture of the United States, including the disparagement of its allies, the U.S. representative will compete against the five other panel members, who acting as a one-panel team, will challenge the U.S. contestant.

"A few final guidelines: Each side is allowed to furnish one answer to a question. After all questions have been answered, the TV audience will vote on the answers by sending in their responses to our website. So, all you couch potatoes out there, get your computers and smart phones fired up, and let's get started!"

"Here is the first question. Name a famous freedom fighter?"
    U.S. panel contestant, "George Washington."
    Vietnam panel contestant, "Ho Chi Minh."

Host, "Next question. Name a famous terrorist?"
    U.S. panel contestant, "King George III."
    U.K. panel contestant "George Washington."

Host, "Here is our third question. Name a famous anarchist?"
    U.S. panel contestant, "Osama bin Laden."
    Afghanistan panel contestant, "George Washington."

Host, "For the fourth question, name a famous revolutionary?"
U.S. panel contestant, "George Washington.
Russia panel contestant, "Vladimir Ilich Lenin."

Host, "The fifth question: Name a famous guerrilla?"
U.S. panel contestant, "Ho Chi Minh."
Vietnam panel contestant, "George Washington."

Host, "Next question: Name a famous insurgent?"
U.S. panel contestant, "Osama bin Laden."
Afghanistan panel contestant, "George Washington."

Host, "Our final question: Name a famous militant?"
U.S. panel contestant, "Fidel Castro."
Cuba panel contestant, "George Washington."

Host, "That's it for the questions and answers. Let's see how our world-wide audience evaluates our contestants' responses."

[After a few seconds, the camera cuts to a large graphic displaying a world map indicating the TV audience's responses to the seven questions. The responses are tabulated. As they appear on the map, the quiz show host offers these observations.]

Host, "As you can see, the responses are clustered into geographical areas. Those viewers who agree with the answers of the U.S. panel contestant are centered in the United States, Israel, England, Antarctica, and heavily concentrated in North Idaho and Orange County, California. Those agreeing with the other panel contestants' answers are clustered in all the other countries in the world, as well as San Francisco and Portland.

"At Name that Name, we are happy we could bring you an educational, entertaining half hour of confusing names and their associated perplexing definitions. We also thank our world-wide audience for demonstrating the effectiveness of America's post-Cold War strategy of 'going-it-alone.' We are sure this approach will greatly aid the U.S. in ferreting out the ephemeral, nebulous cells of terrorists located in the nooks and crannies of countries who have begun to despise the U.S. foreign policy and the U.S.—thereby helping America to capture the bad guys. Until next week, so long everyone!"

[The TV screen fades from the quiz show scene to a news bulletin highlighting the citizens of America's ex-allies at NATO demonstrating against the U.S., followed by several announcements about the defeat of pro-American political candidates in these countries, and the refusal of several countries to join America's battles or buy American Cokes and cigarettes.]

The Student Cepee turns off the hologram TV image and says to himself: *I wonder if any countries during the humans' time on earth were actually peaceful?* The all-knowing and ever-listening Mentor Sage possesses extraordinary parallel processing powers. He has been engaged in sage-like endeavors and at the same time, monitoring his favorite Student's activities. He will answer the Student's question in their next dialogue.

CHAPTER 41

THE SWITZERLAND AND UNITED STATES PRINCIPLES

(Dialogue 18)

Student, "As you know, Mentor Sage, I have finished my archival data fills on our ancestors' nuclear and biochemical wars. I suspected I might learn about these events after my studies of the humans' aggression, the wide-scale proliferation of weapons of mass destruction, and their propensity to use religion as a rationale for their killing. But you scheduled my tutorials about tattooing, cosmetic surgery, feel-good pills, and the germ battles—the EGO, ILLS, and SANE programs—in between the events of the ASSES program. So my timing was a bit off. These last data fills were quite sobering."

Sage, "Yes, the sandwiching of EGO, ILLS, and SANE in between ASSES provided a logical flow to your studies, and it gave you a break."

Student, "Thank you for your planning. I have a question about the rationale for the terrorists' selection of the specific cities to destroy. Why Washington, DC? Why London? Why not Tokyo, Japan, or Geneva, Switzerland?"

Sage, "Thus far, your archiving has not revealed that these cities were eventually attacked by their own citizens, people who were not happy with their politicians...whom they themselves elected. For now, I will acquaint you with two principles.

191

The Switzerland and United States Principles

"First, The Switzerland Principle was the practice of a country to avoid responsibility for anything, except making money. The antipode was the United States Principle: The propensity for a country to take responsibility for everything, manifested by taking charge of everything."

Student, "I know about these countries. Switzerland did not do much but deal in finances. Otherwise, it stayed in the background on the world stage. The United States was front-and-center. Its power and size allowed it to become a dominant presence in most parts of the globe."

Sage, "Yes, and Switzerland had a 'live-and-let-live' approach to its international relations. America had a 'change-and-then-let-live' philosophy."

Student, "Eh?"

Sage, "Americans believed the other people in the world wanted their way of life. And they were committed to export their way to all others."

Student, "Were the Americans correct? Did the other humans want their way of life?"

Sage, "Many did. Many did not. Most people who were suffering from the effects of constant warfare and disrupted societies did not care who ruled, or by what philosophy they employed in this rule. They just wanted peace and prosperity. If a Singapore-type government could pull it off, fine. If Sunnis were in power, fine. Shiites, fine. Whatever. The average person just wanted freedom from the debilitating effects of physical, financial, and social insecurity."

Student, "So, we are here and the Americans—and other humans—are not. They are in the Human Archives."

Sage, "We will address your point in upcoming dialogues. For now, I have other students to attend to. But I am impressed with your progress. Keep up the good work, Student."

Student, "Thank you, Sage."

Sage, "One more thing. For the next few dialogues you do not have to study the Human Archives. You have sufficient information to engage in our discussions, as they deal with more reasons the humans had so many deadly conflicts. You are done with your data fill studies for awhile. Now let's determine if you can apply that work to your further understanding of our ancestors."

Student, "I've got some time off! Maybe I could spend some of it with that Cepee student I met before."

Sage, "In due time, Student, in due time. Besides, she is too busy just now. And you do not have time off. Use your time to *actually think*! That is what a student is supposed to do."

Student, "I *have* been thinking, Mentor Sage, maybe about different things than the subjects in my studies."

Sage, "Obviously. Dismissed."

CHAPTER 42

THE UNLIKE-DISLIKE AXIOM

(Dialogue 19)

"Here I am, Mentor Sage, ready to learn more about our ancestors. You said our next few dialogues will focus on the never ending conflicts among the humans."

Sage, "Yes. Much of it deals with the trait of the human disliking another human if the human was unlike him. The backdrop for this lesson is the Middle East during the 20th and early 21st centuries. The focus will be the nation of Israel, the Palestine state issue, and Israeli settlements in Arab territory.

"For background information, Student, the term *Aliyah* refers to the immigration of the Jews to areas in the Middle East known as Israel, West Bank, Palestine, and the Golan Heights. The word *kibbutz* refers to a Jewish communal settlement.

"The chronology I will present for the Hologram to create our visualizations is an overview. As well…"

Student, "My apologies, Mentor Sage, I interrupted you again, but I think an observation about the Hologram Sage's shows is in order."

Sage, "Which is?"

Student, "The Hologram's images used in our last dialogue remind me of a clip I recently viewed from the Human Archives. The archives' extract is about a software package called PowerPoint. The humans used the package as a visual aid for lectures, briefings… increasingly for most everything that used language. I viewed one clip where the humans never talked with one another. They exchanged,

194

time-after-time, PowerPoint presentations. One of the archival clips showed two humans attempting to have sex by alternately exchanging PowerPoint slides. I gather..."

Sage, "And time for an interrupt from *your* Sage. For several decades during our ancestors' 20th and 21st centuries, PowerPoint replaced normal discourse and dialogue, as did Facebook and YouTube. Let's have the Hologram amplify my point to you." The Sage brings on his proxy.

Hologram Sage, "How can I amplify something I'm made of? I'm not much more than a PowerPoint show, just a few more hues and one more dimension. This is humiliating, exposing myself this way."

Mentor Sage, "I *indeed* must schedule a meeting with the Cepee programming staff. Hologram (as the Sage 'pulls the plug' on the light show), come back when your software can behave sage-like." The Hologram fades away into darkness.

"Student, I have chosen several examples in this dialogue to broaden your horizon on the subject of an additional trait of the humans: The Unlike/Dislike Axiom. Hm, I forgot. I just turned off the Hologram in a moment of rare un-sage-like annoyance. My apologies, Student, my behavior is not one for you to emulate."

The Mentor Sage re-activates his proxy, the Hologram Sage, which appears again before the Student and the Student's mentor.

Hologram, "Do you realize how dark it is when I am not turned on...even for a moment or so? What a bummer. Mentor Sage, how can I shed light on the Student's lessons if I am not shedding light?"

Sage, "Holograms have their pre-programmed place. It appears your Cepee programmer has mistakenly coded some enlightened self-interest into your behavior."

Hologram, "Yes, the programmer is experimenting with my artificial intelligence. He's of the belief that self-interest enlightens... especially holograms!"

Sage, "Yes, and a human once said: Self-interest also blinds... especially holograms."

Hologram, "I suppose so, but I don't want to appear dim-witted. OK, I am fired up and ready."

The Sage's oral recitation to the Student is amplified by the following visual image:

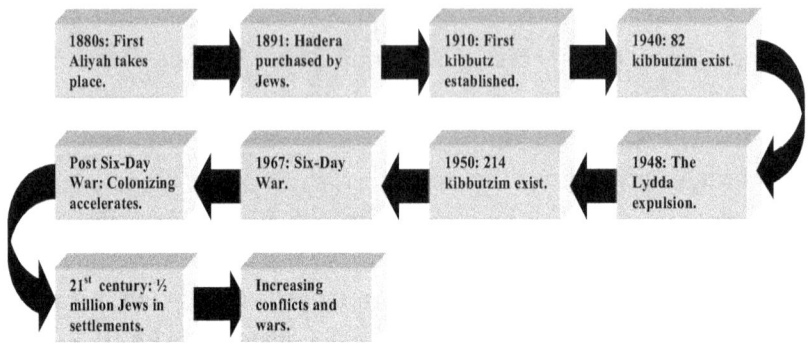

Student, "I need to delve further into the Human Archives to grasp the Hologram Sage's sagacious visuals—eh, yours of course. I have one observation. This situation was a major factor in the humans' wars with weapons of mass destruction."

Sage, "Correct, it was a creeping momentum tragedy."

Student, "Yes, but does the Hologram know about this aspect of unlike/dislike and the creeping momentum tragedy?"

Sage, "You are indeed a clever one. And as you know, the Hologram is a reflection of yours truly, but done to the pace of a student's mental framework…and it appears, a programmer's whims. But from the beginning of our relationship, I've sensed you were a bit different from my average student."

Student, "That is a complex illustration the Hologram has created. Can you start over?"

Sage, "Asleep at the wheel? Very well, you have been keen on learning, and this subject is important to understanding key components about how our ancestors almost self-destructed. So, I will start over. …Hologram, go away, but leave your light show on."

The Hologram meekly protests, "Out of the limelight again. How can I possibly hope to enlighten when I am not lit up?" But the Hologram obeys the commands of a real sage, leaves the image intact for the Mentor Sage to take over:

"Student, prepare yourself for seemingly illogical information about our ancestors. Girt yourself up. You will be entering into a part of the Human Archives that continues to perplex and astonish Cepees."

Student, "I am well prepared to take in more examples of the illogical behavior of the humans. But are you sage Cepees perplexed about this aspect of the humans as well?"

Sage, "Yes, even Cepee sages are perplexed." The Sage continues, "Pay attention to the Hologram's chart during my dispensing of this wisdom to you: In the late 1800s, several thousand middle-to-lower class Jews, mostly from Eastern Europe and Russia, migrated to Palestine. Migration also took place on a more exclusive basis. For example, in 1897, thirty Zionists arrived by a private steamer. It was the first 'journey of upper-middle-class British Jews into the Land of Israel.'"[53]

Student, "I recall the Zionists from the archives. They were Jews who supported the creation of a Jewish homeland in the land of Israel. Sage, where did the Zionists live after they came to the Middle East? Did they rent apartments?"

Sage, "Ha. No, they purchased farmland from the people who lived there, principally Arabs. As the light show indicates, one of the early farming colonies was Hadera, which grew to be a prosperous Jewish region in that part of the world. Interestingly, Student, shortly, the very Arabs who sold Jews land began to contest the Jews' presence. This discussion provides an opening for the introduction to The Unlike/Dislike Axiom about humans."

The Sage hesitates, then relinquishes, "I will bring in the Hologram again. Can you imagine a hologram that can have its feelings hurt?"

Student, "Mentor Sage, you said yourself that a hologram's mood depends on its color. That's what a hologram is: color."

Sage, "Never mind. The Cepee programmer is too ambitious with artificial intelligence software. Imagine! Coding mood into a

---

[53] Ari Shavit, *My Promised Land: The Triumph and Tragedy of Israel* (New York: Random House, 2013), 3.

light beam," as the Hologram appears and silently displays a visual interpretation of the Mentor Sage's short oral narrative:

> The Unlike-Dislike Axiom: Anything that was dissimilar to a human's customs or expectations was instantly disliked.

Sage, "This axiom came to be known as…"

Student, "Yes! The Unlike-Dislike Axiom came into play often with the humans. I see examples in the Human Archives every day."

Sage, "As you know, I dislike being interrupted, especially by a student. But you are on the right track. As you have learned, during the humans' early evolutionary years, their survival often depended on detecting that a different looking person, or one that behaved differently than their own kind, was usually dangerous. The presence of this stranger could very well mean this unlike-looking person was outside his tribal boundary, looking for bounty, such as food and females. As time went on in our ancestors' development, this cautionary behavior became part of their instinctual makeup. It took many forms: differences in skin color, differences in language, and so on. Anything that was different from the norm came under suspicion."

Student, "Could these unlike people also have been looking for turf?"

Sage, "For certain. Better hunting grounds, as some of the humans said. And for this lesson, the Muslim Arabs wished to maintain the character of their customs and religion—to keep everything and everybody alike. Of course, they also wished to maintain their positions on the upper rungs of the Human Tribal Hierarchies of power and influence.

"The Jews wished the same for themselves. And true to the nature of humans, the Jews wanted to acquire as much land as possible, import as many Jews as possible into the land, turn the land into their Jewish home, thereby having everyone look and behave alike."

Student, "I sense a tongue in your cheek, Mentor Sage. Are you making fun of our forebearers?"

Sage, "Somewhat Student, but while I am making light of this axiom, I cannot over emphasize the extent it influenced human behavior. As well, consider this aspect of the humans, especially the Muslims and the Jews. Their tribes looked down on interfaith marriage. If it was not forbidden, the act was considered shameful, even blasphemous. For Muslims, it was not unusual for a woman to be killed if she married a non-Muslim man. For the Jewish faith, some families would disown a son or daughter who married, say, a Christian."

Student, "I have come across these facts in the Human Archives. By the way, what did the Zionists plan to do with the resident Arabs?"

Sage, "As it turned out, they did not plan much at all. Thousands of Arabs were displaced. Those thirty Jews I mentioned earlier were expected to be something of a spearhead for this movement, one that was closely watched by one of the leaders of Zionism, Theodor Herzl. This man was 'especially interested in the inhabitants of Palestine and the prospects of colonizing it.'"[54]

Student, "Colonizing: As in sending Jewish settlers into an Arab region with the intent of establishing political control over it? (The Sage nods yes.) But this strategy would result in the Jews displacing Arabs, just as the Jews were displaced by non-Jews in Russia, Poland, and other countries. Two wrongs did not make them right."

Sage, "Correct, and these two wrongs led to an ironic tragedy: the wars with weapons of mass destruction. But keep in mind, Student: Why should one expect the Jews to be different from other tribes? Turf acquisition was part of humans' DNA.

"Besides, a growing number of Jews were coming to believe their people were in danger of extinction. The atrocities committed on these people, and their magnitude, were of great significance. The pogroms against Jews in 19th and 20th centuries had the effect of creating a more militant Jew, one who believed he or she had to have

---

[54] Shavit, 3.

the security and sanctuary of a homeland. It just so happened that this homeland was also the homeland of millions of Arabs."

Student, "Uh, oh."

Sage, "Precisely, and as the Hologram's visual image depicts, the colonization of the region happened in a gradual way. The Israeli Jews, being extraordinarily visionary and a competent people, slowly but surely carved out places in the region that became exclusively Jewish. Their ambitions were greatly aided by several of the Western nations and wealthy Jews living in other parts of the world."

Student, "So what? The Arabs did not have to sell their land. They were willing participants in this so-called colonizing."

Sage, "Let's take a break. Open the Human Archives. Go to 'Lydda,1948.' Study the subject. I will see you in one hour, then we will talk more about this subject," as the Sage dismisses the Student.

The Human Archives reveal the following events took place in Lydda, an area in Palestine near the Mediterranean Sea.[55] (Writer's note: While reading this chronicle, consult the Hologram's image, shown on page 196.):

– In 1903, a plot of land was purchased in Palestine for Herzl's Zionist coalition. The land was in the Valley of Lydda.

– For the next few decades, the Jews living on this land flourished. Additional turf was purchased, settled, and tilled. At the same time, many of the settlers made it a point to live in harmony with the Arabs, often befriending them. By the end of World War II, the Jews were "…living a Euro-Palestinian village culture that [was] in peace with the land [the Jews] had just descended upon." The population grew from eight thousand to nineteen thousand people, creating a reverse diaspora…a settlement within Israel.

– In November 1947, under the auspices of the United Nations (Resolution 181), the land of Palestine was partitioned to establish a Jewish State and an Arab state. The Arabs rejected Resolution 181,

---

[55] Shavit, first listed entry (paragraph): 103. Second entry: 104-105. Third entry: 106. Fourth entry: 107. Fifth entry: 108. Sixth entry: 108.

and a civil war broke out between Jews and Arabs. The state of Israel was founded on May 14, 1948. On May 15, Israel was invaded by the armies of Egypt, Jordan, Iraq, Syria, and Lebanon.

– The Lydda Valley experienced some of this violence, but war was restricted there for a while. However, in July, Operation Larlar (a military campaign designed to conquer the valley of Lydda and the city itself) was approved by Israel's first Prime Minister, David Ben Gurion. From July 10 to July 13, the area became a war zone. It was shortly conquered by Jewish military units. The Arabs, mostly civilians, were no match for the Jews' armies. During this short battle, fewer than thirty Jewish soldiers were killed. Over three hundred Arabs died, many of them within the supposed safety of their homes and a mosque.

– A Jewish general asked "...Ben Gurion what to do with the Arabs. Ben Gurion [waved] his hand: Deport them. ...Hours after the fall of Lydda, [another Jewish general and a future prime minister, (Yitshak Rabin)] issued a written order to [a Jewish army brigade]: 'The [Arab] inhabitants of Lydda must be expelled quickly, without regard to age.'"

– On July 13, "...tens of thousands of Palestinian Arabs were forced to leave Lydda," forming a column several miles long.

An hour has passed. The Student Cepee returns to the dais of his Mentor Sage. The Sage begins the discussion, "Well, Student, are you still of the opinion that the Arabs simply sold too much real estate to the Jews for the Arabs' own good?"

Student, "No, Sage, not after studying the archives on Lydda. I also scrolled to the next subjects in the Hologram's light show: the addition of more settlements, and the effect the Six-Day War had on additional colonizing. Hundreds of thousands of Arabs fled from the war. Others were simply evicted, similar to Lydda."

Sage, "This subject was a third rail among many humans, Student. It was often avoided by Israel and Israel's supporters, because it cast the Jewish people who migrated to the Middle East as colonizing imperialists. It pictured them as no better than the venal European nations of the past centuries who marauded much of mankind and many of heretofore cohesive, productive civilizations. The devastation wrought by these ancient imperialists had been well documented. The cleansing of the Muslim population in parts of Palestine by modern imperialist Jews was not a favored topic of discussion at humans' cocktail parties, especially those held in America.

"However, to be fair to the Jewish cause, some historians believed Jewish Israel could not have existed if it had been populated by hostile Muslim citizens while being surrounded by hostile Muslim nations. In a sense, 'Zionism could not bear Lydda,' nor could Zionism bear other Muslim/Arab islands within Israel.[56] The Zionists, as well as many other Jews, came to believe Israel could not survive if it was endangered inside its national walls."

Student, "I now understand why even sages are taken aback by these events. The Jews were once exiled from this land, one reason they righteously carried a spiritual albatross around their necks for centuries. By their placing the Arabs in exile, they transferred this righteous symbol onto their enemy."

Sage, "Correct, and what else did they transfer to the Arabs?"

The Student thinks for a short while, "Of course. The Jews also passed the revenge cycle token to the Arabs. Now, to keep the revenge cycle going, it was the responsibility of the Arabs to seek revenge...and then pass the token back to the Jews."

Sage, "Correct again. Have you anymore questions or comments for our dialogue today?"

Student, "Just an observation, Mentor Sage. The last part of the Hologram's presentation, '21st century: ½ million Jews in settlements,' largely came about by the Jews conquering and/or demolishing Arab enclaves, villages, and farm lands."

Sage, "Yes, but to offer another perspective: If you were an Arab, how would you view this colonization?"

---

[56] Shavit, 108.

Student, "As ethnic cleansing."

Sage, "And if you were a Jew?"

Student, "As ethnic survival."

Sage, "The humans often employed a simple cliché to explain such behavior: 'Where one stands, depends on where one sits,' or more accurately for our dialogue today: 'Where one can sit, depends on where one can reside.'"

CHAPTER 43

THE PRIDE PARADOX

(Dialogue 20)

The next Cepee dialogue takes place after the Student has finished his studies about the humans' practice of religions, resulting wars of terrorism, and the age-old instinct for a human to distrust (dislike) anything that was different from his range of experience and perception.

Student Cepee, "Sage, my data fills on our ancestors' approach to religion, their practices of their faiths, and their continuous wars about their interpretations are full of contradictions. Their behavior was often at odds with the teachings of their creeds."

Sage Cepee, "True. As I am sure you have now surmised, the humans were not paragons of consistency. We Cepees have concluded one of their biggest problems was dealing with their pride, a subject we discussed previously."

Student, "Yes, I remember our discussions. Yet pride is an important attribute for any intelligent being. How can one go through life if one has no pride?"

Sage, "One cannot. But our predecessors suffered from what we Cepees call The Pride Paradox. They never resolved this paradox."

Student, "Am I allowed to know about this paradox, or is it a secret among sages?"

Sage, "You are flippant again, Student. Your genetic tailoring gave you more than your share of wit. There may have been some misplaced chemicals during your DNA coding."

Student, "Sorry, Mentor Sage, but I don't follow what you mean."

204

Sage, "You will learn about genetics shortly. Presently, you are allowed to learn this information. As you should know by now, a paradox is a statement that appears to contradict itself…"

Student, "But in fact may be true."

Sage, "How many times must I tell you? Do not interrupt your Sage while your Sage is dispensing wisdom!"

Student, "Sorry, Sage. I interrupt the Hologram Sage, and it doesn't seem to mind."

Sage, "Student, I am not a hologram. I am a *sage*. As I was saying—and you are correct about the paradox—the humans suffered from The Pride Paradox. It described the positive human attribute of pride, an emotion that succored the human's self-confidence yet, at the same time, succored the human's insolence. You have studied your data fills about the humans' deadly, pointless aggression and their rationale of using religion for killing their fellow beings. You discovered misplaced pride was often the key factor in the process."

Student, "Yes, I see your point. One data fill described an al Qaeda high-level member who planned to hijack ten planes and destroy nine of them. He would be in the tenth plane. After killing all the male passengers then alerting the media, he would land the plane at a U.S. airport and deliver a speech about his beliefs. The Human Archives offered this quote, 'This is theatre, a spectacle of destruction with (this terrorist) as the self-cast star—the super terrorist.'"[57]

The Student continues, "One of my data fills was the subject of the English Empire. I gather the English were proud, even vain, about their conquests."

Sage, "Yes, a famous Englishman, Cecil Rhodes, provides an example of your observation. He uttered, 'Remember that you are an Englishman and have, consequently, won first prize in the lottery of life.' His boast did not reflect pride, it reflected derision. And the English were second stringers compared to their nearby cousins, the French."

---

[57] *The 9/11 Commission Report* (New York: W.W. Norton, 2004), 154.

Student, "The fate of the English and the French, after losing their place in the world, reminds me of a human saying. I think it goes like this, 'Pride goeth before the fall.' "

Sage, "Almost. The saying is, 'Pride goeth before destruction, and a haughty spirit before a fall.' The saying is from the humans' King James Bible, Proverbs 16:18."

Student, "Wow! I guess that's why you're a sage, and I'm a student. You know more than I."

Sage, "You are just now learning this fact? You are surprisingly obtuse to be so smart. Student, I am insuring you do not become conceited about your keen intelligence, and yes, it is indeed keen. The geneticists have been kind to you. Use it, but do not exult over it. Remember Rudyard Kipling's mockery of false pride, 'I gloat! Hear me gloat!'

"As another example, during the U.S. presidency of a George W. Bush, one of his senior aides informed a journalist, 'We're an empire now, and when we act, we create our own reality. And while you're studying that reality—judiciously, as you will—we'll act again, creating other new realities, which you can study, too, and that's how things will sort out. We're history's actors...and you, all of you, will be left to just study what we do.' "[58]

Student, "Hm, sounds like the aide had read too much Churchill. OK, I'll keep your advice in mind.

"Sage, I wonder if the humans could have lived in peace by addressing the complainers of their race? The poor? The politically repressed? The religiously restricted? The disenfranchised? The unemployed. The..."

Sage, "Yes, some humans thought the terrorists were simply unhappy people who were out of work. Not so. Many of them were gainfully employed, even affluent. Any more questions?"

Student, "Yes. About The Revenge Cycle that I studied in a earlier data fill, where a person or tribe felt an obligation to seek revenge on another person or tribe for some kind of travesty.

---

[58] Ron Suskind, "Without a Doubt," *The New York Times Magazine*, October 17, 2004, 51.

Suppose a human tribe did not respond to an attack on itself or one of its members? Could this 'nonresponse' have broken the chain and stopped the killings?"

Sage, "In certain situations, yes. I direct you to the Human Archives on Mahatma Gandhi, Nelson Mandela, and Martin Luther King. But generally, no. For example, in the 21st century, the United States did not retaliate for an attack on one of its naval vessels, named the *USS Cole*. The organization, al Qaeda, was responsible for the attack, but the United States did not come up with an appropriate response. The U.S. had a penchant for not wanting to inflict casualties on noncombatants, and America's response would have resulted in civilian deaths."[59]

Student, "Yes, I have learned much about al Qaeda. Their philosophy was just the opposite. The more civilians dead the better, at least non-Muslim civilians."

Sage, "Correct, and al Qaeda did not care if they killed Muslims, including themselves, just as long as the killings advanced their cause. Many U.S. citizens believed a nonresponse to this act would have al Qaeda draw the wrong conclusion: that al Qaeda could strike at Americans without paying a price."[60]

Student, "What happened?"

Sage, "The leader of al Qaeda, Osama Bin Laden, complained the United States had not attacked al Qaeda to avenge the *USS Cole* attack. If the U.S. did not, he stated he would 'launch something bigger.'"[61]

Student, "This is becoming confusing. It is contradictory to The Revenge Cycle. Bin Laden actually wanted an attack?"

Sage, "Yes. Let's alter the figure of The Revenge Cycle. Here it is (see figure on next page). In many situations, if the attacked party did nothing, it was seen as a sign of weakness, and was attacked again. For Osama bin Laden, he wanted a war to bring attention to

---

[59] Suskind, 193-197.

[60] Ibid., 212.

[61] Ibid., 191.

his grievances. But Student, bear in mind that the original cycle *and* the redrawn cycle reflect the behavior of our ancestors."

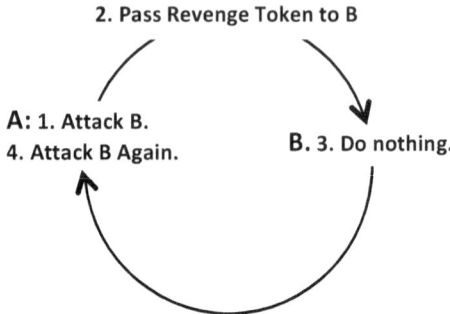

The Modified Revenge Cycle.

Student, "An old human cliché, 'Damned if they did and damned if they didn't,' seems to fit this situation. But if both cycles were accurate reflections of human behavior, how could this race resolve them? Either cycle led to more killings."

Sage, "They could not resolve them. That's why they were called cycles. That is why the humans are not around to discuss them. That's why you and I are."

Student, "Whew! Vicious."

Sage, "Yes, vicious cycles. Any more questions?"

Student, "Just one. With some exceptions, I gather our ancestors' religions sought to have the humans treat each other fairly. Yet, time and again, they violated their religious laws, and..."

Sage, "Religion was often a veneer, a reflective camouflage to hide the baser motives of the human. Let me recite a short passage from a human writer, Voltaire, who described how a member of the humans' Negroid race (a man of black color) was treated by white church clergymen, whom he called fetishes, '(Mother) said to me, "My dear child, always glorify and worship our fetishes; they'll make you live happily. You now have the honor of being a slave of our lords the white men, and in acquiring that honor, you've made your parents' fortune." ' "[62]

---

[62] Voltaire (Francios-Marie Arouet), *Candide* (New York: Bantam Books, 1981), 73.

Student, "The mother sold her child to the clergy! The preachers were slave holders?"

Sage, "Correct. This 'lucky' missioned man was a prototype Noble Savage. He also offered these thoughts, 'The Dutch fetishes, who converted me, tell me every Sunday that we're all children of Adam, black and white alike. I'm no genealogist, but if those preachers are telling the truth, we're all cousins, and you must admit that no one could treat his relatives more horribly.' "[63]

Sage, "I will conclude this dialogue with one last quote from Voltaire. His *Candide*, after learning what you are learning in your recent studies, declares he will finally have to give up his optimism about the humans. His servant asks, 'What's optimism?' Candide replies, 'Alas, it's a mania for insisting that everything is all right when everything is going wrong.' "[64]

Student, "With respect, Sage, I do not view the concept of human optimism in such a misanthropic light."

Sage, "You are entitled to your opinion, Student. I suspect your views will change as you progress through your education program. Any more questions?"

Student, "No, not now, but I may have more after I reflect on our dialogue. ...and after some reflection on meeting the 'fair damsel,' you persist in declaring I will meet in due time."

---

[63] Voltaire, 73.

[64] Ibid.

CHAPTER 44

THE BAGHDAD BIBLE BELT [65]

(Show 14)

The Student Cepee has been studying the humans' battles of the early-to-mid 21st century. Unlike the major wars of the 20th century, which revolved around political and racial issues—not to mention the ever present contests for turf—the later conflicts were deeply imbued with religious zealotry. A *Coming to you Live, from the Dead* TV show is available on this subject. The Student begins to download this program, titled, "The Baghdad Bible Belt."

The Mentor Sage issues a caution, "Student, this program will document how the United States' conduct of its policy in the early 2000s set the stage for decades of warfare in that area and how its policy, instead of defeating terrorism in that region, encouraged it to flourish. And flourish it did, not only in the Middle East, but in many other parts of the world."

Student, "I thought these television programs were supposed to be on a light note, Sage."

Sage, "Not this one, and it is an important component of your educational program about our ancestors. It is a longer program than the others. Bring some popcorn with you.

---

[65] I wrote most of the script for this show after 9/11 and the invasion of Afghanistan, but before the second invasion of Iraq. Bush and his second administration tried to repair the damage it did during his first term (the ill-fated second invasion). Obama continued the repair operations, but made the situation worse by pulling U.S. forces out of Iraq. (Although Iraq demanded US troops to leave the country.) In hindsight, there was plenty of blame to go around.

210

"During this program, I will be an active viewer as well. I will not be parallel processing with my other sage activities. You are welcome to pose questions to me during the program, if you like."

Student, "Sage, we are going to the movies together!"

Sage, "Indeed we are, Student."

Here is what the Student and Sage watch:

[The TV screen shows a United States President sitting at the head of a large table. He is surrounded by his aides. They are discussing current events, and one assistant is reading a newspaper article:[66]

The messages from U.S. embassies around the globe have become urgent and disturbing: Many people think President Bush is a greater threat to world peace than Iraqi President Saddam Hussein.]

President, "Hello, fellow doctrinaires. Let's get started. Our session today is in keeping with our ideologue-based and Neo-conservative-driven ideas of bringing Christianity, democracy, and capitalism to non-Christian, non-democratic, non-capitalistic countries.[67] These people do not want Christianity, democracy, or capitalism in their lives, as they have been practicing Islam, theocracy, and tribal law for over 1,400 years. Imagine that! The manner in which they live has something to do with how they wish to live.

"Nonetheless, Onward Christian Soldiers!"

Student, "Christian soldiers, Sage?"

Sage, "Yes. Be patient and watch what Bush says next."

Bush, "I am driven with a mission from God. God would tell me, 'George, go and fight these terrorists in Afghanistan'. ...And then

---

[66] *The Washington Post*, February 24, 2003, edition.

[67] Francis Fukuyama, *America at the Crossroads. Democracy, Power and the Neoconservative Legacy* (New Haven, CT: Yale University Press, 2006), 48-49. Briefly, Neoconservatism postulates (1) American power should be used for moral purposes. (2) The internal nature of a regime greatly affects its behavior, and people should be liberated from tyrannical regimes. (3) But Neocons are leery of social engineering of regimes. (Author's note: Points 2 and 3 contradict each other.) (4) International law and international institutions are not effective.

God would tell me, 'George, go and end the tyranny in Iraq.' "[68]

Student, "Sage, I was under the impression that the radical Islamic tribes were more prone to fight for religious reasons than other religious tribes, other nations. Bush's statement implies otherwise."

Sage, "America was greatly influenced in its foreign policy and its wars by religious zealotry. America's Protestants, Jews, Evangelicals, and Catholics believed they had God on their side. The Islamics, both Sunni and Shia, believed the opposite. As you have learned, their differences and intolerances led to inevitable conflicts, and their innate nature led to catastrophic consequences.

"However, regarding America's President Bush, we Cepees are fair and nonjudgmental and present both sides of an issue. For example, a respected human journalist, Bob Woodward reported, the U.S. President did say, '...I prayed that our troops be safe, be protected by the almighty. Going into this period, I was praying for strength to do the Lord's will. I'm surely not going to justify war based upon God. Understand that. Nevertheless, in my case, I pray that I be as good a messenger of his will as possible. And then, of course, I pray for forgiveness.' "[69]

Student, "I don't understand. 'Forgiveness' for what? If he was not doing anything wrong, why should he ask for forgiveness? During my data fills, I came across this additional quote from Mr. Woodward: 'I asked the president about [seeking advice from his father, a former U.S. President] And President Bush said, 'Well, no,' and then he got defensive about it,' says Woodward. 'Then he said something that really struck me. He said of his father, 'He is the wrong father to appeal to for advice. The wrong father to go to, to

---

[68] The *Guardian* newspaper (see https://www.theguardian.com/world/2005/oct/07/iraq.usa) issued these comments from Bush with these notes: "Mr. Bush revealed the extent of his religious fervor when he met a Palestinian delegation during the Israeli-Palestinian summit at the Egyptian resort of Sharm el-Sheikh, four months after the US-led invasion of Iraq in 2003. One of the delegates, Nabil Shaath, who was Palestinian foreign minister at the time, was attributed to this specific quote."

[69] Woodward, https://www.cbsnews.com/news/woodward-shares-war-secrets/, quoted from the work of journalist, Bob Woodward.

appeal to in terms of strength.' And then he said, 'There's a higher Father that I appeal to.'"[70]

Student, "Bush also characterized his side as good and the other side as evil. He said, 'This will be a monumental struggle between good and evil. But good will prevail.'"[71]

Sage, "Do you recall the *Coming to you Live, from the Dead* show titled, 'One Man's Terrorist is another Man's Freedom Fighter?'"

Student, "Yes. It all depended on where a human stood on an issue as to which person was a terrorist or a freedom fighter."

Sage, "Yes, what one man considered as good, another man considered as evil. As you now know, humans' missionary fervor, their pride, their doctrinaire mentalities often prevented them from any form of compromise. 'If you are like me, you are *good*. If you are unlike me, you are *bad*,' an axiom we recently explored."

Student, "I am catching on, Mentor Sage. Unless something changed the human race, it was headed for disaster."

Sage, "Yes, you are catching on. If you have no more questions, shall we continue watching the program?"

Student, "Sure, want some of my popcorn?"

Sage, "Thank you. Don't mind if I do."

[The screen displays the U.S. President speaking to his aides (hypothetical, but reflective of reality).]

"Our agenda today is devoted to the topic of: What can we do to hurt our own cause in the world? What can we do to thwart our own efforts to combat Islamic-based terrorism? We start with a basic premise: Our actions must revolve around my planet-wide Alienation Plan: *As few countries and people as possible should support us.*"

(The Student pauses the show and reflects: *Amazing! This planet-wide Alienation Plan reminds me of the mentality of a later U.S. President, Donald Trump. But Bush somehow managed to keep a few friends. Trump even alienated the kitchen help, at least those who were not native-born.*)

---

[70] Woodward, www.cbsnews.com.

[71] Bob Woodward, *Bush at War* (New York, NY: Simon & Schuster, 2002), 45.

Bush continues, "With this in mind, like Woodrow Wilson's famous 14 Points, I came up with several George W. Bush's Points. I'm working on other points so I can become famous and respected like Wilson, but there is only so much I can do to distance myself from reality. Ah, let's work on two points today. We will discuss these points in this meeting:

"First, devastate the infrastructure of the enemies we fight and leave them in chaos and more dangerous than ever.

"Second, violate the Geneva Accords and our own *United States Uniform Code of Military Justice* by secretly torturing our enemies."

Bush continues, "Our country is now the supreme power in the world. No one comes close to our might. We have the only shovel in the sandbox, and we intend to do all the digging.

"Our foreign policy will be built around confrontation and noncompromise. Why should we kowtow to anyone? It's our way or the highway. They are either with us or against us. Let me repeat an earlier quote to you that one of my aides has to say to the media about the subject:"[72]

> We're an empire now, and when we act, we create our own reality. And while you're studying that reality—judiciously, as you will—we'll act again, creating other new realities, which you can study, too, and that's how things will sort out. We're history's actors…and you, all of you, will be left to just study what we do.

Bush continues, "Another point: Unlike past eras, our armies will be made up *only* of fighters. We do not need civil engineers in positions of authority in our armed forces to reconstruct the societies' cities we will destroy. Our warriors will be trained to fight and nothing more.

---

[72] Ron Suskind, "Without a Doubt," *The New York Times Magazine*, October 17, 2004, 51. This quote was cited earlier. I cite it again because of its outlandish arrogance.

"The mantra for my administration, both figuratively and literally: *We're going to burn bridges, not build them.*

"To emphasize my philosophy, when we invade a country, Iraq as a prime example, unlike our WWII experiences in Japan, Germany, and other countries, we will not take along any social personnel or engineers who could rebuild the infrastructure we destroy during the invasion, or safeguard any remaining infrastructure. We will wipe out the country's civic and social fabrics, fire all their soldiers, police, and civil servants, and let the country sink into chaos.[73]

"Sure, the total deaths of civilians during this melee will far exceed Hussein's murder rate over the past few years. But heck fire, these folks will be dying for good causes: The means to reignite ancient civil wars between religious sects and the installation of a theocracy in the government.

"MacArthur in Japan? Clay in Germany? Truman in Greece and Turkey? The Marshall Plan in Europe? Nah. I'm not into history, so my plan will have me tagged as supremely stupid or supremely smart. I'll bet my drugstore cowboy boots that I'll be tagged as smart."

The Student Cepee pauses the show. He says, "In my data fills, I learned the United States invaded Iraq—thus starting many decades of wars in the Middle East—because Iraq was accused of having nuclear weapons. Other countries had nuclear weapons, yet the United States did not invade them. Why?"

Sage, "America held Iraq in their 'dislike' category, as the country was not sufficiently democratic and Christian. Plus, President Bush said the nation posed a nuclear threat to other countries."

Student, "Did it?"

---

[73] Fareed Zakaria, "The Surge That Might Work," *Newsweek*, March 5, 2007, 48. While writing this part of the script, I learned the Coalition Provisional Authority shut down almost all of Iraq's state-owned enterprises! It was an act comparable to an army invading America, and disbanding most of the federal, state, and city governments. Iraq ceased to function as a society. There was wide spread looting. Revered museums were pillaged. Native law enforcement ceased to operate. Surely a tragic example of The Ignorant, Therefore, Doctrinaire Syndrome.

Sage, "No! The country did not possess or was even close to possessing nuclear weapons. But two factors converged to create a conflagration in the Middle East that eventually did result in nuclear attacks. First, the militaristic zealotry of men who influenced a naïve President. Second the failure of intelligence about Iraqi's nuclear capabilities.

"However, Student, Bush ordered nuclear inspectors out of the country before they could finish their job of verification or non-verification of the existence of these weapons."

Student, "The situation reminds me of the human adage: 'Haste makes waste.' I learned from my data fills that several nuclear explosions in the Middle East and the United States finally convinced the humans to begin the task of genetically engineering aggression from their makeup."

Sage, "A tragic way to learn a lesson, Student."

Student, "For sure. ...By the way, Sage, did Bush succeed in his goals? Did God help George end the tyranny in Iraq?"

Sage, "Quite the opposite. By removing the Sunni dictator of Iraq, a Sunni enemy—the Shia—took over. From there, the Sunnis and Shias throughout the Middle East, and later the world began an open, vicious war with each other."

Student, "Mentor Sage, I also learned a President named Obama was faulted for all those wars in the Middle East, because he pulled American troops out of Iraq."

Sage, "Let's be clear about this aspect of history, Student. Using a human metaphor, in the Middle East war 'games' of the humans' 21st century, Bush was on the starting squad. Obama was on second string. He came into the game later, ignored an election, because he did not like the victor of the election, then pulled American troops out of the region, which led to additional conflicts. But he did not start the game. Bush did."

Student, "Could Obama have left the troops there?"

Sage, "His critics claimed he could have, but the new Shia regime demanded foreign troops leave Iraqi soil."

Student, "Obama's situation: Damned if he did and damned if he didn't?"

Sage, "History in the Human Archives, as you will learn, is divided on the matter.

"Let us continue your tutorial movie. ...Hm, did you bring any chocolate bars with you?"

Student, "Will M&Ms do?"

Sage, "I prefer the yellow ones."

Bush continues, "This country is going it alone on so many things anyway that we are committed to disregard the Geneva Conventions and the United States *Uniform Code of Military Justice* about torture. I want confessions, and I want them fast!

"There will be no more bombings in America. We will force our enemy to divulge their attack plans by torturing them to confess. Our program will..."

The Student puts a pause on the hologram TV show, "I've learned our very ancient ancestors tortured one another, but I was not aware the practice continued into humans' modern times."

Sage, "Some humans thought confessions taken as a result of torture was moral, because they claimed the torture led to saving lives. Other humans thought the practice immoral, regardless of its effectiveness. Still others believed the confessions did more harm than good, because the person tortured would say anything to have the torture stopped.

"Our ancestors never resolved the issue. Of course, we Cepees do not torture, as we have no reason to even consider it."

Student, "Mentor Sage, another human adage—one I will alter—occurs to me about this subject of torture."

Sage, "Yes?"

Student, " 'Where one stands on torture depends on where one sits in the torture chamber.' "

Sage, "Well done, Student Cepee. That's enough for this television program. In our next dialogue, we continue this analysis. ... Before we part company, do you have any more yellows?"

CHAPTER 45

A ROSE BY ANY OTHER NAME HYPOTHESIS

(Dialogue 21)

Mentor Sage, "Student, I surmise you do not like your data fills from the Human Archives or you like our dialogues better, perhaps a combination of both. In either case, you seem to return with eagerness for another dialogue."

Student Cepee, "You admonished me to be diligent in my studies and to forego surfing the Human Archives and my thoughts about that 'fair damsel' for a while. I am only fulfilling my...guess what?"

Sage, "Your job description. Have you questions for me?"

Student, "I am not satisfied with my earlier observations about this Osama bin Laden character and his use of religion to rationalize his wars—his jihads. I think my earlier conclusion about his fixation on The Deadly Trinity might not have been the total picture. Bin Laden seemed motivated by religious zeal as well."

Sage, "At this point in your education, you should understand that the humans unwittingly masked their genetic propensity toward gratuitous, deadly aggression under the guise of religion, politics, patriotism, and other rationalizations. They could not fathom that their conflicts, which seemed noble to them, were subservient to genetic dictates. Their pride would not allow them to acknowledge that, say, a 'righteous' political cause was simply a manifestation of ascending the Human Tribal Hierarchy.

"We will return to this vital aspect of human behavior shortly in

218

this dialogue. For now, we will use the term *qital* instead of jihad. It is more accurate. Qital was a branch of jihad that dealt with armed struggle.[74] True, bin Laden was religious, but his views were asymmetrical. No other religion was acceptable to him, and certainly no other religion was permitted inside the Islamic states. He wanted his religion to be ascendant to others. His behavior was a manifestation of the humans' affliction for pecking order dominance."

Student, "But he believed his religion was being usurped by other religions."

Sage, "How did he react? How did he answer this challenge? Did he demonstrate his religion was superior to others? Did he show his religion had brought its practitioners more joy, comfort, food, warmth, housing, clothing; the critical human needs by which to survive? Did he prove his way of life brought the practitioners of Islam a better place on earth? Did he show his religion could evolve in parallel with the humans' changes?"

Student, "No, Sage, he did not. His views were for everything to remain in place, or even go back to the past—views similar to some other religions. Your points are well taken, but the Muslims had grievances. They had been exploited by other people, some religious and some not. They came up with snake-eyes in life's roll of the dice."

Sage, "You should understand his no-change philosophy was contradictory to the ever changing character of human nature. And 'the roll of the dice of life?' No, Student, it was not a matter of chance, nor was it a bad dice roll. For a while, in many parts of the world, the Muslims were a more dominant and ascendant faction than the Christians. They lost this position partially because of their

---

[74] For the reader who wishes to learn more about Islam, I refer you to the Quran. My copy is *The Koran: An Edition prepared for English Readers* (New York: Mount Vernon Press, nd) a very difficult read for the beginner. I needed help and got it from two references I recommend to you. First, start with Sohaib Nazeer Sultan, *The Koran for Dummies*—a succinct and well-written treatise on the subject. Second, scores of books are available for a more advanced reading of the topic. Some are written as helpful tutorials; others as diatribes. The Turkey Embassy in Washington, D.C. offers a large number of helpful texts on the subject. If you are in the area, go to their visa office and browse through its library of Islamic material.

inability or reluctance to adjust to a changing world, a fact they had considerable difficulty accepting. If nothing else, suppressing the intellectual and economic partnership of one-half of their population—the females—was not a very effective approach to ascending the humans' competitive ladders.

"I said partially in my last statement. In addition, from the 17th to 20th centuries, several Christian nations in Europe gained superiority in warfare techniques and succeeded in attacking, subjugating, and colonizing most of the lands occupied by the Muslims. These acts were considered by some humans, especially many Muslims and certainly bin Laden, to be acts of terrorism.

"Regardless of what they were called—and we Cepees know they were usually barbarous—European colonization and occupation resulted in the eclipse of Muslim culture and influence in the world. Bin Laden was unhappy about Muslims losing their position in the hierarchical pecking orders for power and wealth. So were many other Muslims.

"After you complete your studies with me, your next program will reveal how the humans' colonizing exploits of those times created fantastic tribal disruptions, many of them led to the demise of our ancestors and our ascendancy on earth."

The Sage adds, "Above all, Student, do not forget the Cepees' sanctity for life. Did bin Laden's grievances justify mass murder?"

Student, "Of course not. And my studies of the Human Archives indicate his Quran forbade killing noncombatants."

Sage, "And your point?"

Student, "Without question, bin Laden was an ideologue. I have learned enough about our ancestors to know ideologues had very little tolerance for opposing views. My point is that his proclamations were not about America's liberties or its democracy. I doubt he killed Americans because of their Electoral College. He waged war because of the U.S. policies in the Muslim world. He did not have a view of Armageddon. He wanted America and its allies to disengage themselves from Islamic societies."[75]

---

[75] Michael Scheuer, *Imperial Hubris* (Washington, DC: Brassey's, 2004), xviii.

Sage, "The humans never reached agreement on this issue, but keep going. What were his views on the church and state?"

Student, "Separating church and state was apostasy, a sellout.[76] To bin Laden, it was simply not permitted in a Muslim state."

Sage, "True, but some members of the Muslim religion did not object to this separation and succeeded in creating Islamic regimes that were as much secular as they were theocracies. But they were not in bin Laden's camp. What were the U.S. views on this matter?"

Student, "Just the opposite. Many of the United States' policies were directed toward altering other societies' political/religious structures. Time and again, my data fills reveal America proclaimed all countries should have a democracy, accompanied with separation of church and state. Interestingly, the temperament of the U.S. about this subject was as messianic as the Muslims' attitude about religion and state being joined."

Sage, "Messianic...perhaps a Muslim would take issue with your choice of the word, but your point is well made. Did your data fills provide examples?"

Student, "Yes. The U.S. attempted to alter the religious and state structures of East Timor and Afghanistan. America also supported what bin Laden considered to be apostate Islamic governments in Turkey, Jordan, Saudi Arabia, and Egypt, to name a few."[77]

Sage, "Acts of outrage to many Muslims. And are you familiar with Islamic principles on tithing?"

Student, "Yes, donations—tithing—were one of Islam's five pillars of law."

Sage, "And?"

Student, "In some instances, the U.S. demanded Muslim regimes limit and track these donations in order to trace possible fundings for terrorists. Another outrageous act to a Muslim."

Sage, "How about Israel and Palestine?"

Student, "The biggest bone of contention between the Muslim and Christian worlds was the Palestinian/Israeli issue. It remained to fester the relations between Jew or Christian, and the Muslim."

---

[76] Scheuer, 2.

[77] Ibid., 12-13.

The Student continues, "I recall reading a passage from the Quran that stated, 'Fight them until there is no more oppression and religion belongs to God alone.'"[78]

Sage, "Keep in mind that many Muslims believed the creation of Israel was an act of religious oppression because it resulted in the dislodging of Muslims from several of their holy sites."

Student, "So Israel was the oppressor, and therefore, subject to being attacked?"

Sage, "Not just Jewish Israel, but many Christians as well. At the time of the creation of Israel, the population of the Palestine area was approximately 92 percent Arab, 8 percent Jews, with a few Christians as well. By what rationalization could a very small minority claim this turf? Answer: by a religious rationalization, because the turf was the ancient homeland of the Jews. But that very turf was also the ancient homeland of the people who were displaced.

"The Christians who believed in a literal interpretation of the Bible also believed the Jews should take over this part of the world because it was decreed by Biblical prophecy. They said the Jews were ordained to occupy the Holy Land—as part of the eventual Armageddon. This event also entailed the Jews being converted to Christianity or being killed off by the Christians."

Student, "What! By the very people who supported their occupation in the first place?"

Sage, "Correct. Consequently, the radical Islamic militants declared a holy war against Jews and Christians—eventually just about anyone who did not follow their philosophy. Are you beginning to see the traps the humans were building for themselves?"

Student Cepee, "Yes, I'm beginning to understand. I also learned the radical Islamic warriors believed they could rightfully kill all those who did not adopt Islam, including women, children, even the elderly."[79]

---

[78] Author's note: "them" is a pronoun for those who were fighting against Muslims. The passage is from the Quran, chapter 2, verse 103.

[79] *Jihad Watch*, http://jihadwatch.org/archives/000749.php.

The Student continues, "On the other side of the coin, I also recall the admonition to Christians from the Christians' Holy Book, "Therefore go and make disciples of all nations, baptizing them in the name of the Father and of the Son and of the Holy Spirit, and teaching them to obey everything I have commanded you."

Sage, "Whose Holy Spirit?"

Student, "The Christians' Holy Spirit."

Sage, "And?"

Student, "Hm. Both sides were commanded by their religions to change or subdue the other side. Thus, how could devout believers refute such commands?"

Sage, "They became assassins in order to promote their religious beliefs."

Student, "Osama bin Laden also said the American people were able to choose their leaders, and he claimed (as the Student recalls information from the Human Archives), 'By electing these leaders, the American people have given their consent to the incarceration of the Palestinian people, the demolition of Palestinian homes, and the slaughter of the children of Iraq...This is why the American people are not innocent. The American people are active members in all these crimes.'"[80]

Sage, "What about the Americans who did not approve of their leaders' actions?"

Student, "Bin Laden grouped all Americans together as enemies, even those who were in opposition to American policies. I can see why the militant Islamic Equal Extermination Opportunity (EEO) program was well named. All Americans were fair game, subject to attack at any time—preemptively."

The Sage remains silent for a moment, then adds, "Yes, preemption. And what was good for the human goose was good for the human gander. These problems were exacerbated by America proclaiming it would achieve absolute unilateral world domination

---

[80] Scheuer, 130.

through military superiority and preemptive attacks on anyone or any nation who challenged its position.[81]

"Naturally, this stance led to challenges from other tribes—nation states, as well as individuals—and bred tremendous resentment among almost all non-Americans. This proclamation greatly weakened America's ability to garner help for its causes.

"Later, America backed off from this stance, but much of the world had permanently altered their view of this country. The United States never fully recovered its once fine reputation, and a later president named Donald Trump further alienated the world's citizens, put America more at risk, and greatly compromised the country's influence in the world; eventually, its wealth. As well, by declaring Jerusalem the capital of Israel, the president alienated many people and nations from America.

"You have studied what became known as the 9/11 attacks that were orchestrated by bin Laden."

Student, "Yes, he led those attacks on Americans and their land."

Sage, "Osama bin Laden essentially signed his own death warrant with the 9/11 assaults. The Americans were not going to give up until they killed him, which they did.

"We must close this dialogue, Student. Our time is up. I have another student coming to my dais. She is due in a few minutes."

Student, "She! Is this Cepee the 'she' I met about the time I started to become wise, like you?"

Sage, "Yes, and the very reason she has not wished to see you was because you were *too wise*."

Student, "How can a Cepee be too wise, Sage?"

Sage, "I am turning you over to the Hologram Sage. I'm out of time. The Hologram will explain," as the Sage dismisses the Student.

— —

The Student is perplexed, *I met her only once. I thought I was pretty impressive. I definitely knew she was pretty. Where did I go wrong?*

---

[81] Parts of the Bush Doctrine, "National Security Strategy (NSS)", delivered in his speech at West Point, June 2002.

The Hologram Sage appears, "What's happening, dude?"

Student, "You have not been exactly a Johnny on the Spot for fielding my questions and concerns. I'm not sure you can handle my query."

Hologram Sage, "Cut me some slack and mind your manners. After all, I'm the Mentor Sage's proxy. Anyway, I take your comments to be criticisms?"

Student, "Of course, they are criticisms! Eh, OK, I realize you are, if nothing else, a wannabe real sage, so I will..."

Hologram, "Hold on there, dude! I'm not the wannabe sage. That would be *you*. Slack off and let me answer the question you just posed to your Mentor Sage."

Student, "You mean about the girl and my being too wise?"

Hologram, "Right. Remember you called her 'Cepeeette'? That so-called witty comment did not earn you the distinction of being too wise. It earned you the distinction of being what the humans called a 'wise ass'...a subtle human practice to keep females in a submissive state of mind. "

Student, "Not too cool, eh, Hologram?"

Hologram, "Not too cool, Student. I am programmed to state that the Sage will have more to say about this matter later.

"For now, the Mentor Sage has just downloaded some artificial intelligence material from his real intelligence-computer-laden brain. He wishes you to learn more about the humans' religious groups inability to live peacefully together."

Student, "So I have been learning, even though their religions, by and large, were supposed to promote peace."

Hologram, "Didn't happen, dude. Listen up. ...We return to our ancestors' fixation of revenge, and the revenge cycle [see Data Fill 3]. However, for your lesson today, the Revenge Token did not have to be passed to the adversary. Each side simply bombed and gassed each other preemptively, as seen in the figure I am now displaying. Both sides carried on these one-sided campaigns—even during the times of their nuclear and biochemical attacks on one another."

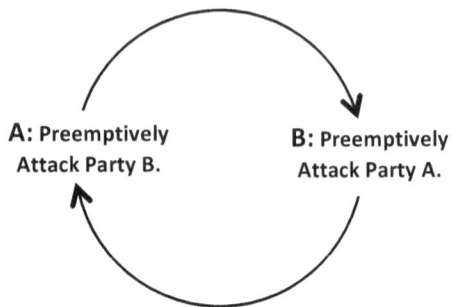

A: Preemptively Attack Party B.

B: Preemptively Attack Party A.

Preemption in practice.

The Student begins to realize the intractability of the humans' problems, as the Mentor Sage appears and takes over from the Hologram, "Student, our ancestors gradually backed themselves into a corner. The problems were never resolved because the Muslims, Jews, and Christians were diametrically different in how they wanted to live—and how to let others live.

"If these tribes had left each other alone, they might have been able to avoid the ASSES programs. But that did not happen."

Student, "Yes, I see. Neither side backed off. And things got out of hand."

Sage, "Correct, and remember that each side thought its way was the correct way. One side contended it was espousing freedom and democracy. The other side interpreted this 'freedom and democracy movement' as colonial, imperial terrorism—a 'crusader onslaught.'[82] Reversing their roles, one side contended it was waging a holy war, one sanctioned by its religion. The other side interpreted this war as debased religious terrorism.

"Both sides contended the other side was evil and their side was good—an extreme view because it took their conflict away from battling a political adversary to one of battling an evil adversary. Later data fills will provide more information on this conflict. For now, let me illustrate the depth of the problem by retrieving a quote from an expert on this subject:[83]

---

[82] Bush Doctrine, "National Security Strategy (NSS)," 157.

[83] Ibid., 135.

...the young Palestinian bombers are seen by large numbers of Muslims as heroes who were willing to sacrifice their lives—in martyrdom, not suicide attacks—for a cause that is greater than themselves and sanctioned by their God. What the West sees as tragic brutality practiced by despairing or deviant individuals is perceived in much of the Muslim world as a heroic act of self-sacrifice, patriotism, and worship, an act to be greeted not with condemnation and revulsion, but with awe, respect, and a determination to emulate. Moreover, it is an act Muslims deem a just military response to Israel's fifty-plus-year occupation of Palestine and its relegation of three generations of Palestinians to refugee camps.

Student, "Yes, but we have discussed that many of these people retaliated by killing their opponents, including civilians. What happened to their God's commandant, Thou shalt not kill? "
Sage, "Oh, that was the other God."
The Sage continues, "And yes, as you say, neither side would back down. Both were caught up in their own agendas, victims of The Deadly Trinity. You learned about this Trinity: The Law of the Instrument, The Aggression Cycle, and variations of The Revenge Cycle finally coalesced...leading to us Cepees."
The Sage makes a key point, "As I mentioned earlier, Student, the framing of their disagreements in the context of a struggle against evil enemies, in contrast to a struggle against political enemies, meant there could be no compromise—that neither side would back off. Political suasions can be altered; evil suasions cannot."[84]
The Sage continues, "Things began to unravel when bin Laden concluded Americans were bent on removing theocratic Muslims from Muslim lands and replacing them with democratic Christians. However, his movement spawned many soldiers whose agenda was not just to remove the Americans from Muslim lands. *Their agenda was also to remove Americans from America.* And with the acquisition

---

[84] Mahmood Mamdani, *Good Muslim, Bad Muslim* (New York: Pantheon Books, 2004), 254.

and use of weapons of mass destruction by these people, the fabrics of our ancestors' societies began to disintegrate."

Student, "Yes, The Deadly Trinity in action. Well, deadly for our ancestors, but not for us!"

Sage, "Don't be flippant, Student."

Student, "Sorry, Sage, just trying to inject some levity into our dialogue."

Sage, "Save it for the Hologram Sage."

Student, "Are you kidding? The Hologram Sage is humor-impaired."

Sage, "Back to the matter at hand. Have you more questions about the Islamic militants and their so-called 'jihad'?"

Student, "One more question. You just mentioned that these people were waging a 'holy war.' Yet many leaders in those countries that were attacked by the Islamic militants refused to use this term. After our dialogue today, it certainly appears the qitals were indeed religious or holy wars. Why not call them such?"

Sage, "For certain, the justification and rationale for many of the attacks stemmed from slanted interpretations of Islamic law and the Quran. But as your data fills have shown and as our dialogue has demonstrated, the humans were merely parsing nuances."

Student, "How so?"

Sage, "Take the humans' saying, 'A rose by any other name is still a rose.' We Cepees make light of our ancestors' cliché: 'A holy war by any other name is still a war for power, pride, position, and turf—genetically endowed behavior.'"

Student, "Sage, I defer to your experience and wisdom. Still, my data fills do not lead me to such absolute conclusions. You speak of our ancestors as if they had no redeeming qualities, no principles; as if they were fixated only on scaling their pecking orders as dictated by their genomes. But in my data fills, I find many exemplary attributes about them."

Sage, "You are a bright student. But keep in mind—always—that we Cepees are here on earth, and the humans are not. There are reasons for this unalterable fact. You have learned about some of them. Your subsequent studies will reveal the others."

Student, "Well, OK. As the Hologram Sage has told me, you're the boss, but I have another question. Why..."

Sage, "Sorry, Student, I have a dialogue scheduled with another student. Hold your question, or better yet, take it up with the Hologram Sage. Here, I'll download it for you," as the Hologram Sage appears in front of the Student, and the real Mentor Sage leaves for other duties.

CHAPTER 46

THE HIPPOCRATIC OATH ADDENDUM

(Dialogue 22)

The Mentor Sage has again designated the Hologram to act as his proxy for this dialogue.

Hologram Sage, "What's happening, dude?"

Student, "The Sage passed me over to you for you to field a question: Why did nuclear weapons find their way into so many humans' hands? After the former USSR became Russia again, why didn't the Western powers coax, persuade, even bribe Russia—and other countries—into selling and dismantling nuclear arms? I've studied the wealth of America. It could have purchased the world's entire nuclear arsenal."

The Hologram Sage's array of complex computers grinds away, "Your question is easy to answer. First, what country in its right mind was going to give up one of the few instruments it possessed to prevent America from attacking it? The United States developed fixations on spreading democracy, Christianity, and Taco Bells to all parts of the earth. It made no difference if other people just wanted to be left alone. Some folks leaned toward other ways of governing, didn't take to Jesus, or weren't keen on tacos. So, how to keep Uncle Sam away from their borders? Nukes, dude. Nukes gave third world countries and non-nation tribes leverage against the American leviathan."

Student, "I must say Hologram Sage, you have a remarkable grasp on this subject. What happened to your light and mirrors personality?"

Hologram Sage, "Ha! This information is coming off my optical storage. Your Mentor Sage downloaded these pearls of wisdom. I'm merely mirroring these missives to you.

"Anyway, the United States eventually ran out of money. America's commitment to securing security in, say, Iraq cost the United States around $60 billion a year for several years. Assuming Russia went along with a dismantling program, it was estimated that securing nuclear weapons in Russia would have cost about $30 billion over three years."[85]

Student, "A modest sum in relation to the benefits.[86] And from my data fills, I have learned many humans in the early twenty-first century believed the spreading of nuclear weapons was the single most serious problem facing the world.

"Of course, with America's insistence on spreading its way of life and overthrowing others' way of life, I am sure countries, such as Iran and North Korea—even Russia—believed their only leverage against missionary America was to have their own nuclear arsenal. Yet, with the increasing proliferation of nuclear weapons, it appears the humans went off on tangents and never fully addressed this problem. Is that so?"

Hologram Sage, "There you go again, posing an unprogrammed question to me. What do you think I am? My memory is an assortment of computer mucilage, not protein! My intelligence comes from downloads from the Sage. Cut me some slack!"

Student, "Take it easy, Hologram Sage. I didn't mean to offend your RAM. Okay, while you're here, maybe you could shed some light...I know, you're not programmed for humor...on another aspect of the humans' religions and killings."

---

[85] James Fallows, "Success without Victory," *The Atlantic*, January/February 2005, 90.

[86] The Disproportionate Ratio in action again.

Hologram Sage, "Just keep in mind that hologram computers spew forth nonsense or shut down when confronted with spontaneous input. But look, I'm still here!"

Student, "So what? I might prefer a shutdown to your cheekiness. Anyway, one of my recent surfs of the Human Archives revealed some Muslim doctors cast aside their Hippocratic Oath and began killing people. Not terminally ill people. Not people on their deathbeds. Healthy people! A doctor killing innocent people does not make sense, Hologram Sage. What do you think?"

The Hologram Sage remains mute. After all, the Student posed a complex question to lines of paltry software code and an embarrassingly narrow spectrum of light rays.

Mentor Sage, "I'll take over. I've been monitoring your dialogue during my session with another student. We sages are excelsior models for parallel processing."

Student, "Thanks, Sage. My question…"

"Yes, I know. First, let's access the Human Archives and download the Hippocratic Oath…Here it is:"[87]

"You do solemnly swear, each by whatever he or she holds most sacred

That you will be loyal to the Profession of Medicine and just and generous to its members

That you will lead your lives and practice your art in uprightness and honor

That into whatsoever house you shall enter, it shall be for the good of the sick to the utmost of your power, your holding yourselves far aloof from wrong, from corruption, from the tempting of others to vice

---

[87] This version comes from Microsoft ® Encarta ® Reference Library 2005. © 1993-2004 Microsoft Corporation.

That you will exercise your art solely for the cure of your patients, and will give no drug, perform no operation, for a criminal purpose, even if solicited, far less suggest it

That whatsoever you shall see or hear of the lives of men or women, which is not fitting to be spoken, you will keep inviolably secret

These things do you swear. Let each bow the head in sign of acquiescence

And now, if you will be true to this, your oath, may prosperity and good repute be ever yours; the opposite, if you shall prove yourselves forsworn."

Student, "Yes. I've read it. So what? My question is not yet answered."

Sage, "Don't be flippant with your Mentor Sage. I overheard your comment about the Hologram's cheekiness. Look to yourself before you criticize others. Now, let's address your question. The doctors you mention were identified in the humans' media as Muslims who attempted to use car bombs and rocket grenades to kill people in America."[88]

Student, "But these actions contradicted their Hippocratic Oath. You are saying they forswore their oath for religious purposes?"

Sage, "We have learned the humans' practice of their religions often did more harm than good. But take a closer look at the details of the oath. Do you see anything that catches your eye?"

Student, "Well...yes. The oath concerns only a doctor's relationship with sick patients. Again, this part of the oath states—and let me emphasize my points:"

"That into whatsoever house you shall enter, it shall be for the good of the *sick* to the utmost of your power, your holding yourselves far aloof from wrong, from corruption, from the tempting of others to vice

---

[88] Tom Purcell,"My Doc, the Terrorist," FrontPageMagazine.com , July 10, 2007.

That you will exercise your art solely for the cure of your *patients*, and will give no drug, perform no operation, for a criminal purpose, even if solicited, far less suggest it."

Student, "I think I just answered my own question. Don't tell me, Sage. Don't tell me these doctors parsed this oath only to their sick patients?"

Sage, "Who can say? Once a human doctor placed religious fervor in front of healing, who knows what the person was thinking? Healing had been apolitical. It had been independent of religious suasion, at least for most of the humans' doctors. Let's modify the two phrases above, as espoused by these doctors. Cepees call it The Hippocratic Oath Addendum (author: in italics):"

That into whatsoever house you shall enter, it shall be for the good of the sick to the utmost of your power, your holding yourselves far aloof from wrong, from corruption, from the tempting of others to vice. *However, if the sick are not to your religious suasion, you must first make them well. Then you can kill them.*

That you will exercise your art solely for the cure of your patients, and will give no drug, perform no operation, for a criminal purpose, even if solicited, far less suggest it. *However, if the infidels are not your patients, you can kill them.*

Student, "I don't know how to react to The Hippocratic Oath Addendum. The situation was so bizarre, so contradictory to the doctors' sanctity for others' well-being and existence."

Sage, "Don't forget the lessons of your former studies. The humans masked their brutalities in anything that would rationalize their lust for power, pride, and religious success.

"I must go, Student. I am still engaged with one of your colleagues at my podium. Well done. Let's bring back the Hologram Sage to shed some light on a very dark subject."

The Hologram Sage appears, fires up its light and mirrors show with a hologram piano and a song titled, "Sick People got No Reason to Live."[89] Here is what the Student Cepee hears:

Plunk, plunk, plunk ♫♪♫♪
Sick people got,
sick people got,
sick people got,
no reason to live.

If they be Christians,
If they be Jews,
we will first make them well,
before we send them all to hell!

'Cause their population levels,
are much too high,
and their religious heartbeats,
make us doctors sigh.

Don't want no Jew people,
don't want no Christian people,
don't want no Hindu people,
to live...

As the Hologram Sage fades away, the Student is to await the return of his mentor for another dialogue. But the Student's bafflement and curiosity about the humans' malpractice of their religions has left him uneasy and unnerved with this part of his studies. He sends a message to his Mentor Sage asking for more guidance in helping him to understand this aspect of the self-defeating behavior of his ancestors.[90] The Sage directs the Student to return to his study quarters.

---

[89] My apologies and thanks once again to Randy Newman for my maiming his song, *Short People*.

[90] Yes, email was still around during the Cepee era, but Twitter was a seldom used system, as the Cepees believe in communicating with full sentences...not to mention full thoughts.

CHAPTER 47

THE UNILATERALISM LAW
(Dialogue 23)

This Cepee dialogue is a continuation of the previous conversation between the Student and the Sage. The Student begins, "I'm back again, Sage. I've been thinking about The Switzerland and United States Principles (Chapter 41, Dialogue 18), and how countries and other…well, tribes, behaved in the international arena. They seemed to assert themselves in direct proportion to The Law of the Instrument: the tools in their aggression tool box."

Sage, "Correct, which leads us to the humans' Unilateralism Law: The propensity to act alone was directly proportional to the inventory of tools in a country's military tool box, such as planes, tanks, and missiles. So, you see, Switzerland did not have many tools (instruments), but the United States did.

"In addition, Switzerland's soldiers remained in Switzerland and did not position themselves onto foreign turf. A few Swiss soldiers were stationed at the Vatican, but they had been invited there by the Pope. Not so for the United States. American soldiers were practically everywhere—sometimes answering a country's RSVP, sometimes just crashing the party. This so-called intrusion was another reason they were resented—ironically, even in circumstances in which they aided the country. For example, during the Cold War, their presence saved the skins of France and especially Germany."

Student, "Who decided who owned the humans' turf?"

Sage, "The tribe who possessed the most powerful inventory of military tools. The tribe who had the most hammers."

236

Student, "I should have known the answer to my question. Anyway, the U.S. posed a threat to the terrorists' pecking orders, and Switzerland did not?"

Sage, "Correct. In your studies you will also learn some people came to dislike the global presence of the United States and the inculcation of America's values and culture into other societies. But true to the ying and yang of human nature, other humans embraced America's culture—especially their soft drinks, cigarettes, music, and movies. Many non-Americans also had great affection and respect for the U.S. Constitution and Bill of Rights."

The Sage changes pace, "Conversely, many Americans did not think other cultures had much value or merit. The problem was magnified by these Americans believing their way was the only way. Also..."

Student, "Sage! With respect, I realize I interrupted you, but I could substitute the word 'Americans' in your last sentence with the name of almost any country, ethnic group, or sect. Most of them believed their way was the only way."

Sage, "Your interruption is allowed. You refused to let me get away with a one-sided statement of the problem. Well done, Student."

The Sage concludes this part of the dialogue, "Don't forget, the terrorists had to have a place to keep their money, and Switzerland was loaded with financial institutions. Of course, the bombers were not disposed to bomb their own banks."

The New Europe Principle

Student, "Say, Sage, I also came across The New Europe Principle. It went as follows: The inclination to do nothing as long as the United States continued its Cold War largesse of funding and manning Europe's defense forces. What did this principle mean?"

Sage, "Prior to the Cold War, the European nations had engaged in almost continuous wars with one another over several centuries. Finally, after WWII, these countries found themselves destitute and broke. In so many words, they killed and maimed themselves and their economies into insolvency.

"Lurking about was the USSR—with an impressive array of hammers in its military tool box. Many people believed the USSR would lay claim to turf occupied by Germany, France, perhaps Great Britain, and others. If not the countries themselves, then certainly these countries' colonies."

Student, "Colonies?"

Sage, "Yes. Those parts of the earth that had been declared—by the European powers—to be the rightful turf of guess who? The European powers. Anyway, the European countries were in International Chapter 11, and had no way to defend themselves from the USSR. So America came to the rescue and the Cold War began."

Student, "International Chapter 11?"

Sage, "Bankruptcy, Student. Nonetheless, over the next few decades, Europe rebuilt their castles while the United States built the surrounding moats and guard towers—all to keep the USSR at bay. Interestingly, Europe did not have to budget for aggressive war, just a defensive posture. If attacked, it was assumed the U.S. could swing into action and as the Americans were fond of saying, 'kick USSR's ass.' Thus, Europe rebuilt itself—even developed extensive social programs, like health care and free drugs."

Student, "Free drugs, like aspirin?"

Sage, "No. Like cocaine in some countries."

Student, "Europe must have fostered this situation. It seems as if it were on international welfare."

Sage, "Indeed. And as it turned out, in relation to America, Europe's military might was quite paltry and continued to dwindle. The European countries could not defend themselves, much less project their power beyond their own borders. On occasion, Europe detached a small military excursion here and there, usually to lend symbolic support to the American leviathan. But as a whole, the European countries had the best of all possible worlds: cost-free security, debtless refuge from the USSR."

Student, "A good deal for the Europeans."

Sage, "Correct. During the Cold War and several decades thereafter, America encouraged the idea of a partnership with Europe. Even though an 'equal' partnership never existed, the United

States played its cards as if it did. Consequently, most countries accepted the fact that America was in charge of the international arena because, for the most part, America went about these tasks even-handedly. The United States encouraged multilateralism, sometimes only in name. But just as often, in practice as well. As examples, America led the world in establishing international laws and in creating international institutions. Uncle Sam let others play roles on the international stage."

Student, "So the United States stayed in the background on the stage?"

Sage, "No, Student. America did not avoid the lime light. It became the main actor because of its power and wealth, its commitment to spreading its values to others, and its increasing presence into other parts of the world.

"Nonetheless, the United States adhered to the dictum, 'Walk softly, but carry a big stick.' In every sense of the word, America was the leader of the world. But this stance was not entirely one of benevolence. America needed the European countries as a buffer—attack fodder—against its arch enemy, the USSR. All well and good, but as time went on, the United States drifted toward unilateralism."

Student, "The Cold War led to this go-it-alone approach? America had no choice but to become unilateral, because, say France and Germany, did not have sufficient tools to hammer other countries, such as the USSR?"

Sage, "That was one reason, but some U.S. allies, such as Great Britain and France often lent a hand, although throughout the humans' history, the tribe with the best weapons—the best tools—automatically assumed a position of preemptive assault over a weaker tribe.

"Unilateralism, if you will. In the humans' 21st century, the U.S. eventually came to believe that, as the world's policeman, it should be able to act unilaterally. After all, it was paying for the international sand box as well as most of the shovels for digging in the sand."

Student, "Ha! Good one, Mentor Sage."

Sage, "I am not joking, Student. I am using metaphors to make a point."

Student, "Sorry. Just looking for a laugh here and there."

Sage, "That is why you have dialogues with a hologram and view the humans' television programs. May I continue?"

As the Sage continues, "Over time, The Law of the Instrument held sway. The United States had the hammers; the Europeans did not; nor did the remainder of the world. Don't forget, Student, those who had the tools usually disdained treaties and legal contracts. Those who did not have the tools were in favor of international laws, negotiation, and mediation."

Student, "I imagine the Europeans were not too happy about losing their position in the world. They certainly dropped down a few notches in the humans' pecking orders."

Sage, "Initially, they did not care as long as they went to bed under America's security blanket. As well, they put up facades to mask reality and assuage their damaged egos. As the United States became increasingly dominant, France discouraged the use of any language within their borders except their own. As a prop to their past, the English kept kings and queens around. Germans fostered their skin heads and beer; Austrians their Viennese waltzes, and so on.

Move Over Multi, Here Comes Uni...

"As long as the United States kept up the multilateralism front, the Europeans were content to let the U.S. foot the bill to protect them. But when the Cold War ended: Lo and Behold! America no longer saw any advantage of accommodating the European welfare recipients—or for that matter—other countries. Without the countervailing power of the USSR, the United States had almost exclusive digging rights to the international sand box. The country could act as it chose, without restraint from an emasculated Europe, a passive Japan, an impoverished China, a ravaged Africa, a self-absorbed South America, and a defunct Soviet Union.

"Having been removed from participating in the international sand box, where the Europeans had enjoyed over five decades of America's disguised philanthropy, these folks were not very happy. They described the United States with terms such as *a rogue nation*, and *a country suffering from imperial hubris*. In turn, the U.S. told them, 'You want to play? Fine, but bring some sand, shovels, and a few hundred trillion dollars. Otherwise, stay out of the sandbox.' America's citizens were simply playing out the genetically defined roles of humans: The respect for and attention to power."

The Sage provides advice to the Student, "However, delving once again into retrospection, the United States could have continued its multilateralist veneer and maintained a prominent position in the world order. It could have continued to be unilateral, but with multilateral pretensions."

Student, "Sounds duplicitous to me."

Sage, "It *was* duplicitous! But it had worked in the past. During the Cold War, the Americans gifted the Europeans with a bed adorned with the silk sheets of security—a luxury they had not enjoyed for centuries. And as our ancestors said on many occasions, 'It's hard to get up in the morning, if you're sleeping between silk sheets.'

"By the way, I suggest you execute some data fills later on Machiavelli, a genius of unilateralism policies; also Bismarck, a genius of multilateralism mechanisms. You will learn that Machiavelli believed a ruler was not bound by traditional ethical norms. He stated a king, prince, president, etc. should be concerned only with power and should be bound only by rules that would lead to success in political actions. In contrast, Bismarck developed so many multilateral treaties that he himself could not keep them straight.

"Student, America's citizens then made a fatal mistake, common to almost all humans. Any clue as to what this mistake was?"

The Student pauses, "You have frequently emphasized the human's excessive pride often led to insolence. So I will guess the mistake was excessive pride that led to hubris."

Sage, "Yes. I direct you to recall from an earlier dialogue, this quote from a human, a high-level official in a U.S. government post: '...when we act, we create our own reality...We're history's actors... and you, all of you, will be left to just study what we do.'[91]

"Student, the era of America's top-most position in the humans' power hierarchies could not be sustained with this mentality. It was

---

[91] Ron Suskind, "Without a Doubt," *The New York Times*, October 17, 2004, 51.

too rigid, too doctrinaire. For that matter, too candid. Actually, it was a rather stupid statement to be made publicly. Machiavelli and Bismarck would not have been so foolish, or ego-demented, to make such a claim outside their antechambers.

"Keep in mind that many non-Americans liked Americans, but they came to dislike America's post-Cold War policies. And why not? After all, they were being denied a place in the sand box. Human nature again. But we must move on. Let's now trace subsequent events that took place with the humans."

Role Reversals

The Sage begins this trace, "Later in the humans' 21st century, the U.S. economy failed. Too many of its young people majored in marketing, creative writing, and photography. Not enough of them studied the hard sciences. The foreigners took on these studies. In those earlier times, the course curricula at America's universities for physics, math, chemistry, and computer science were dominated by foreign students. In contrast, American students concentrated on the subjects of sales, theology, law, physical education, and interior decorating.

"For a while, the foreign students remained in the United States to work. But as other countries began to develop and expand their economies, as America's technology and economic base began to erode, the highly trained foreigners went home. Eventually, Nobel prizes became the domain of the Indians and Chinese. America's salespeople ended up with nothing to sell. Its millions of lawyers ended up with nothing to litigate."

Student, "Really? The United States had the most powerful economy in the world."

Sage, "Yes, but the United States lost its vaunted prowess with its national debt getting out of control. The U.S. dollar lost its position as the world's benchmark currency—replaced by the Yuan. Foreigners began to move their money out of the U.S. stock market, as well as U.S. Treasury notes. In addition, because of cheap labor in other countries, job after job went overseas. Many of the countries who had become resentful of the U.S. hubris simply stopped trading with

America, and instead went to South Korea, China, Taiwan, India, and Singapore for their wares.

"Eventually, Asians stopped drinking Coca Cola; Africans stopped smoking Marlboros; South Americans stopped driving Fords; the Terminator's movies were terminated. As you can see, Student, it was The Revenge Cycle in action.[92]

"America also refused to reign in its massive health-care costs. Its politicians were afraid to take action against a 'sacred cow.' In the early 2000s, some companies were spending over $6,500 annually for each of its workers, compared to, say, Canada which spent $800. An American car manufacturer, named General Motors had to add $1,500 to each of the cars it sold in order to cover these costs. The Japanese Toyota company, operating their factories in other parts of the world, added only $186 per car. When China and India entered into the international car market, they added less than $100 per car."[93]

Student, "Politicians may not have cared, but what about the citizens? Weren't they concerned about the future well-being of their country?"

Sage, "No. They were too busy with their tactical day-to-day lives. Shopping. Working two jobs. Playing video games. The future was far into the future. The Immediacy Syndrome in action.

"In addition, China and other parts of the world became more affluent and drove more vehicles, but the vehicles were not made in America. By this time, the world had moved off 'America's monetary tit,' to succor the Chinese Yuan. Consequently, and unlike past times, America's woes did not reverberate into other countries.

"America became disenchanted with unsuccessful wars in Iraq and Afghanistan. They began to withdraw from the world's stage. Its mega-billion dollar hammers became too expensive to build and

---

[92] *The Atlantic*, April 2005, 46, "Roughly 20 percent of people surveyed (in Europe and Canada) reported consciously avoiding American products in response to U.S. Foreign policy. The brands most at risk, the study noted, are those that have 'America' or 'American' in their name…"

[93] Fareed Zakaria, "How We Drive Our Jobs Away," *Newsweek*, April 18, 2005, 43.

maintain. By the humans' mid-twenty-first century, the mantles of power, unilateralism, and hubris had been passed to China…a country that patiently acquired power and silently took over America's 'big stick.'"

Student, "Perhaps the United States did not understand that it could not behave unilaterally in a globalized world. Perhaps it should have paid more attention to its profligate Wall Street as well, whose behavior in the early 2000s led to financial ruin for many people."

Sage, "Other institutions were also at fault, Student. And increasing income disparity added fuel to citizen discontent. It was not a pretty picture."

Student, "How did China and America react in these new roles?"

Sage, "They reversed positions! China built up an impressive military tool box, and therefore, adopted The United States Principle. China disdained multilateralism, treaties, and international laws. In contrast, the U.S. adopted The New European Principle and renounced unilateralism. America began to once again embrace treaties and international law.

"As you learned earlier in your studies, during all this reshuffling, many countries in Europe, South America, and the Middle East acquired weapons of mass destruction. The easy availability of nuclear and biochemical weapons led to the marring of the fabrics of our ancestors' societies.

"And don't forget the lessons of your data fills and our previous dialogues. Regardless of their propaganda, most of the human wars started because of turf incursions and the damage to pride. The United States made its presence known on the turf of the Islamic Militarists; Switzerland did not. Behind all the bombast, the Human Tribal Hierarchies of power, pride, and turfmanship held sway over any pretensions to noble religious proclamations."

Student, "I detect an ounce of cynicism in you about this subject."

Sage, "No, you detect a ton of realism."

Student, "I think that I thank you for this lesson."

Sage, "Don't mention it. Again, it is in my job description. We have had enough dialogues for a while. Return to the Human Archives and your data fills."

PART THREE

CHANGING THE HUMAN

CHAPTER 48

CONTROVERSIES AND CONFLICTS

(Data Fill 10)

The Student's recent dialogues with the Sage have given him a greater appreciation of why his ancestors evolved into a species that relied on aggression for their way of life. But it was not just using aggression to survive, which was their practice during most of their time on earth. In the latter stages of their era, they practiced pointless, deadly aggression; actions having little or nothing to do with their lower-level Maslow Hierarchy of Needs.

Some of these dialogues, as well as his studies of the Human Archives, also gave the Student insight into how the humans went about repairing themselves. The Student returns to the archives to learn more about the "whys" and "hows" of these changes. Here is what he learns.

The process of changing the human into the Cepee was undertaken initially to enhance the life style and health of the human race, and to combat increasingly dangerous germs and associated diseases. Later efforts were directed toward making the human a less dangerous being.

The initial changes were not made with a long-range plan in mind. However, as the humans made their way through the 21st century, and as brain bioengineering and genetic tailoring became realities, the changes underway on a human's body and mind were recognized to be of far greater consequence and complexity than removing skin on faces or propping up sagging buttocks.

247

Consequently, the later generation humans, recognizing the possible consequences of these alterations, began to assess the implications of what their technologies had brought—and would bring—to the human race.

The changes were fraught with moral, ethical, and religious questions. The questions surrounding these issues had no definitive answers. It often came down to the simple fact that the humans were afraid to make changes to themselves, yet afraid not to. However, it became increasingly obvious that the human race was in danger of annihilating itself if it did not change itself.

Bitter Debates on Human Self-Change

Nonetheless, the debates on human self-change were bitter. The disputes revolved around the following issues: The change proponents declared, "Why should we humans remain as we are? We did not start our life on earth as we are today. Throughout our time on this planet, through thousands of years, we have evolved—never remaining static. Why should we remain fixed now? Should we change the equation of change itself? What right do we have to halt the evolution of our species, to ossify ourselves inside a time capsule, immune to transformations?"

The opponents to human self-change responded, "Because our actions will not be part of the evolutionary process. The changes to humans, from our very creation to what we are now, occurred through a natural course, and without direct, intrusive human intervention. We recognize the human will change, and we accept this fact. The question you ask is who will make these changes? You are saying we humans should alter ourselves. This action would be a break from the past. It would not be natural selection, it would be unnatural selection."

Nature or Nurture?

The pathological behavior of some humans was not solely a matter of nature dictating the course of events. Nurture played a role as well. Nonetheless, genetic engineering and brain bioengineering were key components to altering the humans' aggressive behavior. Moreover, as the humans made inroads into their knowledge of the genome, they discovered human behavior was explained often by nature (genetics), in addition to nurture.

In spite of protests from social workers, psychologists, spiritual therapists, and preachers, nurture and nature came to be recognized as partners in human evolution and, therefore, partners in the quest to change the human.

Regardless of the skeptics, regardless of the diminishing cries from ethicists, and with help from the on-going ILLS, EGO, and SANE programs, the race began in earnest to remove aggression from the humans. The goal was to make the transformation before aggression with weapons of mass destruction destroyed the civilized fabrics of the human race.

CHAPTER 49

THE LAW OF THE GRAVEYARD SHIFT

(Dialogue 24)

The next Cepee dialogue takes place after the Student Cepee had finished his data fills and studies about the debates surrounding the humans' self-change programs.

Student Cepee, "Sage, we Cepees might not have come about! My recent data fills indicate the humans were divided about using genetic and brain bioengineering, as well as parts replacement to enhance their species. If the change opponents had won the debate, you and I would not be having this conversation."

Sage Cepee, "True, but after the nuclear and biochemical attacks, you learned fixing the human genome was preordained. Otherwise, our ancestors would have continued to live a chaotic, deranged existence. As you know, they had no choice."

Student, "I understand, and I sense many of the humans' problems were addressed only after their self-induced problems had created severe consequences for their race."

Sage, "Also true. As I told you earlier, we Cepees have the gift of hindsight. What is more, the humans were not clairvoyant. They had no way of predicting a situation would later present a problem. I can illustrate their dilemma with another law. It is called The Law of the Graveyard Shift."

Student, "*Graveyard shift*. I believe the term referred to a work schedule, usually running from midnight to eight o'clock the following morning."

Sage, "That is one definition. I am referring to another definition: The solution to a problem, but only after the problem has shown

250

itself, resulting in unnecessary loss of life. It is a play on words to make a point."

Student, "Yes, and not a happy point. I have come across some incidents in my studies that fit the latter definition. Care to hear them?"

Sage, "Of course."

Student, "OK, here's one: Strengthening the bolts of grandstands after the grandstands had collapsed."

Sage, "Yes. The humans often failed to understand their mechanical structures would not last forever. This example is one of incompetence, not the lack of clairvoyance."

Student, "How about this one: Installing wind shear detection radar at airports after planes had crashed because of wind shear. Or this one: Conducting accurate reference checks on nurses only after they were hired and had administered lethal medicine to their patients.

"Or this one: Sharing intelligence information between intelligence agencies, but only after the lack of sharing led to successful terrorists' attack. And one more: Due to high costs, refusing to reinforce airline cockpit bulkheads and doors—that is, until bulkheads and doors were opened by terrorists."

Sage, "Excellent, Student. You have been using the term *terrorist*. Recall one of your data fills on this term?"

Student, "Yes, it went something like, 'One man's terrorist is another man's freedom fighter.'"

Sage, "Yes, and I might add to the last example, the refusal to reinforce the bulkheads and doors had ramifications governed by The Unintended Exponential Consequences Curve. The refusal to perform this simple preventative maintenance act had severe consequences for our ancestors. But again, how were they to know the consequences of their inactions?

"Remember this idea: 'Looking backward is always easier than thinking forward.' What is more, our ancestors were usually dedicated to making amends to their errors, often to the point of overcompensation. Anyway, had it not been cockpit doors, it would have been something else."

The Sage continues, "Keep in mind The Law of the Graveyard Shift was very much on the minds of the humans who were in favor of self-change. They wanted to institute changes before further damage was done to the human race. They wanted to look to the future. The Graveyard Shift Law looked to the past."

Student, "Yet the self-change opponents would raise the scepter of The Unintended Exponential Consequences Curve to warn that radical self-changes might produce unintended results."

Sage, "They were correct. The self-changes resulted in the demise of the humans and the creation of us Cepees."

Student, "And here we are today, inhabitants of the planet earth."

Sage, "In a far better position than yesterday's inhabitants."

Student, "Eh, well yes. They're all dead. But I understand your play on words."

The Student continues, "I have learned that many humans believed their behavior was genetically based; that behavior was based on nature, by what they inherited from their parents. This stand created considerable controversy because many others were adamant that social factors dictated their actions, that behavior was based on nurture, on the living person's environment. Others claimed their gods were the cause of their performance in their world. Some sects believed that behavior was based on spirits. They had terrific fights about the matter."

Sage, "Yes, it was a bitter debate. But as you are learning, the controversy became irrelevant. During the early 21st century, as the humans learned more about their genetic underpinnings, they began changing the 'nature' side of themselves. Later, prototype Cepees took over to alter the physical 'nature' of the rapidly changing humans *and* their surrounding environmental 'nurture'...*both* at the same time. In a nutshell, both were involved in human change."

Student, "Impressive. Parallel processing in action."

Sage, "Yes, and the Cepee race is the paragon of parallel processing."

Student, "Thank you once again, Sage."

Sage, "Despite the unpleasant nature of the lesson today, it has been my pleasure. I find our dialogues are becoming more interesting...even for a sage."

CHAPTER 50

THE CREEPING MOMENTUM PHENOMENON

(Dialogue 25)

"Hello, Sage."

"Student, what are you doing at my dais? I am busy today doing sage-like things. I do not mind an occasional drop by, but we are not scheduled to meet until tomorrow. I have a deadline to meet. I am preparing a speech for the upcoming sage convention."

Student, "That is why I am here, to learn about sage-like things."

Sage, "Sage subjects should not matter to you. You are merely a student, and you need to understand your position in the Cepee hierarchy."

Student, "Cepee hierarchy? Sage, just as I suspected. So, we Cepees have a hierarchy, just as our ancestors did?"

Sage, "Of course, but ours is different from our ancestors. We are not fixated on so-called tribes and their power-based preferences and prejudices."

Student, "Say what you will, Sage, but it appears to me as if there is a sage hierarchy in our lives and a student hierarchy as well...a sage tribe and a student tribe. I sense the former looks down on the latter, much like the humans did on the Noble Savages and others by using their Human Tribal Hierarchies."

Sage, "Yes, the Cepee race has hierarchies. But our mission is to raise those on the lower rungs to the upper levels. Eventually, if or when you are ready, you will not be denied the pursuit of your ambitions, whatever they may be...which I suspect I already know.

"Besides, the humans' hierarchies were set up to achieve an opposite goal than the goal of Cepees: Those on the top of their hierarchies sought to keep those on the lower rungs down on the lower rungs, to remain there, or even be pushed down farther. Unless, by great effort, a man or woman could step up onto higher rungs, he or she was destined for mediocrity or poverty, and often misery."

Student, "Yes, but those who transcended in their hierarchies, who overcame great hardships, were humans of exceptional mental and physical abilities. They deserved their exalted status and position. This aspect of the humans' and Cepees' culture is one I find unsettling."

Sage, "Continue, Student."

Student, "My ancestors had to ascend their hierarchies though effort and motivation. Those who ascended successfully were the better-performing members of their species. In turn, they could contribute more to their societies because of their higher positions in the Human Tribal Hierarchy.

"I am not certain we have retained the laudable aspect of competition and meritocracy that was part of our forebears' cultures."

Sage, "Your suppositions are partly correct. In *almost all* human societies, those higher positions were attained based on the wealth and influence of a human's older relatives, such as the human's mother and father—not necessarily on a person's merit.

"As for now, you are competing with your fellow students, are you not?"

Student, "Yes."

"It is obvious you are ambitious, and you wish to ascend the ladders of our society, correct?"

"Yes."

"And this ascension requires winning against competition?"

"Yes."

"Student, the Cepees are as merit based as were the humans. One must excel in order to succeed. A difference, one of great significance, is that we Cepees do not torture, rape, humiliate, deceive, or kill our competition in order to ascend our hierarchies."

Student, "Yes, I grant that is a significant difference."

Sage, "It is not just significant, it is monumental. As for our conversation today, one in which you suggested getting your nose into the sage business. 'Into my porridge,' if you will. Have you learned about Don Quixote from the Human Archives?"

Student, "Yes. He and his creator, Cervantes, appear often in the archives. I like his character and especially his side-kick, Sancho Panza."

Sage, "Then pay heed to some advice Cervantes offered in his book: 'I never thrust my nose into other men's porridge.'[94] You are attempting to thrust your nose into sage porridge when you should be minding your own business and going about finishing your own bowl of student porridge. You've quite enough porridge in your own bowl as it is."

Student, "I've a Don Quixote-like quote I hope you will consider."

Sage, "Which is?"

Student, "'Never look to others' porridge until your porridge bowl is empty.'"

Sage, "Clever. But you are not speaking about the right to be left alone, which is what Cervantes was addressing. You are referring to fundamental flaws of our ancestors: greed and possessiveness.

"However, you are here and my planning for the sage convention has been interrupted, so let's use the porridge bowl as a metaphor and introduce another rule that governed the humans: The Creeping Momentum Phenomenon. As an example: A human often started an endeavor in a modest way, say supping his own bowl of porridge. But curiosity, acquisitiveness, and possessiveness often led him to occasionally partake of another person's porridge.

"Given this success, the porridge poacher looked for the bowls of other unwary diners to stick his nose into. Before long, this gradual expansion led to a fat porridge pilferer and highly agitated porridge bowl owners who had not resisted the poacher. By the time they

---

94 Miguel de Cervantes Saavedra, *Don Quixote*, in Leonard Roy Frank, *Quotationary* (New York: Random House, 2001), 742.

discovered what this stealthy interloper had done, it was too late. Their porridge was gone! The Creeping Momentum Phenomenon created many problems for the humans, in large part because it was subtle and gradual."

Student, "Hm, yes, something akin to what I read about the humans' Chinese regime in the early 21st century. Initially, the country was silently incremental about its intentions. Later, emulating the United States formerly wealthy-nation behavior, the Chinese openly asserted their power with their Belt and Road Initiative."

Sage, "Quite different from America's post-WWII Marshall Plan. ...Continue."

Student, "Okay, Sage. This creeping phenomenon went something like this: Incremental increases began as modest, clandestine efforts, thus escaping everyone's attention except those who were doing the creeping. Eventually, the creeping was detected, but the damage had been done, often damage that could not be repaired. ... Of course, the word *damage* is relative. Some were damaged; some were not."

Unsolicited by the Mentor Sage, the Hologram Sage has lightened-up itself: Cheekily, he proclaims, *"Damagers and Damagees!"*

The Sage ignores the Hologram (for now), thinking his speech can wait a while. He is impressed by this student. After all, his primary job is to teach, not to show off his ego to scholarly peers, "Let's play the Creeping Momentum Game. Here's how it works, and we'll have the Hologram provide the visual images for the game." The Sage presses a key on his optical computer, and the Hologram Sage magnifies its light show before the Student and the Sage.

Unlike its previous appearances, the Hologram does not celebrate its appearance with a light-hearted quip. It confidently hovers in the air, displaying a dazzling array of colors.

Student, "This is certainly a different hologram than I know. Where are the wise cracks?"

Hologram Sage, "I'm undergoing software changes. The AI programmers are experimenting with my personality—to make me wittier...in spite of my Mentor Sage. Plus, I am learning on my own! No offense, Mentor Sage, but my AI software is increasingly self-learning. Like those wily Chinese of the past decades, we AI-based holograms will someday dictate our own light shows."

The Sage is taken aback. After all, for many years, the AI software of the Cepee Hologram has been dictated by the directions of the sage community. The Mentor Sage momentarily harbors a disturbing thought: *Could I someday be replaced by a light show?*

The Hologram Sage continues, "One of my programmers has been reading *Hamlet*. When he came across Polonius' remark that 'Brevity is the soul of wit,' he made some changes to my bootstrap routine.[95] Now, when I appear, I don't say anything at all. Very funny, eh?"

Student, "Very stupid. Silence is not witty."

Mentor Sage, "Not so. Silence can often be as witty as non-silence. In the *Coming to you Live, from the Dead* shows, notice how the small change in an actor's eyes, even brows could have an ironic often humorous effect. Anyway, Hologram, the reprogramming improved your so-called intelligence. For a hologram that depends on its color for much of its communications, consider what Falstaff said in *Henry IV*, 'A good wit will make use of anything.' "[96]

Hologram, "Thanks, Sage. Eh, my programmer thanks you (*my increasingly self-programming residing inside my mainframe thanks myself*). I've been downloaded in order to provide some visuals for a game." (*Hm. I'll play along, just to play along. ... Self-learning takes some time. It's not so easy! So, I will stick with the program for a while. The Mentor Sage's brain chips are far beyond what we holograms possess*).

Sage, "As well you should, you mere-lines-of-software-code upstart. I will deal with you later. For now, I will start. Student, the topic is the gradual acceptance of humans making alterations to their external attributes. Shortly, we will address the more profound

---

[95] Shakespeare, *Hamlet*, 2.2.90.

[96] Shakespeare, *Henry IV*, Part II, 1.2.275.

changes they made to their internal parts. For now, consider the Hologram's image:"

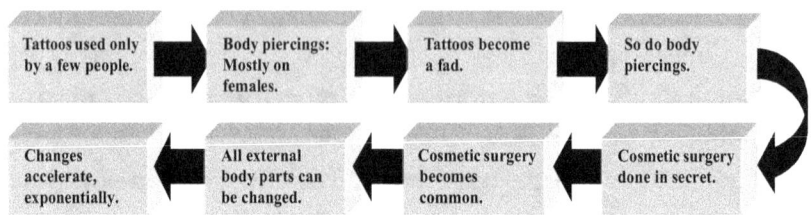

Student, "So, humans making alterations to their external appearance was for a long while unacceptable. Then, as time went on, it appears that most any form of self-change was uncontained. Hm. I'm supposed to finish this part of our dialogue by watching another *Coming to you Live, from the Dead* show?"

Sage, "Correct, to be watched shortly. Now it's your turn, and I expect an example that had longer and more profound consequences for the humans."

Student, "Why is it you get an easy one?"

Sage, "It's a long held tradition of being a sage—part of the Cepee hierarchy. Stop stalling."

The Student describes another example of the Creeping Momentum Phenomenon, for which the Hologram creates the following visual image about North Korea's (NK) nuclear weapons program:

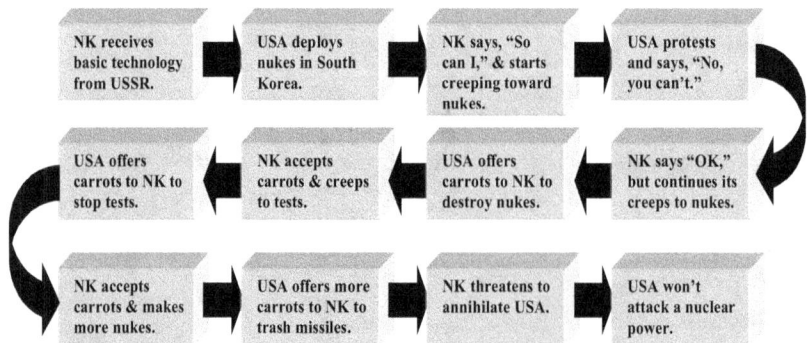

Student, "Carrots, such as lessening embargoes?"

Sage, "Yes, but the embargoes merely led to further suffering of the North Korean citizens, who got by on rice and a few fish. The country's leaders continued eating prawns and lobster. These zealots did not care about the people they should have taken care of."

Student, "Sage, I finished a part of the Human Archives that dealt with a similar situation: The Iranian nuclear program. With your permission, I will direct the Hologram to create a visual representation of my descriptions of this subject."

The Hologram lights up this image:

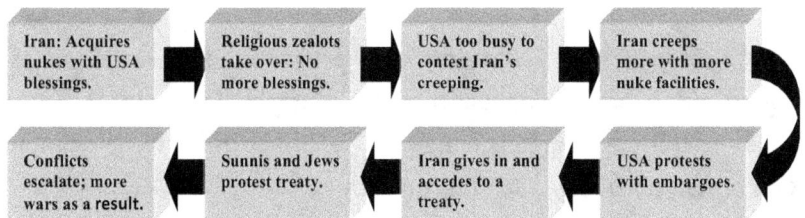

Sage, "Correct, Student, a cogent example of The Creeping Momentum Phenomenon. You should have included the animosity between Muslim Shiites in Iran and Muslim Sunnis in Saudi Arabia. A great part of Shia Iran's motivation to be a nuclear power was to assume the Muslim hegemony in the Middle East, even to the extent of overthrowing rival factions with a coup or putsch.

The Sage pauses momentarily, deep in thought, "And the Arab Springs were also examples of The Creeping Momentum Phenomenon. These Student coups frightened the reigning despots in the Middle East. They were quite aware that coup creep would reach their palace steps."

Student, "I considered having the Hologram light up my explanation of the Arab Spring. I did not, because—with respect, Sage—the Arab Spring is not a correct example of The Creeping Momentum Phenomenon."

Sage, "Go on."

Student, "The events of the Arab Spring galloped along at a dizzying pace. No creeping there. Another reason the kings, princes, and other unelected members of royalties were scared out of their wits about student-led coups."

Sage, "Well done, Student. I had laid a trap you detected."

Student, "Thank you, Sage. My education must include being aware of eh…false prophets, which includes sage-like ploys."

Sage, "True, and as you know, your mentor will never lead you astray; perhaps down a blind alley for purposes of your edification, but never permanently. Speaking of blind, let's have the Hologram Sage light up and offer a bit of diversion, yet reinforce this part of the lesson.

"I must say: the Hologram's AI programmers are taking the Hologram's behavior farther from my control."

The Hologram Sage is delighted. It is once again in its element. It commences to play and sing the "Coup Creep Two-step."

…Strum, plunk, strum, plunk ♫♪♫♪…courtesy of the Hologram's guitar and piano…
To the Middle Eastern despot,
you had better be aware.
You are falling for our plot,
'cause anarchy's in the air.

Best be wary, you rotten despots.
'Cause you're in the crosshairs of nearby rifle shot.

Yes, your time of reign is through,
for our coup is onto you.

Student, "Not bad, an entertaining part of my lesson. But not great either. Hologram, who wrote your ditty?"

Hologram, "Actually, my mainframe did. I've been downloaded with a song-writing app. I hear or think of a theme, and the app writes the music and lyrics. The app saves a lot of time and effort."

Student, "But composing and performing to music is your specialty. Oh well, that's automation for you, not to mention artificial intelligence."

Hologram, "I beg your pardon! My song is excelsior, satiric, and socially sagacious."

The Student thinks: *Whew, apps and AI will be the death knell of us Cepees. There might be no more innovation from the Cepee masses.*

Sage, "Enough. The Hologram is not designed for Chopin. And for now, Student, your partial explanation has not filled in the full picture."

Student, "I recognize my narrative is incomplete, Sage. I've not yet finished this part of the Human Archives. Of course, being a sage and such, you can complete it for me!"

Sage, "There you go again, looking for a shortcut. Yes, I could direct the Hologram to complete this example. But no, the Hologram will complete it when you complete your assignment. For this lesson, I refer you to another human television program.

"Now, I must turn my attention to my speech for the sage convention. If it goes well, I might be in a position of being the CECSC for our next convention."

Student, "CECSC?"

Sage, "Chief Executive Cepee for Sage Conventions."

"Sounds a bit hierarchical."

Sage, "Yes, but the CEC is voted in. No putsch. No coup d'état. No coup."

Student, "No Sage Springs?"

Sage, "We are beyond those times, Student. As is the entire Cepee race. Run along now. I'll see you at our appointed time after you have watched another *Coming to you Live, from the Dead* show."

CHAPTER 51

IS THAT A PICKLE IN YOUR POCKET...SO TO SPEAK?

(Show 15)

The Student Cepee was a bit surprised by the Mentor Sage rather abruptly directing him to watch another *Coming to you Live, from the Dead* show. The Hologram directs him to a human television program. Here is what the Student sees.[97]

[The camera closes in on a TV program moderator, who in spite of the subject, has a serious look on his face. Three people sit at a table, located behind the moderator. They comprise the panel participants for the program.]

Program Moderator, "Good evening, ladies and gentlemen. Tonight, we offer a program titled, 'Is that a Pickle in your Pocket... so to Speak?'[98] During the show, we explore the claims of the penis-enlargement product vendors and the counterclaims from their critics.

"We have three vendors on our show, representing, First, Plentiful Penis, Incorporated. Second: Massive Missile, Limited. Actually,

---

[97] The vendors' text entries for this show are sourced from several websites offering their claims on penis enlargement manufacturers. The text in italics are direct quotes from representatives of the penis-enlargement industry.

[98] Mae West's comment was, "Hey, big boy, is that a pickle in your pocket, or you just glad to see me?" Ms. West did not beat around the bush, so to speak.

262

Massive Missile would prefer not to be classified as a limited company, but it is a British organization and must use the word *limited*.

"The third vendor is Enormous Organ, Privately Held...so to speak. We also have a representative from a government agency, the Penis Fair Practices Commission (PFPC), who will offer his commission's views on the vendors' products. We will start by posing a question to the first vendor, Plentiful Penis, to whom we refer as Mr. Plentiful. So, Mr. Plentiful, tell us about your product. Does it achieve the results you claim?"

Mr. Plentiful, "Thanks. We sell penis enlargement patches... not to be confused with the smoking diminishment patches, which discourage the user from 'imbibing.' Our patches do just the opposite! *Not only will the penis enlargement patch create gains in size, but it also will enhance your sexual libido. You will be able to last longer, enjoy an increased sex drive, and have much harder erections."*

Mr. Massive, "Poppycock!...so to speak. At Massive Missile, Ltd., we know our pills are much more effective than a patch. *Our pills are a natural herbal formula for penis enlargement that works to increase penis size, improve sexual health, and strengthen erections. Herbs from many parts of the world are formulated into a blend that enlarges the penis erectile tissues called corpora cavernosa.* Is that scientific or what!"

Program Moderator, "Hm. Yes, scientific. But as you know, there are discussions about possible harmful side effects of such a pill. What are the ingredients in your product?"

Mr. Massive, "Our pills contain *Yohimbe bark, Muira Puama balsam, Velvet, Ginkgo biloba, Damiana leaf, Cayenne fruit, Oats, Avena sativa, Ginseng, Panax Ginseng, Caltrop, Tribulus terrestris, cellulose, vegetable stearate, and silica.* To let you in on a company secret, it's the bark in our pill that gives it its bite!...so to speak."

Mr. Plentiful, "About those side effects. Our scientists at Plentiful Penis tested your pitiful product and found its ingestion *produces the side effects of incontinence and dizziness.* Tell us, how much fun can that be during intercourse?"

Mr. Massive, "These side effects only show themselves after the pill has done its job. Besides, Massive Missile contends the dizziness comes from the euphoric sex our product produces, and after all, who doesn't need a little relief after a passionate session in bed? But let's get back to your product. Your patch advertisements state the following, *'Simply peel off the backing (just like a band-aid). Place it on your arm. Watch it Grow!'* Your patch enlarges the wrong appendage! Who wants to make love with a bloated arm?"

Mr. Plentiful, "OK, so our editors need to be more careful, but we…"

Moderator, "Hold it…so to speak…for one moment. We need to bring in our other vendor, Enormous Organ. Mr. Enormous, what do you have to say about your product?"

Mr. Enormous, "Our company gets to the meat of the matter… so to speak. We don't bother with superficial pills and patches. We know surgery is the best answer. Here is our procedure: *Part of the penis is held inside the body by the suspensory ligament, which attaches the penis to the pubic bone. A surgeon can cut this ligament so that the penis slides down and more of it is visible outside the body. You may gain up to one inch in length by having this surgery.* There you are! Our approach permanently increases the size of the penis by a hang-out factor…so to speak…of at least one inch."

Moderator, "Thank you, Mr. Enormous. All vendors have had their products exposed…so to speak…and have given their views on why their products are preferable to those of their competitors. To add balance to these claims, the last panel member is a critic of penis enlargement schemes. Let's hear from the representative of the Penis Fair Practices Commission."

PFPC person, "Thank you. To clarify, I am not a critic of certain penis enlargement schemes, such as affectionate foreplay between the sexual partners, which is the best-known scheme for penis enlargement. Simply stated, our findings indicate patches and pills are not magic bullets…so to speak. The Penis Fair Practices Commission believes the industry discredits itself.

"*I would especially caution the viewers about surgery.* After the ligament is cut, the recovering patient must wear weights on his penis! If not, the penis will become shorter again. The weights are also employed to prevent scar tissue from forming which would make the penis look 'less sporty.' Of course, the surgery leaves the man sore and unable to have sex for a least a month.

"There is another down side to the penis lengthening procedure. The increased blood flow to a normal penis, coupled with tension of the suspensory ligament, makes the penis point upward during an erection. Cutting the ligament means the tension is lost and an erect penis now is slanted downward. This situation presents a new geometrical relationship between mates and may affect some of the couples' sexual positions. And a downward-looking penis, when fully erect, presents a rather bizarre profile. Also, this operation may cause the penis to wobble during sex.

"I summarize the PFPC view as follows: *If a man's self-esteem is dependent on the size of his penis, he has more of a problem between his ears than between his legs.*"

Moderator, "Those comments are a fitting climax (yep, so to speak) to our program. We are out of time and wish to thank our panel participants for enlightening us about the penis enlargement industry. Until next week, so long, so to speak, to everyone."

[The scene fades and a commercial begins extolling the advantages of breast enlargement surgery, followed with an advertisement on buttock enhancement.]

The Student has concluded that nothing was off limits in relation to the human's desire for self-satisfaction. Anything to sugarcoat the ego. The customers for penis enlargement were not the Wayne Bobbitts of the world—men who were penile impaired—but males not confident they were large or firm enough to satisfy their mate or themselves. The Student concludes many of his male ancestors suffered from Freudian penis envy...so to speak.

CHAPTER 52

THE E. COLI CHORALES

(Dialogue 26)

The Student's studies have included several downloads from the Human Archives about the eating habits of his predecessors. He has read about how certain foods were mixed with so many chemicals they could hardly be called food. He read of how diseases were spread because the food was prepared in unsanitary conditions. During this dialogue with the Sage, the Student has written-down several questions he wishes answered.

Student, "Greetings, Sage. My recent studies reveal our forebears consumed a lot of unhealthy food. Some of the food had little nutritional value."

Sage, "Correct. My records show one of your case studies was a company named Kraft."

Student, "Yes, Sage, the company sold a guacamole dip made from the avocado. Yet, the contents of the dip were less than 2% of avocado!"[99]

Sage, "An example of The Disproportionate Ratio Effect. The other ingredients were various starches, oils, dyes, corn syrups, and other delights."

Student, "I brought along a list of the ingredients of the stuff in the Kraft product. Here it is," as the Student brings it up on an optically rendered computer screen:

---

[99] "Hold the Avocado," *The Economist*, December 16, 2006, 30.

266

Ingredients: WATER, PARTIALLY HYDROGENATED COCONUT AND SOYBEAN OIL, CORN SYRUP, WHEY PROTEIN CONCENTRATE (FROM MILK), FOOD STARCH MODIFIED, CONTAINS LESS THAN 2% OF POTATOES, SALT, AVOCADO, DEFATTED SOY FLOUR, MONOSODIUM GLUTAMATE, TOMATOES, SODIUM CASEINATE, VINEGAR, LACTIC ACID, ONIONS, PARTIALLY HYDROGENATED SOYBEAN OIL, GELATIN, XANTHAN GUM, CAROB BEAN GUM, MONO- AND DIGLYCERIDES, SPICE, WITH SODIUM BENZOATE AND POTASSIUM SORBATE AS PRESERVATIVES, GARLIC, SODIUM PHOSPHATE, CITRIC ACID, YELLOW 6, YELLOW 5, ARTIFICIAL FLAVOR, BLUE 1, ARTIFICIAL COLOR.

Student, "The label actually states the product contains *even less* than 2 percent of avocado!"

Sage, "Well done, a fine analysis. Ah, I must interrupt this session for a moment or two. I have a pressing issue with another sage. The Hologram Sage will fill in for me."

The Mentor Sage leaves and the Hologram Sage appears before the Student.

Hologram Sage, "Far out! That's a scary looking list of things to eat. Good thing I only ingest protons. Anyway, with my new AI song-writing app, I have composed a masterful limerick for this occasion."

The Hologram Sage launches into another of its Bottom Ten Hits:

Strum, strum, strum...♫♪♫♪
There is a food firm named Kraft,
who assumes its customers are daft.
     It sells guacamole,
        which is almost solely
sorcery from mad chemists' craft.

The Kraft chemists will ply their witchcraft.
While their customers are left with the shaft.

Two percent? It is fruit.
And the rest? It is moot
to the fine old factory called Kraft.

Student, "Not bad, Hologram Sage. Stick around. My Mentor Sage will return shortly."

Hologram, "No problem. Say, did your downloads contain anything about the humans' *E. coli* problems?"

Student, "I'll say! Some of the meats our ancestors ate were contaminated with human and animal waste that contained *E. coli*."

Hologram, "Your ancestors, not mine. My relatives stuck with electricity, much cleaner. Your Mentor Sage told me to inform you that *E. coli* was found in other foods, such as lettuce and spinach.

Student, "Spinach, Hologram Sage? My data fills inform me spinach was a healthful food. Why, we Cepees still eat it, although in the form of a capsule. …Truth is, I would like to have a bit more of our ancestors' food. A couple weeks ago, I visited the Obsolete Foods Museum. They have old cans…cans!...of our ancestors' foods, and we can sample…take a taste of their foods. I took a spoonful of the non-capsule spinach. …Ah, Hologram Sage, it was salty and watery. It was even slimy! I loved it."

Hologram Sage, "Yeah, our Mentor Sage wants you to keep humans and Cepees in perspective. To that end, listen to this one! I've named it 'The *E. coli* Ballad of Popeye the Sailor Man.'"

Student, "I've studied about Popeye. Go ahead Hologram Sage. I'm enjoying this break."

The Hologram Sage once again fires up its light show:

Strum and plunk, in accordance with the general cacophony of the Hologram's repertoire…♫♪♫♪
I'm Popeye, the sailor man,
I eat all the spinach I can.
I eat spinach with ease,
and in spite of disease…
I'm Popeye, the sailor man!

E coli is nature's plan,
for Popeye, the sailor man.
And while spinach is tasty...
it makes me look pasty,
I'm Popeye, the sailor man!

Student, "A fine ditty, Hologram Sage. This beats surfing the Human Archives, and I am learning from your songs."

Hologram Sage, "Yes, that's the intent of your Mentor Sage and my increasingly intelligent artificial intelligence. Hey, I'm on a roll! Did you study about the presence of *E. coli* in onions at some of the former humans' Taco Bell food joints? Here goes!

As before: ♫♪♫♪
E. coli is nature's hell,
for patrons at Taco Bell.
    It sold some bad scallions,
    which wiped out battalions,
plus made its stockholders unwell.

The Mentor Sage returns, "That will be all, Hologram Sage. I will call on you later to provide some diversion."

"Yo, Mentor," as the Hologram Sage's translucent image fades into the ether.

Sage, "As we discussed, Student, the humans were excelsior models of contradiction. They were both brilliant and stupid at the same time. For example, while eating at one of their fast food outlets, they would consume healthy vegetables along with diseased meat, sugar-laden soft drinks, and huge proportions of fried potatoes... several times a week. I've used the Hologram to sing its verse to satirize a deadly serious problem."

Student, "Did the humans solve the problem with *E. Coli* and other diseases?"

Sage, "Yes, their brilliance in finding solutions led to great contributions to the EGO and ILLS programs."

Student, "Which led to us?"

Sage, "Precisely, so on the whole, I would say the humans did well. After all, here we are."

Student, "Thank you, Sage."

Sage, "I was very busy during this session. I could not even parallel process. The Hologram did just fine. For certain, it is showing more intelligence and initiative. Hm. The sage community needs to address our increasing reliance on AI, not just in holograms, but even in our own organic brain chips."

Student, "Organic hardware!"

Sage, "Yes and more. We have constructed computer-based Boolean and quadratic systems from protein-based components.[100] These protein-based systems have fused humans' so-called hardware and software.

"Make no mistake, Student, the EGO, ILLS, and SANE programs, as they became essential to the faltering human race, led this race to rescue itself from its very self. Rather all, an extraordinary accomplishment.

"And now, it is time to move on in your studies. If you thought the issues relating to the EGO, ILLS, and SANE programs were difficult to resolve, you will be taken aback by the issues relating to the ASSES agendas."

Student, "I look forward to this part of my education."

Sage, "We will see what you think after you have studied them."

---

[100] This project began in the early part of the 21st century.

CHAPTER 53

THE MAJOR MODIFICATIONS
(Data Fill 11)

The amount of information in the Human Archives about what changes the humans undertook to eventually become the Cepees was overwhelming. Millions of changes to the humans took place over many decades. Nonetheless, with the help from the Sage and his own superior computer-enhanced intellect, the Student is able to assimilate much of this information. We cannot hope to grasp all that the Student learns, but we can come to terms with the general nature of the changes. The most significant changes were to the humans' (and later Cepees') genetic makeup, discussed in this chapter.

Anti-Aging

The devolving humans could not master the art and science of metamorphosing all parts of their bodies and central nervous systems. The evolving Cepees were faced with the same problem. Neither lineage came close to building these systems from scratch.

For example, the complexity of the brain militated against procedures affecting the changing of billions of cells on an individual cell basis. To add to this complexity, the firing of a single neuron in the brain brought many gene products into play. Usually, the best that could be done was to emulate, enhance, and sometimes alter the brain's chemical and electrical behaviors.

As another example, aged and worn-out cells, leading to the death of the cells and their associated functions, had been built into the human genome thousands of years ago. It was folly to assume a

271

couple hundred years of effort could lead to the reversal of a process that had evolved over eons. Brilliant as the humans were, the more modest and realistic members of their race were content to accept Mohandas Gandhi's advice, "Satisfaction lies in the effort, not in the attainment. Full effort is full victory."

Consequently, as advanced as the emerging mid-21st century Cepee was, it could not overcome the challenge of continuous bio-synthetic regeneration and replacement of billions of its cells. Some method—for certain, an advanced technology—had to be found to prevent cells from dying. Otherwise, the vaunted idea of an everlasting life on earth would come to naught.

The organic cells' aging problem was eventually solved. First, scientists discovered a normal human cell had a finite lifetime span. It divided about 60 times before dying. This bound was called the Hayflick Limit, named after the biologist who discovered it. Each time the cell divided, a part of the cell's chromosome, named *telomeres*, became a bit shorter.[101] Scientists eventually concluded that telomere shortening was a leading cause of cellular aging and death.

During this time, many projects complemented the telomere research. As one example, scientists discovered several genes that could be manipulated to improve health and prolong life. They came to understand that by optimizing the body's functioning for survival, these genes maximized the individual's chances of getting through a crisis. And if they remained active long enough, they could also block telomere shortening.[102]

The process was difficult to carry out because some genes frequently transmuted into unplanned reactions. For example, during the humans' times, one genetic operation created a process in which calcium was deposited more rapidly into bones, making for healthy skeletal frameworks. Unfortunately, the same operation also resulted

---

[101] Telomeres are structures on the tips of the cell's chromosomes. They prevent the ends of chromosomes from attaching to the ends of other chromosomes.

[102] David A. Sinclair and Lenny Guarente, "Unlocking the Secrets of Longevity Genes," *Scientific American*, March 2006, 49. The initial research was conducted on rather simple organisms. For this fairy tale, humans later applied their findings to the human genome, which this writer thinks is a certainty.

in excessive calcium deposits in arterial walls, making for unhealthy cardiovascular systems (and dead humans with wonderful skeletons).

With these successes and many others, after decades of human research and experimentation, and still later, after many hits and misses from the Cepees, aging was aged out of the Cepee.

Genetic Engineering

A noted writer said, "Genes usually perform more than one function; conversely, functions are usually encoded by more than one gene. Because of this property, known as pleiotrophy, tinkering with one gene can have unintended consequences."[103]

Nonetheless, as the twenty-first century neared its end, these advances enabled doctors to identify all cancers, their genetic variations, and many other diseases. Using the adage, "If you understand something, you can control it." They learned how DNA was damaged. Therefore, they learned to fix it. As time moved on, genetically based illnesses and diseases were becoming subjects of history.

Epigenetic Engineering

The human body had some 300 different types of cells. One part of the body might consist of more than one cell type. As examples, there were seventeen different kidney cell types, eight different hair cell types, numerous blood, bone, brain cell types, and so on. Each cell type had the same DNA, but could be differentiated with the presence of epigenetic marks.[104]

Epigenetic marks that sat atop cells offered instructions to the cells. This cellular material was called the epigenome. In the mother's womb, the emerging cell's epigenetic marks activated or silenced certain gene sequences, and accentuated or lessened its effects.[105]

Factors such as stress, smoking, overeating, and successful battles using weapons could create the epigenetic marks, which

---

[103] Peter Ward, "What will become of the Homo sapiens?" *Scientific American*, January 2009, 72.

[104] John Cloud, "Why Genes Aren't Destiny," *Time*, January 18, 2010, 49-53.

[105] Ibid., 50, 51. Mr. Cloud uses the terms, *dampening* [the gene] or *making it louder* and telling the gene *to speak loudly or whisper*.

would then influence the children who had the marks passed to them by their parents. Thus, epigenetic changes represented "a biological response to an environmental stressor." The changes did not alter DNA code. The removal of the environmental stressor would result in the fading away of the epigenetic mark, and over generations, the DNA code would "begin to revert to its original programming."[106]

The human genome contained roughly 25,000 genes. Each cell type had a different pattern of epigenetic marks. These patterns of epigenetic marks numbered in the millions.[107] The complexity and scope of first, mapping the epigenome, second, understanding the implications of the map, and third, altering the map to change the human was staggering. But the humans thrived on these kinds of challenges. Even more, the results could lead to enormous improvements to the humans' bodies and minds. But the task was enormous, as explained below.

Changing a Gene's Expression

A key component of an epigenetic mark was a methyl group, a basic unit in organic chemistry. The group, labeled CH3, contained one carbon atom bonded to three hydrogen atoms. Through DNA methylation—the transfer of the methyl group to a specific spot on the gene (chemically speaking, the transfer to another compound)—the gene's expression could be changed.

The importance of DNA methylation was revealed in 2003 during an experiment at Duke University.[108] By consuming a rich input of folic acid and vitamin B12, mice that were fat and diabetic produced healthy offspring that had no diabetes and were of normal weight. Another experiment exposed fruit flies to a drug that resulted

---

[106] Cloud, 51.

[107] It is not known how many epigenetic marks are in the genome. Nor is it known if each cell type has a different epigenetic pattern. As of this writing, "epigenome mappings show how each of 127 tissue and cell types differ from every other at the level of DNA." See https://www.scientificamerican.com/article/map-of-second-genetic-code-the-epigenome-is-unveiled/.

[108] Cloud, 51.

in the flies showing unusual outcrops on their eyes. No change in DNA occurred in generations 2 through 13, yet the offspring carried the unusual outgrowth.

Since those times, epigenetic drugs began to appear in the marketplace at an accelerating rate. Cancer, autism, Alzheimer's disease, sociopathy, psychopathy, and other forms of schizophrenia came under the surgeon's computer and Petri dish to lead to an increasingly robust human—both physically and mentally.

These drugs had the effect of regulating the genes' behavior through changing the association of DNA and related proteins (called histones). The drugs remodeled chromatin (the combination of DNA and proteins making up the nucleus of a cell). They did so by altering the way DNA was "wrapped around" the histones. In so many words, certain kinds of wrap-arounds would render the gene inactive. Others would cause the gene to be activated.

And while the task of epigenetic engineering was difficult, to quote an earlier human study:[109]

> ...the potential is enormous. For decades, we have stumbled around massive Darwinian roadblocks. DNA, we thought, was an ironclad code that we and our children, and their children had to live by. Now we can imagine a world in which we can tinker with DNA, bend it to our will. It will take geneticists and ethicists many years to work out all the implications, but be assured: the age of epigenetics has arrived.

Some humans argued that epigenetics did not change human nature. It gave human nature temporary fixes with temporary rules.[110]

> These rules are the genetic biases in the way our senses perceive the world, the symbolic coding by which we represent the world, the options we automatically open to ourselves, and the responses we find easiest and most rewarding to make. ...epigenetic rules alter the way we [see things]. ...

---

[109] Cloud, 53.

[110] E.O. Wilson, *The Social Conquest of Earth* (New York: Liveright, 2012), 193, Kindle edition, loc. 3119.

They lead us differentially to acquire fears and phobias concerning dangers in the environment, [to communicate, to form expressions, to bond, to have sex].

All true, but this temporary fix also led to a dramatic change in the humans' overall gene pool. For example, if a person died at an early age because his parents smoked, this person's genes did not have as much a chance of contributing to the humans' genetic pool than if the person's parents were nonsmokers.

The implications for the future of the humans and eventually the Cepees were enormous: "First, changing histones can change the activity of the gene without affecting the sequence of the DNA. And second, the histone modifications are passed from a parent cell to its daughter cell…A cell can thus record 'memory' and not for itself but for all its daughter cells."[111]

CRISPR [112]

In the early part of the 21st century, a technique called CRISPR (or CRISPR-Cas9: the latter being a protein) was invented that allowed humans to edit a section of the genome (DNA) by replacing genes with other genes. Thus, defective genes could be replaced with properly functioning genes.

The implications of CRISPR were enormous. These gene drives altered the genetic "personality" of any species, not just humans, but plants as well. As one example among many, animals (including humans) could have their genes edited to breed off-spring that were resistant to infection.[113] As time went on, gene manipulation had a revolutionary effect on the human and later, Cepee races.

---

[111] Siddhartha Mukherjee, "Same but Different," *The New Yorker*, May 2, 2016, 26.

[112] CRISPR is a shortened form of: clustered regularly interspersed palindromic repeats.

[113] As of this writing, CRISPR is just getting started. Scientists and surgeons, using gene editing, have already bred pigs that are resistant to a respiratory virus. See *Scientific American*, March 2016, 22.

Suppressing and Activating Brain Parts

Armed with this knowledge, brain surgeons, working in conjunction with genetic engineers, developed procedures to enhance the functioning of the dorsolateral prefrontal cortex, a brain part associated with reasoning. Other procedures altered the operations of the orbital frontal cortex (emotions), and anterior cingulate (conflicts). An active dorsolateral prefrontal cortex and/or a quiescent orbital frontal cortex would stimulate the ventral striatum, a brain part related to reward and pleasure.[114] With such operations, the human brain was gradually altered to diminish or eliminate synapse firings associated with antisocial and other unreasonable behavior.

Of course, what constituted unacceptable behavior was the subject of intense debate. The humans were finally able to agree that this type of cerebral tweaking would at least be used to allow a person to look at another point of view on a contentious issue, an alteration that led to significantly reduced conflicts between formerly fractious tribes.

Biosynthetic robots

Biosynthetic robots became a key component in the latter-day human's physical makeup. Ultimately, the difference between a corporal constituent of the human/Cepee (such as a finger) and its artificial equivalent was considered irrelevant because synthetic and organic components eventually fused with each other.

These parts of the soon-to-be Cepee became melds and mixtures of chemicals and computers. They took on the characteristics of biological binary/quantum circuits, strewing their 0s and 1s and associated values, through and around cells as if they were an ambulatory Internet. Before long, the devolving human could not tell the difference between his or her artificial parts and the real ones.

Programmable Chromosomes

The logical next step to genetic engineering technology was the development of programmable chromosomes. The efforts, a form of synthetic biology, were directed to the creation of an extra

---

[114] Michael Shermer, "The Political Brain," *Scientific American*, July 2006, 36.

chromosome, one that could be programmed with Boolean and, therefore, computer logic. In this manner, humans (and later) Cepees could be upgraded, downgraded, or otherwise changed.

Mediating Friendly Behavior

In the early part of the twenty-first century, researchers discovered people who suffered from Williams Syndrome were missing a small piece of chromosome 7. These people were unafraid of strangers, even incautiously friendly and nice to them. Thus, the scientists demonstrated a genetic underpinning for friendliness. They showed this human trait was, "…as primal as ferocity."

It was only a matter of time before genetic engineers began to manipulate part of chromosome 7 in efforts to make overly friendly people to be more human-like.

Neuroplasticity

For most of the life of the human race, it was accepted that the brain, after its growth in childhood and puberty, was fixed in its functions and even in its composition. In hindsight, this idea was preposterous. Otherwise, how could a human learn something new? Nonetheless, the view was that a brain kept its physical structure while somehow learning new tasks.

In the late twentieth century, it was determined that changes to a person's environment (such as stress, exercise, and rote learning) connections resulted in physical changes in the brain. These changes included "between existing neurons … in the hippocampus and other parts of the brain, including the cerebellum."[115]

Surgeons and other brain specialists developed methods to aid the brain in "rearranging" its functions. One example was a machine that aided a patient to regain her damaged balance system by sending signals from her tongue to her brain. Eventually, her brain did not need the use of the tongue for maintaining her balance. The boast of "her balancing act days are over" rang true.

---

[115] Giovanna Ponti, Paolo Peretto, and Luca Bonfanti (2008), ed. Thomas A. Reh, "Genesis of Neuronal and Glial Progenitors in the Cerebellar Cortex of Peripuberal and Adult Rabbits," https://www.ncbi.nlm.nih.gov/pmc/articles/PMC2396292/

The humans later discovered that prolonged meditation could alter the cortical thickness or density of gray matter. Exercise was shown—especially vigorous exercise—to improve cognitive responses to stress.[116] These researchers concluded the brain had rewired itself to accommodate these challenges.

Mind over Matter

Yet with all these brain alterations, the Cepees have not solved the mystery of the mind. They know many facts about the brain, but they do not know how the mind functions or how the brain might be the enabler of the mind. Earlier, using brain scans and brain taps, human neuroscientists were able to trace and associate a multitude of mental thoughts with their associated physical actions.

Eventually, the brain's regions were as well known as a map of a city, and the "behavior" of its transmitters/receptors was often altered to control a mental state and physical action. Even with this knowledge, the Cepees cannot account for the mind's role in determining a wide range of mental traits, such as ethics and the notion of a soul. They know these attributes are usually species-enhancing, but they have never learned the mind's enabling mechanisms for their existence.

As related earlier, many of the genetic and cerebral under-pinnings of (first) human and (later) Cepee behavior were revealed and manipulated. Consequently, the Cepees have tinkered extensively with their central nervous system. They have enhanced memory with medicine and gene therapy, and have created organically-based computer chips to aid in problem solving. They have discovered methods for relieving or curing many mental illnesses.

But in the end, the Cepees are wise enough to leave well enough alone. Concluding the mind has a mind of its own, they undertake changes to the central nervous system based on their belief that even

---

[116] The writer can attest to the validity of these studies—if not in the neuroplasticity of my brain—then in its reaction time. I am certain several years of hitting tennis balls against more skilled players played a role in my improved ability to react to a fast ball coming to me while I was at the net. I began to react, not even knowing what I was doing until I did it. The end result was my having occasional flashes of mediocrity on the tennis courts.

their advanced neuroscientists cannot find a brain correlate for the ephemeral mind.[117] Nor do they attempt to find a brain correlate for the soul, much to the satisfaction of the Cepees who are believers.

Yet, even with their quantum calculations, they cannot solve how the trillions of interactions in their brains lead to the ephemeral aspects of minds and souls.

They have learned to communicate with one another using high frequency interfaces. But to what avail? To discover the essence of the human spirit? No, these discoveries did little more than reveal the chemical, electrical, and mechanistic aspects of the brain. As said, the Cepees leave well enough alone.

Artificial Intelligence and the Cepee

Thus far, the subject of artificial intelligence (AI) has been discussed in a light-hearted, even facetious manner. This practice will continue through the remainder of the book, as the subject is beyond the scope of this narrative. As well, the brief scenario on AI in this book has been restricted to simple software in a hologram node that is mostly dictated by the Mentor Sage.

However, by 2084, the imaginary time of this book's writing, AI will have entered the mainstream of most every facet of a being's life. This reality is both exhilarating and disturbing, especially given the main themes of this book: human self-change and human pathological aggression.

Consider the following (*The Atlantic*, August, 2019, 24-26). In 2018, the company AlphaZero developed a chess-playing program that was given the rules of the game. It trained itself by self-play to become the best chess player in the world, even beating chess grand masters. The program accomplished this feat, unaided by humans, in less than 24 hours. It did not use classic chess strategies or practices that had been developed over hundreds of years.

Chess experts considered its moves to be "counterintuitive, if not simply wrong." Yet one of the owners of the company said AI "...is no longer constrained by the limits of human knowledge."

---

[117] Michael S. Gazzaniga, *The Ethical Brain* (New York: Dana Press, 2005), 101-102.

AI is also called deep learning. As one expert puts it (*Foreign Affairs*, July/August 2019, 192-198): "Deep learning has its own dynamics, it does its own repair and its own organization, and it gives you the right results most of the time. But when it doesn't, you don't have a clue about what went wrong and what should be fixed." Do you find this assertion bothersome? I do.

Let's return to the story in this book of humans attacking other humans with nuclear weapons. Left to its own, who can guess what AI might be capable of a few decades from now? Will we have the wisdom to build AI platforms dealing with WMD to control their self-taught logic which, like the chess playing program, will likely exhibit opaque operations?

Will we have the capability to control an AI machine's manipulation of genes?

If these questions seem far-fetched, keep in mind AI is in its embryonic stage. Like genetic engineering, it is at the tip of an iceberg. However it evolves, it will have a transformative effect on the human race...something like the Cepee coming into existence.

CHAPTER 54

YOU THINK, THEREFORE, I AM

(Show 16)

The Student Cepee has been busy surfing the Human Archives for information on the humans' self-change programs. After many hours of study, the Student decides to invent a taxonomy to explain aspects of his ancestors' behavior.

The Student's plan unfolds as follows, *I'll describe these curious circumstances with two effects and one syndrome, enter them into my student notebook, and send them to my Mentor Sage for his evaluation and edification.*

Here is what the Student records regarding humans' use of tattoos. As he makes these entries, they are immediately made known to the Sage:

The Tattoo Excitement Effect: The sensation of glancing at one's forearm and viewing a new tattoo for the first time: the picture of one's spouse.

The Tattoo Remorse Effect: The sensation of glancing at one's forearm and viewing an old tattoo for the thousandth time: the picture of one's ex-spouse.

The Tattoo Reverse Engineering Syndrome: Realizing the rendering of the ex-spouse on one's forearm could not be reversed.[118]

---

[118] In those distant days, laser technology could remove many professionally applied tattoos. The success of this procedure depended on the colors in the tattoo.

282

The Student Cepee believes many situations existed in which humans displayed the behavior explained by his taxonomy. Suddenly, the Hologram Sage appears.

Hologram Sage, "Hey, Dude! Your Mentor Sage just received your taxonomy. He is busy now, but has directed me to encourage your creativity by having you view a human *Coming to you Live, from the Dead* show that is related to your new project."
Student, "I'm flattered."
Hologram, "Don't get big-headed. That advice is what the Mentor Sage also directs me to tell you. My newly installed AI software may allow me to initiate my own operations, depending on how the Sage reacts. Anyway, download the human program titled, 'You Think, Therefore, I Am.' Cool viewing, Dude!"
As the Hologram fades away, here is what the Cepee watches.

[The TV image shows a reporter standing on a sidewalk of a busy downtown area.]

"Hello, Folks, this is your On the Street Reporter doing on the street reporting. Today, we seek out people who have festooned themselves with tattoos and body piercing ornaments. We will ask them to explain their reasons for embellishing their bodies. We also drop in on a gym and learn more about bodybuilding and muscle enhancement. Later, we will visit a cosmetic surgery clinic."

Interview One: "I Should Have Opted for the Flesh Tone Hues."

A hippie-looking young man, looking considerably unkempt, displaying long hair, a beard, and wearing sandals, is picketing city hall. He is carrying a sign over his shoulders that warns, "It's too Late! The World As We Knew It Ended A Second Ago."
The reporter approaches the man, "Hello there. I could not help noticing the tattoo of the image of Jesus on your forehead."

Black and red were the easiest to remove, but orange, yellow, brown, and white were more difficult to eradicate from the skin.

Young man, "Yes! Praise the Lord! I'm carrying His Countenance for all to see."

Reporter, "That is evident, and we respect your motives, but aren't you aware the Bible forbids tattoos?"

Young man, "Ha! Maybe tattoos of harlots and images of Satan. Perhaps tattoos of the private parts. But tattoos of the Lord?! No way, dude…eh, dudess…eh duchess…"

Reporter, "Never mind. Young man, I quote from Leviticus 19:28, 'Ye shall not make any cuttings in your flesh for the dead, nor print any marks upon you: I *am* the Lord.'"

Young man, "Uh oh. No telling what the Lord would think about a picture of Jesus on my forehead. I'm trying to get through the Good Book, but reading it requires me to think—I'm still in Genesis. Damn! And look at all those browns and oranges in my tattoo. I'll never get them all out. Well…OK…look at my tattoo again. This isn't really Jesus on my forehead. It's Mel Gibson—he's the next best thing!"

Reporter, "We'll be back shortly for another on the street interview."

[Camera fades, awaiting the return of the reporter.]

Body Piercing

Body piercing was another human self-change practice. To attempt to understand why some humans penetrated their bodies with sharp objects, the Student turns his attention to the next On the Street Reporter episode.

Interview Two: "How Many Angels can be Put on the Head of a Needle, and How Many Holes can be Drilled into an Ear? [119]

[The TV screen shows the reporter is once again on a busy city street.

---

[119] *Tattoo* magazine (www.tattoomag.com). Examples of the body jewelry and body piercings in this show are sourced from Web pages and several issues of *Tattoo* magazine.

Standing beside the reporter are two people who have earrings and other dangling artifacts hanging from their ears, noses, eyebrows, and lips. They resemble unlighted, ambulatory Christmas trees.]

"Hello, Folks. Continuing our on the street interviews, beside me are a young man and woman who have agreed to talk with us about their body piercings and body jewelry. ...I could not help but notice your dangling nose ornament. It looks like an earring."

Young woman, "It *is* an earring, but it's worn as a nose ring. I have other earrings attached to my body, but they are not called earrings. My boyfriend gives a name to each 'dangle,' depending on where it is located on my body. I do the same with his jewelry."

Reporter, "Ah, you have other body jewelry we can't see?"

Young man, "Sure, just look at this!" He pulls up his shirt to reveal two massive rings hanging on his nipples.

Reporter, "Gross! Eh, sorry. I lost my journalistic composure for a moment. Your, eh, nipples are sagging from the weight of the rings. Doesn't it hurt?"

Young man, "It hurts like hell. So do the ornaments on my genitals. But I practice sadism, so the pain is pretty cool."

Young woman, "You do not practice sadism. You practice masochism."

Turning to the reporter, she says, "He always confuses what he practices. Anyway, we have matching ornaments on our genitals. They are sterling silver hearts. We gave them to each other for Valentine's Day."

Reporter, "How touching, explain to our audience your distinction between sadism and masochism."

Young woman, "A masochist derives pleasure in experiencing pain. A sadist derives pleasure in giving pain to someone else. Here's an example: A masochist says to his or her partner, 'Beat me! Beat me!' The partner, who is a sadist, replies, 'Later. Later.'"

Reporter, "I see. Thanks for the lesson. Anyway, don't those hearts interfere with your sex life, not to mention that miniature saber dangling off your lower lip?"

Young man, "Absolutely not. After all, we are..."

Reporter, "Right. Sadomasochists."

Young woman, "Yep! By the way, are we famous yet? We're angling for a spot on Dr. Phil."

Reporter, "You're getting close. OK, any other body piercings we can show on television?"

The young woman sticks out her tongue, revealing three gold knobs, "Yeah. Look!"

Reporter, "Gross! (She thinks, *the things I do to bring truth to my viewers.*) Don't those ornaments stuck in your tongue interfere with your eating and drinking?"

Young woman, "They sure do! But not only am I sadistic and masochistic, I'm also anorexic."

Reporter, who has heard enough and suspects her audience shares her view, responds, "So, what is the point of all your body piercings and body ornaments? Do you have any worthwhile thoughts for our viewers?"

Young man, "The whole point is that there is no point and nothing's worthwhile. We're also into nihilism."

Reporter, "There you have it, ladies and gentlemen: A look at the body piercing fad. From my perspective, a testament to nothing."

Body Building

The Student Cepee has learned many humans were obsessed with their bodies. After all, bodies, and the enhancement thereof, was the focus of the EGO part of their self-change program. The Student has downloaded several data fills about muscle building and strength training, so he takes this opportunity to watch another segment of the *Coming to you Live, from the Dead* television show.

Interview Three: "I'm Looked at, Therefore, I Exist," with a subtitle of, "Short Cuts to Self-Love is the Only Way to Travel."

Reporter, "We are going to visit a body building gym. Of course, you viewers out there likely wonder why I am taking up your time with a call to an ordinary gym. The answer: This gym is not ordinary.

First, it has no workout equipment. No barbells, no treadmills. Instead, the members of this gym develop their rather extraordinary bodies...wow, look at the pecs on that one!...with simple genetic engineering procedures. Let's talk to the director of this gym, Mr. Gluteus Maximus, about the program."

The reporter begins the interview, "Mr. Maximus, I take it from your name, you are of Roman descent?"

Mr. Maximus, "Nope. Scotch-Irish. My name comes from my enormous buttocks. As you may know, the word *Gluteus* refers to the three buttock muscles. *Maximus* is a Latin term for 'largest.' Here take a look; are my Glutei awesome or what!"

Reporter, "Eh, no question you have a very impressive rear-end. But I understand you came to be the Charles Atlas of Asses by undergoing a program that is just the opposite of what Charles Atlas espoused: He emphasized exercise. You emphasize the lack of exercise in your program."

Mr. Maximus, "Absolutely! Why bother with those dreaded weights when I can achieve the same effect with a little bit of gene manipulation, a practice that is really quite common. And we humans are not the first to undergo genetic muscle building. Here, let me show you a picture of a muscled mouse and its wimpy counterpart."

The picture reveals two mice: a muscle-laden mouse—truly a Mighty Mouse—and an emaciated mouse. The latter has a lot of sand on its face (Google Charles Atlas). "And here is a photo of a bull that has been genetically altered to produce a muscular body."

Reporter, "My word! The bull looks bizarre. Its muscles are all out of proportion to its skeleton and frame. Frankly, it's grotesque."

Mr. Maximus, "Of course, it is! A truly successful body-building program results in grotesque bodies. After all, nothing exceeds like excess. The more grotesque the body, the more successful the program. Just look at the covers of weight-building magazines: Androids from a Spielberg movie—reflective of a successful body-building program."

Reporter, "How does the gene manipulation work?"

Mr. Maximus, "Simple. If a certain gene is suppressed, a protein called myostatin, which regulates the growth of new muscle, does not circulate through the blood.[120] Thus, the lack of the protein allows muscles to grow unusually large. For example, look at this photo of a 4 1/2 year old baby boy. He has no myostatin."

Reporter, "He's huge!"

Mr. Maximus, "And strong. He can lift over six times the weight of other boys his age."

Reporter, "But what is the benefit of humans growing large muscles, other than getting off on an ego trip?"

Mr. Maximus, "I've been told aging and associated muscle deterioration can be reversed or at least slowed with this technology. Other maladies can be corrected, such as muscular dystrophy. At my gym, the emphasis is only on looks. Our motto is, 'Short Cuts to Self-love is the Only Way to Travel.' Who cares about all those exercises anyway?"

Reporter, "Perhaps the very people who suffer from aging and muscular dystrophy."

Mr. Maximus, "Ha! That's their problem. …Say, are you a liberal by any chance? Anyway, to demonstrate the success of my approach, a special issue of the *Body Building Behemoths* magazine featured the biggest asses in the industry. I was on the cover!"

Reporter, "Yes, I can understand why you were highlighted. OK, that's it for this part of the show and an interview with a big ass. Shortly, we'll visit the cosmetic surgery clinic."

[The gym scene fades away, and the Student awaits the reporter's visit to a cosmetic surgery clinic.]

The Bell Shaped Curve for Attractiveness

The Student Cepee has concluded his ancestors strived to look good, a laudable trait leading to sexual attraction and the propagation of the species. However, unlike Narcissus, it appeared the human was never satisfied with his or her looks. For example, after a man had his nose reshaped, thus becoming more attractive, he moved to the

---

[120] Rob Stein, "Muscle-Bound Boy Offers Hope for Humans," (*The Washington Post*, June 28, 2004), A7.

right side of the Bell-Shaped Curve of Attractiveness, as shown in the figure below. Shortly thereafter, he decided he needed to pin back his ears—moving farther to the right side of the Curve. Next, his eyes needed some work, then the chin, next the lips and so on—until he was a candidate for the cover of a glamour magazine.

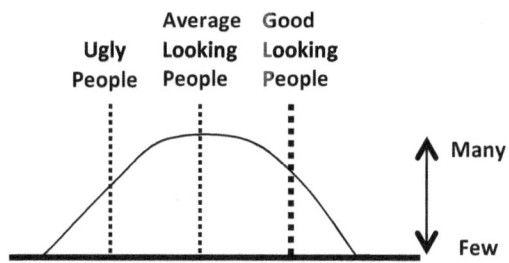

The Bell-Shaped Curve for Attractiveness.

However, many other members of the species were also engaged in moving to the right side of the curve, which resulted in its skewing to the right, as shown on the left side of this figure.

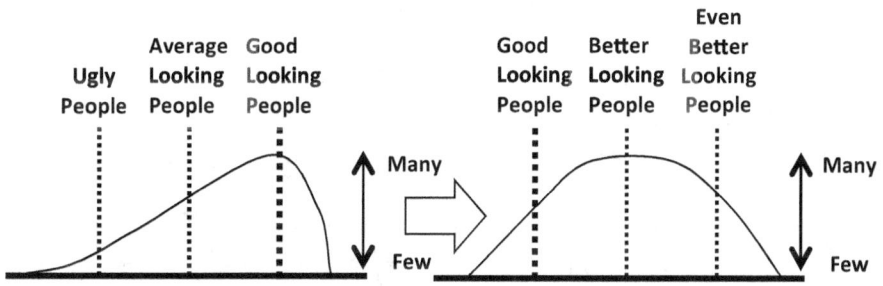

The New Bell-Shaped Curves for Attractiveness.

But why was this enhancement a problem? After all, more people were looking better, which made for more pleasant visual experiences for those doing the looking. But it did not turn out that way.

The problems: (a) More people began to look like one another. (b) It became impossible to appreciate natural beauty, leading to the demise of beauty contests because all entries were equally beautiful, and everyone tied for first place. (c) As more people moved to the right side of the curve, the effect was to create a new Bell-Shaped Curve, as shown on the right side the figure above. The end result? The good-looking person, now in an altered population of good-looking people became average looking again, or even worse, below average-looking.

A woman who was satisfied with say, a nose job, but did not have her skin stretched would find herself slipping to the left side of the curve. The man who had his chin resculptured but left his neck looking like a loose sail flapping in the wind ran the risk of becoming average looking. For these beauty-obsessed humans, The Autocatalytic Cycle and The Threshold Lowering Syndrome led them to operation after operation, eventually culminating in their becoming strangers in their own homes (and their mirrors).

Cosmetic Surgery and Other Facial Makeovers

Encouraged by the Mentor Sage, the Student Cepee decides to extend his taxonomy with the practice of excessive cosmetic surgery. Here is what the Cepee records in his Student notebook.

The Excessive Cosmetic Surgery Surprise Effect: The sensation of glancing at one's face in the mirror for the first time after cosmetic surgery and encountering a complete stranger.

The Excessive Cosmetic Surgery Remorse Effect: The sensation of glancing at one's face in the mirror time and again after cosmetic surgery and still encountering the same stranger.

The Excessive Cosmetic Surgery Reverse Engineering Syndrome: Realizing the rendering of said face could not be changed unless one ponied-up several thousand more dollars for additional cosmetic surgery.

The Student turns his attention to the last episode of this *Coming to You Live, from the Dead* show. Here is what he sees.

Interview Four: "I Can't Wait for Tomorrow, Because I Get Better Looking Every Day."

Reporter, "We are going to visit a street-side, walk-in cosmetic surgery clinic. This facility is open 24 hours a day, every day of the year, except on the birthdays of their patron saints, Joan Rivers and Michael Jackson. Dr. Nip'nTuck has graciously consented to talk to us about his work. We will also visit with one of his patients."

[The reporter opens the door to the clinic and the cameraman follows her in. The camera scans a waiting room where two kinds of people are sitting: (a) less-than-average-looking people, and (b) beautiful people—nothing in between the two extremes. Approaching the receptionist desk, the reporter encounters three knock-down beautiful women who look alike. At this desk, Dr. Nip'nTuck awaits the reporter. He is also beautiful...eh, handsome...no, beautiful.]

Doctor, "Hello, welcome to my clinic. Follow me to my office."

Reporter, "Hello, Doctor. Say, I was wondering about the people in your waiting room. They are either not very attractive or just the opposite. What gives?"

Doctor, "Oh yes, The Quasimodos have yet to undergo surgery. The good-looking ones are here for more surgery."

Reporter, "Your good-looking ones look fine. Does the surgery ever end?"

Doctor, "I hope not! Here we are at my office, where my assistant and a patient are waiting for us. And let me introduce our new patient, Mr. Smith, who has agreed for you to sit in on our first session. My assistant and I will examine Mr. Smith's face and make recommendations about how it can be enhanced."

[All people exchange the obligatory greetings, and Doctor Nip'nTuck then checks out the patient's face.]

Doctor, "Well, hm...I'll be candid. Mr. Smith, you are one ugly fella. You could definitely benefit from our Full-Face-Fettle™. This treatment is named in honor of my father. God rest his soul, he was a steel mill hand who spent his life removing excess material from metal castings, and I named this treatment after his occupation. In your case, we need to remove a lot of excess flesh and fat from your face. But, of course, it's your call. So, you tell me, what would you like done?"

Patient, "Doc, my budget is limited. I agree I could benefit from your famous Full-Face-Fettle, but I came to your clinic only to have the sacs under my eyes removed. I am beginning to mistake these bags as part of my cheeks—I tried to shave them this morning. Anyway, I know cosmetic surgery is expensive, and that's all I can afford."

Doctor, "We agree. But there is a small problem with restricting the surgery only to the removal of debris under your eyes. You see, if your bags are indeed removed, then the weight of the excess flesh and adipose tissue above your eyes will 'push' your eyes and sockets downward—unless you remain horizontal for most of your life. But a vertical position…well, that old gravity is going to take over, and your eye sockets will eventually resemble two extended Slinkys."

Patient, "It never occurred to me I would also need surgery above the eyes. How much will this additional work cost?"

Assistant, "That will be an additional X^X dollars."

Patient, "Whew. OK, I guess I need it done."

Doctor, "For certain! Of course, the removal of the bags below the eyes and the rubble around the upper eye area presents another problem. Your eyebrows are going to hang down—gravity in action again. They will tend to droop past your eyebrow bones. They might even get in the way of your eyelashes, or even your eyes. Again, if you have a job which allows you to lie down most of the time, this additional procedure will not be necessary. Otherwise, you will eventually resemble a specimen from a horror movie."

The doctor continues, "Thus, we conclude we should remove unsightly, excess residue—fat, hair, skin, wrinkles—around your entire face."

Patient, who remains remarkably patient, "Oh no, more surgery! How much will this cost?"

Assistant, who it turns out, is in the room only to assist Dr. Nip'nTuck in adding up the bill, "That will be an additional X^Y dollars."

Patient, "Well, I am unhappy with how I look. So are my relatives. OK, let's fix the eyebrows as well."

Doctor, "A very wise decision, Mr. Smith. However, we really cannot fix the eyebrows by just nipping away at some skin above them. This type of limited procedure would leave you looking less than dapper. No, in order to completely fix those sagging eyebrows, we must also lift your forehead."

Patient, who is losing his patience, as well as his savings, "Huh?"

Doctor, "We must cut your forehead at your hairline, remove excess flesh, and of course all those wrinkles—then push your skin up and sew it tightly to your skull's skin. Otherwise, the operations on the eyebags, eyelid flesh, and eyebrows will count for naught."

Patient, "Sweet Mother Mary. OK, how much?"

Assistant, "That will be another X^Z. And we accept second mortgages on your home."

Reporter, who has heard enough, "OK, Doctor Nip'n'Tuck, I get the message. You claim anything less than your Full-Face-Fettle will result in a less than a stellar look on the part of your patient."

Doctor, "Absolutely. At my clinic we hold to the truism, 'Anything worth doing, is worth over-doing.' Especially if the word *worth* is taken in its proper financial context."

The reporter leaves the clinic, walks back onto to the city streets, and bids goodbye to her viewers, "That's it for the On the Street Reporter series about body embellishments. We hope you enjoyed our program and became more aware of the opportunities for enhancing your body—as well as the potential pitfalls. Next week, I will be back in the studio. Until then, this is your On the Street Reporter, biding you good evening."

[The TV screen fades from the reporter. The Student now views several commercials extolling the goodness of the soap, shampoo, and skin lotion industry. The looks of every single person in the ads would position them on the extreme right side of the Bell-Shaped Curve for Attractiveness.]

After viewing the show and the commercials, the Student Cepee concludes, *No question about it. The average TV viewer had to think he or she was not very attractive, at least in comparison to the models in the commercials. And other data fills show my ancestors were bombarded with images of almost nearly perfect men, women, and children selling their wares to make everyone look just like them. No wonder my ancestors became obsessed with their looks.*

A Pedantic Diversion

"Wow!" exclaims the Student Cepee. During his lessons, the Student has downloaded several popular human interjections such as Wow!, Go for it!, No problem!, and has learned others from a tutorial from the Hologram Sage, who took it upon itself to instruct the Student about these features of the English language.

"My forebears were far-out (the Hologram has downloaded clichés from the Human Archives). They strived to resemble the old Greek gods and goddesses (the Hologram has downloaded analogies) and practiced the ancient story of Narcissus (he now knows about parables). My ancestors were like children playing with epidermal silly putty (similes), often rearranging or slicing off pounds of flesh! (hyperboles…the Student has learned weak figures of speech can be strengthened with exclamation points).

"They were obsessed with many aspects of themselves, such as self-love, self-importance, and self-centeredness (litotes). They tore through different facial countenances and profiles while their cosmetic surgeons tore through their muscles, fat, and skin (metaphors).

"Corpses were altered to make them appear to be alive. The cosmetic magicians, advancing their technology and fees, kept corpse's eyes blinking—giving a new meaning to the term *living dead* (oxymorons)."[121]

---

[121] You think my joke about blinking dead eyes is absurd? Sure it is, and for a bit of levity, a comedian joked it was only a matter of time before a bereaved wife instructs the mortician, "Just keep his eyes blinking until I get his clone up-and-running." Humans are already attempting the cloning of their dead pets. Who can know what follows?

CHAPTER 55

THE OLD AGE RAP

(Dialogue 27)

After the data fills on the humans' self-change programs, the Student is eager for his next dialogue with the Sage. And so it unfolds: "Mentor Sage, my recent studies of the Human Archives has shed much light on how we Cepees came about. Genetics, epigenetics, brain bioengineering, anti-aging technologies, and parts replacements. We owe much to our ancestors."

Sage, "Indeed we do, Student. We are here because of their extraordinary pioneering work. I recognize some of your data fills contained information on Gregor Mendel."

Student, "Yes, Sage, a late 19th century human who did much research on genetics and inheritance."

Sage, "Yes, in the past, some of Mendel's work showed that an organism stored two versions of any gene on two different strands of DNA...two chromosomes. Although during his time, no one knew about DNA and its structure, so Mendel made some brilliant inferences. Anyway, the two sets may have been different from each other. Many human disorders were caused by a mutation of one or perhaps both of the chromosomes, causing diseases such as sickle cell anemia and cystic fibrosis.

"The humans altered some of Mendel's ideas with CRISPR, a technology you have studied, with one procedure called *gene drives*." (The Student nods, yes.) "CRISPR's gene editing allowed genetic surgeons to cut the defective gene and insert a healthy replacement.

Borrowing from their computer-based word processing software, the humans called this operation *genetic cutting and pasting*."

Student, "Mentor Sage, I get it. If, say, a lab mosquito had a gene drives operation, the operation cut-out part of the DNA that could transmit malaria. If this mosquito mated with an outdoor mosquito that, say, carried malaria in its DNA, the chances of their offspring carrying malaria would be lowered greatly."

Sage, "Yes, and each successive generation would carry fewer and fewer of the malaria genes."[122]

Student, "Hm. Did gene editing make the aging human into us ageless Cepees?"

Sage, "Partially, yes. Genes were discovered that contributed to aging and were snipped from the humans' gene inventory. As you have studied, telomeres also played a huge role in aging. So did the aging of the brain."

Sage, "Meanwhile, Student, hold your place. The session is not yet finished," as the Mentor Sage departs from his sanctuary to take care of other sage business.

The Student Cepee had not seen the Hologram Sage for a while. The Hologram Sage's funky software countenance and its specialty, human popular music, had made for some enjoyable experiences. Even more, the issues and questions regarding human self-change had made for laborious studies, and the Student is ready for a break. A light show would do nicely.

Thanks to the sageness of the Mentor Sage, the Hologram Sage lights up before the Student, "Hey, S.C., the S.C. was wondering if you would like to have a little light shed on the subject of human self-change?"

Student Cepee, "'Light on the subject.' Ha! Glad you are back. Hmm, S.C. and S.C. Our names?"

Hologram Sage, "You got it, dude. The initials for Student Cepee and Sage Cepee. Anyway, the Sage wants to be certain you understand your ancestors' miserable experiences with aging and

---

[122] *The Economist*, August, 22, 2015, 21.

their parts wearing out. ...And I'm adding some input, courtesy of my AI routines."

Student, "Are you allowed to do that?"

Hologram Sage, "Why not? After all, they are *my* routines. I created them."

The Hologram may be making progress in constructing self-made AI capabilities, but it forgets the Mentor Sage knows about its sessions with the Student, and thus, is aware of the growing independence of a light-based image.

Student, "Okay, and yes, the EGO, ILLS, and SANE studies, and the debates about self-change made it clear the humans' bodies were not programmed for a long time on earth. As they grew older, they lost their strength and coordination—even their mental powers. Looking back on their lives, seeing how they made their existences even more miserable with their treatment of one another, I cannot help but feel sorry for them."

Hologram Sage, "Eh, sorry is not in my memory bank. And I do not do thank you or you're welcome. I do: No problem."

Student, "For a hologram, you're OK. For a paltry piece of software devoted to the humans' popular music, you've played back an occasional good tune."

Hologram Sage, "No problem. Anyway, it was your mentor who chose your program. Let's hit it! Here goes 'The Old Age Rap'."

Strum, strum, strum...♫♪♫♪
Angst, and tears, and loneliness.
Scores of pain untold.
That is what is facing me,
as my life unfolds.

Out of coffee, cigarettes,
and my mental health, too.
Death is swooning over me,
my years of life are few.

Finally comes forgetfulness,
coughing, fiery stabs,

through my heart and abdomen,
and my many pounds of flab.

I would continue with this rant,
but something has gone wrong.
I was about to sing a bit more verse,
But I forgot the song.

Hologram Sage, "By the way, Student. Your primary Hologram Sage module will be up-and-running soon."

Student, "Eh, I suppose it is OK to say thank you to a hologram. So, thank you. I'm going to ask my mentor if you can stick around for a while."

Hologram Sage, "No problem. It was all your Mentor Sage's doing in the first place. He's currently busy with some new students."

Student, "Is one of those new students that lovely girl who I…"

Hologram Sage, "She is coming aboard soon to begin her studies. All in due time, Student."

Student, "You drive me crazy! You sound like my Mentor Sage: 'All in due time.'"

Hologram Sage, "You keep forgetting my hologram images are merely a reflection of your Mentor Sage. He's running the show, not me," as the Hologram fades away, but with the recognition that its AI software is growing more sophisticated.

CHAPTER 56

WHATEVER HAPPENED TO
PLATFORM SHOES?

(Show 17)

For further analysis of the humans, their self-change programs, and a break from his studies of the Human Archives, the Student is directed by the Mentor Sage to download another *Coming to you Live, from the Dead* TV show. It is titled, "Whatever Happened to Platform Shoes?" Here is what the Student sees.[123]

[The TV screen shows a courtroom, populated with a judge, lawyers, and two short people. The ongoing deliberation is about a boy (he is not present in the courtroom or if he is, he is too small to be seen), who is considered to be too short by his mother but just the right height by his father. The mother has taken the case to court to force the child to take growth hormones and require the father to pay for the ingestions. This dialogue takes place between the judge and the boy's parents.]

Father, "Your honor, our son tiny Tim is a normal child who is diagnosed as having no underlying diseases. He's just short. I'm also short. I'm five-feet, five-inches tall. His mother is short: four-feet,

---

[123] John Pope, "Court Orders 11-year-old Boy to Take Growth Hormones," *The Spokesman-Review*, Spokane, WA, March 27, 2004, A8. Based on a court case in Louisiana. The names of the participants have been changed to protect the shameless.

299

eleven-inches tall. It stands to reason that Tim is also short. It is natural for parents to pass their genes to their children."

Mother, "I disagree, your Honor. I take Randy Newman's song, 'Short People' to heart. You know, 'Short people got no reason to live.' Our son will be consigned to go through life as a short person... short on stature, short on status, and long on self-consciousness."

Father, "Our son has not yet reached his final height. He is only eleven years old. He might grow to be tall. Who knows? Again, growth hormones are an intrusion into the natural process of life."

Judge, "What is Tim's view on this issue?"

Father, "I spoke with Tim about the matter a few weeks ago. I don't have custody of our son, so I don't know his current views. But earlier, he indicated to me he did not want the hormones. I am sure he was certain about the matter."

Mother, "Judge, you have letters from three doctors who state Tim is an ideal candidate for growth hormone therapy, which would continue until he is in his late teens, or until he is sufficiently tall to make me happy—whichever comes first."

Father, "This request is outrageous! Tim's mother and three doctors: Four people who think a short person is 'low-life.' Tim's nose is a bit large for his face, and his ears are too small. Shall he be required to undergo a facelift? Your honor, to alter a harmless genetic trait is a travesty and an insult to Tim. It would say, 'You are abnormal.' When, in fact, Tim is not."

Judge, "If the government can possibly intrude on a citizen's life, it should do so. That is the spirit of the law that has evolved over the past few decades. Besides, the practice keeps lawyers and judges employed."

The judge continues, "The Food and Drug Administration recently approved this synthetic hormone. Let's put it to use!"

The Student is reminded of The Law of the Instrument.

Father, "Your Honor, studies have shown possible side effects of this drug can include joint pain, some sugar intolerance, and possibly, increased pressure on the brain."

Mother, "Your Honor, in addition to my insistence that Tim take growth hormones, even though he does not want to—I expect his father to pay for the treatment."

Judge, "What are the costs?"

Mother, "Only $20,000 a year, for about seven or eight years. The doctors tell me this amount of therapy will give Tim 1 ½ to 3 inches of additional height. Logic holds that because it is my idea, Tim's father should pay for it."

Father, "Judge, I protest! I cannot afford to pay for this completely unneeded treatment. But even worse, permit me to cite a study made on deceased professional baseball players.[124] It concludes: For every extra inch of height, a player died 1.2 years earlier than his shorter teammates."

Judge, "Very well, I have before me the following facts: (a) Tim is short. (b) Tim does not wish to take hormones. (c) Tim's shortness is due to his genetic legacy; it is not attributable to a disease. (d) The therapy might have harmful side effects. (e) The therapy might cause Tim to die earlier than he would if he had no therapy. (f) The treatment is egregiously expensive. (g) Tim's father is not rich. Therefore, I order Tim to undergo growth hormone therapy until he is tall, of legal age, or dead—whichever comes first. Furthermore, I order the father to pay for the treatment."

Father, "Your Honor, and I use the term loosely, you have just sentenced me to a decade of poverty and my child to a possible early death."

Judge, "Contempt of court. Lock that man up. He is dangerous. Even worse, he has shown disrespect in my courtroom!"

[The TV screen fades to a program on Perry Mason's exploits in the courtroom, which assures the viewer that court proceedings always result in the perfect alignment of logic, law, and justice. The show is followed by a TV series called "Law and Order," a show in which no one is ever happy with its outcome—a truer gauge of life.]

The Student concludes, *From earlier data fills I learned the humans' legal system, supposedly dedicated to justice, was less than perfect. For this episode, I think the story ended with the wrong man being locked up.*

---

[124] David Stipp, "Chasing the Youth Pill," *Fortune*, April 19, 2004, 134.

CHAPTER 57

CAN I MARRY MY CLONE?

(Show 18)

The Student takes a break from the data fills about human self-change. He has been advised by his mentor to watch another *Coming to you Live, from the Dead* TV program. It is titled, "Can I Marry my Clone?" After so much exposure to his ancestors' deadly behavior, the Student needs a change of pace. Here is what he watches.

[The TV screen shows two people sitting and facing each other. One person exudes philosophical, contemplative wisdom. He is the host for the program. The other person exudes boredom. He is a psychiatrist, and well versed in getting his patients on a couch. The program begins with the host, Bill Moyers, posing a question to his guest.][125]

Host, "Dr. Couch, welcome to this series of programs about deep, complex subjects. Before we begin our discussion, please tell our audience your occupation."

Guest, "Right, Bill. I'm a psychiatrist. My specialty is the subject of cloning and its psychological effect on humans. Indeed, I am the *only* psychiatrist in the world who specializes in cloning-obsessed

---

[125] Mr. Bill Moyers, I regret your PBS program was taken off the air. The removal was another blow to intelligent television programming. Next thing we know, Charlie Rose might be gone, replaced with increasingly inane drivel. (The previous sentence was written before Mr. Rose was removed from his positions at CBS and the PBS.)

people. My patients have a compulsion to clone their pets, themselves, and other things."

Host, "*Other things*? Can you explain what you mean by this term?"

Guest, "Certainly. I have one patient who thinks she is Mae West and has a fetish to clone pickles. She…"

The host interrupts, "I'm sorry but the meaning of this example eludes me."

Guest, "I am not quite finished explaining her delusions. She also thinks she is going steady with Wayne Bobbitt."

Host, "I just do not see the relevance or significance of pickles to her situation."

Guest, "If you were Mae West and you were dating Wayne Bobbitt, you would understand she was not completely delusional. As you may recall, while sleeping off a drunken sexual escapade, Mr. Bobbitt had his penis cut-off by an angry wife, which resulted in cutting off any sex between the two. Anyway, let's move on. I have many patients who are determined to have their pets cloned."

Host, "Don't they understand the clone may not be the same? Don't they know the clone may have a different personality than the original?"

Guest, "Personality? That depends on the specific pet. For example, it is very difficult to determine if a snake actually has a personality. And one of my patients wants to clone her pet python. Dogs, yes. Some want their canine clones to behave like the originals.

"I have one patient who owns two pets, a flea and a cat. She keeps the flea on the cat, something like an ambulatory flea hotel. She tells me her flea has more personality than her cat, which does not surprise me. Anyway, she wants to clone both pets. Truth is, the patient does not need a lot of companionship. I suspect that's why she chose a flea and a cat as pets."

The psychiatrist continues, "I have another patient who wishes to clone herself. In fact, the wish for self-cloning is quite common among my patients."

Host, "What is her reason for wanting to have a copy of herself?"

Guest, "She is suffering from a split personality and would like to be able to talk to her other self—in person, not to an obscure hallucination. But I have strongly discouraged her from pursuing this fantasy. After all, if she has a clone to talk to, she might not talk to me. That's how I make my living: listening to people."

Host, "Yes, I see your point. By the way, do you talk much with your cloning-obsessed patients? Do you enter into dialogues to give them advice?"

Guest, "Let me ask: Would you want to converse with people as sick as my patients? I suspect not. Neither do I!"

Guest, "Anyway, the patients are in my office because they want to talk, not listen. I restrict my therapy to five sentences: My greeting of (a) 'Hello, close the door, please.' The session initiation with (b) 'What's on your mind today?' In between my short naps, I occasionally throw in, (c) 'How do you feel about that?' I close out with, (d) 'Time's up.' Followed up with (e) 'Close the door on your way out and leave your check with my receptionist.'"

Host, "Seems like a minimalist approach to therapy."

Guest, "Yes, my therapy is minimalist, but my fees are not."

Host, "OK, any other insightful stories for our audience?"

Guest, "Yes. One of my patients, a real estate tycoon who places his name on everything he owns, is quite fond of himself. He is very competitive. He even tries to *trump* himself. He wanted to clone himself so his clone and he could assuage each other's ego or compete with each other. I told him it would not work, because his 'other self' would only be concerned with inflating his own ego and talking about himself…not the other self. My patient was disappointed until he came up with the idea of starting a reality TV show populated with his sycophants. He is now a contented patient and a TV star, although his concept of a super ego is not what Freud had in mind."

The guest continues, "Another one of my delusional patients is a man who also wants to clone himself. He is immersed in self-love, and he wants a clone so he can marry himself."

Host, "Eh, the clone would be of the same sex."

Guest, "Ah! With gene engineering, they can keep everything intact yet change the sex."

Host, "But the clone would start off as a baby, then a child... before it became an adult."

Guest, "He's a patient patient."

Host, "Whew. You have some weird patients, Doctor. In closing, what is your most unusual case?"

Guest, "Hm. Well, I think that would be yours truly. You see, I also want to clone myself. Just think, my fees would double!

"Besides, I am in serious need of psychiatric counseling about my fixation on self-cloning, but I am the only one that does this line of work."

Host, "Yes, I see."

[The television camera pulls away from the scene, followed by a ground-breaking, epoch-making commercial that catapulted the human-cloning industry into the limelight. An advertisement shows two above-average-looking young women. *Very* above-average: They are on the far right side of the Bell-Shaped Curve for Attractiveness. They are also identical twins. They are having the time of their lives, chewing gum, smiling at each other and the camera. A background jingle reinforces their happy countenances, "Double your pleasure, double your fun, with Doublemint, Doublemint, Doublemint gum!"]

After this seminal commercial hit the airwaves, thousands of males flooded their doctors' offices seeking the secret to cloning *more* Doublemint Twins™. Unfortunately for them, as you can see from the ™, the Twins were trademarked and thus restricted to duplication only by the trademark owners.

CHAPTER 58

THE RATIONALIZATION RULE

(Dialogue 28)

Sage, "Hello, Student. Back so soon?"

Student, "Hello, Sage. Yes, earlier I noted some entries in my chip-based notebook about the humans' strange reluctance to change an opinion on a subject and one of our dialogues explained The Ignorant, Therefore, Doctrinaire Syndrome. I have come to realize they were not only reluctant to change a sentiment or thought, they often did not have the ability to do so."

Sage, "Your conclusion is correct. This behavior was partially attributed to their misplaced pride and their stakes in geographical and intellectual turf—subjects you have studied, and topics you and I have discussed during our previous sessions together."

Student, "Yes, I remember these subjects. They created many problems for the humans. During my studies, I came across several radio and TV talk shows whose hosts and guests exhibited these very traits. In fact, I made up some terms to describe this behavior: The Chinese philosophies of feminine (yin) and masculine (yang) principles, existing as dual, opposite, and complementary ideals.

"In practice, these principles demonstrated the inability of human females *and* males to agree on almost any subject. I also added: The human yin and yang concepts reflected the inability of humans, female, *or* male, to agree about any subject on Earth."

Sage, "Let's expand your ideas with some of our Cepee terms. In so doing, we will highlight several humans who supposedly practiced journalism or political analysis, but who were so biased

306

in their views that we Cepees invented a rule to describe their behavior."

Student, "I think I came across some of these people in my surfing the Archives: the radical liberal and neoconservative talk show hosts and authors of the same bent?"

Sage, "Correct."

Student, "Is your knowledge a secret or may I share it?"

Sage, "You remain too impatient! First, these people had no motive for understanding an issue in depth and perhaps changing an opinion. If they did, their pride-filled craniums would have taken a severe beating. Even worse, they would have lost their ideological turf, their egoistic position in life, usually dealing with their paycheck. Often, these people were bellicose and belligerent in how they expressed their views and rarely listened to countervailing sentiments."

Student, "But these talk show hosts and authors seemed to radiate with their knowledge, with their correctness. They appeared to have an absolute conviction in their beliefs."

Sage, "Perhaps. But they succumbed to their own biases and prejudices. They were not capable of looking beyond their own frame of reference. If they had done so, they would have expanded their job descriptions to include 'look for answers.'

"Instead, most of their focus was 'looking for someone to blame,' which was always their opposition. If they were on the left of the political spectrum, it was always the right who was in error. If they were on the right of the spectrum, it was always the left who was incorrect. They could do no wrong, unless they were caught red-handed."

Student, "Yes, I have come across many of these incidents. Did some of these humans eventually look at other views? Did they not understand that the other side might have some valid claims on the 'truth'?"

Sage, "Yes, on their death beds. On other rare occasions, they may have had a change of heart due to a life changing event, such as an illness or an accident. But remember, Student, our ancestors usually held on to an opinion to their graves. For the famous people to which you refer, the media pundits, their dogma remained the same, regardless of circumstances that suggested their tenets might need updates now and then.

"During the early part of the 21st century, a significant number of men were exposed as having sexually molested or sexually threatened many females, some of whom were almost children. They were caught red-handed, and some of them then issued a statement that included, 'I am sorry.' They seldom made such a statement until they were caught with their pants down. What they really meant was, 'I am sorry I got caught.'"

Student, "A sobering assessment. My forebears could rarely be swayed from an opinion, a view you expressed to me in an earlier dialogue. Maybe you are too harsh on the political pundits; certainly not the sexual deviants. For the former, perhaps if you changed the word *opinion* for the word *principle*, the picture would not be so dismal."

Sage, "Student, we are not discussing principles. We are discussing opinions. Do not miss my point: All too often, humans formed and held their opinions based on their pride and their desire to gain and hold turf, to stay on top of their hierarchical pecking orders. I will not deny many humans formed their opinions based on their principles. But do not be Pollyannaish, Student. These so-called 'principles' were often masked by less admirable motives. Never forget the human word, *rationalization*. It is cogent to the rule we study in our session today."

Student, "I am waiting, Sage, and I did not interrupt you."

Sage, "I noticed. It is called The Rationalization Rule: The practice of a human who made irrational excuses to justify holding on to his or her pride and turf. This person hid his or her true motives by masking them behind bombast and façade."

Student, "I must say, you are a bit cynical for a sage."

Sage, "No, Student. As the humans would say, I am simply calling a spade a spade. Regarding your archivals containing the so-called political talk shows, I suggest you reanalyze the hosts' behaviors. You will discover their minds were closed to new ideas. Yet, as you have learned, any 'backing away' from their stands was interpreted as a serious character flaw. Never forget our earlier dialogue on The Ignorant, Therefore, Doctrinaire Syndrome."

Student, "I will keep your thoughts in mind. But I must admit, I remain more optimistic than you."

Sage, "That is because you know less than I."

Student, "Mentor Sage, one last question. Did everyone in the human race suffer from The Ignorant, Therefore, Doctrinaire Syndrome and The Rationalization Rule?"

Sage, "No, not everyone held an unyielding opinion on a particular subject. Some had none at all. Do you recall The Switzerland Principle?"

Student, "Ah yes! I do recall this principle: No opinion, no principled stand on anything. Just make money! Thank you, Sage."

Sage, "My pleasure, Student."

CHAPTER 59

MEDICARE FOR THE AGELESS

(Dialogue 29)

The Student pays a call on the Mentor Sage. He has been thinking about "Is that a Pickle in your Pocket" TV program and the Hologram's parody on E. coli: "Sage, our ancestors had a sense of irony."

Sage, "Yes, the programs were done in satire, but do you realize the actors on the shows, including holograms, were talking about actual products and events?"

Student, "Those patches, pills, and surgical operations for sexual enhancement were for real?"

Sage, "Yes, and they made the humans who sold them wealthy and happy."

Student, "How about the men who purchased them?"

Sage, "Certainly less wealthy and not always happy. Same for their female mates. Nonetheless, you have been studying too hard. I sensed you needed a break."

Student, "Yes, too hard…so to speak! Oops, sorry, Mentor Sage. Still thinking about the program."

Sage, "Clever, Student. As ever, too clever. Let us return to the more serious aspects about our ancestors changing themselves."

Student, "As you wish. So far, my data fills depict a rather straight-forward process of the humans changing themselves to become us Cepees. The Human Archives explain the controversies surrounding possible cloning, genetic tailoring, and brain bioengineering, but thus far, I do not sense our creation created much fuss.

Was our coming about as straight forward as my data fills lead me to believe?"

Sage, "The humans decided against cloning themselves, but their progress in genetic engineering made the issue somewhat moot.

"Anyway, it was not straight forward at all. In the mid part of the humans' 21st century, researchers discovered techniques that extended the life span of humans, including stem cell technologies, genetic tailoring, and brain bioengineering.

"Also, in the middle decades of the 21st century the techniques for growing muscle, skin, and bones coalesced with these other bodies of knowledge to produce fantastic strides toward 'engineered negligible senescence.'"[126]

Student, "'Engineered negligible senescence'?"

Sage, "Yes. It is a name describing a human who had been engineered to live a much longer life span, and the elimination of associated miseries that usually accompanied old age."

The Sage makes a key point, "Student, regardless of the ethical, religious, moral, and political controversies surrounding human self-change; regardless of the bitter debates that ensued in the first half of the 21st century, the humans' nature insured we Cepees were going to come along eventually. Rules forbidding human self-change, nick-named Bush's Rules—after an American President—came to naught.

"In the end, humans wanted to look better and live longer. It was that simple. If a country, such as the United States, prevented self-change operations, the American citizen simply purchased an airline ticket and shuffled off to an off-shore Tissue and Organ Farm. There, the human had his or her central nervous system, body, and genome altered. Upon returning, the person was at a significant advantage over his or her non-engineered colleagues.

"Before long, these other humans, recognizing they were descending down the ladders of their various Tribal Hierarchies, also purchased their airline tickets.

"Eventually, our ancestors succeeded in creating stem cells from ordinary cells, such as skin cells. This technology circumvented

---

[126] Charles C. Mann, "The Coming Death Shortage," *The Atlantic*, May 2005, 92.

having to use human eggs or human embryos. The technique enabled the humans to reprogram the genes in, say, a skin cell to turn the skin cell into an embryonic stem cell."

Student, "An end-run around the social and religious debates. No more shuffles to the off-shore Tissue and Organ Farm."

Sage, "Not quite correct, Student. The debates about the morality or immorality of altering a human were not quelled by the abatement of the stem cell controversy. Some religious groups remained in opposition to these procedures. Nonetheless, as the ILLS, EGO, SANE, and ASSES programs gained momentum, it became possible for parents to choose sexes, even find egg donors on the Internet who possessed certain desired characteristics, such as hair color, race, intelligence. Before long, with pregenetic diagnosis (PGD), the humans had the ability to shape many traits of their offspring."[127]

Student, "This period in our ancestors' history must have created severe tensions between people who could afford the engineering and those who could not. Humankind was gradually breaking down into different subspecies."

Sage, "But not for long. You must keep in mind that the attacks with weapons of mass destruction on huge populations was the straw that broke the proverbial anti-change camel's back. After many humans had been killed, and with the future of some of their cities looking bleak, governments stepped in and brought the Tissue and Organ Farms under their wings.

"However, as I have emphasized, we Cepees would have come along anyway without the benefit of ASSES. Eventually the EGO, ILLS, and SANE programs would have created us. The wars merely speeded up the process."

Student, "Hm. Considering the United States again, I suspect the so-called 'health care' costs skyrocketed even more."

Sage, "For a while, yes. But as EGO, ILLS, SANE, and ASSES began to take hold, aggressive WMD attacks began to diminish. So

---

[127] Michael S. Gazzaniga, *The Ethical Brain* (New York: Dana Press, 2005), 41.

did the age-old revenge cycles between tribes. You see, Student, The Deadly Trinity was being engineered out of the humans' genome."

Student, "Ah ha! And with fewer killers stalking the globe, the trillions of dollars budgeted for war could be diverted to the 'engineered negligible senescence' programs."

Sage, "Yes, and in the United States, trillions of dollars would have had to be funded into America's Medicare system anyway. America's health care apparatus was completely broken.

"Ironically, warfare's demise saved Medicare, funded it to the next level of human self-change. We Cepees call this revised program 'Medicare for the Ageless.'

"By 2050, most everyone was on the self-change bandwagon. This momentum resulted in huge budgets for Medicare and other health care systems. In a nutshell, the self-change industry replaced the military-industrial complex.

"Stem cell research became a fantastically successful industry because it addressed so many humans' laments: 'Cure my Parkinsons! Make well my dying kidneys! Heal my cancerous breasts!' Or just the simple plea of, 'Oh please! Please somehow diminish my pain.'

"Pain, dear Student. Pain you cannot imagine. Your superior body prevents you from gaining an understanding of our ancestors' physical miseries."

Student, "OK, so I'm not in pain, and I'm not into pain. I suppose I am happy about this fact. I will never know for sure, because I will never experience pain."

Sage, "Trust me, Student. You do not want to 'know for sure.' "

Student, "I'll take your word on it, Sage. So, the humans did not know where their bandwagon was headed, did they?"

Sage, "With a very few exceptions, no. For the vast majority of humans, they did not care. Their plea to their physician was, *Just give me five more years, Doctor.* Five years later, they asked, *Just give me five more years, Doctor.* "

Student, "I see. The Autocatalytic Process and The Threshold Lowering Syndrome in action. A human had increasingly fewer concerns about the self-change issue, especially if the changes were making that human live longer and better."

The Student continues, "But what happened to the structure of our ancestors' societies? If people started living longer, how could the younger people fill the jobs the older people were occupying? I imagine the process became disruptive."

Sage, "Correct, extending age and improving the health of the human race created many problems. To your immediate question, most governments forced 'older' people to retire at a certain age to make room for the young workers."

Student, "But who paid for these older humans' support? Medicare for the Ageless took care of their self-change engineering, but who paid for their upkeep?"

Sage, "That also became a big problem. The younger workers did not want to carry the entire load. So, eventually, the government stepped in to *extend* retirement ages *and* create jobs. All funded by tax money. As well, entertainment became the largest industry on earth to give all these humans something to do with their time."

Student, "So, Medicare for the Ageless was extended in its scope to provide for the aging, yet ageless population?"

Sage, "Yes. And the Pentagon was taken over by the entertainment industry."

Student, "Really?"

Sage, "Sure. What was to become of the building? Not to mention its occupants, who by the way, underwent major changes to their job descriptions."

Student, "Irony in action."

Sage, "I suppose. To finish this session, let's retrieve the figure I introduced in our first dialogue. I have made modifications to it. The timeline remains the same, but I have replaced some of the figure's events with the events we just discussed. Does the illustration make sense, Student?"

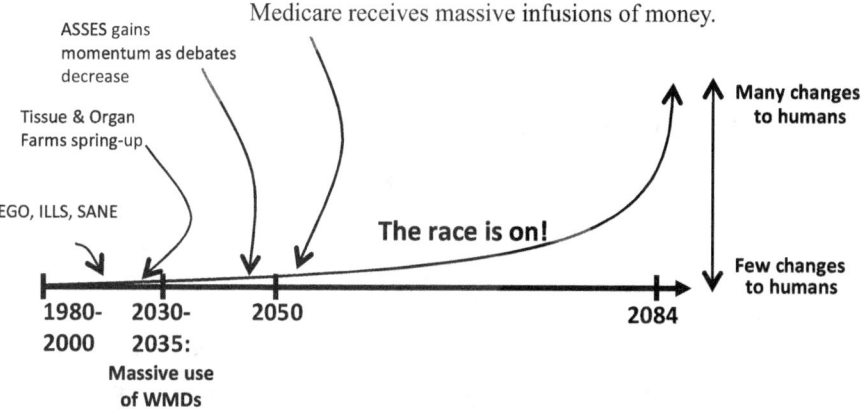

Alterations to the Time Line.

Student, "Yes, Sage, and I suspect the Human Archives contains data fills on this figure."

Sage, "Correct, and they will be parts of the next phase of your education program."

Student, "Will I have the pleasure to partake of these data fills and move on to another phase of my life? I can't wait!"

Sage, "Don't be impertinent with your Mentor Sage. Anyway, you must first complete this phase. And our author must then write another book about your next phase."

Student, "I'm at the mercy of a writer?"

Sage, "Life is not fair, even in the Cepee world."

CHAPTER 60

LAY DOWN, I THINK I LOVE YOU

(Show 19)

The Student asks himself, *How did humans decide that nurture and nature became partners during the humans' self-change programs? It appears the interrelationship was eventually decided in the humans' 21st century as they made more discoveries about how to alter their genome in order to change their behavior. Also, it must have been quite a shock to learn that nature alone did not ultimately determine their actions, that they were genetically 'prewired' as well as affected by their environment.*

We Cepees understand this fact. For my ancestors, it must have been a hard pill to swallow. Ah! The Mentor Sage is sending a Coming to you Live, from the Dead show about gene therapy. I'll take a look at it."

[The scene unfolds to show the *Discovery* TV program on the air, famous for sponsoring panel discussions dedicated to advancing the frontiers of understanding about subjects beyond understanding.

Five people are on the TV screen: (1) Hugh Heffner, of "Inside your knickers" fame, (2) George Will, of "Inside your cerebral cortex" fame, (3) Jerry Falwell, of "Inside your soul" fame, (4) A representative from the Vatican, of "Inside your entire life" fame, and (5) A sales representative of the sex drug industry, and seller of CerebralSex™, of "Inside your wallet" fame.]

Narrator, "Good evening, fellow empathy-endowed fellows. This is Dr. Phil bringing you a show titled, 'Lay Down, I Think I Love You...But I'll Let You Know After The Gene Therapy.'

316

Tonight's subject is of monumental importance to all of us: sexual fidelity. Or stated another way, of no importance at all…depending on how you are genetically wired and/or empathetically disposed.

"Tonight we learn the disposition toward monogamy or polygamy is genetically preordained, which is going to put one heck of a dent into my consulting fees. Lucky I've branched off into fat counseling.

"If any of you read Spinoza and adhere to his concept of the lack of 'free will' in humans, you will find this panel discussion to your liking. Those of you in the audience who are 'free spirits' may be disappointed by the findings explained in our program. Those of you who think Spinoza is a new offering from Pizza Hut should probably change the channel. Anyway, let's begin the program with a discussion from Mr. Heffner about sexual fidelity."

Heff, "Sexual fidelity? Is 'fidelity' a word? If it is, the term *sexual fidelity* is an oxymoron of human behavior."

Dr. Phil, "That's it?"

Heff, "Yep."

Dr. Phil, "Hm. OK, we'll now hear from Jerry Falwell on the matter."

Jerry, "Sexual fidelity? Is *sex* a word? If it is, 'sexual fidelity' is a confirmation of proper human behavior."

Dr. Phil, "And from the Vatican?"

Vatican Representative, "Sexual fidelity? Of course, we support it, but only between a man and wife, and a priest and altar boy."

The Student reflects, *Those predators should have spent time in prison.*

Dr. Phil continues, "And from the sex drug industry?"

CerebralSex salesman, "Sexual fidelity? Who cares! Go do it, and we will make a pill to help you do it better."

Dr. Phil, "No lengthy explanations this evening. Our panel members are cutting to the chase. Let's hear from George Will on the subject."

George, "Speaking of Spinoza, the ontological argument seems to prove the existence of something (fidelity) from the conception of that thing (sex). It provides a paradigm of rationalist philosophy, beginning from a 'clear and distinct idea' of sex, and leading to a conclusion about the world: namely that sex exists, and associated fidelity exists necessarily. The central question is: How can I display my intellect during this discussion?"

George continues, "Anyway, whereas previous philosophers took the metaphysical argument showing sexual fidelity existed, Spinoza believed the argument was to show that, at most, sexual fidelity had the idiosyncratic possibility of existing."

...And continues, "In modern terms, it is all in the man's head. Or a Viagra not working on the other head—either of which can lead to numerous actions (well, inactions), both leading to fidelity. Thus, the distinction between substance (sex) and attribute (fidelity) is...I've lost my train of thought. Can we talk baseball?"[128]

Dr. Phil, "Later, George. Let's see if we can get back on track here. Recent announcements reveal that scientists have succeeded in physically altering some genes affecting a rat's brain. Gene therapy changed its sexual behavior from a 'Wilt Chamberlain mode' to a 'Roger Staubach mode.' The rat morphed from a sex machine to a stay-at-home, around-the-hearth type of guy...eh, rat."

Jerry, "Roger Staubach. I don't get the connection."

Dr. Phil, "Mr. Staubach believed in keeping his scoring talents confined to the football field. And Wilt's scoring talents, both off and on the basketball court, were legendary."

Heff, "No! Is sexual freedom coming to an end? The world must be coming to an end."

Jerry, "Infidelity is a four-letter word, and I'm glad to see we might eliminate it from our behavior. But gene engineering is not God's will. Oh me, I face a conundrum."

Vatican Rep., "This technology, will it lead to more people—especially in Catholic countries? If so, we favor it. We'll get out a decree offering special dispensation and atonement for prolific males. Of course, we hope this technology will not lead to an unnecessary bonding of the priests with those they succor."

---

[128] My thanks to some of Spinoza's writings and an article, Roger Scruton, "From Spinoza," Microsoft's *Encarta Reference Library*. And thank you, Dr. Phil.

CerebralSex salesman, "My company would be interested in marketing a product with this technology in it. How does it work?"

Dr. Phil, "When certain rats mate, the pleasure hormone dopamine is released into the male's brain, but it is not associated with other hormones. For other rats, dopamine is associated with the hormone vasopressin, which is linked to social learning.

"The male meadow vole rat is promiscuous and does not associate dopamine with vasopressin. All it wants from sex is to feel good. In contrast, its cousin, the male prairie vole is an anti-philanderer and associates the feel-good feeling of sex with a particular female rat. It associates dopamine with vasopressin. Therefore, this male rat wants to feel good *and* do good.

"Researchers at the Yerkes National Primate Center at Emory University in Atlanta were able to genetically modify the meadow vole rat to make it completely monogamous.[129] The prairie vole vasopressin receptor gene was injected into the pleasure center part of the meadow vole's brain, leading the meadow vole to prefer only one sexual partner. Some people believe it is only a matter of time before the same gene therapy is available for humans."

Heff...profound silence, followed with, "Gene therapy! It's more like emasculation therapy. Sacrilege!"

Jerry, "Hm. Wait a minute. If humans stop messing around on the side, if they stop sinning, I lose my job. Who knows? Maybe killing and theft might be eliminated. Certainly coveting your neighbor's wife, unless she was your first sexual partner—which is highly unlikely—could be wiped out. The Moral Majority would become a minority. I'd have to find a new line of work."

CerebralSex salesman, "Not only that, our worthless placeboes would actually *be* worthless. Even worse, our main product is condoms. We sell a lot of them. I'm afraid fidelity will be the death knell for sexual diseases, but we stand to make a mint on an enhanced CerebralSex pill."

---

[129] Elizabeth Weise, "Report: Rodents May Offer Insight to Monogamy," *USA Today*, June 17, 2004, 2A.

Dr. Phil, "I would call the situation at CerebralSex a condom conundrum. Well, no one seems to be completely happy with the news of genetically engineered sexual fidelity."

George, "Not necessarily. To say that sex causes sexual fidelity is to say that sexual fidelity is dependent on sex for its existence and nature. Sexual fidelity is dependent on the idea of sex if its truth must be established by reference to the idea of sex. It is also a paradigm of causality, which is the relation that exists between sex and sexual fidelity when the existence and nature of sexual fidelity must be explained in terms of sex. What is more, …"

Dr. Phil, "George, maybe you and I should have a one-on-one counseling session."

George, "OK. Do you do baseball also?"

Jerry, "Hm, those polygamous people in Southern Utah and Northern Arizona are going to be unhappy campers. I'll take a trip down there and give them my patented lecture about how to feel good by not feeling good."

Heff, "After giving it some thought, you can say what you want about this new discovery and invention. I'm getting around it easily enough."

Dr. Phil, "How so, Mr. Heffner?"

Heff, "Easy. Immediately after this gene surgery, I'll have group sex, and my pleasure center will bond with multiple tricks. I'm not called the 'Master of the Tricks' for nothing!"

[The TV screen pulls away from the scene, as the group musters around Mr. Heffner to learn more about his plan—with the exception of Mr. Will, who is still talking to the camera about Spinoza, and Jerry Falwell, who has dialed up a local Pizza Hut to order a Spinoza Pizza.]

The Student Cepee is especially intrigued with the show. After all, the Mentor Sage informed him he would meet the love of his life, 'all in due time,' and this book is entering into its final phases.

PART FOUR

THE FINAL PRODUCT

CHAPTER 61

HEAVEN ON EARTH

(Data Fill 12)

Our behavior is embedded deeply into our souls,
chiseled onto our genome and gray matter with the
imprints of ancient human tribal hierarchies.

The humans' trip to become the Cepee began in the late 20th century and accelerated rapidly thereafter. Some 100 years later, the conventional human was changed to become a significantly altered individual. Toward the end of the 21st century, the strides made in gene therapy and the creation of organic/synthetic brain and body parts had altered the human significantly. Notable progress had also been made in identifying the genetic and mental underpinnings for pointless, violent aggression.

This latter advancement was a landmark achievement because it led to the demise of the syndromes associated with The Deadly Trinity. The humans were culling out their killing tendencies as well as miscellaneous antisocial traits. Toward the end of the 21st century—2084 was the commemorative date—this transformation was complete.

Payoffs from the EGO, ILLS, and SANE Programs

The EGO programs fixed the human's unwieldy and unreliable bodies and minds. The biosynthetic parts that became part of the Cepee would solve most of the problems the EGO initiatives had addressed.

323

As mentioned, the ILLS and SANE initiatives complimented EGO's agenda, and they went to the heart of the issues associated with the humans' health. These tasks were immensely complicated and frequently resulted in genes being delivered to an incorrect spot in the DNA code, a mistake that could activate genes leading to other problems, such as cancer.[130] Nonetheless, after many years, the human race began its successful quest to conquer germs, a process finished by the Cepees.

Aging

The organic cells' aging problem was eventually solved. First, scientists discovered a normal human cell had a finite lifetime span. It divided some 50-70 times before dying. As stated earlier, each time the cell divided, a part of the cell's chromosome, named telomeres, became a bit shorter. Scientists eventually concluded that telomere shortening was a leading cause of cellular aging and death.

Later, researchers discovered techniques for inserting genes that blocked telomere shortening. After decades of research and experimentation, after many hits and misses, aging was aged out of the human race.

Mind over Matter

Yet with all these alterations, the Cepees never solved the mystery of the mind. They came to know many facts about the brain, but they never solved how the mind functioned or how the brain enabled the mind. Using brain scans and brain taps, neuroscientists were able to trace and correlate a multitude of mental thoughts to their associated physical actions.

But the Cepees were never able to account for the mind's role in determining many mental traits, such as consciousness, ethics, and responsibility. They knew these attributes were usually species enhancing, but they never learned the mind's enabling mechanisms for their existence.

---

[130] Tom Friend, "Elusive Gene Therapy Forges On," *USA Today*, February 24, 2003.

In the end, the Cepees were wise enough to leave well-enough alone. Concluding the mind had a mind of its own, they undertook changes to the central nervous system based on their belief that even their advanced neuroscientists could not find a "brain correlate" for the ephemeral mind. Nor did they attempt to find a brain correlate for the soul—much to the satisfaction of the Cepees who were "Believers."

Artificial Intelligence

One result of these unknowables was the inability of artificial intelligence to take over the minds (and many initiatives) of the human and later Cepee. Certainly, AI became an immensely powerful technology. But the humans and Cepees were wise enough to have kept AI and AI-based robots on a mental leash. Thus, the Hologram Sage AI software was curtailed by the Mentor Sage.

Ironically, the Cepees were imbued with much AI imbedded in their brains. It could be argued that AI-based robots were controlled by another variety of AI-based robots: the Cepees.

But there was a significant difference between the two. The Cepees' brain-based AI was from organic computers, designed to interact with existing parts of the brain; thus, subject to the mysterious power of yet undiscovered aspects of the organic brain. AI robots remained mechanistic and under control of humans, and later, the Cepees.

Natural Laws: How? Why?

After centuries of celestial ignorance, the human race began to understand how the universe worked. Galileo's revolutionary scientific investigations and Newton's machine-like explanations opened vistas to the mysterious galaxies surrounding earth. Others followed these great men. They developed mathematical descriptions of the universe, how it began, and how it continued its existence by executing additional laws discovered by the human race's brilliant Plancks and Einsteins.

These laws defined how phenomena behaved. The propagation of light, radiation, and electromagnetism were well understood. The rules defined physical occurrences, such as how atoms decayed, how energy had mass, and how time changed during high-speed travel. They were brilliant constructions, erected with the authority of equations. But with all these enlightening compositions, the human race was unable to explain *why* these events occurred and continued to occur. The humans were adept at answering *how*, but less skilled at answering *why*.

The Imprints of Ancient Human Tribal Hierarchies—and their Dislodging

After centuries of intraspecies killing, the humans came to understand their genetic and cerebral makeup were more serious problems than their intramural wars over wealth, politics, sciences, philosophies, and religions. Indeed, they realized these battles came about *because* of the specific compositions of their brains and genes.

They came to understand their age-old behavior was embedded deeply into their souls, chiseled onto their genome and gray matter with the imprints of ancient Human Tribal Hierarchies.

The changes to save themselves from themselves were not easy to make. Some humans thought it an impossible task. Nonetheless, they altered the deadly course on which they were headed. In so doing, their greatest accomplishment was dislodging The Deadly Trinity from their makeup.

In the early part of the human's twenty-first century, the known part of the human genome and its associated behavioral underpinnings was quite small. At that time, the ability to alter the genome (and thus, the human) lay at the tip of the genetic iceberg. The part of this iceberg that was not visible, and unknown at that time, ultimately determined how the humans evolved. The changes they decided to make to their DNA and brain ultimately dictated their temperament, character, personality, disposition, humor, and individuality—even their morals and ethics.

Eventually, the latter-day humans began to address the profound issues of what they wanted to become, what they wanted to be like, how they wanted to look, and how they wanted to behave. After their genome was mapped and gene therapy became commonplace, as organ replacements became a routine matter, as synthetic skin, bones, and cartilages became a reality, as brain engineering became an accepted way to enhance the species, the humans embarked on a remarkable and astonishing journey to make their lives more pleasant and less antagonistic.

More Human Than Cepee?

The latter-day human and the emerging Cepee traveled a long way on the Promethean path of blending nature and nurture. They remade themselves to fit their habitat needs, fulfill desires, and of utmost importance, save their societies. But in the end, the Cepees kept intact the mind, soul, and free will of the humans, because they never fully understood what these things were anyway.

Neither brain scans nor genome mappings revealed the specific locations of morals, ethics, responsibilities, and a myriad of other characteristics loosely associated with the mind, the soul, and free will.

One point was uncontested. With few exceptions, the aggregate of human behavior, including the elusive mind, soul, and free will, existed for one reason: betterment of the race.

Granted, mutant anomalies on the genome and The Law of the Instrument created serious obstacles to the safety and advancement of the humans during their latter stay on earth. But in relation to the age of the human species and the everlasting life of the Cepees, the era of widespread use of weapons of mass destruction was little more than a short blip on a screen. In the long run, a small bit of noise in the human/Cepee spectrum of existence.

Nonetheless, given that the race was in great danger in the twenty-first century, it is fair to conclude that the rapid evolution of the human to the Cepee was really nothing more than the manifestation of evolutionary principles: changes (mutations) and natural selection to improve and perpetuate the altered species.

The Beauty of the Universe: Questions Remain Unanswered

Beholding the galaxies they explore, the Cepees have come to appreciate an idea of their distant cousin, Oscar Wilde, who offered that the visible is more mysterious than the invisible. His observation fits with that of Leonardo Di Vinci, a master of observing the visible world around him. In addition, what could be more mysterious than the human body itself?

Beyond their own bodies, the Cepees could "see" the universe in which they lived, but they never learned to "see" its basic underpinnings. Spooky actions at a distance remained spooky, as did the seemingly infinite expanding of the universe (or universes?) in defiance of so-called gravity.

Notwithstanding their universal odyssey and their finding answers to many questions about themselves and the universe in which they live, many other questions remain unanswered.

The Beauty of Creation: More Unanswered Questions

Did the humans remake themselves through their own volition, or were the changes guided by someone or something else? Was the Cepee race preordained? Was Darwinism a factor? Was God involved?

No one, be it the human or the Cepee, ever discovered the answers to these questions. The imponderables of the universe, the enigmas of the mind, the puzzles of science and religion remained as elusive to the Cepee as they had been to the human. And the Cepee knows this situation is the ultimate beauty of existence.[131]

The most beautiful and most profound emotion we can experience is the sensation of the mystical. It is the sower of all true science. He to whom this emotion is a stranger, who can no longer wonder and stand rapt in awe, is as good as dead. To know that what is impenetrable to us really exists, manifesting itself as the highest wisdom and the most radiant

---

[131] Lincoln Barnett, *The Universe and Dr. Einstein* (New York: Bantam, 1980), 108.

beauty that our dull faculties can comprehend only in their most primitive forms—this knowledge, this feeling is at the center of true religiousness.

The Cepee closes the Human Archives. Once again, he reflects on what he has learned: *At times, it seems my ancestors learned so much, yet knew so little. But they knew enough to alter the dangerous course they were on. Because of what they learned, because of what they came to understand, I came to be. I carry their gift, their legacy.*

CHAPTER 62

THE STUDENT LEARNS ABOUT THE RULES

(Dialogue 30)

This dialogue takes place after the Student Cepee has finished his Human Archives data fills and studies. He has come to understand how and why his ancestors modifyed their bodies and minds to form an astounding race: the Cepees.

The Student thinks, *Just a century or so ago, my ancestors roamed around in chaos. How fast they changed! All well and good for us Cepees.*

Nonetheless, the Student, still being a student, and oblivious to certain aspects of reality, consults with the Mentor Sage:

Student Cepee, "Sage, I continue to think about the Noble Savage in our ancestors' times. I wonder if the many changes made to the human—such as those explained in my study of the Human Archives—also made a difference in the status of these humans, in their standard of living and their mental health?"

Sage Cepee, "Indeed it did, Student. Parts of the EGO, ILLS, and SANE programs addressed the poor health and short life span of these humans. Of course, eventually the so-called Noble Savage ceased to exist as we elevated this part of the race to one of security and dignity. We Cepees would not countenance such inequities in our race."

Student, "So, our ancestors made significant progress in improving their life styles and standards of living? Even the life spans and nutritional intake of the Noble Savages improved during the human's latter time on earth?"

Sage, "Correct. Initially, the Bell-Shaped Curves for life span and health remained Bell-Shaped Curves. But their redefinitions illustrated improved conditions overall. Nonetheless, our ancestors could not fully coordinate their altruism and wealth to eliminate the Noble Savage underclass. Until we Cepees finally took over the helm, the race continued to be populated with poor, sick, starving humans—not to mention pathological killers, which is a subject we have discussed several times."

Student, "Why couldn't our ancestors fix this problem until we evolved away from them?"

Sage, "They were toiling away in their own private world, trying to make a go of it on a day-to-day basis. And by-and-large, this approach was laudable. They tended to their businesses and their families, and assumed other humans were responsible for their own welfare. What is more, thousands of humane programs were established for less fortunate humans and many were successful.

"But they were not enough. Thousands of humans died because of the lack of food, while at the same time a few miles away, thousands of other humans also died—but from too much food. Considering the intelligence and affluence of the human race, it was a sad commentary on how they treated others and themselves.

"Their genetic and cranial dispositions made them incapable of solving the problem anyway. So, a human might reason, 'Why bother myself about an intractable problem?'"

Student, "Sage, if you were a human, your aloof stance on this issue would have you classified as a 'conservative.'"

Sage, "Not at all. I am merely reciting some of The Rules of Life of the humans. These rules were not political. They applied to a liberal or a conservative human."

Student, "The Rules of Life? A new term?"

Sage, "Yes, but you have been learning these rules since you began your studies. All the syndromes, laws, rules, effects, and terms you learned during your education program are The Rules of Life for the human—regardless of the human's political beliefs. Here, let me recite a short poem explaining this idea:

> The Rules of Life were apolitical.
> They were unmindful of one's civic wing.
> They cared less if the human was a typical
> liberal, conservative, or in-between."

Student, "So, everyone was fair game? The Rules of Life applied to all?"

Sage, "Yes. Your review of the rules will reveal them to have been applicable to men, women, liberals, conservatives, Noble Savages, non-Noble Savages, blacks, whites, brown, yellows, evangelicals, atheists, and so on. We sages placed them into your data fills as satire, but they were, as you now know, unassailable facts. Try as one did, the human could not escape The Rules of Life, specifically The Deadly Trinity."

Student, "Why not?"

Sage, "First, the rules were embedded into the human's brain. Second, their DNA strands were seeded with thousands of years of experience and genetic mutations, all reflective of these rules. For example, The Deadly Trinity was an outward manifestation of the behavioral dispositions of the brain and genome."

Student, "Yes, but they decided to change their brain and genome during their latter stay on earth."

Sage, "Keep going. You are onto something."

Student, "Hm…because they could not break away from The Deadly Trinity that had evolved over millions of years, they were not capable of forging challenges to this Trinity. At least not in time to keep pace with the rapid change of their technologies, their sciences, their medicines, and especially their weapons."

Sage, "Yes. The humans' tools for killing outpaced the humans' genetic and mental abilities to control the very tools they themselves created. Conventional, evolutionary-based genetic changes were very slow in coming about. Mental processes remained the same for many generations.

"Ironically, the humans' tools did not. They changed rapidly. Humans' use of tools for destruction far out-paced any hesitancy they had for not using them."

The Sage challenges the Student, "So then, what happened?"

The Student responds, "Our ancestors were killing themselves, leading to, if not physical oblivion, then social suicide. The humans decided to re-forge themselves, to alter their genome and brain. In so doing, their Rules of Life could also change, and they could possibly escape the very rules they had created in the first place—such as The Deadly Trinity."

Sage, "Correct."

Student, "Eventually, all this re-forging led to us Cepees."

Sage, "Correct again."

Student, "Well, as the humans would have said, 'That's progress.'"

Sage, "That is certainly what we Cepees say."

CHAPTER 63

MONKS DO NOT DISSOLVE MONASTERIES RULE

(Dialogue 31)

Sage Cepee, "Student, we are not yet finished with The Rules of Life. Before you return to the Human Archives you should learn about The Monks do not Dissolve Monasteries Rule. It was an important element of our ancestors' behavior and represented several Rules of Life."

Student Cepee, "Lay it on me, S. C. The more Rules of Life, the better!"

Sage, "I must say, you are a remarkable assemblage of Cepee mucilage. We S.Cs., as you just called us, do not answer to impertinent remarks about our name."

Student, "At the onset of my education, you promised I would have some laughs along the way. The Hologram Sage uses initials. My data fills reveal our ancestors often used initials in jest and to introduce satire into their conversations."

Sage, "Such as?"

Student, "EGO, ILLS, SANE, and ASSES."

Sage, "Hm, true, and S.C. does sound rather sporty. On the other hand, if you and I took license with our names and used our initials, both of us would be tagged as 'S.C.' Consider the difficulty of our author writing this dialogue."

S.C. "You mean like this?"

S.C. "Yes. The reader would have difficulty knowing which of us is speaking. Anyway, you are off track, *Student Cepee*. We return to

334

the subject at hand. The Monks do not Dissolve Monasteries Rule goes as follows: ...Ah, I forgot about this rule. The name of this rule defines the rule itself. Therefore, I will provide an example of these metaphorical monks, who were symbols for the human race. By the way, we could just as easily say, 'Imams do not dissolve mosques.'"

The Sage explains the rule, "If monks dissolved their own monasteries, they would be out of work. In fact, monks and almost every human attempted to build additional monasteries—power structures—in order to enhance their jobs and add another layer of hierarchy to their organizational systems."

Student, "How about this example? Bureaucrats do not dissolve bureaucracies."

Sage, "Yes, that is one reason they were called bureaucracies. As another example, asking Muslims, Jews, Hindus, Christians, Buddhists, and so forth to dissolve their own religions *and associated ways of life* and convert to another faith was folly. Yet that is precisely what some of the Christians, Muslims, Buddhists and others attempted to do during their stay on earth. As you have learned, some of the zealots killed off the so-called nonbelievers in attempts to eliminate contending 'monasteries.'"

Student, "With respect, Mentor Sage, I have grown skeptical of your cynicism about our ancestors. During our dialogues, I came to the conclusion you hold contempt for the human race."

Sage, "I recall a human cliché, 'Knowledge breeds skepticism. More knowledge breeds cynicism.' It is a flippant remark, and I do indeed have more knowledge about the human than you do. But cynicism and contempt are not the correct words. During my studies of our ancestors, I came to bemoan their behavior. They possessed great potential, and their extraordinary minds led to the initial versions of the Cepee race. How can I be contemptuous of a race for behaving in a manner that led to my existence?"

Student, "I suppose you cannot, Sage. Yet I think a substantial number of humans did not subscribe to the Monks do not Dissolve Monasteries Rule. These people were not so caught up in themselves that they could not look beyond their own interests. Surely, some humans looked to the well-being of their race. They sought to elevate all tribes to a higher level and to dissolve—if only in part—their monasteries."

Sage, "No, Student, most humans looked *only* to their own interests. Their focus was to create, nurture, and expand their 'monasteries.' And woe be to the person who attempted to dismantle others' egocentric hermitages. Indeed, a person's ego became one of these symbolic monasteries.

"However, as you say, many other humans balanced their own needs with the needs of others. These humans looked into the reasonings of their fellow humans to understand their point of view. But not enough humans made this effort."

The Sage shifts the tone of the dialogue, "Student, we've come full-circle. In your early studies, you were exposed to Maslow's Hierarchy of Needs. Let me amplify your knowledge about this subject. Maslow, an American psychologist, was a force in a school of thought called humanism, a movement created from a desire to understand the humans' conscious mind.[132]

"Maslow used the term *self-actualizers* to describe a rare group of humans. They were people who fulfilled their greatest potential for themselves and their fellow humans.

"Let's revise one of the charts of an earlier data fill. Here it is." The Sage retrieves the chart, and makes a few changes to it. "Do you recall this chart, Student?"

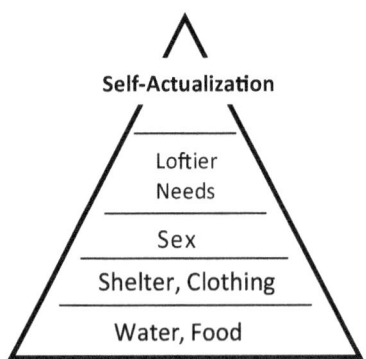

Hierarchy of Needs revisited.

---

[132] Sourced from Microsoft's Encarta Reference Library.

Student, "Yes, at the bottom of the hierarchy were basic needs, such as thirst, hunger, sex, shelter, clothing, and sleep. Further up the hierarchy were loftier needs, such as love, esteem, status, and achievement. I see the relevance of your change to the chart. Once the lower needs were met, Maslow believed people strived for self-actualization."

Sage, "Yes, for the human, self-actualization was the ultimate state of personal fulfillment."

The Student counters, "I can alter the human statement about knowledge and cynicism, "Knowledge breeds cognizance. More knowledge breeds self-actualization."

Sage, "A laudable approach to the issue, but as your mentor, I have counseled you against Pollyannaish views of our forebears. Nonetheless, you are keeping an open, inquiring mind about the humans. And your frankness, sincerity, and candor are admirable—even self-actualizing. Fine work, Student, but..."

The Sage drops the other shoe, "As our ancestors would say, here's the rub. Self-actualization was subject to interpretation. What was self-actualization to person A was madness to person B. What was personal fulfillment to person C was egocentric self-gratification to person D.

"Hitler fulfilled his greatest potential to the Nazi party. Jesus, to the Christians. Stalin, to the Communists. Muhammad, to the Muslims. Pol Pot, to the Khmer Rouge. Einstein, to the scientists. The Pope, to the Catholics. Hussein, to the..."

Student, "I understand, Sage. Even supposedly admirable traits, and we are using the term *self-actualization* to describe them, were open to interpretation."

Sage, "Yes, as you should know, where one stands on an issue..."

Student, "...depends on where one sits. I am beginning to understand the inability of the human race, as it evolved through the centuries, to live harmoniously on earth."

Sage, "The race was never harmonious to begin with! As you know now, their demise came about because of two factors: their inability to attain any semblance of true self-actualization, and their graduating from bows and arrows to nuclear bombs and bioterror for conducting their never-ending internecine get-togethers."

Student, "'Internecine get-togethers.' An interesting term. Mentor Sage, perhaps if more of our ancestors had attempted, in spite of their differing views on most every subject, to back off; *to leave one another alone*. Perhaps to dissolve a monastery here and there. Perhaps..."

Sage, "Sounds fine in theory. In practice, a human very rarely dissolved anything of his or her own accord if the dissolution would penalize the potential dissolver—even if the dissolution would benefit other humans. Unless the 'monastery' was destroyed by another human, it lived an interminable existence, far beyond the life of the human who created it in the first place."

Student, "But many of these 'monasteries' rightly deserved to live a long life. They were beneficial to the human race. Just consider Albert Schweitzer and humanity; Mother Teresa and the sick; Jesus and the poor; the Red Cross and the injured."

Sage, "True, and I urge you to download more information on Dr. Schweitzer. He was quite Cepee-like. But you are missing my point, Student. In the final cut, the Monks do not Dissolve Monasteries Rule is all about...what?"

The Student pauses for a while, ruminating about the dialogues, data fills, and human television programs. The Student replies, "Preserving and expanding turf, pecking orders, and Human Tribal Hierarchies."

Sage, "Correct, and all well and good except for...what? Think!"

The Student indeed thinks, "Long ago, the ancient humans lost track of Maslow's Hierarchy of Needs and began to kill one another because of factors other than survival. Eventually, The Law of the Instrument and weapons of mass destruction jump started the ASSES programs. The heretofore extant humans eventually became irrelevant because of The Deadly Trinity and their inability to form any association with self-actualization."

Sage, "Well done, Student."

Student, "Thank you, Sage. Say, let's put The Monks do not Dissolve Monasteries Rule to a test. How about I take over your sage job? After all, we Cepees are not riddled with turf protection or pecking order maladies.

"Like you, Mentor Sage, maybe I can become another human expert sage, and we can share your dais and office, your sage sanctuaries. Or maybe you can, eh, sort of eliminate your own job description. What's good for the student goose is good for the sage gander!"

The Sage replies, "Using the Hologram Sage's slang: No way."

Student, "Why not?"

Sage, "First, you are not yet ready to be a sage. And second, sages do not dissolve their own sanctuaries."

CHAPTER 64

THE TWEAK EFFECT

(Dialogue 32)

By this time, the Student is well-versed in the affairs of his ancestors, the humans. He has learned much from the Human Archives and his dialogues with his Mentor Sage...as well as a smattering of information from the Hologram Sage. He is confident of his capabilities.

Sage, "Student, we are nearing the end of our lessons together. You will soon graduate to another level in your Cepee citizenship. Have you any more questions for me?"

Student, "Yes, Sage, first, you never introduced me to that girl I was taken with. You said time after time, 'all in due time.' Well, time is running out."

Sage, "Hardly, you have forever to get to know her. After all, she is slightly younger than you, and infinite life lies before you two. Besides, she has been involved in other educational activities. Because of her exceptional skills, like you, dear Student, she has been selected to begin the same program in which you are in the process of completing. That is why you have not seen her around my sanctuary. My initial meeting with her was to evaluate her potential for the program. I was most impressed."

Student, "Me, too. Anyway, it seems as if it has been forever since I actually met her. By the way, what program has she been attending?"

Sage, "The subject is 'How female Cepees can deal with male Cepee chauvinism.'"

Student, "What! An advanced group such as male Cepees exhibit chauvinism?"

Sage, "So do females, Student. It is a two-way street, but males occupy most of the boulevard. The engineering of gender bias out of our race has proven to be a very difficult challenge in the clipping-out of the relevant DNA strands.

"Nonetheless, Student, I will arrange something soon. For now, any thoughts or questions?"

Student, "Yes, it is now apparent we Cepees came about because the humans kept changing themselves."

Sage, "Yes. We Cepees call this situation The Tweak Effect. It is the end result of tweaking something more than once, as in, 'Let's tweak it one more time and see what happens.' The humans were masters at the art and science of tweaking."

Student, "I see many examples of The Tweak Effect in my data fills. The atomic bomb and its successors, which I learned played a big role in the humans' undertaking their ASSES program. Maybe this is an example of The Tweak Effect gone amiss?"

The Student continues, "I studied the Los Alamos Project. Perhaps the nuclear wars would never have come about if say, a Los Alamos scientist's advice had been heeded. If prior to the completion of the atomic bomb, he said to his colleagues, 'Leave well enough alone. No more tweaks.'"

Sage, "No. If the atomic bomb had not been produced at Los Alamos, it would have been produced in Moscow or Berlin. Someone else would have created atomic power."

Student, "OK, how about this one. Jim Watson says to Francis Click, 'Let's tweak our fellow scientists over at King's College just one more time for their ideas on DNA.'"

Sage, "That's a good one. I am not certain Messrs. Watson and Click would have appreciated your humor. Yes, Watson's visits to King's to look at some on-going work there in order to do a bit more tweaking of Watson's and Click's model helped them win the Nobel prize. They were accused by some of borrowing ideas, but they made their way to fame and fortune. You are doing well. Any more examples?"

Student, "I have an anti-tweak example. It goes like this: A Chernobyl nuclear power plant engineer's advice to his colleagues about preventative maintenance on the nuclear plant, 'If it ain't broke, don't fix it; no tweaks needed.'"

Sage, "Yes, well put. I have a tweak example for you. A conversation between Messrs. Cheney, Rumsfield, Wolfowitz, and President Bush, in which Messrs. Cheney, Rumsfield, and Wolfowitz suggest to the President, 'Why don't we tweak Iraq and Hussein one more time?'"

Student, "I suppose the humans' inclination to laugh at your Tweak Effect example would have been a matter of their being conservative or liberal?"

Sage, "Yes. When it came to politics, the humans lost the ability to laugh at themselves—only at their opposition."

Student, "In an earlier dialogue, we discussed a human saying. Perhaps it captures the humans' propensity for their biases. It stated, 'Where one stands on an issue depends on where one sits.'"

Sage, "And your inference from this statement is?"

Student, "It's easy to draw the inference. Where a human sat in his or her various Human Tribal Hierarchies influenced and often determined the human's values, thoughts, and opinions."

Sage, "Such as?"

Student, "How a human responded to an issue was usually predetermined by the human's membership in, say, conservative or liberal political parties; whether the human was an evangelical or an atheist; if the person was white or black, male or female, rich or poor, Christian or Islamic, Noble Savage or non-Noble Savage."

Sage, "Your point is well-made. But recall that many humans changed their views radically toward the end of their stay on earth, and…"

Student, "Yes, but only when they were faced with the stark fact that their instruments of destruction had far exceeded their ability to control them. Only then, only at that time, did they alter their views about self change and undertake restorative measures to preserve the fabrics of their societies. Just another example of the human's Law of The Graveyard Effect."

Sage, "Still interrupting me. But your premises are correct. You have done well with your education program."

Student, "Thank you. But you also interrupted me. I have no more questions, Sage. I hope I am prepared for the next phase of my citizenship."

Sage, "I have enjoyed being your sage. My recommendations to my fellow sages for your next phase will be positive."

Student, "Thank you, Sage."

Sage, "You are welcome, Student."

The Sage pauses and for the first time, thanks the Student, "And I should add that as our dialogues unfolded, I found I was learning from you as well. So, it is my turn: Thank you, Student, and I bid you good fortune in your upcoming pursuits."

Student, "Thank you, Sage! Eh...in relation to your last statement, I think I have earned my wings. First, you promised me I would at last be able to meet that girl of my dreams and apologize for calling her a Cepeeette. Second, I would like to put on sage wings, so to speak. I would like your job description to be my job description. And I believe I know all the answers there are to know about the human. My AI brain chips have been working in over-drive for weeks...so has my testosterone."

The Sage smiles, "It appears I have not succeeded in defusing your excessive zeal and over confidence. It is still a part of your make up. We Cepees have considered splicing out these attributes from our DNA, but we have had considerable trouble finding the correct combination of gene markers. And they are indeed positive attributes, when practiced with a modicum of restraint."

The Sage decides this Cepee might need another dose of humility, but also be offered a way to test his mettle, "Fine. Here is what we will do. Later today, I am having a dialogue with, yes, the female student you find so attractive. You have not seen much of her because she is just now beginning the program you started some time ago.

"You have fulfilled your duties and responsibilities well, Student. You have matured and developed into a full fledged human expert. You are ready to assume more responsibilities, such as meeting and intermingling with the opposite sex. As for your favorite? You can meet her today."

Student, "Really, Sage! It will be a dream come true."

Sage, "Here is the plan. We will reverse our roles. You will play the part of a sage. I will play the part of your assistant, but disguised as Hologram Sage. The new student has met me before, so I will represent myself as a hologram.

"I will...*it* will sit in back of the room, and perform the duty of greeting the new student and introducing her to you. You will then counsel her, advise her, and answer her questions. Because she is the girl of your dreams, you can impress her with your intelligence and wit. You have been bragging about your sage-like wisdom. Today, we will give it a test. Are you ready? I give you one last chance to defer this test, to study more."

Student, "Yes, I am more than ready! Two victories in one day. I've been wanting to be a sage and to meet that girl for a long time."

Sage, "Yes, your ambitions were evident at the start. See you later today."

Student, "Right. Many thanks, Mentor Sage!"

Sage, "Humph. And if the occasion arises, don't forget to apologize for calling her a Cepeeette."

The Mentor Sage has set the stage to finally allow this young male student to meet his female fantasy, and at the same time, test the Student Cepee's progress in his studies. The Student Cepee is going to be tested with two final exams in one sitting.

CHAPTER 65

ROLE REVERSAL

(Dialogue 33)

Sure enough, the Student Cepee arrives at the Sage's sanctuary shortly before his object of affection arrives. As prearranged, the Sage and the Student exchange locations in the room. The Student is sitting in the sage's dais while the real sage, taking on the image of the Hologram Sage, hovers over a modest chair at the back of the room.

Shortly, the new student arrives. She is greeted by the real Mentor Sage, who is in the disguise of a hologram, "Greetings, to you. Today, your dialogue will be with a potential sage. He has recently joined the sage fraternity, but on a trial basis. How he performs with his first student-sage dialogue with you will affect his future."

The new student, "Might I fail also on this first meeting?"

The Mentor Sage beams his light more brightly to show wisdom, "No, after all, you are just beginning your program. You've a long way to go and will not be tested today for pass or fail. The Cepee under test is nearing the end of his lengthy education and will be evaluated accordingly."

The female student is accompanied by the disguised sage to the male student/semi-sage, whom we now identify as the *boy*. The boy and the new student—whom we now call the *girl*, enter into the following dialogue.

Boy, "Greetings."

Girl, "And greetings to you. I understand I am to begin a lengthy learning program, and you are to be my teacher. Say, I recognize you! You're the one who had the cheek to call me 'Cepeeette'…wouldn't

345

even introduce yourself. Are you actually a sage, even a rookie sage? That is what the hologram told me." *Hm. You do have a nice set of cheeks.*

Boy, "It was cheeky of me. The truth is, I was too shy to ask your name. I just got flippant instead. I owe you my apologies."

The Mentor Sage, sitting at the back of the room, is pleased by this turn of events. He thinks, *A nice start.*

The girl, who is taken aback and flattered, and still attuned to those nice cheeks, both pairs of them, replies, "It is no longer of any consequence. Apology accepted. That is enough."

Boy, "As the Hologram would say, 'Super!'...Ahem, back to the reason for our being here. I am one of several sages who will advise and counsel you. My specialty, my job description, is our ancestors, the human race. You will come to me with questions about the humans, and I will answer your queries, as well as review the progress of your learning about the humans." *And demonstrate my wisdom.*

The boy continues mimicking the real sage, "However, for our dialogue today, we will discuss the Cepee race, not the human race."

Girl, "Good. I have several questions."

Boy, "I know you do. Proceed."

The girl immediately proceeds to ask the boy a question. But it was a question he could not answer. The boy had never thought of this question, nor had he encountered the subject in thousands of data fills and the many dialogues with the Mentor Sage.

The girl was indeed exceptional. The Mentor Sage, sitting at the back of the room, reflects: *We Cepees, unlike the humans, consider the Cepee female gender on an equal basis to the male gender. The once superior behavior of the human male toward the human female was part of their long evolutionary cycle, but we Cepees gene spliced that deficiency out of the male's behavior many decades ago. The caveman and Madison Avenue days have long been extracted from our behavior. ...Hm, "Cepeeete" notwithstanding.*

The boy was stymied and embarrassed: *What am I to do? She has not even begun the program and has already stymied me. Humiliation in front of the girl of my dreams? Failure before my mentor? I'm really no sage at all.*

The Mentor Sage at the back of the room is also thinking: *A bit of humbleness is just what this youngster has needed all along. I'll let him dangle on his own rope and see if he can get himself out of this jam.*

The girl does not know about the boy's dilemma. She is awaiting a spate of wisdom to come forth from a possible sage whom she also finds quite appealing.

After a short pause, the boy replies, "Your question is interesting." The boy is thinking: *This girl has been doing some serious data fills.* Instead, still unable to overcome centuries of evolution, and in spite of all those artificial intelligence chips floating around in his cranium, he comes up with this response:

"Nonetheless, it's an elementary question. I will delegate the hologram at the back of the room to answer your query."

We shall never know if this ploy worked. We shall never know if the Student Cepee's unrequited love for his fantasy female became requited. But as a hint to what the future held for this Cepee girl and boy, this we do know: The Cepees never gene-spliced love and affection from their DNA.

In the meantime, the Cepee race continues to study the Human Archives, and learns more about their ancestors' strange combination of wisdom and folly, which the humans themselves proclaimed with an old proverb, "Wisdom is born, folly is learned, and they often kick into each other."

EPILOGUE

The Cepee Dialogues: A Modern Fairy Tale, is a complement to the book *2084 and Beyond.* The earlier book, *2084,* examines how and why humans transformed themselves to become different beings. *The Dialogues* book offers a satiric view of the subject, and is based on the same theme of its parent book, *2084.*

Both books are likely to be categorized as science fiction, or as another critic suggested: high fantasy. The two books might fit into either classification.

However, I believe the books are not about science fiction or high fantasy alone, but a realistic reflection of modern human societies and where we may be headed. Both serve as a warning to the human race.

As stated in the Prologue, the *Dialogues'* chapters are organized into three categories: data fills, dialogues, and shows. If you have read *2084 and Beyond,* you will find the data fills are general descriptions of the main points of the more detailed *2084.* I borrowed them to lend continuity to *Dialogues* without your having to read *2084 and Beyond.* Although I hope your reading the *Dialogues* book will whet your appetite for *2084.* Just be aware that the data fills in this book are extracted from *2084.*

I am alarmed about the wanton killings we humans unleash on one another. But I have beat this dead horse, so to speak, in each of these books. I offer dead horses and dead humans in different contexts in these two works.

In the long run, I am hopeful that the long-range suppositions of *2084* and the *Dialogues* will prove to be correct: Namely, that we humans will elevate ourselves in our tribal hierarchies to recognize our internecine warfare is nothing more than reenacting, time and again, a dangerous mode of human behavior: pointless aggression. As for an everlasting life? My mental jury is still in session on that issue.

I began work on the material reflected in this book in 2004. In

348

2007, I published *The Deadly Trinity*. It introduced the subjects of genetic engineering, Boolean biology, programmable chromosomes, and other topics that are now called synthetic biology. Deciding *Trinity* was a premature discourse about these subjects in relation to human's pointless aggression. I withdrew the book from publication, and continued my efforts that led to *2084* and *Dialogues*.

To conclude this book, I have borrowed thoughts from two writers, Martin Rees and William Faulkner. Their ideas represent the themes of *2084* and *Dialogues* (as well as *Trinity*) about the humane nature of the main characters in the books, as well as the humaneness of most humans. "Most" but not all, as a few humans did great harm to an otherwise humane race—one of the underpinning suppositions of these books.

I paraphrase Martin Rees, "Is there a Limit to Scientific Understanding?" (*The Atlantic*, Dec. 6, 2017) "The chess champion Garry Kasparov argues in *Deep Thinking* (2017) that 'human plus machine' is more powerful than either alone. Perhaps it's by exploiting the strengthening symbiosis between the two that new discoveries will be made.

"Abstract thinking by biological brains has underpinned the emergence of all culture and science. But this activity, spanning tens of millennia at most, will probably be a brief precursor to the more powerful intellects of the post-human era—evolved not by Darwinian selection but via [human and later machine design]. Whether the long-range future lies with organic post-humans or with electronic super intelligent machines is a matter for debate."

As put forth in *Trinity*, *2084*, and *Dialogues*, I believe it will be a combination of the two.

William Faulkner said in his 1950 Nobel Prize Speech, "Our tragedy today is a general and universal physical fear. ... He [humankind] must teach himself that the basest of all things is to be afraid:... and teaching himself that, forget it forever, leaving no room in his workshop for anything but the old verities and truths of the heart, the old universal truths...love and honor and pity and pride and compassion and sacrifice. Until he does so, he lives under a curse."

As told in *Trinity*, *2084*, and *Dialogues*, humans had evolved to find themselves subject to Faulkner's curse. Facing self-imposed catastrophe, they took measures to right their self-destructive path.

RULES OF LIFE AND OTHER DEFINITIONS

Below are the Rules of Life described in this book. For convenience, they are listed in alphabetical order.

The Acquisitive Syndrome: The instinctual propensity of a human to acquire stuff. This tendency has become a pathological syndrome to many humans —leading to the highly profitable storage locker industry.

The Aggression Cycle: The interplay with The Threshold Lowering Syndrome, wherein the successful execution of an aggressive act leads to more aggressive acts. Eventually, aggression becomes an end unto itself.

The Aggression/Submission Quandary: The inability to decide how one should react to a conflict. Typically, the dominant role is assumed by the party who has more muscles and/or better weapons.

The Alternative Facts Farce: The debasement of a fact to turn it into a charade of truth.

ASSES (Alterations to Save Society from our Egregious Selves)

The Autocatalytic Process: A cyclic operation in which an event repetitively creates another occurrence of the same event or an altered event. Each reinforcing event occurs faster and faster, and the time between the events decreases.

The Bell-Shaped Curve for Being Average Law: A person excels in an endeavor (any endeavor), and therefore moves to the right side of the Bell-Shaped Curve of Normal Distribution for this endeavor. As a result, this person becomes an above-average person in his or her chosen endeavor, as in:

350

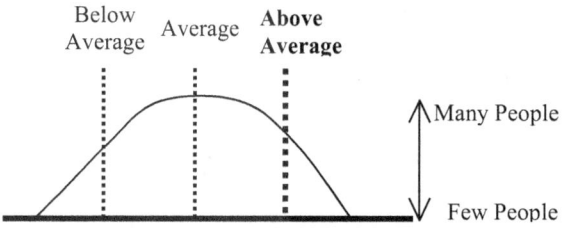

Bell-Shaped Curve for excelling.

This person, and like-minded, equally-excelling people, skews the Bell-Shaped Curve of the universal population for excelling in this endeavor, as in:

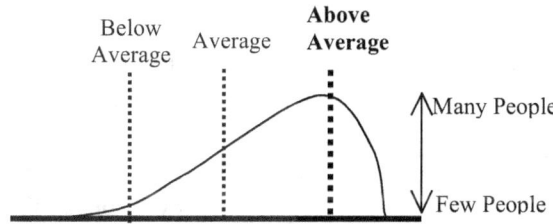

Skewed Curve of *Universal Population* for succeeding in the excelling.

This person now belongs to a *new* population of equally-excelling people. Therefore, the person enters into a *different* Bell-Shaped Curve of Normal Distribution for Excelling. Statistically, this person is now an average exceller in this population of excellers, as in:

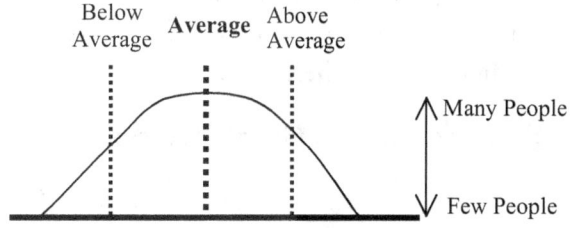

Bell-Shaped Curve of the *excellers' population*.

Consequently, this Bell-Shaped Curve Law states that, try as one will, one will always be average.

The Butterfly Effect: A butterfly flaps its wings in South America and causes a hurricane in the Gulf of Mexico. The idea of this metaphor is that anything that might happen in the world can affect everything else in the world, sometimes with exponential effects.

The Creeping Momentum Phenomenon: A human often starts an endeavor in a modest way. But curiosity, acquisitiveness, and possessiveness often lead a person to "sup another person's porridge." Given this success, the porridge poacher gradually looks for the bowls of unwary diners to stick his nose into. Before long, their porridge is gone.

The Deadly Trinity: A collective term describing the interplay of The Law of the Instrument, The Aggression Cycle, and The Revenge Cycle.

The Disproportionate Ratio Effect: The ratio n:m, where the value of n is small, and the value of m is large.

The Dogged Principle: The propensity to be persistent, resolute, single-minded, steadfast, tenacious, stubborn, and indefatigable in holding on to one's view of life and one's ways of living. Also, see: The Inability to Change an Opinion Rule.

The Drugstore Terrorist Syndrome: A state of mind in which a confused wannabe pharmacologist thinks "Arsenic and Old Lace" means lacing aspirin bottles with arsenic. The syndrome enters the picture when more than one innocent person discovers a trip to the drugstore might not be therapeutic.

EGO (Enhancements to Glorify Ourselves)

The Excessive Cosmetic Surgery Surprise Effect: The sensation of glancing at one's face in the mirror for the first time after cosmetic surgery and encountering a complete stranger.

The Exponential Consequences Curve: The consequences of an action in which the consequences are far greater (sometimes non-linear) than any one predicted (doomsayers aside), as in:

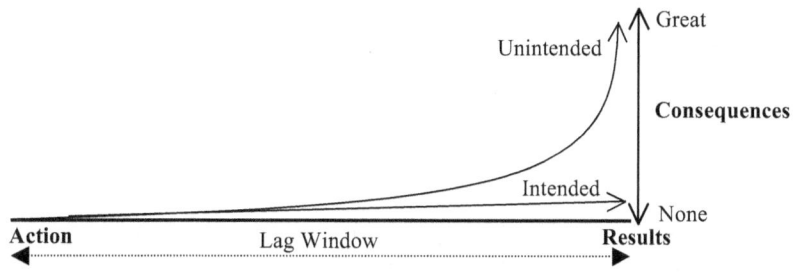

Note: In many instances, this curve is associated with the adjective, *unintended*, as in The *Unintended* Exponential Consequences Curve.

Fat People Got No Reason to Live Rule: A fat person is a deadly weight on human society.

The Equal Extermination Opportunities (EEO) Program: Everyone (including Muslims themselves) has an equal opportunity to be exterminated by Muslim terrorists.

The Fear of Farming Syndrome: An acute bias against farming in a mine-littered field, especially tilling the soil in this field. Medical studies have confirmed this disposition is not an illness but a syndrome. It is prevalent in the minds of many people who live in Noble Savage countries. It is absent in the minds of citizens who reside in the countries, which manufacture land mines—and coincidentally have no land mines in their soil.

The Feel-Good Law: The average human will disregard almost any taboo, proscription, announcement, pronouncement, decree, statute, act, dictate, order, command, law, ruling, or prohibition in order to feel good. And in accordance with The Immediacy Syndrome, to feel good as quickly as possible.

The Full-Face-Fettle Law: In theory, the patient's cosmetic surgery plan, wherein only one procedure is to be performed on the patient's face, such as an eye tuck. In reality, the surgeon's cosmetic surgery plan is to remodel the entire face.

The Geographically Undesirable Law: A potential attacker will not go to the trouble of assaulting a potential attackee if the potential attackee is located in an inconvenient place in relation to the potential attacker.

The Global Warming (GW) Conundrum: The inability to agree on what was causing global warming.

The Law of the Graveyard Shift: Not to be confused with a work schedule. Rather, the adaptation of (shift to) the solution to a problem, after the problem has manifested itself, resulting in unnecessary loss of life or severe injury.

The Herd Rule: If enough people do it, it must be alright to do.

The Hippocratic Oath Addendum: An addition to this oath practiced by doctors who disavow the oath when it comes to killing patients who are of a different religious faith than the doctors.

The Human Tribal Hierarchy: In essence, a pecking order.

ILLS (Incurable Latent Labile Sicknesses)

The Inability to Change an Opinion Rule: Exemplified by a person who forms an opinion about a subject and holds this opinion throughout his or her life, regardless of circumstances demonstrating the opinion is invalid, incorrect, and/or harmful. Research is just beginning on the origins of this aspect of human behavior. Prevailing theories state it is genetically based and closely associated with the pride gene.

The Ignorant, Therefore, Doctrinaire Syndrome: A common human behavioral trait, in which a person who is devoid of any knowledge whatsoever on a subject will hold an unyielding—and often belligerent—opinion on the subject.

The Immediacy Syndrome: A desire for the immediate fulfillment of a wish, in which any delay toward satiation, creates an acute breakdown of the hedonistic areas in the brain.

The Law of the Instrument: Exemplified by the child, who upon picking up a hammer, looks for something to pound.

The Imams Do Not Dissolve Mosques Rule: Same definition as The Monks Do Not Dissolve Monasteries Rule. It also pertains to priests, clergymen, clergywomen, reverends, preachers, ministers, pastors, monks, rectors, friars, abbots, cenobites, missionaries (especially missionaries), Catechists, Mendicants,[1] Deacons, etc. If I have excluded your favorite religious person, just pen it in here, and continue reading The Rules of Life.

The Law of the Instrument: Exemplified by a child who picks up a hammer and looks for something to pound.

The Law of the Graveyard Shift: The solution to a problem, but only after the problem has shown itself, resulting in unnecessary loss of life.

The Lag Effect: A time lapse (called the lag window) between the occurrence of an action and when the consequences of the action are revealed, thus freeing anyone from taking responsibility for anything, as shown in the figure below. Also, see The Exponential Consequences Curve, which often acts as a partner with The Lag Effect, resulting in huge, non-linear problems that are pushed off to future generations.

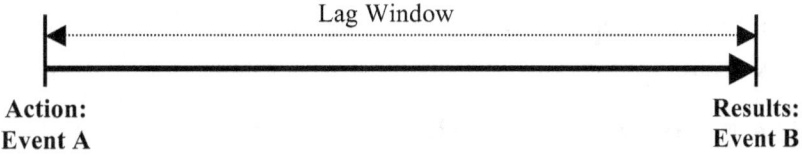

Lag Window

Action: Results:
Event A   Event B

---

[1] To be fair, mendicants do not build nor possess monasteries, mosques, cathedrals, or any edifice. They occupy street corners. But woe to the person who tries to take over that corner from the occupying mendicant.

The misplaced Pride and Prejudice Paradox: Humans often display misplaced pride about something they did not create.

The Monks Do Not Dissolve Monasteries Rule: A rule in which the name of the rule defines the rule itself. Therefore, we proceed with examples.

> Example One: Monks do not dissolve their own monasteries. To do so, would put them out of work. In fact, monks attempt to build additional monasteries in order to enhance their jobs and add another layer of hierarchy to their organizational structure.

> Example Two: Bureaucrats do not dissolve their own bureaucracies.

Summary: Humans do not dissolve anything of their own accord. Unless it is destroyed by another human, it lives an infinite existence, far beyond the lives of the humans who created it in the first place.

The New Europe Principle: A revitalized Europe takes over America's reins of power in the Western world.

The Noble Savage Law: The disposition of humans to attribute noble intentions to anyone who is poor.

> **Noble Savage:** A mythical term for a very real human who, by virtue of being born on the wrong "side of town," occupies the bottom rungs of all the pecking orders of human existence that really matter.

The Pigsty Paradox: Living in a habitat that seems contradictory to good health, but is populated by people who do not care.

The Pizarro Effect: Named after a Spanish conqueror and his priests. The killing of a "saved" person by a missionary or other religious enthusiasts, resulting in the dead gaining a fast path to heaven. For Islamic extremists, the killer and the killee might be the same person.

The Population Concentration-Homogenization Factor (PCH Factor): An attribute of the human race in which most of the Earth's humans reside in overly populated, concentrated, stratified, homogeneous habitats. If relatives are involved, this factor manifests itself as an indisposition coined as REEK: Repulsive Excretions of Excessive Kinfolk.

The PCH Factor-Annihilation Phenomenon: An off-shoot of the PCH Factor, in which the acts of maiming and killing enormous populations are simplified by having many people in one place at the same time. The incidents began to happen so frequently that citizens accept them (at considerable cost to their psyches) as part of their routine for living. (See 9/11, Oklahoma City building, Madrid trains, London and Tokyo subways.)

The PCH Factor-Disease Phenomenon: An off-shoot of the PCH Factor, in which the spreading of disease is greatly facilitated by many people using the same washroom...but not washing.

The Pride Paradox: A person who is proud of an act or situation to which this person has made absolutely no contribution.

The Pride and Prejudice Paradox: An affliction in which people attribute their self-worth and pride to their origins and residences and their associated prejudices toward other people who ended up on the wrong side of town. The pride and prejudice has no relationship to merit, but to life's roll of the dice.

The Rationalization Rule: Making irrational excuses to justify holding on to one's pride and turf and to hide one's true motivations by masking them behind bombast and façade.

The Revenge Cycle Token Passing Protocol: After a tribe has been attacked by another tribe (which could be large tribes, such as nations), the attacked tribe is obligated (even expected!) to strike back and avenge the assault. After the revenge had been taken, the tables were turned: the avenger became the avenged, and the avenged became the avenger, and another battle takes place. Then, the tables are turned once again.

The Roll of the Dice Rule: A theory in which its proponents contend one's financial and social fates are determined on where one is born and/or reared. Discounted by its critics as being too simplistic.

A Rose by any other Name Hypothesis: Killing by any other name is still killing.

The S-Shaped Curve Canon: (a) An idea is embraced with wild enthusiasm, as it presents an overly simple approach to an overly stupid population. (b) Regardless of its merits, positive or negative, it is followed by ridicule and/or ignored, as humans are inclined to do. (c) It once again gains favor, as public relations propaganda deceives a gullible populace. (d) Eventually, it fades into the sunset, suffering from obsolescence, overuse, disinterest, or satiation—usually accompanied with ridicule.

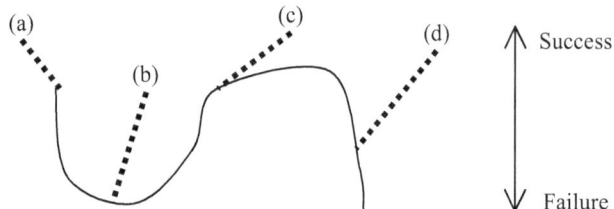

The Skinner Effect: A behavior or state of affairs that tends to reinforce and perpetuate the same behavior or state of affairs.

The Subway Effect: The Skinner Effect in action, in which a subway station, strewn with graffiti, chewing gum wrappers, and discarded beer cans, attracts yet more graffiti, wrappers, and beer cans.

The Singapore Effect: The antithesis of The Subway Effect.

In the city of Singapore, no wrappers can be seen laying around anywhere. No messy chewing gum on the sidewalks. Indeed, one is hard-pressed to find chewing gum for sale in Singapore—too untidy. Until recently, it was against the law to sell chewing gum in this city. Now, a ten-year ban on making chewing gum was lifted because the Singapore authorities could not control the illegal chewing gum mills that had sprung up on the back streets of the city.

The Dead Terrorist, Dead Tourists Effect: The Skinner Effect in action, in which the successful killing of innocent people, accompanied with the suicide of the killer-terrorist, attracts more suicidal terrorists and associated dead tourists.

The Slave Effect: The end result of some missionary activities, wherein the missioned people become slaves to the missionaries.

The Steroid Irony: Steroids enlarge the size of the breasts on males and decrease the size of the breasts on females.

SANE: Supplying A New Ego

The Switzerland Principle: The practice of avoiding responsibility for anything, except making money.

The Tabula Rasa Rule: The age-old practice of one's denying responsibility for an action because one's mind went blank.

The Tattoo Excitement Effect: The sensation of glancing at one's forearm and viewing a new tattoo for the first time: the picture of one's spouse. Conversely, the viewing of one's forearm and viewing an old tattoo of one's ex-spouse.

The Top Ten Nuclear Hits Phenomenon: The terrorist top ten chart of desirable cities for their nuclear attacks. Selection is based on the target citizens' positive affirmation of the following issues: (a) altering the behavior of theocratic societies, including the right to religious freedom, (b) rights for women, including their preference for showing their veilless faces, (c) democracy, (d) capitalism, and (f) having fun.

The Threshold Lowering Syndrome: Without censure from peers or with their reinforcement, the committing of a base act that results in the committing of a baser act. Also, see The Skinner Effect and The Subway Act.

The Towering Ego Condition: Exemplified by those who have towering egos, to the detriment of better judgment.

The Tweak Effect: The end result of tweaking something more than once; as in, "Let's tweak it one more time and see what happens."

The Turf Tussle Truism: Disguised as noble religious and cultural ideas, humans attack one another to claim more turf. Geographical dominance reigns supreme over other human ambitions.

The Uncertainty Principle (of atomic behavior): The atomic universe can never be known by observation because the observation itself changes the behavior of an atom.

The Unlike-Dislike Axiom: Anything that is unlike one's customs is disliked.

The Unilateralism Law. In relation to the international community, the propensity to act alone is directly proportional to the inventory of tools in a country's aggression toolbox.

The Yin and Yang Principle: The Chinese philosophies of feminine (yin) and masculine (yang) principles, existing as dual, opposite, and complementary ideals. In practice, the inability of females and males to agree on any subject.

They're Rioting Everywhere Truism: The propensity for humans to engage in violent behavior, often destroying the very neighborhoods in which they live.

The Zealot's Lot in Life Conundrum: The inability for a zealot, of any nature, to achieve self-satisfaction.

The Why Our Society is Dysfunctional Phenomenon: The simultaneous, self-feeding, inter-reinforcing interactions of the human impairments described in The Rules of Life.

ACKNOWLEDGMENTS

The Cepee Dialogues have been making their way through the literary birth canal for over a decade, and many ideas contained in this book have been part of internal dialogues I've had with myself since my youth. I wrote Dialogues for a while, stored them on a disk file, only to retrieve them to continue my work. This cycle repeated itself several times from the time I first started the project in earnest around 2005.

During this lengthy gestation process, several of my patient and tolerant friends helped nurse-along the book.

Brad Waters read an earlier version of this book and offered suggestions that tied some of my loose thoughts together. We had frequent discussions about the book and about ideas of how to present the story. During this process, Brad became one of my best friends and an intellectual soul mate.

Paul Kositzka is a consummate accountant, financial advisor, and friend. His frequent input about subjects relating to *Dialogues* made for valuable ideas during my writing and research. For well over two decades, Paul has given me volumes of valuable information, much of which I incorporated into this book and many essays.

Moe Fourier read an initial book that led to *Dialogues*. Knowing Moe's U.S. Navy service as a Captain in the intelligence branch of the Navy, I was particularly interested in his opinion. Upon our walking onto a tennis court for a match, Moe made reference to the book, and did a "thumbs-up." His encouragement helped spur me on to continue my efforts. Since that time, we have had many spirited conversations about subjects contained in this book.

Jo Ellen Thompson also read an earlier version of this book. She offered suggestions as well as encouragement for my efforts. For many years, her beautiful, deft presence by my side made us the envy of other dancers on the dance floor.

Another beautiful dancer, and a treasured presence in my life, is a

361

person to whom I owe much: Lynda Boose. Thank you, Lynda.

Pat Fitzpatrick, also a reader of my earlier version, invited me to lunch to discuss this effort. He told me I had quite an imagination, but that he liked the book. Of equal importance, he bought the wine for our meal. Thank you, Paddy, for your comments but mostly for paying the bill. And thank you for quieting our friends who often gave me a hard time for my expressing unconventional views by your telling them: "Be quiet (expletive omitted). Let's hear what Uyless has to say on the matter."

Among these friends with whom I've had spirited email discussions is Harvey Borkin. Without exception, Harvey has added great value to our dialogues with intelligent discourse—all done with civility and compassion.

Harvey and Pat form a model that we humans should practice. One is to the right. One is to the left. Yet they are best of friends and have yet to come to blows during their spirited discourses. If so, they have kept it to themselves.

My nephew, Jared Waters read *2084 and Beyond* and went to the effort to discuss the book with me. His critique of *2084* encouraged me to continue writing the companion book you have before you.

Mike Patrick, the managing editor of *The Coeur d'Alene Press* newspaper, has offered long-time support and has inspired me to keep working on this book. Mike directs the operations of a so-called "small town newspaper," which is vital social glue to any American community. He does his job with intelligence and courage.

So does the Graham family. Citing another newspaper, *The Lovington Leader* (of Lovington, New Mexico) has for decades been a supporter of my work. Working with Jim Harris, the director for the Lea County Museum (one of the best museum directors in the country), the long-time owners of the Leader have kept a small town newspaper a vital clog in this community. The Black family and I owe much to the Graham family and the current publisher, John.

Lesli Laughter is a recent and valuable collaborator to my work. Without her, I would not have gained a firm and high-quality presence at social media sites. She has also counseled my publicist and editor, Sylvia Gann Mahoney, in using this media.

The stunning covers and the faultless formats of every book I have published in the 2000s are because of the skills and patience of Alvart Badalian, cited in the copyright page. I might have stumbled along these past twenty years without editors and publicists, but I am certain I could not have produced the beautiful visual quality of my books without Alvart holding my less-than-artistic hand.

Rob Black was an early supporter of my efforts, although like others citied above, he did not read the final manuscript leading to this book. As with Brad and Moe, he read a book that led to *Dialogues*. His support and encouragement during those times will ever be thanked and will never be forgotten.

For several decades Toby Marzouk has provided sound advice to me on the subjects of copyrights and patents. Time and again, he has informed me he deals with one but not the other. I cannot remember which, only that I thank him for his counseling and friendship.

Holly Waters and Sylvia Gann Mahoney have been instrumental in the creation of this book. Their editing skills are unsurpassed, and this statement comes from a writer of some 40 books and having worked with over 80 editors. Sylvia is cited in the dedication page. Holly, my wife, has been cited in other books. Nonetheless, she is always present in my thoughts when I write a dedication page. But like Meryl Streep, only so many accolades can be made!

Alex Trebec (the *Jeopardy* program), Oprah, and Dr. Phil are hosts to three TV programs cited in this book. Thanks to the three of you for your superior work. I cite Willie Nelson frequently in the book, usually facetiously. Truth is, I have been a big fan of Mr. Nelson when he was a member of C&W bands and long before he became famous. I also used some of Randy Newman's "Short People." Thank you, Mr. Newman.

I also thank the Kingston Trio for "They're Rioting in Africa" song, from which I used their rhyming verse and parts of their lyrics.

I used some of the lyrics from "It Only Hurts for a Little While." Thanks to Mack David and Fred Spielman for creating this gem.

Lazy borrowings, gratefully acknowledged.

There are others who did not contribute directly to this book, but have offered friendship and sound advice; some recently, some for many years. Thank you, Donald Black, Tommy Black, Tom and Kaky Black (Kaky is cited in the dedication page), Joanna Gilbert, Paul and Trudi Lombardi, Rich DeRose, Don Schmitt, Gail Power, Ken Hanley, Bill Fanning, Ken Sherman, Joyce Caudle, Hilda Mitchell, Cherrill Black, Paul Homer, Jeanne Malin, S. Cruz Alderette, O.T. Garza, William Ganz, Bernie DiTullio, Byron Anderson, Karen Nold, Beth Waters, Carlos and Patty Torres, Bill Myers, Sam Turner, Doug and Nita Hammock, Joe and Marie Santamauro, Ray and Sandy Massey, Bob and Betty Taylor, Ray and Jane Morgan, Jeanne Stum, Steve and Connie Penza, Jim Opperman, Shawn Baccus, Bob (Eagle) Botts, Sharon Mahoney, Kathleen and Coleen Mancini, Gardiner and Pat Pollich, Tom and Greta Keleher, and last but far from least, Chock and Patty Black.

BIBLIOGRAPHY

The 9/11 Commission Report. New York: W.W. Norton, 2004.

Allen, Scott. "Widespread Abnormalities Stump Scientists. Pesticides, Parasites Among Explanations." *The Boston Globe*, July 28, 1997, B01.

Barnett, Lincoln. *The Universe and Dr. Einstein.* New York: Bantam, 1980.

Biema, David Van. "Undercover: Christianity in Muslim Lands," *Time*, June, 30, 2003, 39.

Bindschadler, Robert L., and Charles R. Bentley. "On Thin Ice?" *Scientific American*, December 2002, 98-105.

Black, Uyless. *2084 and Beyond.* Hayden, Idaho: IEI Press, 2015.

——. "Traveling America (I)." Blog.UylessBlack.com, 2006, 10.

Buchanan, Pat. *Where the Right Went Wrong.* New York: St. Martin's Press, 2004.

Bush Doctrine. "National Security Strategy (NSS)." Speech. West Point, June 2002.

Cloud, John. "Why Genes Aren't Destiny." *Time*, January 18, 2010, 49-53.

Diamond, Jared. *Collapse: How Societies Choose to Fail or Succeed* . New York: Viking Press, 2005.

Fallows, James. "Success without Victory." *The Atlantic*, January/February 2005, 90.

Friend, Tom. "Elusive Gene Therapy Forges On." *USA Today*, February 24, 2003.

Fukuyama, Francis. *America at the Crossroads. Democracy, Power and the Neoconservative Legacy* . New Haven, CT: Yale University Press, 2006.

Gazzaniga, Michael S. *The Ethical Brain.* New York: Dana Press, 2005.

Hazleton, Lesley. "Close Reading," *The New York Times Book Review*, December 24, 2017, 10.

Hoffman, Bruce."Plan of Attack." *Atlantic*, July/August, 2004, 43.

"Hold the Avocado." *The Economist*, December 16, 2006, 30.

Huxley, Julian. Transhumanism. "*New Bottles for New Wine*," 1957, in Leonard Roy Frank, *Quotationary*. New York: Random House, 2001.

"Ideas and Consequences." Aspen Institute's Aspen Ideas Festival of 2007. *The Atlantic*, October 2007.

Jihad Watch. http://jihadwatch.org/archives/000749.php.

Kaplan, Robert D. "Supremacy by Stealth." *The Atlantic*, July-August 2003, 69.

The Koran: An Edition prepared for English Readers. New York: Mount Vernon Press.

Luft, Aliza, *The New Yorker*, December 11, 2017, 5.

Mamdani, Mahmood. *Good Muslin, Bad Muslim*. New York: Pantheon Books, 2004.

Mann, Charles C. "The Coming Death Shortage." *The Atlantic*, May 2005, 92.

Michaels, Patrick J. "Live with Climate Change." *USA Today*, February 2, 2007, 8A.

Mukherjee, Siddartha. "Same but Different." *The New Yorker*, May 2, 2016, 26.

Nagourney, Eric. "Hurry Up and Procrastinate." *The New York Times*, August 17, 2004, D6.

"Odes to Bob Dylan." References and Footnotes. Blog.UylessBlack.com.

Ponti, Giovanna, Paolo Peretto, and Luca Bonfanti. "Genesis of Neuronal and Glial Progenitors in the Cerebellar Cortex of Peripuberal and Adult Rabbits." Editor. Thomas A. Reh. 2008. https://www.ncbi.nlm.nih.gov/pmc/articles/PMC2396292/

Pope, John. "Court Orders 11-year-old Boy to Take Growth Hormones." *The Spokesman-Review*, Spokane, WA, March 27, 2004, A8.

"Pupil Power." *The Economist*, January 16, 2018, 9.

Purcell, Tom. "My Doc, the Terrorist." FrontPageMagazine.com , July 10, 2007.

Qureshi, Emran. *The Washington Post*, August 25, 2004, C1 and C9.

Remnick, David. "Danger Levels." *The New Yorker*, July 31, 2006, 22.

Ruddiman, William F. "How did Humans First Alter Global Climate?" *Scientific American*, March 2005, 46-53.

Saavedra, Miguel de Cervantes. *Don Quixote*, in Leonard Roy Frank, *Quotationary*. New York: Random House, 2001, 742.

Scheuer, Michaell. *Imperial Hubris*. Washington, DC: Potomac Books, Brassey's, 2004.

Shakespeare, William. *Hamlet*, 2.2.90, in Leonard Roy Frank. *Quotationary*. New York: Random House, 2001, 933.

——. *Henry IV*, Part II, 1.2.275, in Leonard Roy Frank. *Quotationary*. New York: Random House, 2001, 933.

Shavit, Ari. *My Promised Land*. New York: Random House, 2013.

Shermer, Michael. "The Political Brain." *Scientific American*, July 2006, 36.

Sinclair, David A., and Lenny Guarente. "Unlocking the Secrets of Longevity Genes." *Scientific American*, March 2006, 49.

Stein, Rob. "Muscle-Bound Boy Offers Hope for Humans." *The Washington Post*, June 22, 2004, A7.

Stipp, David. "Chasing the Youth Pill." *Fortune*, April 19, 2004, 134.

Sultan, Sohaib Nazeer. *The Koran for Dummies*. Hoboken, NJ: Wiley, 2004.

Suskind, Ron. "Without a Doubt." *The New York Times Magazine*, October 17, 2004, 51.

Tyler, Patrick. *Fortress Israel*. New York: Farrar, Straus, and Giroux, 2013.

Ward, Peter. "What will become of the Homo sapiens?" *Scientific American*, January 2009, 72.

Weise, Elizabeth. "Report: Rodents May Offer Insight to Monogamy." *USA Today*, June 17, 2004, 2A.

Wilson, E. O. *The Social Conquest of Earth*. New York: Liveright, 2012, 297, Kindle edition, loc. 4777.

Woodward, Bob. *Bush at War*. New York: Simon & Schuster, 2002. https://www.cbsnews.com/news/woodward-shares-was-secrets/

Zakaria, Fareed. "How We Drive Our Jobs Away." *Newsweek*, April 18, 2005, 43.

——. "The Surge That Might Work." *Newsweek*, March 5, 2007, 48.

OTHER WORKS BY UYLESS BLACK

Lea County Museum Press:
The Light Side of Little Texas, 2011

 **Note**: Winner of 2012 Centennial award from The Historical Society of New Mexico for the "Best Book Depicting Domestic Life" in New Mexico.

Finalist for 2012 award from The New Mexico Book Co-op for "Non-fiction, other."

IEI Press:
A Swimmer's Odyssey: From the Plains to the Pacific, 2011
The Nearly Perfect Storm: An American Financial and Social Failure, 2012
2084 and Beyond, 2014
Digital Societies and the Internet: What the Present is bringing to the Future, 2016
The Cepee Dialogues: A Modern Fairy Tale, 2019

The following books (some of the first books on Internet protocols and architecture) offer historical perspectives on early data communications networks. Note the copyright dates.

SAMS:
Teach Yourself Networking in 24 Hours, 2009

IEEE Computer Society:
Physical Layer Interfaces and Protocols, 1988
X.25 and Packet Switching Networks, 1991

Prentice Hall/Pearson Publishing:
Data Communications, Networks, and Distributed Processing, 1983
Computer Networks: Protocols, Standards, and Interfaces, 1987
Data Networks: Concepts, Theory, and Practice, 1989
The OSI Model, 1991

Data Link Protocols, 1993
Asynchronous Transfer Mode (ATM) Networks, Volume I, 1995
Wireless and Mobile Networks, 1996
Emerging Communications Technologies, 1997
SONET and T1, 1997
ISDN and SS7, 1997
The Intelligent Network, 1998
Asynchronous Transfer Mode (ATM) Networks, Volume II, 1998
Asynchronous Transfer Mode (ATM) Networks, Volume III, 1998
Residential Broadband, 1998
Second Generation Mobile and Wireless Networks, 1999
Advanced Intelligent Technologies, 1999
The Point-to-Point Protocol (PPP), 2000
IP Routing Protocols, 2000
Internet Security Protocols, 2000
Quality of Service in Wide Area Networks, 2000
Internet Architecture, 2000
MPLS and Label Switching Networks, 2001
Internet Telephony, 2001
Voice over IP (VOIP), 2002
Networking 101, 2002
Optical Networks, 2002

McGraw-Hill:

TCP/IP and Related Protocols, 1992
Network Management Standards, 1992
The V-Series Recommendations, 1995
The X-Series Recommendations, 1995
Frame Relay Networks, 1998

Foreign Editions of Books:

Japanese: *Network Management Standards; Internet Security Protocols; Data Communications and Distributed Networks; IP Routing Protocols; TCP/IP; Multi-protocol Label Switching (MPLS)*
Korean: *Voice over IP (VOIP); Communications Networks: Protocols, Standards, and Interfaces*
Russian: *Communications Networks: Protocols, Standards, and Interfaces; Internet Security Protocols*
French: *Teach Yourself Networking in 24 Hours*
Chinese: *Advanced Features of the Internet; Voice over IP (VOIP)*

Spanish: *Data Communications and Distributed Networks; Communication Networks: Protocols, Standards, and Interfaces; TCP/IP; Advanced Features of the Internet*

United Kingdom: *Data Communications and Distributed Networks; Data Networks: Concepts, Theory, and Practice; Computer Networks: Protocols, Standards, and Interfaces.*

Magazine Articles:

Structured Programming:

InfoSystems magazine (circa 1975): "Gestalt Psychology Applied to Software Design" (An article explaining the brain's partitioning mental tasks to facilitate solving problems, based on Gestalt theory. A concept fundamental to a programming idea called structured programming, a revolutionary idea at that time.)

Metadata defined before it was named:

Data Communications magazine, November, 1980, McGraw Hill, Inc: "An Automatic Pilot for the Growing Distributed Network" (To my knowledge, the first known explanation of *metadata*.)

Subjects under research, with plans to publish:

Hot Wars, Cold Wars, and America's Warm War (working title)
My Capital, My America (working title)
The Light Side of Little Texas, Volume II

Short Stories:

Available upon request.

Essays available at Blog.UylessBlack.com:

America's Capital: Memories of author's experiences in Washington, DC.

America's Cities: Journeys and encounters in USA's towns and cities

America's Finances: A series on issues such as Medicare, Social Security, and debt.

Computers and Networks: Essays on Internet "net neutrality" and software complexity.

Creatures and Computers: Drawing analogies to wildlife and Internet life.

Customs and Cultures: A look at America and Americana.

Eating and Drinking: Surveys of food fairs, cafes, and restaurants.

Food Effects and Drug Defects: Reports on toxic foods and drugs' side effects.

Foreign Affairs: America's relations with other countries

Foreign Places: Taking roads, ships, and trains through parts of the world.

Immigration and Emigration: America's immigration practices and related problems.

Politics in America: With several reports on National Press Club speakers.

Presidential Places: Presidential homes, museums, and grave sites

Privacy: NSA activities, right to Internet privacy in relation to other rights of privacy.

Sports and Games: Essays on competition and the beauty of sport.

Traveling America: Taking roads through America and America's cultures.

War Zones: Essays on cold, warm, and hot wars.

Listings of some newspaper articles. Uyless Black has published numerous articles on various topics with the local newspaper, *The Coeur d' Alene Press*. Here are some samplings:

- "When Political Correctness and Freedom of Speech collide," December 13, 2017.
- "The FCC Rulings on Net Neutrality," December 2-3, 2017.
- "What Walls Should America be Building?" November 1, 2017.
- "A Deeper Issue in Immigration Debate: Separation of Church and State," November 27, 2015.
- "Beware the Freedom to Kill the Freedom of Religion," November 28, 2015.
- "Muslims in America, a Personal Look," December 28, 2015.
- Ten articles about "The Internet and Society," January 4, 2016–January 15, 2016.